EVERYTHING IS JUST FINE

ALSO BY BRETT PAESEL

Mommies Who Drink

EVERYTHING IS JUST FINE

————

BRETT PAESEL

GRAND CENTRAL
PUBLISHING

New York Boston

Grand Central Publishing
Hachette Book Group
1290 Avenue of the Americas, New York, NY 10104
grandcentralpublishing.com
twitter.com/grandcentralpub

First Edition: April 2019

Grand Central Publishing is a division of Hachette Book Group, Inc. The Grand Central Publishing name and logo is a trademark of Hachette Book Group, Inc.

The publisher is not responsible for websites (or their content) that are not owned by the publisher.

The Hachette Speakers Bureau provides a wide range of authors for speaking events. To find out more, go to www.hachettespeakersbureau.com or call (866) 376-6591.

Library of Congress Cataloging-in-Publication Data

Names: Paesel, Brett, author.
Title: Everything is just fine / Brett Paesel.
Description: First edition. | New York : Grand Central Publishing, 2019.
Identifiers: LCCN 2018039321| ISBN 9781538745649 (hardcover) |
    ISBN 9781549175503 (audio download) | ISBN 9781538745632 (ebook)
Subjects: LCSH: Family secrets—Fiction.
Classification: LCC PS3616.A33634 E95 2019 | DDC 813/.6—dc23
LC record available at https://lccn.loc.gov/2018039321

ISBNs: 978-1-5387-4564-9 (hardcover), 978-1-5387-4563-2 (ebook)

Printed in the United States of America

LSC-C

10 9 8 7 6 5 4 3 2 1

For my parents
Fred and Audrey

EVERYTHING IS JUST FINE

It takes more courage to examine the dark corners of your own soul than it does for a soldier to fight on the battlefield.

—*William Butler Yeats*

Train yourself to let go of everything you fear to lose.

—*Yoda*

Losing is only ever your third option!

—*Coach Randy*

Monday, November 8, 5 p.m.

THE SMACK OF A WAVE hitting the beach, loosening rocks as it recedes. As if to drag something—anything—back with it. A smooth stone. A crab. A bottle cap. Coach Randy stands on the shore. Not too close, because it's insanely cold. He bounces up and down a bit and forces himself to contemplate the bigger picture. He read somewhere—or maybe it was in a movie—that there is freedom in understanding how insignificant you are in the universe. He closes his eyes and concentrates on his insignificance. But no dice. In seconds, his mind is dragged back to the unholy mess he's made of the past few months. He is the stone, the crab, the bottle cap.

Would he be standing on the beach today, alone, if he had made a handful of other choices? How would someone who is not him have handled everything differently? What would Yoda say?

Goddamn it's cold and windy and getting dark. Not ideal conditions for making a big, life-changing decision. He bends down to pick up a rock and tosses it into the ocean. Watches the waves for a minute, rubbing his hands together.

Enough of this. He straightens up and drops his hands to his sides. No more stalling. He pivots, the rocks crunching beneath his feet, and marches to his car. There are moments that define every man's life, and this is the moment Randy Tinker will be remembered for.

CHAPTER 1

From: FavoriteCoach@gmail.com
To: Beverly Hills Orange 10 M   sent Tues, Sept 7 3:33 pm

Subject: Note from your favorite coach! (kidding)

Dear Parents and athletes:

Hi from Coach Randy! I hope you all enjoyed your last free Saturday before the season begins next week. For those of you who missed the "meet and greet" last Sunday, you didn't miss a thing. I'm joking, seriously you missed a lot. First off, you'll have to get your uniform from Jacqui, our Team Mom who worked side by side with me last year. She always wears a visor and is only about 4'11". I hope that doesn't offend you Jacqui! Kidding, I know her and she won't mind!! Anyway, you can't miss her, she also carries a huge bag. That's where she'll have the uniforms and stuff you never even knew you needed!

It looks like we have a mixed group of talent and experience this season (some total beginners up to a superstar or two), which is what the Beverly Hills Jr. Soccer league is all about. Remember everyone plays—absolutely everyone, even if you don't like it and it's your just your mom or dad who signed you up! This will be my third year coaching and experience tells me that it's the most reluctant players who get the most out of it in the end. Just ask my own kid, he can't wait to get on the field now.

OK, let's do this!

If you missed the "meet and greet" you might not know that we need a team name that starts with the letter 'M'. I was hoping not to get 'M' because kids always want to start the team name with the word "Magic"...something, Like Magic Ninjas, and, if you know me, you know I don't believe in magic, just hard work, passing, playing your position, and listening to me, your assistant coach (still finding one), and our private skills coach, Al (or Alejandro, as he also likes to be called)recruited and paid for by some of the dads to keep us sharp.

I don't want to go on too much here, and seriously would not have to if a whole third of you hadn't missed the "meet and greet".

Oh, and, for those of you who were on my team last year, notice that I'm not using my work e-mail anymore. You guys were cramming my inbox last season and, frankly, I shouldn't be doing team stuff at work anymore, right?

OK. This Saturday, 9:30 sharp, and be ready to play at 10:00.

Go M team!
Coach Randy

––––––––––

From: Mako@Shakrayoga.org
To: Beverly Hills Orange 10 M   sent Tues, Sept 7 3:35 pm

Subject: Re: Note from your favorite coach! (kidding)

Hello team parents: If I had known the Meet and Greet was optional and not mandatory (like the invite said) I would have gone to my older son's academic pentathlon final. As it was, his team came in first and I missed it.

Sincerely,
Mako (Mason's Mom)

Diane Platt snaps the lid of her laptop closed and takes another swig of wine. Isn't there some kind of regulation about getting the same coach twice in a row? Not that Randy is a bad guy. It's like T said last season, Randy's simply over the top in ways that can exhaust a person.

She leans back in her chair and closes her eyes against the memories that threaten to stream through her mind at the mere thought of T. Eight months since the divorce, and she's still in a constant state of pining and regret. Beyond painful, it's boring as hell.

She breathes in, opens her eyes, reaches for her glass, and raises the lid of the laptop. There's no tonic like reading the inevitable stream of Reply Alls to make her feel a little less fucked up.

From: Visorgrl@mac.com
To: M Team list   sent Tues, Sept 7 3:47 pm

Subject: Snack sign-up

Hey team and parents,

I'm Jacqui, the Team Mom. My son is Calvin and this is his second year playing so go easy on him. I'm only kidding. He's pretty good. You all are. You ALL are superstars! ☺

By now you got Coach Randy's welcome e-mail. I'm sorry I didn't meet all of you at the "meet and greet", but that's OK, because we all have other stuff going on and I understand that. Speaking of which, please choose a day for snack sign up that works FOR YOU. Other Team Moms just sign people up without asking, but I like you to pick your own day so you don't feel stressed. Beverly Hills Jr. Soccer is all about fun. The first six games aren't even competitive, so you can really relax and not worry about your kid crying or hitting players on the other team out of some pretty under-standable frustration.

I will have extra health forms in my bag. Diane and Mark, I need new health forms for your kids even though they played on our team last year. Also, for those of you who are new, I have extra sunscreen, water bottles, sanitizer, and a small first aid kit in my bag. Randy says that the kit isn't that small, but he doesn't realize how much stuff the other Team Mom's carry. Seriously, I'm relaxed in comparison. You'll get to know that! ☺

Remember that we're still looking for an assistant coach. So any of you Dads who have been dreaming of being a part of this season, I'm talking to you! It could even be a mom, or someone between jobs, or a manny, or even a sibling who's not going to college right now and is looking for something to do. Now's the time to get involved. It'll be the best thing you've ever done.

Jacqui Hirshorn
Calvin's Mom

———————

From: Alejandro.Navaro@Pepperdine.edu
To: M Team list   sent Tues, Sept 7 3:53 pm

Subject: Re: Snack sign-up

Hello boys,

I look forward to working on your soccer skills.

Alejandro Navaro

———————

From: Visorgrl@mac.com
To: M Team list   sent Tues, Sept 7 3:56 pm

Subject: Re: Snack sign-up

Hello Team M:

Seriously, Alejandro is being modest. He's not just working on your skills—he's the real deal and played professionally in Columbia before coming to our country to study Forensic Dentistry!

He's going to be a great asset to the team and the league—and to my son, Calvin, who looks up to you already, Alejandro! The boys loved wrestling you to the ground at the Meet and Greet. You are SO GREAT WITH KIDS!!! Calvin can't wait to ambush you again. ☺

See you out there, Alejandro!

Gentle reminder: don't forget health forms and shoelace guards.

Jacqui Hirshorn
Calvin's Mom

———————

From: FavoriteCoach@gmail.com
To: Beverly Hills Orange 10 M   sent Tues, Sept 7 3:55 pm

Subject: No fighting over numbers

I'm sending a quick note about choosing your number. If you are picking up your uniform at the game, you do not get to choose. Choosing happened at the "meet and greet". Now you get what you get, and that's it. Like my wife, Missy, says, "Soccer is a life lesson for our kids. We win or we lose, and we don't get everything we want, when we want it." I could give you a list of things that I want and don't get, and I'm still a happy guy!

By the way, Missy said to tell those of you who don't know that I am Aiden's dad. He made all-star last year and is an asset to the team.

Another 'by the way': I like to write my e-mails to parents and kids as if you are all the team, because really you all are—we can't do it without the parents! It's your choice about what e-mails you share with your kids or not!

Go Aiden and M Team!
Coach Randy

From: MSonnenklar@GSachs.com
To: Beverly Hills Orange 10 M　　　　　　sent Tues, Sept 7 3:57 pm

Subject: Re: No fighting over numbers

What numbers are left? Ben couldn't make it because it was his mother's weekend and she forgot. He shouldn't be penalized.

M

From: MSonnenklar@GSachs.com
To: M Team list　　　　　　　　　　sent Tues, Sept 7 3:57 pm

Subject: Re: Snack sign-up

Are we playing on the north field or the south? Please be clear this year.

M

From: Visorgrl@mac.com
To: M Team list   sent Tues, Sept 7 4:08 pm

Subject: Re: Snack sign-up

That's a good point about the fields, Mark. Coach and I will try to tell you which field, WHEN we know which one it is. We don't always KNOW ahead of time. So it's good to get there early anyway. This Saturday will be North.

The numbers that are left are 4, 5, 7, 10, 11, 13. The Woo's already contacted me about getting the number 7 for luck. Which is easy enough. Mark, do you want 10 like last year? Ben did pretty well with 10.

We're still looking for that special dad (or Mom or older sibling who's looking for something meaningful to do) who wants to be assistant coach. You don't even have to go to the clinic. Coach Randy will get you up to speed. ☺

Go Team M!

Jacqui Hirshorn
Calvin's Mom

From: JWoo@DesignX.com
To: M Team list   sent Tues, Sept 7 4:14 pm

Subject: Re: Snack sign-up

Patrick would not be at the "meet and greet" for his violin concert. He can be early and will bring health forms. Also his idea for 'M' title.

Jung-ah Woo

_____

From: FavoriteCoach@gmail.com
To: Beverly Hills Orange 10 M   sent Tues, Sept 7 4:14 pm

Subject: Re: No fighting over numbers

Coach Randy, here. I'm at work and don't have time to get into a big thing.
I shouldn't even be on my personal e-mail, but I'm just writing to say, that's
enough! No more numbers will be reserved.

Coach Randy

_____

From: MSonnenklar@GSachs.com
To: Beverly Hills Orange 10 M   sent Tues, Sept 7 4:17 pm

Subject: Re: No fighting over numbers

Jacqui,

#10 is good for Ben.

Thanks for hanging onto it. Ben's mom will be coming early to pick up the
uniform.

M

_____

From: ParadiseB@gmail.com
To: Beverly Hills Orange 10 M   sent Tues, Sept 7 4:19 pm

Subject: Re: No fighting over numbers

Hi, I'm Dashiell's mom. Did I miss something? I thought that we weren't allowed to reserve a number if we hadn't gone to the Meet and Greet. My apologies for not making it. My schedule changes all the time and I didn't want to send the Nanny because it was specifically about meeting and greeting!

Since it appears that people are going ahead and choosing numbers, may I request 5 for Dashiell because it's a prime number. He loves primes.

Beth Paradis

Diane's hands hover over the keyboard. To jump into it or not? How can anyone give a serious fuck about jersey numbers?

She reaches for her wineglass. What she should do right now is get off the computer and not read any more e-mails. That would be the totally responsible, grown-up thing to do. She should pour her wine into the sink, get into some street clothes, and take a brisk power walk through the neighborhood. Then she should come home and read something intellectually stimulating before getting some tasty snacks ready for the kids when T drops them off tonight. That's exactly what she should do.

She looks out the window at her possible power-walking path. The sidewalk running in front of neat lawns across the street. She gazes at the geometrically precise hedges that mark each lot. Then downs her wine.

From: DPlatt@ca.rr.com
To: Beverly Hills Orange 10 M　　　　　　　sent Tues, Sept 7 4:23 pm

Subject: Re: No fighting over numbers

Well, hell. What was the point of going to the Meet and Greet if everyone gets to choose their numbers anyway?

Joking. I'm joking.

Diane

––––––––––

From: FavoriteCoach@gmail.com
To: Beverly Hills Orange 10 M　　　　　　　sent Fri, Sept 10 8:41 am

Subject: Let's pump it up for the big day tomorrow

Hey M Team!!!

OK, I guess that number thing got handled. Whatever, I can bend. Sometimes you can't control everything. Jacqui, did you get all that about the numbers?

It's a good thing I don't have to handle the small stuff because I'm totally a big picture guy. I'm the guy with the vision that gets implemented. I mean, seriously, you should see my sundeck. It was just a dusty heap of nothing when we bought our place seven years ago, and now you can't get people off of that deck. It's like you're on perpetual vacation out there, and it was totally my vision. Of course, hats off to my lovely other half, Missy, who drew up the design and had the idea for the stone fireplace in the middle. We went totally over budget, but when you are thinking about the rest of your life in front of that fireplace, you know you have to have it and you make it happen.

So the deck is like the team, and I've got a big-picture plan of how it's going to look, but I need a Missy, or in this case, a Jacqui to actually implement it!

So, this is my big picture for tomorrow: We will get there early, get uniforms, pick our 'M' name, and get our heads in the right mindset to dominate.

Then Al will take us through drills, and if you want to pitch in for Al's fee, see Jacqui. It's totally worth it. We had a Brazilian semi-pro helping us last year and made it to the tournament. We would have had Paco again this year if Dan Majors hadn't swiped him. As luck or fate, or whatever-you-call-it would have it, we'll be playing Dan's team for our second game this season. So that's one you might want to focus your voodoo energies on. Just kidding!

When your kid gets up tomorrow morning, I would like you to read the following poem that was read by Morgan Freeman in the movie about the South African Soccer team who took a mediocre group and won the world championship. Words inspire!!!!

"Out of the night that covers me,
Black as the Pit from pole to pole,
I thank whatever gods may be
For my unconquerable soul.

In the fell clutch of circumstance
I have not winced nor cried aloud.
Under the bludgeonings of chance
My head is bloody, but unbowed.

Beyond this place of wrath and tears
Looms but the Horror of the shade,
And yet the menace of the years
Finds, and shall find, me unafraid.

It matters not how strait the gate,
How charged with punishments the scroll.
I am the master of my fate:
I am the captain of my soul."

—I could not say it better myself. Go Team!!! Remember! There is more to winning than plain luck.

Coach Randy

—————

From: MSonnenklar@GSachs.com
To: Beverly Hills Orange 10 M   sent Fri, Sept 10 7:20 pm

Subject: Re: Let's pump it up for the big day tomorrow

North field. Still. Right?

M

CHAPTER 2

COACH RANDY STANDS ON HIS deck wishing he were the kind of guy who smoked cigars. He should have a snifter of cognac too. That would complete the picture of a man at home, on his own deck in front of the outdoor fire pit, the sun sliding behind the row of trees that marks his property line, watching his younger wife play horseshoes on the recently mowed lawn with their ten-year-old son. But cigars make him nauseous. And cognac makes his throat burn so much that his eyes water and he looks like he's crying. Instead, he has poured himself a glass of red wine from one of the leftover bottles in the kitchen. Make that *two* of the leftover bottles. He combined the remnants of both into one glass since no one was around to see him do it.

"Maybe Daddy wants to play," Missy says loud enough for him to hear.

He twitches with annoyance, but checks it almost immediately. After all, he tells himself, the request is reasonable. Dads on decks should want to play with their sons in the yard. Especially so they can show their wives how great they are with kids and how athletic they are and, on top of that, how relaxed they can be when they're not thinking about work or the bills. He watches Missy bend over to pick up a horseshoe, her tight, pale thighs ducking into her shorts; her shiny straight hair swinging.

"Be right there," he says, setting his glass on the blond wood railing that Missy first showed him in an issue of *Dwell*. Seeing the gleaming oak rail has an almost medicinal effect, dissolving vestiges of irritation at the base of his neck. Now smiling big, he hops down, ignores the twinge in his knees, and runs over to clap Aiden on his shoulder blades. "Let me show you how it's done, son."

"Great," says Missy, handing him her three horseshoes.

Randy stiffens. "I thought we were *all* playing."

"I have to marinate pork."

"Now?" he says, before he can soften his tone. He quickly tousles Aiden's hair to keep it casual.

"It takes three hours," she says, and turns to go. "You want to eat dinner at nine?" she adds over her shoulder, like it's a preposterous thought and he's an idiot for suggesting it. Randy looks down at Aiden, who peers back. Does the kid even want to play horseshoes? Randy sure as hell doesn't. He feels the moment when each of them could acknowledge this and do something else slip by.

God damn it. He keeps missing his moments. He used to be a moment-grabber. But now, because of work, not hitting his numbers, the reorganization, and because of Missy not touching him lately, he's off his game.

He watches Aiden turn his head toward the tree line.

All right. Shake it loose. Randy tosses two of the horseshoes aside and brings one up to his face like it's a mustache. Squinting his eyes and pulling his lip back over his top teeth, he says in his best Chinaman, "I am Mr. Fu. World horseshoe champion. I here to give you great secrets of the toss." And bows.

Aiden turns and looks at him, bringing his hand up to shade his eyes.

"Mr. Fu's first secret: Keep wrist straight. Not floppy like that woman does." He nods toward the house, then back at Aiden. "Mr. Fu say, that woman your mother, yes? She very beautiful." Aiden shifts his weight, smiling or squinting. Randy can't tell. "Tell me, honorable young man. Your mother. She is single, yes?"

Aiden looks down at the ground and says, "That's so racist."

Randy stares at the kid for a second, then drops his horseshoe mustache. "It's just a joke." He waits for Aiden to look up and give him a sign that he understands. But the kid only digs the toe of his shoe into the grass. "Okay. Okay. All I was trying to say was to keep your wrist straight as you toss." He pulls back his shoe, keeps his wrist straight, and throws. It thuds onto the ground halfway to the stake. "Ha. Not like that, right? But you get the idea." He hands Aiden a horseshoe. "Straight wrist."

Aiden narrows his eyes at the stake, pulls his arm back, and underhands the horseshoe high into the air above him like a leaden pop fly. He looks up, standing under the soaring horseshoe, unmoving.

Split-second, Randy sees the horseshoe crest. And reverse. He grabs Aiden by the arm. Jerks him backward as the iron shoe plummets to the ground, right where Aiden had been standing.

"What the hell?" Randy yells.

"You said to keep my wrist straight!" Aiden screams back.

"Yeah, but you threw it way up into the air. You weren't even throwing it at the stake."

"Yes I was!"

"Aiden. The stake is way over there, for Christ's sake!" he yells, pointing.

Aiden balls his fists, screeching, "I don't even want to play this dumb game!"

"Well, neither do I!" Randy yells back. They face off, both breathing heavily. The boy glares at him, a bubble of snot inflating with each exhale, then disappearing on the inhale, only to blow up again. The kid is a mess. He needs a damn Kleenex. Randy kicks the horseshoes. "Forget it, then," he says. "We're not playing."

"Fine." Aiden turns and runs into the house. The kitchen screen door slams.

Randy imagines the scene inside. Aiden burying his face in Missy's lap. Should he go in? No. That'll make things worse. It'll only result in more yelling, and he lets the thought go.

Instead, he goes over to the deck to retrieve his glass of wine, his pulse still jumping. He takes a sip. What the hell is it with Aiden? Randy bets that half the soccer team wishes he were their dad instead of the boring one they actually have. At the end of last year's season, kids came up to him crying and hugging. Giving him Starbucks gift cards. That's how much they were going to miss him. His Mr. Fu routine would have gone over gangbusters with those kids. They would be falling all over themselves to get horseshoe lessons from him.

Why not Aiden? Something's off between them. The day Aiden was born, Randy waited to feel like a changed man. Everyone said that as soon as he saw the baby, he'd feel this rush of overpowering love. Books said it. Fathers at work said it. Moms said it all the time. But the feeling never came. Still, he waited. All through Aiden's infancy. And it never, ever came.

Sure, he liked the kid. Loved him, even. But that blast of chest-hurting, eye-stinging, can't-stop-yourself-from-doing-and-saying-the-stupidest-things-and-showing-pictures-all-the-time kind of love he had heard about never came. Not automatically. Not like a birthright, like they promised. And so Randy had worked at it. Forced himself to play with the boy. Determined to forge the bond that nature had denied them.

Hell. That was what started the whole coaching thing in the first place.

Randy looks at the door to the kitchen and shakes his head. He has to get back in the game. Be the master of his fate. Grab his moments. Sure, it's harder now. With more work and less time. Unpaid bills. The nagging feeling that it's all going to come crashing down. But nothing's lost yet.

He runs his hand across the varnished rail. Takes another sip of wine and wonders if he should wait ten minutes or twenty before going inside and pretending nothing happened.

CHAPTER 3

From: Visorgrl@mac.com

To: Manatees   sent Sat, Sept 11 10:43 pm

Subject: Shake it off, Manatees!

I hope that my e-mail finds you relaxing tonight, after the big game, which was AWESOME!!!! EVERYONE LOOKED SO HANDSOME IN THEIR UNIFORMS. ☺☺ I know that the boys are super disappointed that we didn't get a second goal. Seriously, after the other team scored their eighth in a row, the refs were supposed to call the game. But they're all new to the job this season, so we're going to give them a pass!

Here's something to cheer you up, though. Calvin said the most amazing thing afterwards. He said, "Mom, just think. If we had scored twelve more goals, we would have won." Don't you think that if everyone thought like that we wouldn't have wars?

Sometimes when we lose, it's hard to remember that a lot of great things are still happening. I mean, Patrick Woo putting his arm around Aiden like that?!! What a great learning lesson: Even when you mess up and let a goal through, the team will still love you. And Patrick doesn't even know Aiden from last year.

Let's give a big shout-out to Dashiell for coming up with the awesome name. ☺ Manatees are noble beasts and seem very peaceful and cooperative. And that's going to make a great team.

We are still looking for an assistant coach, by the way. Alejandro isn't technically our assistant coach since we're paying him.

Also, I will be creating a dropbox for pictures, so share away!

XOXO,
Jacqui

————————

From: MSonnenklar@GSachs.com
To: Manatees   sent Sat, Sept 11 11:11 pm

Subject: Re: Shake it off, Manatees!

Seriously? Manatees are sea cows.

M

————————

From: JWoo@DesignX.com
To: Manatees   sent Sun, Sept 12 7:43 am

Subject: Re: Shake it off, Manatees!

Patrick was thinking Aiden could not see for his tears.

Patrick was happy also to make the only goal. We thank Coach Randy for bringing us from Hancock Park League, which is lower.

Jung-ah Woo

From: ParadiseB@gmail.com
To: Manatees   sent Sun, Sept 12 10:48 am

Subject: Re: Shake it off, Manatees!

Jacqui, thanks for your encouraging words and for complimenting Dashiell on coming up with the name. I can't believe I missed it. I would love to
have seen his little face when his suggestion got voted in!

Best to everyone,
Beth

From: Visorgrl@mac.com
To: Manatees   sent Sun, Sept 12 11:54 am

Subject: Re: Shake it off, Manatees!

You're welcome, Beth. These little boys are only ten years old and so
cute you want to eat them up! We just need to keep telling them that it
DOESN'T MATTER who wins, it's playing the game that counts—being a
team, and meet and greets, and snacks afterwards—and passing the ball
so everyone gets their own shot, regardless of talent or who their parents
are. ☺

XO,
Jacqui

From: Mako@Shakrayoga.org

To: Manatees   sent Sun, Sept 12 6:18 pm

Subject: Re: Shake it off, Manatees!

Dear Team: I thought that we had agreed on one healthy snack option. Which was the healthy option? The mini-oreos? Or the Diet Snapple? I'm assuming it was the Sun Chips. Can we all agree that Sun Chips are just as bad as the other options? If you don't know that, you are kidding yourself.

Sincerely,

Mako

———————

From: PPousaint@mac.com

To: Manatees   sent Sun, Sept 12 7:13 pm

Subject: Re: Shake it off, Manatees!

Paul here, Claude's dad. Why didn't the kids have a practice before the first game? That's insane. It's like setting puppies up in front of a firing squad and blowing their brains out. I mean, give the kids something to work with. Isn't that what we're paying Alejandro for?

Paul

———————

From: Visorgrl@mac.com

To: Manatees   sent Sun, Sept 12 7:23 pm

Subject: Re: Shake it off, Manatees!

Paul, the game schedule was handed to us by Bev Hills League, and it shouldn't matter anyway, because it wasn't supposed to be a competitive game!!! No one's supposed to be keeping score!!!! But no matter how hard the team moms work to remind people of this, boys and dads end up keeping the score anyway. It happens like this every year! ☹

XO to everyone!

Jacqui

———————

From: MSonnenklar@GSachs.com

To: Manatees   sent Sun, Sept 12 8:21 pm

Subject: Re: Shake it off, Manatees!

Sea cows. I'm just saying.

M

———————

From: DPlatt@ca.rr.com

To: Manatees   sent Mon, Sept 13 2:26 am

Subject: Re: Shake it off, Manatees!

Writing late. Probably no one up right now to get this. But, come on, people. Let's stop with all the noise, noise, noise. Here's some much needed straight talk.

Mark, the team name is going to be the Manatees. And while they are known as sea cows, that's the chosen name. Get over it. Unless you have some other beef that you are not making clear, like maybe a beefiwth the coach having to do with last year. Perhaps. If that's the case then write to Randy on your own time.

Jacqui, I know you mean well, from all the uplifting e-mails we got last year. But, seriously, please stop acting like there's an upside to the total slaughter out there on the field today. It was humiliating and Reece came home and locked our cat in a closet for hours, just to make a point. If the league is so touchy-feely-everyone=plays-evenif they can't stand the game (just because their over-agrressive dad is making them to prove that they aren't gay), then they should have a mercy policy. They probably even do, but the refs don't know about it. Anyway, Jacqui, the point is that it hurts like hell to lose and no amount of sunnying it up and saying that there were good things that happened out there is going to make up for a cat who pooped all over Reece's shoes in the closet. That's a fucking reality.

Sorry it's late and I admit that I've had two glasses of wine.

And, lastly, I was the one who brought snacks. And, yes, sun chips were the healthy option. You know why? Because NO ONE EVER EATS THE ORANGE SLICES PEOPLE. THEY JUST DON'T. ANOTHER REALITY.

Sorry, it's late. That's all I have to say. Has anyone talked to coach post game? I didn't want to interrupt his thing with Alejandro (sp?), which looked kind of intense. Hold on, I have to remove the coach's and Alahanedro's e-mail from the list.

OK. Did that.

I guess that's all I have for now. Sorry again.

Diane

CHAPTER 4

DIANE PEERS AT THE TIME on her computer. It's 2:44 a.m. Damn, she's done it again. Wasted hours e-mailing and messaging. She should never have opened that second bottle of crappy wine. Her bare ass sticks to the vinyl chair and she wiggles it loose. The skin of her full breasts glows a cathodic pale green from the screen. She is staring at a post on Facebook, a video of a customer yelling at a Starbucks barista. Three hundred and eight outraged comments already. Should she watch the video and add to the outrage? Hell, she doesn't even need to see the video to know how she feels. No way does a Starbucks barista deserve that kind of abuse.

She picks up her glass of wine, takes a sip, and sets it down. Fuck. Go to bed, for God's sake. She stands up, her ass stinging from the vinyl tug, slightly woozy and soggy with regret. The carpet beneath her bare feet is reassuring, though. Scratchy. She stamps her feet, breasts bobbling. The carpet is honest. Solid. The carpet would never yell at a barista. The carpet simply is.

She considers sitting back down and writing the carpet stuff as a comment. How it's more noble to be a lowly carpet than an asshole who yells at service people. But now that she is standing, she feels fatigue filling her up like sand and she'd better get to bed or she'll fall asleep in the chair. Which happens sometimes.

She makes it over to the foyer and starts to pull herself up the stairs by the handrail. This isn't entirely necessary. But it's fun swinging off of it, feeling the breeze on her bare skin. After hoisting herself into the upstairs hallway, before flipping the light switch, she peers into Reece and Sabine's room.

Even though there is plenty of space, Reece and Sabine have insisted on sharing a bedroom since the divorce. The light from the hall illuminates the curve of Sabine's back as she sleeps.

Diane leans against the wall outside, feeling its coolness against the length of her body. From here she watches Sabine's shoulder rise and fall. She gives in to the rhythm of it, times her breath to Sabine's.

Time passes and Diane keeps breathing. Who knows how long she does this. But soon, she is suffused with contentment. How can anything possibly be wrong as long as that tiny shoulder goes up and down with every single breath her little girl takes? Jesus, the world is so fucking beautiful.

Reece is on the other side of the room. Diane shifts slightly to see him better. But he remains in darkness. For a second, she goes cold. Where is he? She quickly bumps the door open farther to allow for more light. Where is he? Where the hell?

Shaky, she steps into the room. Muscles in her feet working. Getting her balance. Reaching for him. Her hand finds his head. Sweaty hair. He mumbles and smacks his lips. She pulls her hand back. Oh thank God. He is alive. The children are here. They are breathing. Nothing else matters.

She stands between the two beds, listening to their breath, feeling the dampness in the air from the open window, wishing she knew how to pray.

She is now fully awake.

She turns. Walks out and back down the stairs. There's a bounce in each step. Isn't this fun? In the living room, the computer has gone black and she can barely see. But she knows this room. The distances between things. And she walks across the trusty carpet with blind confidence. Ass meeting vinyl, she sits at the computer, which lights up at her touch, and begins to write.

From: DPlatt@ca.rr.com

To: TPlatt@ca.rr.com   sent Mon, Sept 13 3:02 am

Subject: Thinking of you

Hi my sweet love. I am thinking of you tonight, the way you were when we were happy and a family. A year after Sabine was bron. And I can't for the life of me remember how it went wrong so fast. What were the steps we took toward this split? A split right down the center of thiss family. A split that neither one of us wanted.

That Thanksgiving after Sabine turned one, we went to Joshua Tree and stayed in that ratty motel because we forgot to make reservations before-hand. First we were upset about the motel and the mold I found in the refrigerator. But then we kind of relaxed somehow. Because it was just us. Our little family alone in the world. Iloved all of us that day, even myself.

And remember that night? The walk that we took in the dark, with Sabine in the bjorn on your chest and Reece holding both of our hands? The gravel crunching under our feet and the night sky was so bright that the road didn't need lights. We could see everything. Joshua trees, lizards, the earth brown and gray against the cold black sky.

Had the split started before that? Like a little tear at the edge of fabric? If so, I had no idea. I thought that we would go on forever, like the desert sky.

OK. That was hokey. I admit it. Surprise. Iv've had a few drinks.

But I'll let it be because this is true. This is real:

I honestly don't know when we started to be so angry with each other. I mean, I can remember the arguments. And I know that I did some things—not as big as you think. I never actually slept with any of them.

I know it's too late for reasons, but I think I know why I kept throwing myself at other guys now. It's crazy, but I was so unhappy and I didn't know how to tell you, I didn't have the words, because I wasn't supposed to be unhappy. Our life looked like everything I ever said I wanted. If I was unhappy with living this dream, then that would make me the most selfish person ever. So I was trying to let you know that I was unhappy without having to say it in words. What I never got to say was that I was unhappy with myself, not so much with you. OK, you could have spent fewer late nights at work, but that's just logistics.

The night you told me you didn't love me anymore. OK, I deserved that. But I can't pinpoint the actual time when you stopped loving me. It had to be after Joshua Tree because you lloveed me that day and six years later you were gone.

I want us to try again. I want to be a family. I want to make love to you again. Not the angry/hungry sex we had near the end. But the long, sweet, talky sex we had when we loved each other.

I'm sorry. Now I sound desperate, right? Well, you always wanted me to be more vulnerable and here I am. Needing you. Hah. You're getting what you wanted.

Baby. Please come back. I'm sorry for everything I ever said or did.

I love you. I never stopped.

Me

Diane sniffs and wipes the tears off her cheeks. If she weren't so sloshed, she'd admit to herself that there's a lot she left out. After all, T barely ever confronted her about her micro-infidelities, stolen sloppy kisses with his faceless work colleagues, mostly. He'd even encouraged her to find a job or a passion (not his colleagues, admittedly). He'd even offered to go to counseling, which she refused. Because she couldn't imagine confessing to even half the stuff she thought and felt.

Snot is running out of her nose and she needs a Kleenex. But she remembers that she's out. She turns on the desk lamp, unsticks her ass again, and pads over to the hallway bathroom. Reaches in and pulls off a piece of toilet paper.

God, she's a mess. She wipes away her snot and dabs at her eyes. Foolish. She probably looks like hell. She shivers. She should put a T-shirt on.

She blows her nose into the damp toilet paper and tosses it into the trash can. Turning back to the living room, now brighter from the lamp, she can't remember the feeling that made her write all that.

Self-pity is so unattractive.

She walks over and stands in front of the computer, moving the cursor.

But Joshua Tree was real. He'll remember. It was perfect. How many perfect days do we get in a lifetime? Not counting births and weddings (which are, let's face it, never as perfect as they're supposed to be). Four? Five? That's why everyone remembers them. Returning to them again and again in our minds, polishing them until they gleam even more perfect in memory. Flawless and ultimately irretrievable.

She moves the cursor again, now resolute, hits Delete.

Are you sure you want to delete?

Yes.

CHAPTER 5

From: DPlatt@ca.rr.com

To: Manatees   sent Mon, Sept 13 9:19 am

Subject: Sorry everyone

For my late night rant. I was just blowing off steam. My apologies to all. I'll keep my thoughts to myself next time.

Diane

From: Missy@skintastic.com

To: Alejandro.Navaro@Pepperdine.edu   sent Mon, Sept 13 9:46 am

Subject: A couple of things from Missy

Dear Alejandro:

Hi, it's Missy, Randy's wife. and I wanted to reach out to you about a couple of things, if that's OK. The first is to privately make apologies for Randy being tense at the game on Saturday and for not allowing you to coach from the side. He's been under a lot of stress at work and I think that the team is a place where he feels he can shine. I bet that he will welcome you coaching from the side once the team has bonded with him as their coach. Right now if you and Randy split the coaching fifty/fifty, the boys might glom onto you more because you're younger and a pro from a foreign country. You can see where he's coming from.

The other thing I wanted to ask about was you coaching Aiden secretly. This is a little awkward and it has to do with Randy's work, stress, ego, etc. If Randy thought that Aiden had to get coaching from anyone else but him, he would be upset. But Aiden needs it and his dad is on him all the time to make All-Stars, and things would go smoother for everyone if Aiden improved and the team had a great season. I wondered if you could meet on Tuesday afternoons right after school. I'll tell Aiden that it's a surprise for his Dad or something. Anyway, it'll be a secret between the three of us. I can pay in cash, your usual rate plus half, and I can also give you free men's skin care products. That might sound silly, but I thought since your a student you might like some free products.

Thanks, Alejandro.

Missy.

From: Alejandro.Navaro@Pepperdine.edu
To: Missy@skintastic.com   sent Mon, Sept 13 12:01 pm

Subject: Re: A couple of things from Missy

Dear Missy,

I can coach Aiden on Tuesday afternoons. Send me the details and tell Aiden to bring his ball.

Alejandro

To: Missy@skintastic.com
From: order-fulfillment@apieceofpeace.com sent Mon, Sept 13 5:32 pm

Subject: Order 328-11598 has been shipped!

Dear Ms. Tinker,

Your recent order(s) from A Piece of Peace (#328-11598) is now being shipped to the following address:

Missy Tinker
42 S. Maple Street
Beverly Hills, CA 90212

Your order included:
Gratitude Is Attitude
by Susan Spiro Sanders

It's Not Me, It's Myself:
How to Find the YOU You're Hiding From
by Tessa Messing

The Heart Place
Meditations on the Self
by Harold R. Asmin

Declutter Your Soul
Easy Steps to an Organized Home and Heart
by Hoosik Gupta Khatri

Delivery Estimate: September 15–September 26

Track your order's delivery status here:
www.apieceofpeace.com/tracking/11598

Questions? Call our Help Desk at 888-555-PAIX

Interested in similar books? Click here for more: www.apieceofpeace.com

We value your FEEDBACK! Please tell us about your experience at: www.apieceofpeace.com/feedback

THANK YOU FOR YOUR ORDER!

From: FavoriteCoach@gmail.com
To: Manatees   sent Mon, Sept 13 7:12 pm

Subject: Words from your Coach!

Hellooooo Manitees!

My apologies for not weighing in on Saturday's game sooner. As your coach, I should be the first to speak—especially after a loss. But I had some work stuff piling up that just had to be handled pronto. Plus, with a couple days to think about the game, I have a cooler head.

Here goes nothing. Just kidding, I've got a lot to say.

First of all, that loss was a hit, but now we know where our weaknesses are. Remember that regs say (and I say!) that we will always respect the other team. Calling the other team "douchebags" is not going to get us into the playoffs. Plus, we will lose important points for calling out! Remember, we don't just need to win games to get to the tournament, we also need to have at least twenty participation and sportsmanship points.

First, the game wrap-up:

Patrick Woo was a powerhouse out there. Thanks for that beautiful goal, Patrick! You were right where you had to be and sailed it in. And Aiden, that was a sweet assist. It had all the things we've talked about at home before, except you had problems on defense and let a couple goals get by. We'll talk about that at home. Calvin, you brought a massive amount of energy to the game, now focus on running towards the other team's goal. It's usually where most of your teammates are running. Mason, you're my man who takes all my coaching, every time. Now work on taking initiative and not stopping in the middle of the field for instructions. Lets give Reece a shout-out for stepping up to goalie, without any coaching. Ashish has never played soccer before in his life and he avoided getting kicked. Don't be afraid to get in there, Ashish. Ben, we talked about calling out the other team. Anger can be fuel but put it into passing and strategy instead. Dash and Claude, you are going to get so much out of working with Al, I'm excited for you. Isaac and David, still getting to know you. But, remember, let's leave it on the field. Not cool, if you are flipping off the opposing team. Especially if a ref catches it.

We had a lot of near misses out there. But let's not fool ourselves, the other guys were the stronger team. That kid Kobe, was unstoppable. Look. There's talent and then there's hard work. We don't have a Kobe. So we're going to have to win on hard work. So come to practice on Wednesday, ready for drills and strategy. If kids want to stay late with Al, I will see to it that we pay him overtime.

We will be facing Dan Major's team, the Tigers, on Saturday. As many of you know my former friend and assistant, Paco, is training the Tigers. They're a tough combo, but I'm not worried. I know how to get into Majors' head and I will be coaching the kids accordingly at practice.

Coach Randy

"Every man dies, but not every man truly lives."
Mel Gibson as Braveheart

From: Visorgrl@mac.com

To: Manatees   sent Mon, Sept 13 7:27 pm

Subject: Re: Words from your Coach!

I'm so excited to have our first real practice! ☺ I just know that the kids are going to get so much better! Not that they aren't perfect in their own ways now. Thanks, Coach, for keeping us focused on the hard work aspect, because even if the kids lose like they did on Saturday, they'll learn about teamwork, responsibility to each other, and reaching for the stars!

And, here's a reminder: There aren't even supposed to be winners and losers for the first six games. So technically SATURDAY'S LOSS ISN'T EVEN A LOSS!!!! IT'S JUST A GREAT EXPERIENCE! ☺

Anyone who hasn't handed in their health forms, please bring them to practice. Technically, I wasn't supposed to let you play without a form, but I went ahead and let everyone play so there wouldn't be any hurt feelings. Life is bigger than a piece of paper, right?

Go Manatees! XOXO,
Jacqui

From: FavoriteCoach@gmail.com
To: PPousaint@mac.com, MSonnenklar@GSachs.com

sent Mon, Sept 13 7:27 pm

Subject: Confidential

Coach Randy, here.

Paul and Mark, I've talked to you guys at practice about this kid Coach Majors has named Angel. We'll be facing him next week and he is a demon on the field, and there's something about his sudden emergence in the league that doesn't add up. His name is Angel Gonzales and league registration lists his address as:

22893 Brentwood Drive
Zip 90210

I propose that one of you go over to the alleged address and knock on that door, because if Angel's family works in the house (instead of actually living there) he is not allowed in the league. I would do this recon work, but the team could forfeit the whole season if this looks like a team action rather than a couple of rogue dads.

Rogue dads, while not sanctioned, are not unusual and kind of expected.

Obviously, this e-mail never happened.

"Every man dies, but not every man truly lives."
Mel Gibson as Braveheart

————

From: MSonnenklar@GSachs.com
To: FavoriteCoach@gmail.com, PPousaint@mac.com

sent Mon, Sept 13 7:28 pm

Subject: Re: Confidential

I'm on it.

M

—————

From: PPousaint@mac.com
To: MSonnenklar@GSachs.com, FavoriteCoach@gmail.com

sent Mon, Sept 13 7:31 pm

Subject: Re: Confidential

Do we really need to knock on the door? What about a simple phone call?
Paul

—————

From: FavoriteCoach@gmail.com
To: PPousaint@mac.com, MSonnenklar@GSachs.com

sent Mon, Sept 13 7:32 pm

Subject: Re: Confidential

Any challenge to Angel's residency claims must be airtight. Are there, for
instance, other residents in the guesthouse? A live-in nanny?

"Every man dies, but not every man truly lives."
Mel Gibson as Braveheart

_____

From: MSonnenklar@GSachs.com
To: FavoriteCoach@gmail.com, PPousaint@mac.com

sent Mon, Sept 13 7:33 pm

Subject: Re: Confidential

Check. I will go over there and verify the nanny's status by gaining her confidence.

M

_____

From: PPousaint@mac.com
To: MSonnenklar@GSachs.com, FavoriteCoach@gmail.com

sent Mon, Sept 13 7:41 pm

Subject: Re: Confidential

Hey Randy and Mark,

I have to say that I feel very uncomfortable about all this. Aren't we making some racial assumptions here? This doesn't sit well with me. And even if we find out that the kid doesn't legally reside in BH, are we really going to bust a talented kid trying to make good? It seems very anti-Beverly Hills Junior League to me.

Please, let's drop this.

Paul

From: MSonnenklar@GSachs.com

To: PPousaint@mac.com, FavoriteCoach@gmail.com,

sent Mon, Sept 13 7:42 pm

Subject: Re: Confidential

With due respect, Paul, we are only playing by the rules here. Does anyone know if the nanny is single? Any details would help in gaining her trust.

M

.From: PPousaint@mac.com

To: MSonnenklar@GSachs.com, FavoriteCoach@gmail.com

sent Mon, Sept 13 7:44 pm

Subject: Re: Confidential

Mark,

We know nothing about the nanny. We don't even know if there is a nanny and if there is, if the kid is even hers. We don't know these people at all and it's none of our damn business.

Seriously, have we even checked to see that all of our own players are residents? Singling out this one kid is massively unfair and ethically questionable. Do we really want to get into this petty stuff? Randy, can you weigh in here?

Paul

From: FavoriteCoach@gmail.com
To: PPousaint@mac.com, MSonnenklar@GSachs.com

sent Mon, Sept 13 8:32 pm

Subject: Re: Confidential

Sorry guys, Randy here. I had to finish dinner with the wife and kid, and I just got back to these e-mails. Yes, Paul, I've been thinking about it more and I agree that we are opening ourselves up for more scrutiny if we challenge Angel. It takes a big man to admit to a bad idea, but this was a bad idea and I'm a big enough man. Mark, thank you for your unquestioning loyalty, but I think that it is best to abort.

Courage,
Randy

"Every man dies, but not every man truly lives."
Mel Gibson as Braveheart

From: MSonnenklar@GSachs.com
To: FavoriteCoach@gmail.com, PPousaint@mac.com

sent Mon, Sept 13 9:07 pm

Subject: Re: Confidential

I want to go on record as predicting that the decision not to pursue Angel Gonzales will haunt us. I am, however, suspending any further plans to gain access to the nanny.

M

CHAPTER 6

AIDEN IS FINISHING UP HIS story about a joke or a game or a lesson of some kind having to do with his teacher or something like that. It's that precious block of time before Randy comes home from work. Precious because Missy loves breathing in the chubby-cheeked adorableness of her son without having to engage with him a whole lot. He doesn't ask what she's thinking, like Randy occasionally does. A question that makes her feel bristly and defensive. If she wanted to share what she was thinking, wouldn't she have already said it?

Right now, she clears Aiden's plate. She rinses it before stacking it in the dishwasher, even though she could have easily left it for Rosa. Missy feels good about being the type of wife and mother who still does a lot of her own dishes and cooking. It makes her feel useful. She slides a dish towel along the edge of the sink, then folds it in thirds so that the image of a hen faces out and drapes it over the center of the rack next to the draining board. She notices that the ceramic fruits on the windowsill have been moved and she lines them up again, spacing them evenly.

By the time she turns back around, Aiden has finished talking and is staring at something on his phone. She sighs at having completely missed his story, which is not unusual these days. She often finds herself dropping out of conversations as if she's taken a trip somewhere in her mind, returning only to find that the world has moved on without her and she doesn't know what was said or what happened. This wandering is normal, she's been telling herself. It's just that lately her little mental trips are taking longer and longer.

She looks at the oven clock. Five more minutes until Alejandro comes for Aiden's lesson. If he's punctual, that is. Which, Missy guesses, he will be. Because he's being paid.

She thinks about applying lipstick but decides against it. After all, Alejandro is coming over to teach Aiden, not to talk to her.

"Do you know where your cleats are?" she asks Aiden over her shoulder.

"Sure."

"Really? Where are they?"

"In the hall."

"I bet Rosa moved them. Why don't you check your closet now? We don't want you wasting time looking for them when Alejandro is here."

Aiden slides off the kitchen stool with exaggerated effort and clumps into the hall.

The doorbell rings and Missy turns back to the sink and the window on the backyard while she waits for Rosa to get the door. Her thoughts drift to the show she finished watching earlier. An episode of *Hoarders* in which a daughter tells her hoarder father that his grandchildren aren't going to come over anymore unless he completely cleans out everything, which looks like an impossible task. There's so much junk on his front lawn that you can't even see the front door, and that's just for starters. The hoarder dad has stopped living in his upstairs, because there isn't even enough room to stand. Now he's sleeping at night in his kitchen, in a chair, and he still doesn't want to clean up for his grand-kids' sake because he doesn't think there's anything wrong with his place. It's impossible to understand people like that. It's like he can't even control the most basic things.

"Where is the little man?" she hears. And turns to see Alejandro in her kitchen.

Even though she's expecting him, even though she asked him to come over and she's paying him, she's surprised to see him there.

"What?" she says.

"Aiden." Alejandro smiles as if it's the easiest thing in the world to be standing in a strange woman's kitchen. He's holding a stack of orange cones, and she notices his hands have just the right amount of hair on the knuckles.

"Right. Aiden's coming down." In fact, she hears him shuffling in the hall behind Alejandro. "Here he is."

Alejandro makes room for her son, who scoots around him, shouts, "C'mon!" and runs out the back door. Screen slamming. Alejandro smiling broader with his white teeth, but not moving. He's staring at her.

She can feel the delicate chain on her neck against her skin. The air in the room. Why doesn't he move? Her mouth tightens. It's almost like he's insulting her, standing there like that. Looking at her like it's no big deal.

She turns away, back to the sink, looking for something to wash. Something to do with her hands.

"Is okay," she hears him say. She feels him walking toward the door, hears the screen open. A jostling with the cones, but she doesn't make a move to help. Can't, in fact, bear him looking at her again.

The snap of the door shutting. She hears, "Aiden! My man."

Without turning her head, she sees them both out the window, out of the corner of her eye. Bouncing. Placing the cones. Calling out.

And after a short while the air is normal in the kitchen again. She puts her hands on the edge of the sink. Closes her eyes. Thinks of his hands on the cones. And then of his messy, curly hair.

Dumb. Dumb, she tells herself, why is she thinking of Aiden's soccer coach? This is nuts. And she shakes off the thought.

What she *should* be thinking about is all of the things she's grateful for. Because there are a lot. She opens her eyes and turns away from the sink and the window.

It's a good kitchen. A better kitchen than she ever would have dreamed of before meeting Randy. She feels gratitude for her kitchen. And for Aiden, who is healthy and is pretty easy, when you consider everything that could go wrong. She breathes in gratitude. You should make sure to spend time every day being grateful. It's one of the seven habits of happy people. Being grateful. She's read it in two different books on happiness. She takes another breath. She has a good life and Randy is a good man.

She pulls a kitchen stool out from the center island and sits. Her shopping list is there. Almost done. She picks it up and looks at her neat handwriting.

That hoarder dad finally gave in because of the grandchildren, and let the trucks take some of his stuff away. And after most of it was gone, he turned to his daughter with tears in his eyes. At first Missy thought he was crying because he was so thankful. Years of junk had just been carted out of there. He could move around his house again. And you can bet the neighbors were happy about it.

Instead he said, "What am I going to do with myself now?" See? He wasn't thankful at all, and you knew that he was going to go back to being his unhappy hoarding self.

But the main thing—the reason why she keeps thinking about hoarding dad and all hoarders in general—is, how can they be so oblivious to how bad things have gotten? Wouldn't you think that they would look around at their disaster of a house and know that something was seriously wrong in their lives?

That is why you have to work on your state of mind all the time. Which obviously the hoarder dad didn't do. Take something simple like gratitude. It might not be the thing you're thinking in the moment. You have to practice it. You have to pick an ordinary moment and look around.

Missy looks up at the ceramic fruits on her windowsill. Aligned perfectly. Neat and ordered. The total opposite of a hoarder.

She mouths the words *Thank you.*

CHAPTER 7

From: FavoriteCoach@gmail.com

To: Manatees   sent Thur, Sept 16 10:47 am

Subject: A few words about Saturday's Game

Just a quick note from your favorite coach! Just kidding. Where would we be without Al? And the coaching staff is about to get bigger. Let me introduce our brand new, is-it-a-bird-is-it-a-plane, flying in from his office every day, ASSISTANT COACH: Paul Pouisant! Claude's dad.

Seriously, thanks to Paul for devoting time to the team's ultimate success.

More about success and how to achieve it in a minute. First off, mark your calendars right now. On Saturday the 25th Missy and I are hosting a post game party at our place. There will be kids, BBQ, and a horseshoe toss. We opted for a deck instead of a pool, so leave those trunks at home. Invites are going to follow shortly.

Now for success: Al's going to help everyone on their dribbling and side-passing, which is going to give us a lot more opportunities across the middle—especially for passing to Patrick's thunder foot. When in doubt look for Woo. Reece, Ben, and Aiden, keep working on your set-ups. I know that everyone wants to score goals, but remember that assists make games! That's coming from a proud assist guy—ME!

Calvin, Dashiell, Ashish, Claude, David, and Isaac keep working with Al. The main thing, guys is to want to get close to the ball.

Parents, I'm going to let you all in on a coach's dilemma right now. To tell, or not to tell, the players about a particular strength on the opposing team. This time, I am choosing to tell you about a particular strength that goes by the name of Angel Gonzales. Guys, we have to stay on this scoring demon like white on rice. The sole focus should be to disable Angel, because without him, the Tigers are average at best.

In order to maximize our chances against the Tigers and Angel specifically, I would like you to share with your kids a technique I like to call, "Focused Rage". It's when you take all of your old losses (say you did badly on a test or a friend sat with someone else on the bus)—and focus all your leftover anger on one target. I guarantee that if we all do it, Angel won't be able to function. Now, does this mean kicking, trash-talking, or taking him down? Absolutely not! We will be kicked out of the league for this!!!!! Do not, do not, absolutely do not, resort to these tactics! Keep the rage all in your mind. It's a powerful mental tool, believe me. All star athletes use anger to get results. The trick is to keep it focused on one outcome.

And that outcome is contain Angel and BEAT THE TIGERS!!!!!!!!!!!

Who wants TIGER MEAT?

"Every man dies, but not every man truly lives."
Mel Gibson as Braveheart

From: Visorgrl@mac.com
To: FavoriteCoach@gmail.com   sent Thur, Sept 16 11:28 am

Subject: Re: A few words about Saturday's Game

Randy, this is just a quick, little note. I don't think that the kids are ready for techniques like "focused rage". I'm not even sure you should be saying things like this inside the league. To remind you, these are not competitive games. There is no winning and losing, and saying we should eat tiger meat is against the mission of the league.

I loved working with you last year. You were so POSITIVE AND FUN. ☺ Let's access that guy again! The guy who throws team parties on his deck, not the tiger meat-eating guy.

No offense, I'm just using my power as Team Mom to suggest that you send a more upbeat e-mail, like the Morgan Freeman poem.

XO
Jacqui

FROM: PPOUSAINT
TO: RTINKER

Rage stuff way over the top. I can't assist if you keep suggesting covert missions and rage talk.

Paul

FROM: RTINKER
TO: PPOUSAINT

Really? I said no force. Keep it mental

FROM: PPOUSAINT
TO: RTINKER

They are TEN. They don't even have
rage.

FROM: RTINKER
TO: PPOUSAINT

mine does. But I get point.

FROM: PPOUSAINT
TO: RTINKER

Also, Alejandro's name isn't Al. I've been
meaning to say something. Noticed it in
your e-mail.

From: Mako@Shakrayoga.org
To: Manatees   sent Thur, Sept 16 12:06 pm

Subject: Re: A few words about Saturday's Game

Dear Coach (and fellow parents),
I have a real problem with the tone of your last letter on rage, and will not
be sharing it with Mason. I agree that team sports are all about getting
your kid competitive and, as an adult, I certainly understand that power in
turning negative feelings into a motivational force. Professional jealousy, for
example, has motivated myself and many a CEO. But for our kids, please
keep the rhetoric on the importance of practice, hard work, and sacrifice.

Regards,
Mako

From: DPlatt@ca.rr.com

To: Manatees   sent Thur, Sept 16 1:47 pm

Subject: Re: A few words about Saturday's Game

Rage and tiger meat? What the hell was that about?

Sent from my iPhone

From: FavoriteCoach@gmail.com

To: Manatees   sent Thur, Sept 16 5:47 pm

Subject: A few NEW words about Saturday's Game

From the desk of your not-so-favorite coach right now! I get it. My apologies for treating our players like pros instead of the kids that they are. I hear you and we are definitely working on team-building, skills, and a positive spirit according to the Beverly Hills Junior Soccer League charter. I certainly didn't want to turn them into rage machines, all I'm doing is looking for that extra edge that winning teams have. I know that these games aren't competitive but, believe me, those boys want to win. And once they get a taste of it, they can't get enough. That's all I meant with the meat reference. It's like lion cubs digging into a dead gazelle. If you give them a tiny taste, they'll fight the others for more gazelle.

And, believe me, Dan Majors is talking this exact way with his team. I've heard him. He was a Navy Seal and has referenced night raids and drone strikes.

Regardless, I got your objections loud and clear. I'll keep it positive in my game speech on Saturday. Go Manatees!

Coach Randy

"Every man dies, but not every man truly lives."
Mel Gibson as Braveheart

From: Visorgrl@mac.com
To: Manatees   sent Thur, Sept 16 5:55 pm

Subject: Re: A few NEW words about Saturday's Game

Go Manatees!

Thanks, Coach. Great stuff and we're a GREAT TEAM!

The Sarins are on for snacks (Ashish's parents) and there are still a couple of health forms out. This happens every year. Parents who forget and start to think it doesn't matter because I let the kids play anyway. PLEASE, don't forget the forms. You know who you are!

On a personal note, Calvin says that someone stole his Star Wars water bottle. Maybe someone simply mistook it for theirs. That sounds like a more likely story. Anyway, if you find that you have it, could you return it to me? I know it was only ten dollars, but Target stopped selling them, and Calvin is really attached to it. Thanks! And no questions asked!!!!! ☺

See you out there on the field!

XO
Jacqui

From: MSonnenklar@GSachs.com
To: Manatees   sent Thur, Sept 16 6:27 pm

Subject: Re: A few NEW words about Saturday's Game

I think you're all overreacting to focused rage. Coaches say stuff like that all the time. Will be sharing rage email with Ben.

M

From: JWoo@DesignX.com
To: Manatees   sent Thur, Sept 16 6:30 pm

Subject: Re: A few NEW words about Saturday's Game

We are sorry that Patrick found the water bottle. He did not know it Calvin's. Patrick will bring back the bottle and he will make his apology for doing this to the team on Saturday.

Sincerely,
Jung-ah Woo

From: Visorgrl@mac.com
To: JWoo@DesignX.com   sent Thur, Sept 16 6:32 pm

Subject: Team apology

Dear Ms. (?) or Mr. Woo (forgive me, I can't tell from "Jung-ah"),

It isn't necessary to make a team apology for something that is so clearly an accident. Patrick is such a great kid and so polite, not to mention our high scorer, even with just one game under our belt! Really, a whole apology to the team is not necessary. In fact, why don't you tell Patrick that he can keep the water bottle as a gift? Our pleasure. I didn't mean to make it a big deal. I'm sorry to have upset your family.

XO,
Jacqui

——————

From: DPlatt@ca.rr.com
To: Visorgrl@mac.com   sent Thur, Sept 16 6:32 pm

Subject: (No Subject)

Jacqui, I thought you should know. Reece says he saw Patrick steal the water bottle. It wasn't an accident. Let's all keep an eye out. Maybe Patrick is already figuring out how to focus his rage. Just saying.

——————

From: Visorgrl@mac.com
To: DPlatt@ca.rr.com   sent Thur, Sept 16 6:33 pm

Subject: Re: (No Subject)

Dear Diane, It's hard to tell where the truth lies with these kids. Right? Let's just close this incident and love our boys. ☺ It's being handled.

XO,
Jacqui

CHAPTER 8

THE WALLS OF PATRICK'S BEDROOM are freshly painted blue and his desk is clean and white. He sits on the edge of his bed with the *Star Wars* water bottle in his hands. He stays very still. He is good at this. His mother told him to sit in his room and consider his crime. He slows down his breathing so that even his stomach doesn't move. That's how still he can be.

He tries to remember soccer practice and the precise moment that he wanted the water bottle. Was it the first time he saw it? Or was it the couple of times after that? Did he even like it? He doesn't know. His parents could have bought him one just like it. In fact, he knows that they would have, after a game. After he scored the most goals. He could have said to them, "I want a water bottle like Calvin's." And they would have bought it for him. They would have gotten him anything he wanted.

But he hadn't wanted to wait. And, anyway, he didn't want to get a water bottle from his parents because he scored goals. He wanted to get it for no reason at all. What's wrong with getting something for nothing?

He has compromised his excellence. That's what his mother said. She cried and smacked him hard on the cheek. He knows that it is not just his own excellence that has been compromised. It is his family's. And that is why he must be punished.

If only he had hidden the water bottle. What was he thinking? Putting it on his desk? Next to the pencil case he took from David on the bus. He should hide the pencil case right now. But he likes looking at it and his mother hasn't noticed.

He rolls the water bottle between his hands. He wishes he hadn't been born this way. Wanting things. Always wanting more. He wishes he were like other kids who lose things and never even look for them, that's how much they don't care. Now he has to apologize to the whole team. Why does he have to apologize? Aiden and Mason are so bad at soccer, he practically has to make the goals all by himself. And there is no defense. Ben just yells inappropriate things at the other team, like "douchebag" and "fag." That's Ben's idea of defense. Reece is an okay player, but he won't always pass to Patrick. And Coach will end up putting him on goal anyway. The others can't play at all. Dashiell runs and cries like a girl. Calvin forgets which way to go. It's all up to Patrick. So what if he takes a water bottle?

He hears cars go by on the street outside. It's going to be dark soon and he doesn't know when his mother will come and get him. Sometimes it's over by dinner, and sometimes he waits so long that it's nighttime and he goes to bed without anything to eat.

He looks down at his stomach and makes the decision. He breathes so that he can see his tummy move this time. He moves his stomach purposefully, in and out with his breaths. Then he speeds up the breaths. In, out, in, out, in, out, in, out. Fast breathing. Stomach going in and out.

He drops the water bottle. In, out. Stomach in and out. He scrunches his face and breathes hard through his nose like a horse. His nostrils are wide. He breathes so fast, so hard that he makes a snorting sound. He keeps it up. Faster and faster. Snorting through his nose. His limbs are numb. In, out. In, out. Then he feels it. Something about to release. He has done this before.

He stops snorting.

Now he slows. Slows. Even more. Slows his breathing down. Slowing it, finally, into one long smooth inhale. Then, oh, so stealthy on the exhale, he slips, pop, out of his body.

Hovering slightly above the boy sitting on the bed with a water bottle at his feet, he is now vapor. Does he feel sorry for the boy? Not really. It is time for him to leave all that for a while. Time to leave all feeling.

He floats over to the window. Passes through it without making a sound. He would not want the boy's parents to hear. Not that they would, above the television and their tight, low voices arguing. And what would it matter? If they were to come into the boy's room, they would not notice him missing.

He drifts above the street in the twilight, watching lights go on in his building and the one across the way. But he is not interested in using his gift for spying. He rises higher and higher. He starts to dip, swoop, and gain speed. Up and up. Faster and faster until he is soaring over roofs, over parks and soccer fields. Ever gaining in speed and momentum, he flies up, up, up to the stars and beyond, into the dark that is darker than nothing. Where he is free.

CHAPTER 9

From: PPousaint@mac.com

To: Manatees   sent Sat, Sept 18 4:39 pm

Subject: Great game!

Wow, Manatees! We really did it. On behalf of your coaching staff, headed by fearless Coach Randy (who had to take off to work directly after the game), may I say congratulations on your first and well-deserved win.

As Coach has pointed out many times, it's not all about goals. In Soccer, everyone has to play their position in order for good things to happen. Good things like Patrick's unbelievable three goals, Aiden's one goal, and Reece's corner goal. Sweet. That's five goals! Five! To Angel's two.

Everyone, everyone, did a magnificent job! Great defense staying on top of Angel just like we planned.

Now, get some rest, and we'll see you at practice.

Coach Paul

From: Visorgrl@mac.com

To: Manatees   sent Sat, Sept 18 5:11 pm

Subject: Re: Great game!

Go Manatees! That was SO EXCITING!! You were awesome out there, every one of you!!!!! And even though these games don't count, it shows that wins are possible. Every team has to win sometime, right? And we can feel good about it when it's our turn!

You know what also makes me feel good? Health forms! There's still one out. I don't want to name names, but you know who you are!

Calvin felt so good about the game that he came home and started kicking a ball around in the back yard. He's never chosen the outdoors over the IPad before. That's the power of team sports and now he's internally motivated to help the team be the best they can be. Frankly, I think that that's where real power comes from. Not from rage, but an inner drive to help others. Calvin wants to be a veterinarian when he grows up.

Speaking of team spirit and internal motivation, thanks so much to Patrick for his little apology before the game. It was completely unnecessary, but manners like that are so impressive in such a young man. You are going places, Patrick!

Applause to everyone! This is going to be a great season and I am humbled to be a part of it!!

XOXO,
Jacqui

From: ParadiseB@gmail.com
To: Manatees   sent Sat, Sept 18 5:39 pm

Subject: Re: Great game!

Jacqui, so well said! I just wanted to check if anyone found Dashiell's Pokemon cards? I should have looked harder when I was picking up, but his sister was having a meltdown in the car and I was just hoping some-one would keep them for him.

Best to all of you,
Beth

———————

From: MSonnenklar@GSachs.com
To: Manatees   sent Sat, Sept 18 5:39 pm

Subject: Re: Great game!

Can we call the team the Magic Manatees now? ☺

M

———————

From: JWoo@DesignX.com
To: Manatees   sent Sat, Sept 18 5:45 pm

Subject: Re: Great game!

Patrick is very happy to score goals and to give the apology.
Jung-ah Woo

From: Alejandro.Navaro@Pepperdine.edu

To: Manatees   sent Sat, Sept 18 5:50 pm

Subject: Re: Great game!

Great game, men.

Alejandro

From: FavoriteCoach@gmail.com

To: Manatees   sent Sat, Sept 18 6:04 pm

Subject: Save the Date Manatees!

Hello Manatees!!! Next Saturday, Sept. 25—after the game! Please save the date for our victory (hope so!!!!!) celebration BBQ at Casa de Tinker! We will have meats and meat substitutes on hand for grilling! Bring a salad or a side! We'll have everything else that our warriors and their hungry (and thirsty!) parents will need! Go Manatees! Go parents! Let's have some rocking fun!

Coach Randy and Missy

"Every man dies, but not every man truly lives."
Mel Gibson as Braveheart

From: KSonn@gmail.com

To: MSonnenklar@GSachs.com   sent Sat, Sept 18 6:18 pm

Subject: Team BBQ

Are you going? It's my Saturday and I thought I'd take Ben, but don't want to go if you are there.

————————

From: MSonnenklar@GSachs.com

To: KSonn@gmail.com   sent Sat, Sept 18 6:28 pm

Subject: Re: Team BBQ

Seriously? Since when were u interested in the team?

M

————————

From: KSonn@gmail.com

To: MSonnenklar@GSachs.com   sent Sat, Sept 18 6:30 pm

Subject: Re: Team BBQ

Not interested in the team, personally. But Ben wants to go and I'm his mom. So, I'll go. Just answer the question, are you going to be there?

————————

From: MSonnenklar@GSachs.com
To: KSonn@gmail.com   sent Sat, Sept 18 6:31 pm

Subject: Re: Team BBQ

Was planning on going w Kelli

M

_____

From: KSonn@gmail.com
To: MSonnenklar@GSachs.com   sent Sat, Sept 18 6:32 pm

Subject: Re: Team BBQ

I don't give a fuck if you bring Kelli, you narcissistic asshole. I just don't care to run into your fat face at a BBQ and have to pretend that you are a normal human being. You take Ben and drop him off at my place afterwards. I'll skip the game too because I can't look at you without wanting to vomit.

_____

From: MSonnenklar@GSachs.com
To: KSonn@gmail.com   sent Sat, Sept 18 6:33 pm

Subject: Re: Team BBQ

Nice coparenting skills ur exhibiting.

M

_____

From: KSonn@gmail.com
To: MSonnenklar@GSachs.com   sent Sat, Sept 18 6:33 pm

Subject: Re: Team BBQ

Just being honest, you fat fuck. I'm not jealous of Kelli, I feel sorry for her.

From: MSonnenklar@GSachs.com
To: KSonn@gmail.com   sent Sat, Sept 18 6:33 pm

Subject: Re: Team BBQ

"Fat Fuck"? Nice. Really civilized.

M

From: KSonn@gmail.com
To: MSonnenklar@GSachs.com   sent Sat, Sept 18 6:34 pm

Subject: Re: Team BBQ

I wasn't attempting to be civilized. Just accurate. Asswipe.

From: MSonnenklar@GSachs.com
To: KSonn@gmail.com   sent Sat, Sept 18 6:34 pm

Subject: Re: Team BBQ

R U sure ass wipe isn't 2 words?

M

———————

From: KSonn@gmail.com
To: MSonnenklar@GSachs.com   sent Sat, Sept 18 6:34 pm

Subject: Re: Team BBQ

One word. Cocksucker.

———————

From: MSonnenklar@GSachs.com
To: KSonn@gmail.com   sent Sat, Sept 18 6:34 pm

Subject: Re: Team BBQ

Creative.

M

———————

From: KSonn@gmail.com
To: MSonnenklar@GSachs.com   sent Sat, Sept 18 6:35 pm

Subject: Re: Team BBQ

Testical licking lizard from inside the crack of someone else's ass.

––––––––––

From: MSonnenklar@GSachs.com
To: KSonn@gmail.com   sent Sat, Sept 18 6:38 pm

Subject: Re: Team BBQ

I refuse to participate in this. Kelli is making dinner.

M

––––––––––

From: KSonn@gmail.com
To: MSonnenklar@GSachs.com   sent Sat, Sept 18 6:38 pm

Subject: Re: Team BBQ

Tell Kelli that she's married to a scrotum sucking flea who hangs off of a pig's ballsack. Oh, sorry. That's BALL SACK. TWO WORDS. Fucker.

CHAPTER 10

EVEN THOUGH HE'S ALONE AT the office on a Saturday afternoon, Randy cannot stop smiling. Hot damn, it feels good to win at something. Anything. Jesus, he feels so alive.

He paces back and forth in front of his desk, barely looking out of his eleventh-floor panoramic window to see the glare of the noonday sun made hazy by smog and heat.

The pacing isn't burning off his excitement, so he adds a few hops up and down. Woohoo. Man oh man. The team was totally on fire this morning and this was what, only their second game? The moms hated the rage stuff. But really, it took rage to coalesce the team. The kids had felt defeated, humiliated by last week's loss. So before the game, he gathered them tightly around him and played them the big speech from *Lord of the Rings* on his phone. The volume was weak and Calvin was shoving everyone out of the way, but man, they still got it. Especially when he recited the speech along with the clip.

He stops in front of his desk and bounces on his toes. Man, he is amped. He bounces, remembering Missy throwing her arms around him the second the last whistle blew. Remembering the boys charging at him, jumping on him. Aiden smiling and burying his face into Randy's stomach. That's all he ever wanted. Right?

Enough of this. He should sit down. Get some work done. Hell, if he finishes everything here and gets home before the good feelings wear off, maybe Missy will give him a little action.

Okay. Focus. He forces himself to stop moving. He puts his hand to his neck and feels his pulse jumping even though he is now still.

Maybe some coffee. Nah. Tea. Without caffeine. Something soothing, like chamomile.

He giggles at the idea of chamomile. But seriously, it's not a bad idea. How else should he calm down?

He could jerk off.

Here in the office? In front of the window?

Why not? He did it after the Office Depot deal.

Yeah, but that was at night.

Right. When he was even *more* visible! Seriously, anyway. Like people on the street are going to look all the way up at his tiny window, look *through* the window and see him going at it.

Randy rounds his desk, plops into his chair, and considers. To jerk off or not to jerk off? This is the constant question.

If he jerks off, he might get sleepy, and he has a shit load of work to crank out. Yeah, but he'll be able to focus, which is the main issue right now.

Then there's the problem of his pants.

Fuck, this is stupid. He could just do it in the bathroom. No window. No mess.

But not nearly as exciting. And, let's face it, the bathroom's a little sad. Desperate.

The night of the Office Depot deal had been pretty epic, even though it was just him. Randy leans back in his chair, resting his hand on his crotch. What to do. What to do.

He feels himself get hard. Man. Hard like a rock. He grabs his dick through his pants and squeezes. AAAAHHHHHH!

God, now he has to fuck everything. The desk. His chair. His fucking computer. Slide his cock along the keys. Stick his dick into something warm and wet. God, why can't he suck himself off?

Fast. He unbuttons his fly, starts to yank down his pants.

And.

What?

Stops.

What?
Wait. No. Wait.
Not this. Don't waste it on this.
Keep the energy going. Keep the feeling.
Use it like fuel.
Like rage.

CHAPTER 11

From: RTinker@OneStopOffice.com

To: Dan@DanMajors.com   sent Sat, Sept 18 5:33 pm

Subject: Today's game

Hey Dan! Great game today and great to see you and Paco out there! I have to say that even though we prevailed, your Tigers are going to be hard to beat in the playoffs. Nice work and, by the way, it would be great to have you and Jeanne over for dinner sometime. Has it really been a whole year since we've seen you two? I guess I got pretty bent out of shape over losing Paco, but now that things have worked out with Al, I can see that it was all business and nothing personal.

How about the Saturday after next? I can't do next weekend because we're throwing a BBQ for the team families. Hopefully, we'll be celebrating our second win of the season!! Not that I'm counting any chickens, it's just this Woo kid is a dynamo and my own kid, Aiden, is showing some promise too. Anyway, let me know if the 2nd works for you.

Randy
P.S. Hey, that Angel is some player! I don't remember him from last year. New to the neighborhood?

Randy Tinker
Executive Director of Sales
OneStopOffice
739 La Jolla Drive
Los Angeles, CA 90042

From: RTinker@OneStopOffice.com
To: SReidel@OneStopOffice.com   sent Sat, Sept 18 8:09 pm

Subject: Confidential to Sam

Attachment: EFY.Projections

Hi Sam,

I am writing to let you know that End of Fiscal Year projections are complete as of this Saturday afternoon. The reason why they were incomplete at end of day, yesterday, is because despite most of our best efforts, we are undermanned and overworked. I don't know what corporate thinks we do all day, but it certainly isn't sitting around thinking of ways to handicap ourselves—as they are currently doing!

I came in this Saturday (my third in a row) as a favor to you and the department. Liz and Jeff said they would be putting in time this weekend and, so far, I'm the only one who showed. Jeff sent a text about his wife getting on his case, and I got nada from Liz. You know me, Sam, I'm a company guy, but I cannot continue to carry the department alone—and, guess what, my wife gets on my case too. I could be celebrating my son's soccer victory (Yes, I am also the coach) right now, but I'm here, getting it done.

Look, this isn't just a complaint, and the solution is simple. Since restructuring, Liz, Jeff, and I are doing the job of seven people. The austerity experiment isn't working. We need to add two more people at the very least. I admit that Gina was a drain, so her position is indeed irrelevant as it was when she was here. But moving Radcliff and Marcia was insane. What was Jeremy thinking? Basically, corporate looked at a fully functioning department and said, hmmm, let's chop off one arm, one leg, a testicle—and see if it can continue to produce at the same rate.

What would make the most sense is to have me out there selling more and back here, doing a whole lot less. This is the one and only reason why sales have been down—my having to do so much work at corporate that I don't get to the job of doing what I do best. SELL! Not to mention the personal hit I'm taking financially. Those commissions are not nothing to me.

When we spoke two weeks ago, you indicated that you might take this matter up with Jeremy yourself. Have you been able to approach him yet? Nevermind, maybe it's about time for me to go straight to him myself. I know it's messy since he's been "seeing" Liz (worst kept secret in the history of the company) but someone has to get this ship back on course.

I know that I can speak about this to you in confidence, with all we've been through. It's just that I really do not want to pull another weekend here. Has Liz stepped up once? The answer is "no", and being Jeremy's flavor of the month shouldn't protect her from doing her share of work at corporate. Too bad I'm not Jeremy's type, right?

Going home.

Randy

Randy Tinker
Executive Director of Sales
OneStopOffice
739 La Jolla Drive
Los Angeles, CA 90042

———————

From: Recall notification
To: RTinker@OneStopOffice.com   sent Sat, Sept 18 8:23 pm

Subject: Recall Failure

Message Confidential to Sam, <SReidel@OneStopOffice.com>
Status: Recall Failed

———————

From: SReidel@OneStopOffice.com
To: JHandHR@OneStopOffice.com   sent Mon, Sept 20 9:36 am

Subject: Fwd: Confidential to Sam

Dear Jenny,

I am apprising HR of a recent e-mail I received from Randy Tinker. See
below. Let me know how you would like me to proceed.

Sam Reidel

Sam Reidel
Senior Vice President
OneStopOffice
739 La Jolla Drive
Los Angeles, CA 90042

———————

From: Missy@skintastic.com
To: Alejandro.Navaro@Pepperdine.edu   sent Mon, Sept 20 7:23 pm

Subject: From Missy

Dear Alejandro,

I wanted to thank you for the great job your doing with Aiden, and I'm not just talking about soccer skills, I'm talking about the bond that you are creating with him. Your so firm, without being short-tempered. That's a tough balance to strike, because, as you now know, Aiden tends to want to give up easily.

I know that Randy seems like an easy-going guy and he is. He's a great coach and a good man all the way around, but he's tough on Aiden. Sometimes I feel guilty that I didn't have another child. That way, it wouldn't all come down to Aiden, at least in Randy's mind, if Aiden doesn't succeed, then what does Randy have as his legacy?

I mentioned to you before that Randy has a lot of job stress. That doesn't seem to be letting up, at the moment, and I'm not sure what it's all about because Randy won't talk about it.

I don't know why I'm telling you all this, except to say "thank you" for coming into our lives when you did.

Thank you.

Warmly,
Missy

———————

From: Alejandro.Navaro@Pepperdine.edu

To: Missy@skintastic.com   sent Mon, Sept 20 10:23 pm

Subject: Re: From Missy

Dear Missy,

Thank you for your e-mail. Aiden is a great kid. I am happy to help always. I am sorry to hear everything is difficult at home. You have the love of a mother and a wife. It is good that you care so much.

Alejandro

From: Missy@skintastic.com

To: Alejandro.Navaro@Pepperdine.edu   sent Mon, Sept 20 10:40 pm

Subject: Re: From Missy

Alejandro, how very kind of you to say so. Sometimes I don't feel very loving, in fact, the troubles of the last year make me feel small-minded. After all, there are so many people in the world who have much harder lives than mine. They don't have enough food to eat, and some of them don't even have houses or jobs. I mean, look at us, we're really very lucky. Aiden wasn't born with a deformity or anything like that. Aiden isn't autistic, like some boys born in California (there's a higher rate here than other places, did you know that? Also, by the way, Calvin—is probably autistic, Jacqui may be in denial). Believe me, living in Beverly Hills doesn't save you from autism, I see it all the time.

So you see, I have a lot to be grateful for. Randy doesn't have cancer or anything, he just has job stress.

And I am perfectly healthy. We have a great house and all I have to do is apply myself more to my skin care business, so that we have a safety net.

Thank you for saying I'm a good mother and wife. I really try, and I guess that's what's important.

Warmly,
Missy

_____

From: Alejandro.Navaro@Pepperdine.edu
To: Missy@skintastic.com   sent Mon, Sept 20 10:48 pm

Subject: Re: From Missy

Dear Missy,

It is beautiful that you care so much. You are a beautiful woman on the inside and the outside.

Alejandro

_____

From: Missy@skintastic.com
To: Alejandro.Navaro@Pepperdine.edu   sent Mon, Sept 20 10:50 pm

Subject: Re: From Missy

OK. Now you just made this married lady blush. Thank you, Mr.

See you tomorrow.

Missy

CHAPTER 12

MISSY WATCHES RANDY THROUGH THE kitchen window. It's dark. Aiden has finally fallen asleep after arguing and crying when she wouldn't let him keep his iPhone in bed. She wanted to give in, because it's so much easier when he is happily engaged and she can sit next to him and sniff his hair for a few minutes. But recently, Aiden's teacher has been stressing a max of only two hours of screen time a night. And even though it might cut down on hair-sniffing time, Missy's got to start accepting that Aiden's getting bigger and has got to start working on life skills. Like self-restraint, the teacher says.

She can see Randy leaning against the railing of the deck, because he has lit the faux tiki torches she scored at the Rose Bowl Flea Market.

She is tired and wants nothing more than to curl up and watch *What Not to Wear* on her computer, wrapped in a comforter, with her socks on. But Randy looks so alone and she can feel the need emanating from his core like a laser grid. Heat seeking. If she does not go out to meet it, it will find her.

She grabs her sweater and pushes the screen door open. Randy turns and sees her. The delight on his face almost breaks her. Why didn't he come into the kitchen and get her? Why is he always waiting for her like a wounded puppy? It wasn't always like this. When did it change?

"Hi," she says, stepping onto the deck and sliding in by his side, her shoulder touching his biceps. They look out at the tree line. "How was practice?" Better to talk about the team than work. Whenever it's work, he goes off on the exact same rant about Liz and the new boss changing things so that sales are down. It makes her anxious.

"Looking good," says Randy, taking a sip of his glass of wine. "Al's got them dribbling up and down the whole field, not just the half field. They're learning to open it up a bit and look for Woo. Sometimes Aiden. Reece isn't half-bad." He sighs. "Calvin's a nightmare. He still cries if no one passes to him. Even Dashiell thinks he's a pussy. And that's saying something."

She leans against his arm. "You should go easy on Calvin. I don't think he can help it."

"Help it? There's no way of knowing for sure what's going on with that kid. But it's definitely something. Jacqui always interrupts whenever I try to give him constructive pointers. I'd take her on, but she might quit and nobody else will be team mom. It's too much work."

Missy pulls away. She sure as hell isn't doing it. Is that what he's suggesting?

Randy slides his arm around her waist and pulls her close again, "Forget it. Jacqui's fine. I'll go easy on Calvin. Hell, I *do* go easy on him. He should have been suspended for two games after licking that kid's hand last week."

"At least he wasn't biting. That's progress."

"Now you sound like Jacqui."

She laughs. And Randy tightens his grip.

This should feel good, she thinks. They are acting like a couple. They are couple-ish. She fits neatly under his arm, her shoulder slotted into his armpit.

She looks up at his face. He is looking out at the yard, lit by torches. Which makes him happy. And she knows—it's such a simple thing, really—what would make him even happier. Before she can talk herself out of it, she pops up on tippy-toes and gives him a quick kiss on the cheek.

He looks down at her with grateful eyes, then goes in for the big kiss. Slamming into her mouth. Scratchy and rough. His pointy tongue working her lips apart and darting in. She wills herself to stay put. Give him this one thing. She reaches up and grabs his shoulders, pulling him closer. Feels his yearning. The tightness of what he cannot ask for. She presses into him.

Give him this. Give it and be done.

CHAPTER 13

From: DPlatt@ca.rr.com

To: Manatees   sent Sat, Sept 25 10:55 pm

Subject: Great game!

Another win! Go maneteess

From: DPlatt@ca.rr.com

To: Manatees   sent Sat, Sept 25 10:55 pm

Subject: Re: Great game!

Sorry. Mispelled that. A little looped still.

Go Manatees! And great party Randy!

Diane

From: DPlatt@ca.rr.com
To: Manatees   sent Sat, Sept 25 10:56 pm

Subject: Re: Great game

Shit! I forgot. And thanks to missy too. Great quiches and dips. I remember them from last year and was secretly hoping you'd make them again!

———————

From: DPlatt@ca.rr.com
To: Manatees   sent Sat, Sept 25 10:58 pm

Subject: Re: Great game!

Nothing like a great BBQ after another win for our boys. Randy you are really pulling it togther out there on the field. And now, that BBQ. I don't know whyour always apologizing about the swimming pool. That outside fireplace is genius. Don't' hachnge a thing. And some of the karaoke was hot. Seriously. I would've gotten up ther to sing, but I wasn't about to follow. Aljjjandro! That was soo forget about it.

———————

From: Mako@Shakrayoga.org
To: Manatees   sent Sat, Sept 25 11:00 pm

Subject: Re: Great game!

I'm not sure that I can match Diane's exuberance, but thanks to the Tinkers for a lovely afternoon. Hi Diane, did you drive home? Hope not.

Regards and thanks to all,
Mako and Edward

———————

From: Visorgrl@mac.com

To: Manatees　　　　　　　　　　　　sent Sat, Sept 25 11:07 pm

Subject: Re: Great game!

Wow!! We are a REAL TEAM now, and thanks to our awesome coaching staff for taking us to another victory. It's fun to win!

I want to apologize for Calvin having a meltdown at the BBQ. He gets like that when he's tired or hot or hungry or bored—and he was probably all FOUR!! ☺

Randy, I know you're getting lots of great feedback on your party, but let me be the first to say, who knew you could sing like that?!!!! GET OUT OF TOWN!!! ☺☺☺ You sounded just like Freddy Mercury on "We are the Champions"! I'm SERIOUS! That Karaoke machine is so much fun!

XOXO,
Jacqui

———————

From: MSonnenklar@GSachs.com

To: Manatees　　　　　　　　　　　　sent Sat, Sept 25 11:10 pm

Subject: Re: Great game!

Kelli and I had a great time too. How about Kelli and Missy heating things up with, "What's Love Got To Do With It?" I'd pay good money to see that duo dirty dance again. Here's to another great year of Tinker gatherings! Goodnight everyone.

M

From: DPlatt@ca.rr.com

To: Manatees   sent Sun, Sept 26 10:55 am

Subject: Re: Great game!

Good morning, all. And so sorry for my late night ramblings. I was really tired and hadn't had much to eat so that glass of wine really went to my head.

Best, Diane

From: FavoriteCoach@gmail.com

To: Manatees   sent Sun, Sept 26 11:31 am

Subject: Re: Great game!

Go Manatees!

Wow, you all know how to make a coach feel special. What a great time was had by all (sometimes a little "too" great a time, but—hey, it's the weekend!). Missy is sleeping in, so I'll send her thanks along with mine.

Strictly for the adults: I'm not sure I should quit my day job to start a "Queen" tribute band, but I do know that Alejandro could make some extra dough at Chippendales! That fake stripper routine was something else—and I'm a man!!! Did you collect all your dollars, Al? I think I saw a couple of bills behind the couch! (HAH)

Go Team parents!

From your favorite Coach,

Freddy Mercury!!

"Every man dies, but not every man truly lives."
Mel Gibson as Braveheart

From: Mako@Shakrayoga.org
To: Manatees   sent Sun, Sept 26 12:01 pm

Subject: Re: Great game!

It sounds like I missed a lot by leaving the party early. I hope there are no regrets! Just kidding. I'm sure everyone was on their best behavior with the kids around and everything.

Best,
Mako

From: RTinker@OneStopOffice.com
To: DPlatt@ca.rr.com   sent Sun, Sept 26 12:01 pm

Subject: From Randy

Hey Diane. Randy here.

I'm not sure you'll recognize my e-mail, since I'm not using the team e-mail address. I just wanted to check on you to see that you're feeling OK. I know you didn't have a lot to eat, and the wine and sun went to your head, like you said. Seriously, just me saying it, but you really can give yourself permission to eat. You're never going to be someone who has to watch their calories! Have you lost weight from last year? I know some women get on a whole regimen after they get divorced. I'm sorry about that, by the way. Thomas seemed like a great guy last season.

Anyway, I am glad I got you the cab. Do you want me to drive over and get you today so you can pick up your car?

Also, some things were said under the influence. I didn't want you to worry about that—unless you want to!

Regards,
Randy

Randy Tinker
Executive Director of Sales
OneStopOffice
739 La Jolla Drive
Los Angeles, CA 90042

―――――――――

From: Alejandro.Navaro@Pepperdine.edu
To: Missy@skintastic.com   sent Sun, Sept 26 12:04 pm

Subject: (No Subject)

Missy,

I hope I don't embarrass you at the party. It was silly and I wanted to make the others laugh.

You are beautiful and sexy when you sing. Is it wrong for me to think it?

Alejandro

From: Missy@skintastic.com
To: Alejandro.Navaro@Pepperdine.edu   sent Sun, Sept 26 12:07 pm

Subject: Re: (No Subject)

Dear Alejandro,

What a sweet thing to say. No, it is not wrong to tell a woman that she is sexy and beautiful. Women love to be admired, even when they are married. In fact, sometimes it's more important to hear those things when your married. People forget that your a living, breathing woman when your a mom and married to someone who is as funny as Randy is.

Thank you for being so sweet, and I wasn't embarrassed by your fake strip tease. It was funny and I think that you were the hit of the evening, especially with the moms! It was all good, clean fun. Most of the kids were outside, but Reece thought you were hilarious. I don't know if you have a girlfriend, but if you do, I'm sure she loves seeing you with kids, because you are so natural.

All the best,
Missy

From: Alejandro.Navaro@Pepperdine.edu
To: Missy@skintastic.com   sent Sun, Sept 26 12:13 pm

Subject: Re: (No Subject)

Dear Missy,

I do not have a girlfriend. American girls are not serious. They are too young for me.

Alejandro

From: Missy@skintastic.com
To: Alejandro.Navaro@Pepperdine.edu   sent Sun, Sept 26 12:22 pm

Subject: Re: (No Subject)

Dear Alejandro,

I hope that you don't give up on all American girls, Alejandro, you have a lot to offer.

Aiden and I are looking forward to seeing you on Tuesday.

Missy

From: DPlatt@ca.rr.com
To: RTinker@OneStopOffice.com   sent Sun, Sept 26 12:51 pm

Subject: Re: From Randy

Hi Randy.

I will be around all afternoon. If you could drive the car over, that would be great. Fortunately, T took the kids this morning so I could go back to sleep. I'm feeling better now.

Thanks for your words about the divorce. I'm hanging in there.

Randy, I have to admit that I don't remember if I said anything I shouldn't have said at the party. If so, please accept my apologies and forget it happened. I hope you have some sympathy for a single mom who was just letting her hair down a little.

You are a great sport. Thanks.

Diane

———————

From: RTinker@OneStopOffice.com
To: DPlatt@ca.rr.com   sent Sun, Sept 26 12:54 pm

Subject: Re: From Randy

That's me! A great sport who does a kick-ass version of "We are the Champion's" according to you!! But, sure, consider it all forgotten!

This great sport will be over in the 1ish to 2ish time frame to pick you up and drop you off at your car.

At your service,
Randy

Randy Tinker
Executive Director of Sales
OneStopOffice
739 La Jolla Drive
Los Angeles, CA 90042

CHAPTER 14

DIANE GLANCES AT THE BIG digital clock on the kitchen counter. One p.m., exactly. She would smile if it didn't hurt her scalp. Ever since she was little, she's had a knack for looking at the clock exactly on the hour. T used to make fun of her "so-called talent," saying that she must have been glancing at the clock leading up to the hour. But it wasn't true. Sometimes she awoke exactly at seven o'clock, and she couldn't have possibly been sneaking peeks at the clock in her sleep.

She guesses Randy will arrive closer to one than two. He's that kind of guy. Her stomach burbles and she forces herself to eat another forkful of scrambled eggs. The eggs aren't helping. But the Diet Coke is. She takes another sip and the aggressive fizz of soda seems to scrub her throat and the inside of her esophagus as it goes down. Her frontal lobe hurts. And the center of her forehead. Not just from the hangover, but from guilt. Every time a flash of memory hits, she squeezes her eyes shut and tries to erase it.

Her exaggerated, lecherous ass-grab when Alejandro did his stripper dance.

Squeeze eyes tight. Erase. Erase.

Everyone must have seen her. Drunk and frowzy. T used to hate it when she got that way, although she'd make up for it later in bed.

The ass-grab, while embarrassing, is forgivable. Sexual energy was pinging around that living room. The way Missy danced with Mark's wife, rubbing her ass into her crotch. Everyone stuffing dollars into Alejandro's jeans. Jesus, that guy is closer to the kids' ages than most of the adults in the room. Wonder what tales he will bring back to Colombia?

Eyes tight. Pain. Drink of fizzy Diet Coke. Ah.

What is not forgivable came later. In the kitchen. With Randy. She can't remember much of the conversation. But what she does remember and hasn't been able to erase is leaning against him, pretending to be giving a friendly hug, while grinding her hip into his hard-on.

Eyes tight, tight, tight. Shooting pain. Take another sip.

She puts down the can of soda and confronts the eggs. Picks up the fork and takes a deliberate bite. She can hear her stomach acids churning as they ravage the paltry forkful of floppy yellow mush.

Maybe a beer would cool it down better and even out other biological calibrations.

The thing is, she never noticed Randy before. Not in that way. He's a bit of a doof. With his bad jokes, unconscious sexist and racist comments, and big, always smiley face. Had he made suggestive comments? She doesn't remember. But it's fair to assume that she was the aggressor. After all, she had ass-grabbed Alejandro minutes before. It was a ramp up from there. She knows what she's like when she gets that way. When she'll take practically anyone. And Randy is tall. She remembers liking how tall he was when she hugged him and, later, when she slid her hand down.

Ouch. Eyes tight, tight, tight. Motherfucking regret.

Yeah. Maybe a beer.

She gets up from the table and opens the fridge. The cold blast feels good and gives her hope. She grabs a beer. Pops it. Ah. Sits back down.

She reminds herself to brush her teeth before answering the door. Randy will think she has a serious problem if he smells beer in the morning.

Although why should she care what Randy thinks?

Grabbing his hard-on, wanting it to bounce out of his jeans.

Eyes tight. Fuck. Ouch. Fucking pain. Swig of beer. Yes.

Jesus. When is she going to stop this? The drinking. Embarrassing herself.

It's all T's fault for leaving. Okay. She wasn't perfect, she gets that.

She'd thrown herself at a few guys, just to get his attention. But she had been fun too, hadn't she? Loving? Great in bed. Giving up her career. Making healthy dinners with kale. Trying not to complain, and mostly succeeding, when he came home later and later from the office.

Whatever. She feels tears coming on and takes another sip of beer.

She hears someone walking up the driveway on the loose gravel. Shit. She jumps up and pours the beer down the sink like a guilty teenager. She runs down the hall. In the bathroom, she pulls open the cabinet above the sink and grabs her toothbrush and toothpaste.

There's the bell.

She brushes and brushes, swish, swish. Spit. Head up. Slams right into the edge of the cabinet door.

"OWWWWWWWWWWWWWWW," she yells. Then forces herself to be silent.

But OWWWWWW keeps going in her mind. MOTHERFUCK-ING OWWWW. SEARING PAIN. BACK OF HEAD. FUCKING CABINET. FUCKING, FUCKING CABINET. OWWWWW. GOD, OH GOD.

She puts the brush and toothpaste back with a shaking hand. Wipes her mouth with the back of her other hand. Steadies herself against the sink. OWWWW. OWWWWWW. OK.

Doorbell.

"All right," she yells.

FUCKING CABINET. OWWWWWWW.

She wants to cry. Cry and cry and curse T for leaving. For making her throw herself at a big goofy guy who is nothing to her and now she has to pretend she doesn't remember and endure the most tedious, stupid car ride ever. With a guy whose dick she grabbed because T isn't here.

She breathes in and reaches up to test her head. It's killing, throb-bing, but no cut. Her eyes sting with welled-up tears. She sniffs. Grabs a Kleenex and blows.

Okay. Let's fucking do this. She puts her hands on her face. Breathes. Right.

She walks down the hallway to the door, where she can see a dark round head moving behind the mottled glass.

She breathes. Fixes her face. Ouch. And opens the door.

There he is with his big dopey grin.

"Hello, my lady. Your chariot awaits."

"Thanks, Randy." She smiles up at him. Ouch. "You really are a sport."

CHAPTER 15

From: Alejandro.Navaro@Pepperdine.edu
To: Missy@skintastic.com   sent Tue, Sept 28 8:37 pm

Subject: (No Subject)

Dear Missy,

I am sorry to make you cry today at practice in front of Aiden. I was only to say your hair is pretty when it is away from your face. That is all.

Alejandro

––––––––––

From: Missy@skintastic.com
To: Alejandro.Navaro@Pepperdine.edu   sent Tue, Sept 28 8:47 pm

Subject: Re: (No Subject)

Dear Alejandro,

It's not your fault at all, it's been a hard week and you were being so nice to me. I feel like I'm doing everything wrong these days.

Have you noticed Aiden improving? I hope so. It would mean so much to Randy for him to get into All Stars again. He only got in last year because one kid had to move out of district and wasn't eligible. Plus, I think that the league fudged it a bit because they love Randy, I mean, who doesn't?

I'm sorry again for crying.

Warmly,
Missy

––––––––––

From: Alejandro.Navaro@Pepperdine.edu
To: Missy@skintastic.com   sent Tue, Sept 28 8:50 pm

Subject: Re: (No Subject)

Dear Missy,

I do not know "fudge", but I think I know. I am happy that it was not me that makes you cry. Beautiful ladies should not be unhappy. Is it wrong for me to ask for you to meet without Aiden? We should talk about his skills. To make Coach Randy happy.

Alejandro

––––––––––

From: Missy@skintastic.com
To: Alejandro.Navaro@Pepperdine.edu   sent Tue, Sept 28 8:53 pm

Subject: Re: (No Subject)

LOL about "fudge". Really, I haven't smiled like that all week! To fudge something means to cheat just a little bit. Not in a big way, or in a way that means anything really.

Of course, we can meet without Aiden. I can get together when he's at school, or if you have to do later in the afternoon, our housekeeper can keep an eye on Aiden. Also, we should meet out of Beverly Hills, because I wouldn't want anyone to see us and get the wrong idea. Not that they have any reason to think anything, but this is a pretty back-stabby town. I'm not worried though, because there's nothing going on but me trying to make Randy happy.

Warmly,
Missy

———————

From: Alejandro.Navaro@Pepperdine.edu
To: Missy@skintastic.com   sent Tue, Sept 28 8:55 pm

Subject: Re: (No Subject)

Dear Missy,

Yes. I know we must fudge the meeting. On Thursday, I am out of class at 3:45. If you can drive to Pepperdine, there is a restaurant it is called, "Today's Catch" on the beach. We can meet there at 4:00 to talk about Aiden and I promise that I will not make you cry this time.

Alejandro

———————

From: Missy@skintastic.com

To: Alejandro.Navaro@Pepperdine.edu   sent Tue, Sept 28 8:56 pm

Subject: Re: (No Subject)

Dear Alejandro,

LOL and that is a great place to fudge our meeting. I used to eat there years ago, before we had Aiden. I love sitting on the balcony, under the heat lamps. Can you get us a reservation?

Warmly,
Missy

———————

From: Alejandro.Navaro@Pepperdine.edu

To: Missy@skintastic.com   sent Tue, Sept 28 8:57 pm

Subject: Re: (No Subject)

Dear Missy,

I will make the reservation. Allow me to pay for the meeting too. I wish to make you happy after I make you cry.

Alejandro

———————

From: Missy@skintastic.com
To: Alejandro.Navaro@Pepperdine.edu   sent Tue, Sept 28 8:57 pm

Subject: Re: (No Subject)

Dear Alejandro,

Your spoiling this married lady, but if we are talking about Randy and Aiden, I'm sure that a glass of wine out somewhere in public won't hurt.

Missy

CHAPTER 16

ALEJANDRO SITS AT THE END of a long table at Henderson's Brew Pub with his hand loose around his second pint of pale ale. The others at the table are his classmates from geology at Pepperdine. They are all three or four years younger than him, except maybe the guy who calls himself Moose and hasn't passed one test or turned in one piece of homework. Why is he even taking the class?

Moose raises his glass and yells, "Let's get wasted, motherfuckers!"

Everyone laughs, even though Moose has said the very same thing every single Tuesday after class. Alejandro smiles and takes a sip of overpriced beer. It's his last one. The others will stay here and drink into the night. Not Alejandro, who has left early ever since that first Tuesday when his pockets were stuffed with cash from two back-to-back private coaching sessions with separate clients. The following morning, he had awakened on the floor of his room, sunlight slicing through the blinds, searing through his eyelids, forcing him awake, barely able to lift his head, most of the night erased from memory, with his pants around his knees and his pockets completely empty. *Mi madre.* This is not what he came here for. Not to lose money but to make it.

The girl on his left looks at him over her tanned shoulder. "Moose is a connector. In Psych we learned about social clusters, and usually there's someone who is the glue. That's Moose." Alejandro nods. What is her name? Dakota? Ava? Olivia? She smiles. "You're always so quiet."

Alejandro shrugs. "I only speak when it is important to say something."

A girl at the end yells, "Olivia, is your card open behind the bar?"

Olivia turns away from him. "Yeah. Go ahead, get anything you want. My dad pays it." She turns back. "So you're not a connector, right? I know, you're an outlier. You live outside society norms."

"Your society is not mine. In my society, I am inside very much."

He isn't sure why he's keeping up the conversation. Except to be polite. He knows he could have her. But he has no interest in spending an hour making her feel smart. Which, he can tell, is what she wants. What it will take to get her into bed. American girls require a minimum of one hour of talk, sometimes as much as three.

"Tell me about Colombia," she says, biting her lower lip in a way that tells him that it is not his country that interests her.

Nothing in him stirs. She might as well have asked him to tell her about being Catholic or a man. It cannot be described in a requisite one or two sentences. His country is mountains so high you cannot breathe and cities that are lit up all night. It is dirt roads where boys like him play soccer using painted rectangles on stone walls for the goal. It is where his mother and sisters live, and it is where his father and brother died.

"Colombia is very beautiful and also cruel."

She pauses and considers this, eyes soft, round. "That's sweet," she says.

Now he stirs.

But it is not lust. This is a darker, shadowy cousin. Not kind at all.

Contempt.

He leans forward, lips pulled into a purposeful smile. Reaches out and, his fingers almost trembling, tucks a strand of hair behind her ear. She places her slight hand on his forearm as he leans closer to whisper in her ear, "Do you want to fuck?"

She pulls back. Eyes confused. Cheeks red. "What?"

"Is that not what you want?"

Her back straightens and he can see who her mother must be. A dry white woman, with broken yellow hair, who wears necklaces of big stones over gem-colored tunics.

Olivia's face is a mask of disbelief. "What made you think that?"

He smiles, congenial. "Then I am sorry."

He watches her confusion. Watches her decide if she should accept the apology or continue the pretense.

Before she has a chance, he stands. He has already paid for his beer in cash. "I see you later, everybody," he says to the group, and turns to zigzag through the other tables, out into the night.

Outside, the sky is clear. He looks up and listens to the ocean receding and advancing, each new wave covering more and more of the beach. He thinks of Missy, who quivers every time he looks at her. Of the women who stuffed dollars in his jeans at Randy's party. Receding and advancing.

A beautiful game.

And up there is some bright star that he should know the name of but has forgotten.

A breeze. He feels his mother pressing her wet cheek against his lips when he left. Hears her saying, "Go. Go now and do not look back."

CHAPTER 17

From: RTinker@OneStopOffice.com
To: SReidel@OneStopOffice.com   sent Fri, Sept 29 8:37 am

Subject: (No Subject)

Sam. Meeting with HR today and I have a bad feeling. I hope that what I said to you in confidence was kept in confidence. I'm curious about why I am the sole person from my department who is meeting. Seriously, Liz doesn't have a meeting? Not that I have anything against her. Something doesn't add up here. Is it because she's a woman?

Randy Tinker
Executive Director of Sales
OneStopOffice
739 La Jolla Drive
Los Angeles, CA 90042

From: SReidel@OneStopOffice.com
To: RTinker@OneStopOffice.com   sent Fri, Sept 29 8:39 am

Subject: Re: (No Subject)

Liz is staying on because she's on the Bay Area account. Not because she's a woman. I have not betrayed your confidence. But, make no mistake, e-mails are unwise.

Missy is working, I believe?

Sam

Sam Reidel
Senior Vice President
OneStopOffice
739 La Jolla Drive
Los Angeles, CA 90042

From: RTinker@OneStopOffice.com
To: SReidel@OneStopOffice.com   sent Fri, Sept 29 8:41 am

Subject: Re: (No Subject)

I still think it's the woman thing. Sure, my numbers are down, but so are everyone's. To be honest, I've been considering a change ever since J came aboard, this will just be speeding up the process!

Will you keep an ear to the ground for me? You know my skill set. When the dust settles let's have a drink and tell tales out of school. (HAH)

Randy Tinker
Executive Director of Sales
OneStopOffice
739 La Jolla Drive
Los Angeles, CA 90042

From: RTinker@OneStopOffice.com
To: SReidel@OneStopOffice.com, JRosenthal@OneStopOffice.com,
JHandHRasst@OneStopOffice.com, JHandHR@OneStopOffice.com,
BSullivan@OneStopOffice.com, JKellam@OneStopOffice.com,
JPacheco@OneStopOffice.com, LCassandra@OneStopOffice.com,
DBrazda@OneStopOffice.com, MEpstein@OneStopOffice.com,
LLedbetter@OneStopOffice.com, RRappaport@OneStopOffice.com,
FBarchesi@OneStopOffice.com, DCharles@OneStopOffice.com,
MRisopoli@OneStopOffice.com, KHaynie@OneStopOffice.com,
GMoody@OneStopOffice.com, CLowen@OneStopOffice.com,
SYoung@OneStopOffice.com, KHill@OneStopOffice.com, (39 more)
                                          sent Fri, Sept 29 9:17 am

Subject: Probably Randy's last e-mail

Dear Friends and Co-workers,

Some of you might already know that I will probably be leaving the company this afternoon. If you don't know, I'm glad that it's me telling you
and not someone who may never have wanted me to succeed anyway.
If my meeting at HR proves to be about something else, then delete this
message!

Since you all like my bullet-point e-mails, I am not going to fail you this
time. Here we go:

- Do not believe everything you hear unless it's about me being a hand-
  some genius! (HA)
- I bequeath my magnetic nail sculpture to Tessa. Just don't sit on it!
- Don't be strangers. I can be reached at FavoriteCoach@gmail.com
  and you have my cell. I might even surprise you by showing up at
  "Willy's" some Friday afternoon!
- Don't say anything to my wife until I've had a chance to break the
  news.

- Don't ever express your work frustration in e-mail form EVER. Even to your friends, even if it's true, even if you were just blowing off steam, and even if it's the one and only time you would do anything stupid like that.

You are welcome and THANK YOU for being great people to work with every day. Even the ones who aren't. Because I am filled with appreciation today. My last bullet point should have been—Don't worry about me!

I hope we'll all see each other soon. You have my e-mail and my cell.

Always yours,
Randy Tinker

Randy Tinker
Executive Director of Sales
OneStopOffice
739 La Jolla Drive
Los Angeles, CA 90042

From: JWoo@DesignX.com
To: FavoriteCoach@gmail.com   sent Fri, Oct 1 9:24 am

Subject: Saturday game

Patrick can not come to Saturday game tomorrow. His mother says he is sick.

Jung-ah Woo

From: FavoriteCoach@gmail.com
To: PPousaint@mac.com   sent Fri, Oct 1 9:31 am

Paul,

I'm sorry to be brief, but lot's going on at work and I can't stop right now. I wanted to give you a heads up that we don't have Woo tomorrow. Can you call Alejandro and reassign positions to minimize damage? Don't make it look too obvious that you are putting strong players up front. Maybe sprinkle Dashiell in there somewhere to make it look like we're giving everyone a chance. I'll go over the list tomorrow before the game.

Randy

"Every man dies, but not every man truly lives."
Mel Gibson as Braveheart

From: Alejandro.Navaro@Pepperdine.edu
To: Missy@skintastic.com   sent Fri, Oct 1 9:38 am

Subject: Re: (No Subject)

Dear Missy,

It is for me to apologize again. You are very beautiful and sad. There are no girls for me here and it does not matter to me you are married. In Colombia it is different. We want who we want. It does not mean anything. Like a fudge. It is healthy to be happy some time and then to go back to the husband and children. No one is hurt.

But if I make you more sad. Forget it. I cannot do it. Right now it is only a kiss. That is all. I know you like it. I like it very much. But I will not do more to you. You must decide.

Alejandro

_____

From: Missy@skintastic.com
To: Alejandro.Navaro@Pepperdine.edu   sent Fri, Oct 1 11:01 am

Subject: Re: (No Subject)

Oh Alejandro, I thought we were really going to talk about Aiden, I really did and I didn't mean to lead you on. In America, we do not do these things easily. It is true that I am very sad, these days, but am also thankful for everything that I have, and sometimes we have to go through sad times in order to keep our families together.

I cannot lie. Of course, I liked the kiss. I haven't been kissed in a very long time, not like that, if you know what I mean. You are right that there is no harm done, it was harmless, so lets us forget about it and keep meeting with Aiden. I really think that he is making progress.

Can you keep our Tuesday practice session?

Warmly,
Missy

_____

From: Alejandro.Navaro@Pepperdine.edu

To: Missy@skintastic.com   sent Fri, Oct 1 11:07 am

Subject: Re: (No Subject)

Dear Missy,

Now it is for me to be sad. I do not want to meet only with Aiden. I wish to make love to you. It is not wrong. You will see. I cannot practice with Aiden when there is something that is not finished between us. This would be a lie.

Alejandro

———————

From: Missy@skintastic.com

To: Alejandro.Navaro@Pepperdine.edu   sent Fri, Oct 1 11:09 am

Subject: Re: (No Subject)

Alejandro, I am crying now, because you have made me sadder. I want to see you. It is important to Aiden, and he will wonder why we stopped practicing. I cannot give myself to you, because it would kill Randy if he ever found out.

Missy

———————

From: Alejandro.Navaro@Pepperdine.edu

To: Missy@skintastic.com   sent Fri, Oct 1 11:10 am

Subject: Re: (No Subject)

I agree. Randy must not know. I do not mean to hurt anyone. Can we meet and I will only kiss and touch your body. We do not even to lie down. We can keep our clothes.

Alejandro

––––––––––

From: Missy@skintastic.com

To: Alejandro.Navaro@Pepperdine.edu   sent Fri, Oct 1 11:21 am

Subject: Re: (No Subject)

If I do this, with clothes, will you keep coaching Aiden?

––––––––––

From: Alejandro.Navaro@Pepperdine.edu

To: Missy@skintastic.com   sent Fri, Oct 1 11:21 am

Subject: Re: (No Subject)

Of course I will teach Aiden. I will be a happy man just to touch your body and your breasts.

––––––––––

From: Missy@skintastic.com
To: Alejandro.Navaro@Pepperdine.edu   sent Fri, Oct 1 11:23 am

Subject: Re: (No Subject)

OK.

Missy

———————

From: FavoriteCoach@gmail.com
To: DPlatt@ca.rr.com   sent Fri, Oct 1 4:54 pm

Subject: From Randy

Hey Diane,

I just wanted to let you know that I just got fired from my job this afternoon. Yup, Coach is out of a job. I guess that means more time for the team and for the family.

I'm writing to tell you because I needed to tell someone and I think that you are a person who can keep a secret.

Randy

"Every man dies, but not every man truly lives."
Mel Gibson as Braveheart

———————

From: DPlatt@ca.rr.com
To: FavoriteCoach@gmail.com   sent Fri, Oct 1 5:12 pm

Subject: Re: From Randy

Dear Randy,

I am so sorry to hear about your job. You are right. I can keep a secret and I promise to keep yours.

But, certainly, you'll be telling Missy soon. It's better to be a couple facing tough times together, than facing them alone. Trust me. I know what I'm talking about.

It will get better. Things just take time.

Diane

From: FavoriteCoach@gmail.com
To: DPlatt@ca.rr.com   sent Fri, Oct 1 5:14 pm

Subject: From Randy

I can't tell Missy.

"Every man dies, but not every man truly lives."
Mel Gibson as Braveheart

From: DPlatt@ca.rr.com
To: FavoriteCoach@gmail.com   sent Fri, Oct 1 5:17 pm

Subject: Re: From Randy

Dear Randy,

You will have to tell her eventually. Why don't you tell her now and get it over with?

Diane

———————

From: FavoriteCoach@gmail.com
To: DPlatt@ca.rr.com   sent Fri, Oct 1 5:19 pm

Subject: Re: From Randy

Not until I have something better, she already thinks I'm a loser.

"Every man dies, but not every man truly lives."
Mel Gibson as Braveheart

———————

From: DPlatt@ca.rr.com
To: FavoriteCoach@gmail.com   sent Fri, Oct 1 5:22 pm

Subject: Re: From Randy

Dear Randy,

Missy does not think that you are a loser. I've heard her tell lots of people
that you are funny and everyone loves you.

Diane

From: FavoriteCoach@gmail.com
To: DPlatt@ca.rr.com   sent Fri, Oct 1 5:24 pm

Subject: Re: From Randy

Not everyone. Not her.

"Every man dies, but not every man truly lives."
Mel Gibson as Braveheart

From: DPlatt@ca.rr.com
To: FavoriteCoach@gmail.com   sent Fri, Oct 1 5:27 pm

Subject: Re: From Randy

Dear Randy,

Please don't give up on your marriage like that. T and I gave up too fast and now I regret everything. Give Missy some credit. You have Aiden. There's so much there.

Diane

From: FavoriteCoach@gmail.com
To: DPlatt@ca.rr.com   sent Fri, Oct 1 5:29 pm

Subject: Re: From Randy

I said too much. Thanks for listening and keeping my secret.

Also, don't worry, I'll find something soon! Maybe it's time to start a Queen cover band!!!!

Randy

"Every man dies, but not every man truly lives."
Mel Gibson as Braveheart

OneStopOffice

CORPORATION

Mr. Randy Tinker
42 S. Maple Street
Beverly Hills, CA 90212

Dear Mr Tinker,

This letter confirms our discussion on October 1 that your employment with OneStopOffice Corporation is terminated for cause, effective immediately.

Your employment, as discussed during the termination meeting, is terminated because you committed company resources to a client without informing your department head.

This breach of standard protocol, as it pertains to the proper notification to superiors of gifts to clients, was a gross violation of both our company policy and our code of conduct.

Additionally, your attempt to cover up your transgression and involve other employees in your deception is behavior that cannot be countenanced, and it also violates our code of conduct.

Payment for your accrued PTO and any regular salary still owed after termination is to be held by the company until a more thorough investigation of all improper disbursements can be discerned.

You can expect a separate benefits status letter that will outline the status of your benefits, if any, upon termination. The letter will include information about your eligibility for Consolidated Omnibus Budget Reconciliation Act (COBRA) continuation of group health coverage.

We have received your security swipe card, your office keys, and the company owned laptop and cell phone at the termination meeting.

You will need to keep the company informed of your contact information so we are able to provide information you may need in the future such as your W-2 form, and any other legal inquiries.

Regards,

J Hand

Jennifer Hand
Director, Human Resources
OneStopOffice Corporation
739 La Jolla Drive
Suite 318
Los Angeles, CA 90042

CHAPTER 18

DIANE STANDS IN FRONT OF the open refrigerator, staring at an unopened bottle of wine—which could be her second this evening—next to a fancy bottle of fizzy grapefruit juice. The choice she should make is obvious. Even to her.

Mind made up, for now anyway, she reaches in and pulls out the sparkling grapefruit juice, shutting the door with her foot as she turns. She grabs a glass from the cabinet, feeling virtuous as she pours the juice into the glass. Tonight is a night that she could get looped with impunity. The kids are with T. She doesn't have to get up early in the morning. Not only is she completely alone, but she can be pretty sure that no one on the planet is even thinking about her at this precise moment. Which is more than alone. It's insignificant.

And not in the way she felt insignificant with T. This is cosmic insignificance, the kind that lets you off the hook because you're no more or less important than anything else, even a bug. With T, her insignificance was born (or so it seems to her) the moment she decided to stay home with the kids. Noble enough, at the time. Although now she suspects she chose it because she didn't know how to sell herself as a photographer and it was an easy out. Had she been angry that T hadn't pushed her more to keep up with her photography? Maybe that was it. He had liked her bargain with domesticity a little too much and she hadn't been able to forgive him for it.

She doesn't put the juice back into the fridge. Nor does she screw the cap back on. She simply leaves it there on the counter—why not—and barefoots it into the living room.

She stands in front of the coffee table in her panties and nothing else. She puts her glass down and listens to the quiet of her life when the kids are gone. It's the sound of absence, and it can get a woman down, if she lets it. Which is hilarious in a pretty depressing way. Because when the family was together, here in this house, she couldn't wait to get away from the kids. She loved them like her own breath. But they were her jailors too. Oh, the interminable hours she spent pretending to drink tea from a tiny cup with Sabine. Whole afternoons discussing minute differences between thousands of Pokémon characters with Reece. She had dreamed endlessly about escaping in the middle of the night and starting a new life as a hot, single woman somewhere far away—another state—at a typical office-type job doing something undefined—not too complicated, but requiring some kind of skill that only she had—that involved a sexy wardrobe with short, short skirts and head-banging sex in supply closets with higher-ups and lower-downs.

Now she gets every other weekend to herself and she's pining?

The light from the windows is blue and falls across her feet. She follows its cast, making fantastic shapes across the shelves and the rug. She lifts her hand, curving it through the shadows, sliding her hip to the side and lifting her other hand as if it's reaching for something over her head. She turns slowly, crossing one leg over the other in one continuous motion. Like a slow spin underwater. Now she slides one foot over the nap of the carpet, then the other. Gliding almost, with an occasional hitch to recover her balance.

Rounding the corner of the coffee table, her toe catches and she topples onto the couch. Her face hits a pillow and she takes a moment to right herself, tossing a smaller pillow and another to the ground, before finally sitting up.

Wow. The quiet.

She thinks about the spiritual riddle. If a tree falls in the woods and no one is around to hear, does it make a sound? Ha! If a single mom dances drunkenly alone in her living room and no one is around to complain, tell her to come to bed, or dance along, who's to say she's dancing? Who's to say she's doing anything at all?

She leans forward and picks up her glass of fizzy juice. Leans back.

She really, really, really needs to get fucking laid.

CHAPTER 19

From: PPousaint@mac.com

To: Manatees   sent Sat, Oct 2 7:03 pm

Subject: Tough game, guys

Dear Manatees and Parents,

I'd like to say a few words from the coaching staff. Coach Randy and I discussed the game afterwards, but he had to run off to a dinner. This is why you are getting a post-game e-mail from the assistant coach. I'm sure that Coach will weigh in later.

First of all, 6-0 is a crushing defeat, any way that you look at it. Yes, Jacqui, I know that the game technically doesn't count. Please don't feel the need to remind us of this again. But it's a simple fact that we lost. I know that the coaches always say that the game isn't only about goals, but you do have to make some, eventually. And we were down a kicker today. Not just any kicker, either. Patrick we hope you get better soon and we're sorry to lay a defeat at your door.

Reece, we will be taking you off of defense and trying you out as a forward again. There will be other changes made at practice on Wednesday. Please don't miss. I know that it's Rosh Hashana for a handful of you. If you must miss, by all means, Happy New Year and Shalom. But that means get to the game earlier so you can go over details with Alejandro.

Now, to address "the incident". Ben let his temper flair today and got thrown out of the game for trash-talking a referee. Parents, when an incident like this happens, we need you to stand down. You will only get us docked more points. We don't get into the tournament by simply winning games, we need sportsmanship points too.

Ben was only suspended from the game and will be joining us on Saturday. He will not be at practice on Wednesday, not because of the incident but because he is Jewish.

That is all for now. I will see most of you on Wednesday.

Sincerely,
Coach Paul

———————

From: Visorgrl@mac.com
To: Manatees　　　　　　　　　　sent Sat, Oct 2 7:13 pm

Subject: Re: Tough game, guys

Dear Coach Paul and everyone else!

Just a reminder that Calvin will not be at practice on Wednesday either.

I know that the game was hard for everyone. Calvin's grandma was in from Philadelphia and it sure would have been more fun for her to see the team be their usual happy selves!

I think it's awesome that the kids stayed on the field and played to the end. I didn't see one kid sit down and refuse to play. THAT'S PROGRESS!!! ☺
Last year, Calvin, himself, refused to play a couple of times, and he wasn't

the only one. There was one kid that would get so mad, he would just sit down in the middle of the field and refuse to move. Remember that, Coach Randy? I know Coach will remember when he reads this later.

Go Manatees! I have faith in you, win or lose!!!! ☺

XOXO,
Jacqui

———————

From: MSonnenklar@GSachs.com
To: Manatees   sent Sat, Oct 2 7:13 pm

Subject: Re: Tough game, guys

Dear Manatees,

Ben wanted me to apologize to everyone for losing his cool. He's been having a tough time going between his mother and me. Everything escalated when I married Kelli two months ago. We're working it out.

M

———————

From: Alejandro.Navaro@Pepperdine.edu
To: Missy@skintastic.com   sent Sat, Oct 2 7:05 pm

Subject: (No Subject)

When will I see you?

———————

From: Missy@skintastic.com
To: Alejandro.Navaro@Pepperdine.edu   sent Sat, Oct 2 7:06 pm

Subject: Re: (No Subject)

Not this weekend, because Randy is home the whole time. He's on the deck right now lighting torches. I'm in the bedroom getting ready for dinner.

From: Alejandro.Navaro@Pepperdine.edu
To: Missy@skintastic.com   sent Sat, Oct 2 7:06 pm

Subject: Re: (No Subject)

Lie down.

From: Missy@skintastic.com
To: Alejandro.Navaro@Pepperdine.edu   sent Sat, Oct 2 7:07 pm

Subject: Re (No Subject)

What?

From: Alejandro.Navaro@Pepperdine.edu
To: Missy@skintastic.com   sent Sat, Oct 2 7:07 pm

Subject: Re (No Subject)

Lie down and change to the IM. It is faster.

From: Missy@skintastic.com

To: Alejandro.Navaro@Pepperdine.edu   sent Sat, Oct 2 7:08 pm

Subject: Re (No Subject)

OK, but why am I lying down?

Alejandronavaro: because
Missy: why
Alejandronavaro: so I can touch your body
Missy: you aren't here
Alejandronavaro: yes I am. I am touching your sad face
Missy: wait a minute
I'm lying down but I have to sit up a bit to type
Alejandronavaro: relax and let me touch you all over
Missy: ok
Alejandronavaro: can you feel me touching the back of your neck
Missy: yes it feels good. But randy may come in
Alejandronavaro: then he will only see his wife typing
Missy: right
Alejandronavaro: I am kissing you with my mouth open
My tounge is finding yours
I go deeper into your mouth with my tounge
Missy: ok. Are you on my side or above me
Alejandronavaro: above you
I am only wearing brief underwears
Missy: I dont think I know how to do this
Alejandronavaro: there is no right or wrong
I am touching your breasts
Can I lick them?

Missy: ok

wow. I can really feel you

maybe this is all we should do

Alejandronavaro: I am taking a nipple in my mouth and biting it

I suck and suck and want to touch your cunt with my hand

Missy: dont say that

Alejandronavaro: it is what it is

Missy: makes me think you dont like me

Alejandronavaro: may I touch your lower parts?

Missy: yes

Alejandronavaro: I am sticking my thumb inside you

Im rubbing and rubbing while I suck your breasts

Missy: this is getting hard to do with clothes

Alejandronavaro: take them off

Missy: but randy

Alejandronavaro: take off only your panties and I will take off my underwears

Alejandronavaro: my underwears are off

Missy: sorry I had to find the chord for my computer

Alejandronavaro: I am putting two fingers inside you

and now I lick your stomach

Missy: I cant stand this. Its very hard

Alejandronavaro: is very hard. do you want to touch me?

Missy: im scared

Alejandronavaro: do youwant to touch my cock

Missy: I cant do this. im scared

Alejandronavaro: I want to lick your pussy

Missy: please dont. Just breasts

Alejandronavaro: I want you to cum

Missy: I cant. Im stopping

CHAPTER 20

"FIRST YOU GET KICKED OUT of a soccer game, and now this." Mark stands before his son and ex-wife, who are sitting on the couch, their heads raised in collusive contempt. He waves the report card in front of his son's face. "Well, what have you got to say about it?"

Ben's glare turns molten. Karen puts her arm around the boy, which he immediately shakes off. And even though this pleases Mark, he's in no mood to enjoy it.

"Honey," Karen says, turning to their son, using that high-pitched only-for-Ben voice that Mark hates, "we're sitting here together to come up with solutions. You seem to be unhappy. You were such a good student last year. Remember? You made all those A's, and now your father..."

Mark forces himself to sit. He wiggles around in the overstuffed chair, trying to find a position that makes him look relaxed yet in control, when all he really wants to do is to pound on the coffee table with his fist and tell them both exactly how things are going to go, and that will be the end of it. It's easy. Lay down a series of punishments escalating in scale—for starters, maybe threaten Ben with military school.

But Mark is trying like a motherfucker to rein it in, because now—since the divorce—he and Karen are engaged in a battle over Ben's allegiance. And so far, Karen is winning.

She pats Ben's hand. "Your father and I..." She says this phrase like it's pricking her in the throat with a thousand pins. "Your father and I want to help you."

Mark takes a deliberate breath. "Answer your mother," he says, trying like hell to keep his voice even. "You made all A's last year and now, an F and a D? How is that even possible? Mr. Patten says you haven't turned in any of your science homework." He can feel his neck tighten, but he's sure he's keeping his tone cool. "Is that true?"

"I don't know," Ben says, like it's a challenge. Everything the kid says to him is said like this. Even "Pass the milk." Like, *I dare you not to pass the milk.* Or *Wanna say something about how much milk I'm drinking? Go on, old man.*

Mark gives up trying to find a relaxed position and catapults from the chair. He starts to pace, if only to keep from smacking the kid across the face. "You either turned in the homework or you didn't. What's not to know? Do you write it down in your planner? Whenever you're with Kelli and me you say you've done it all at school. Clearly that isn't the case."

Karen puts her arm around Ben again and this time the kid lets it stay. "Mark, sit down."

"I'm upset. Can't a guy be upset?" What the fuck? It's not a crime to get a little fired up. It's always been like this with Karen. You get the least bit excited, and suddenly you're a, what was it, an "emotional terrorist"?

"But you're upsetting Ben," she says, smoothing the kid's hair.

"I'm not sure I care. He's the one with the D and an F. I never made below a C in my entire life. How does he ever hope to get into college?"

Karen's lips tighten into such a thin line that she can barely get her words out. "Mark. He's only ten. Calm down."

He pivots and eyeballs his son. "Well, you're not getting an iPhone now."

Karen jumps up from the couch, clenching her fists. "For God's sake, Mark. It's not about the fucking iPhone!"

Mark glares at her. They hold each other's hard stare.

Then, he sees her reassess. Sit back down. Arm around Ben again. Thick as fucking thieves.

Now it's Ben's turn. Without leaving her maternal grasp, he screams at Mark, "You can't take away my iPhone!"

"You're right!" Mark yells back. Two steps, and he's looming over the kid. "I can't take it away because it doesn't exist yet. You have to have something first in order to get it taken away. I said you'd get one *if* you behaved at soccer and *if* you got, at least, a B average. You didn't do either of these things. So you don't get a phone." He looks down and quickly realizes that if Ben takes a swing at him, he's going to get a punch in the nuts. He turns abruptly and resumes pacing.

No one says anything. It's like they're all considering their next move.

Karen pulls Ben tighter and stares out the window. Plainly choosing to wait for Mark to work himself into a black rage so that she can feel like the reasonable one. Always her way. Lie low. Watch him torque into a tight ball of combustible fury, smoldering past all restraint, until the inevitable blast. When she will finally look at him with that heavy-lidded, *you did it to yourself* smugness that makes him want to shoot himself. Oh, let's be honest. Not himself. Her. Shoot *her*.

Fuck her! Fuck her!

Damn it. He stops pacing. Stands still. Heart pounding. Looks at the boy. Tries like mad to focus through the hazy scrim of his rage—on the boy. Only on the boy. Not Karen. Just the boy.

Karen's hand cupped around his little-boy shoulder.

His little-boy shoulder.

And from somewhere in the back of his mind, he hears a voice from his distant past—although it isn't a voice he knows (sure as hell not his father's)—telling him to go back to sitting in the chair. Take a different tack. Talk to his son, man to man. Tell him about a time when he, himself, didn't do so well, and how he ultimately triumphed. Shit, it took him two years to go varsity.

Why the hell didn't he go inspirational instead of punishing and mean?

Caught up in self-recriminations and second guesses, his gaze drifts back to Karen's slack and impassive face.

Except for a slight curl of her lip.

"I hate you!" Ben screams, breaking the triangular stalemate.

Mark looks over to see his son standing, red-faced and shaking. And, now, running out of the room. Stomp, stomp, stomp up the stairs. Another "I hate you!" Slam.

Mark turns to see his ex-wife sitting still and smiling.

Like a dead fish.

Well, score one for her.

CHAPTER 21

From: RTChampion@gmail.com

To: DPlatt@ca.rr.com   sent Mon, Oct 4 9:16 am

Subject: Diane, from Randy's new e-mail

Hi Diane,

Randy here. I hope that, by now, you can keep all my e-mail addresses straight! I opened up a new address for personal and job hunt e-mails, and guess what? You are my first correspondence at my new address. Lucky you, huh? Kidding!

By now, you probably think I'm some loser guy who doesn't have any friends. I mean, why does this guy (in this case, me) keep writing to you? And the truth is I have lots of friends, but I can't talk to them about what's really going on. You remember the coach of the Tigers, Dan Majors. Well, he was over here with his wife Saturday night and do you think I'm going to say anything to them about losing my job AND my last game? Hell, no. In fact, that night it felt like I hadn't lost anything at all. Missy made bacon wrapped trout, which is not as hard as it sounds, but everyone is always impressed and wolfs it down. Majors loved the bamboo planters on our deck and said that Missy looked great in her new green dress. Which she does, especially compared to Jeanne who, let's be honest, Dan married for her personality. Not that she doesn't have a great personality, she does and props to Dan for recognizing that.

Dan Majors isn't someone you want to be vulnerable around. As soon as you hesitate, or even can't remember something, he moves in.

Thanks for listening to me talk, Diane. I know you have busy days with the kids and whatever else it is that you do. I guess I don't know what else you do. If you want to tell me sometime, that's OK.

Anyway, I'm just saying that I appreciate you letting me confide in you. You don't even have to respond, unless you want to.

Thanks!
Randy

From: FavoriteCoach@gmail.com
To: JWoo@DesignX.com   sent Mon, Oct 4 9:22 am

Subject: From Coach Randy

Dear Mr. and Mrs. Woo,

Coach Randy here. I hope that everything is going well in your family. I am writing to see how Patrick is doing. Was it just a cold or something more serious?

Also, I hope that you haven't had any problems using the address of your business for a permanent address. Once the league starts to notice Patrick's talent, you might get some questions. In cases like this, it is best to pretend you don't speak any English at all.

I know that we have gone over this before, but as playoffs start happening, and then All Stars, it's best to review strategy.

Go Team. Go Patrick, unless he's still resting!
Coach Randy

"Every man dies, but not every man truly lives."
Mel Gibson as Braveheart

From: Kelli.Sonnenklar@Sonnenklar.com
To: KSonn@gmail.com   sent Mon, Oct 4 9:47 am

Subject: keeping an open mind

hi karen,

it's kelli. in other words, probably the last person you want to hear from this morning. please don't just delete this without hearing what i have to say because its just about ben and not about mark or us or the past. that's why i put "keeping an open mind" in the title—because, you, and mark and me are all going to have to have one when it comes to helping ben.

i am writing this while ben is in his bedroom on day two of his "silent treatment" about mark not giving him the iPhone. as you know mark can be pretty stubborn himself and so it's a pretty quiet house. its too quiet and all you have to do is read the news to hear stories about angry kids that really, honestly hurt people. they even beat up their mothers and kill their own pets. that's why i moved the fish tank in here. so before all this bad energy gets even worse i thought i would try to get some peace going.

my first idea is to find some way to give ben the IPhone so that he just calms down and listen to reason. then I think we need to look into medication. i am suggesting that you and me set aside our differences of the past and get some help for ben before things get worse and we have to give him the IPhone anyway because he's threatening a fire or something.

so let's all keep an open mind and get ben the help he needs.

sincerely,
kelli

—————

From: KSonn@gmail.com
To: Kelli.Sonnenklar@Sonnenklar.com   sent Mon, Oct 4 9:50 am

Subject: Re: keeping an open mind

Dear KELLI: Are you fucking high? Do not give him ANY drugs or an IPhone! I will deal directly with Mark on this.

—————

From: Kelli.Sonnenklar@Sonnenklar.com
To: KSonn@gmail.com   sent Mon, Oct 4 9:53 am

Subject: Re: keeping an open mind

dear karen,

that's kind of what i expected but i thought it was worth a try. just remember that I am trying to actually make a situation better and not worse.

i'm going to buy the phone today and keep it in my nightstand in case it comes to that.

sincerely,
kelli

—————

From: DPlatt@ca.rr.com

To: RTChampion@gmail.com   sent Mon, Oct 4 9:56 am

Subject: Re: Diane, from Randy's new e-mail

Hi Randy.

I'm glad that you had a good evening with your wife and friends. I bet you'll find tons of support from people who know and love you when you tell them about being laid off.

It's funny that you seem confused about what I do, since I'm going through a bit of questioning about that too. I get enough money from T to keep me from being motivated to find any purpose beyond bringing up my kids—who—even though I seem pretty casual about parenting—are my whole focus. Not that that's a healthy thing. In fact, I'm pretty sure it isn't. I've been thinking of getting back to photography. My very last project before I quit was a series of photos of kids' toys—especially ones that had been defaced somehow. That was a few years ago. Now I look at the photos and instead of being a reflection on impermanence, they seem cheesy and obvious.

Randy, I'm flattered that you are confiding in me but, trust me, I'm a lousy confidant. T used to say I had all the subtlety of a drag queen. I'm loud, inappropriate, opinionated as hell, with a big butt and a past. You need someone out of a Jane Austen novel, the plain girl who isn't ever going to get married and has nothing but time to listen. That's my two cents.

Don't worry though. I won't say anything to anyone else about your situation. You are right about one thing. I can keep a secret. I've kept lots of them. So I'm good for something.

Here's what I think. TELL MISSY ABOUT THE JOB!!!! It's not too late to go through this together. If you wait any longer to tell her, she'll feel foolish and betrayed. Because other people will start knowing about it soon. For all you know, that guy who came to dinner and his homely wife already know—and they praised the trout and Missy's dress because they felt bad for you. It's better to beat people to the punch than have them pity you. That's my philosophy. I don't need anyone's pity. Except T's and I'm never going to get that.

While we're "talking", what's Jacqui's deal? This is my second season on the same team as her, and I've only seen her husband a couple of times. Calvin seems to have some developmental/behavioral challenges, but I don't see her taking them in. She even makes it sound like he's an easy kid, when that doesn't seem to be the case. There some kind of disconnect that I can't quite figure out. Maybe she self-medicates?

Diane

From: RTChampion@gmail.com
To: DPlatt@ca.rr.com   sent Mon, Oct 4 10:38 am

Subject: Re: Diane, from Randy's new e-mail

It's great to hear from you Diane. I really like having someone to write to in the middle of the day when I'm at the Echo Park Library. Missy thinks I'm working and I'm pretty sure no one's going to run into me here! I'm a genius, right? I get it. I get it. You're going to say I can't do this much longer. And I know you're right. But I've been dropping my IPhone off in an envelope under a bush near the office. That way the GPS says I'm at work.

That will buy me the time I need to send out feelers, and once there's some hope (a second interview or, maybe, a real offer!), I'll tell her. I promise!

In the meantime, to answer your question about Jacqui. I don't know about her husband. I think that Steve doesn't like soccer, or maybe doesn't like Calvin, or both. I met him twice and both times he was in another room watching cooking shows. As far as I can tell, Jacqui's upbeat manner is for real and not due to anything other than that's how she is. She doesn't see anything unusual about Calvin and it's hard to tell a woman like that. She thinks it's normal for a ten year old to bite, hit, and eat rocks when he's mad. I figure it's not my place to tell her anything.

I feel really good that you can tell me about your ex-husband. He doesn't know what he's missing! You're so honest and you don't need a lot. Maybe I'm comparing you to Missy. She isn't exactly dishonest, but I never know what's going on with her. She always says that she's fine and then shows me something in a catalog or asks about work. I can't remember the last time she told me anything about herself.

I'm going to have to get off the computer here in the library because we're only supposed to be on for half an hour at a time, but if you feel like writing back, I'll get it in about an hour when I can get back on.

You're great, Diane.
Randy

_____

From: DPlatt@ca.rr.com
To: RTChampion@gmail.com sent Mon, Oct 4 10:40 am

Subject: Re: Diane, from Randy's new e-mail

Calvin eats rocks?! That's not good. How many does he eat at a time? How big are the rocks?

Speaking of potentially "not good". Do you and Missy have sex? I mean, what's holding you together?

Diane

From: KSonn@gmail.com
To: Kelli.Sonnenklar@Sonnenklar.com   sent Mon, Oct 4 10:45 am

Subject: Re: keeping an open mind

Kelli, do NOT buy Ben that phone. If you give it to him and I find it, I will flush it down the toilet. I didn't agree with Mark using it as a bribe, but now that it's an issue we can't go back on our word.

Every day I ask myself how I could have been so blind as to hire you! You clearly know nothing about raising kids and everything about stealing husbands when wives are working twelve-hour days! Whoops, did I say that? I guess I'm still not cured of my anger issues surrounding—what was it my therapist said last week—the "circumstances" of our break-up.

Do not give that kid the phone or I will tell Mark all about our little e-mail exchange!

CHAPTER 22

Patrick's mother calls him out of his bedroom and he stops, midstep, in the hallway. What is Coach Randy doing in his living room? On a school day?

Coach peers down the hall at him. "Hi, Patrick. How're you doing?"

The Pokémon cards.

His heart pounds. In a second, the boy's palms are wet, and he clenches his fists. No. No. No. Why did he have to have them? Why didn't he leave them wrapped in Dashiell's bandanna? His fists are so tight that he can feel his nails digging into his palms.

He wants to run into his room, snatch the cards, and throw them at Coach. He wants to scream that he never wanted those stupid cards anyway. But his mother is looking at him with a bare-teeth smile that makes escape impossible. "Hello, Coach Randy," he hears himself say, starting to walk toward the two of them, with a hesitating hitch. Each step is deliberate. Questioning. What does Coach know?

"You see. He is very well," his mother says, with a nicey-nicey dip of her head. She looks so pliant that it's impossible to imagine her lifting her hand in anger. Impossible to picture her smacking Patrick's face and yelling that he is lower than a worm.

"The doctor says pneumonia," she says. By the slow way she pronounces *pneumonia*, Patrick can tell she's been practicing it.

"So that's it," says Coach Randy, with his always smiling face. "You look great now, Patrick. Did you get a pack of super antibiotics? Those'll kick the sickness right out of you." Coach kicks the air, all silly.

Patrick smiles and feels his shoulders loosen. He figures, by the goofy way Coach is acting, that he isn't here to throw him off the team for stealing. Patrick lets his fists uncurl. Coach reaches out to squeeze his shoulder. "Yeah. You look just fine. Maybe you'll even be able to play on Saturday."

"Yes. I'm much better and I can't wait to play," Patrick says, looking at his mother to see if this sounds right. She smiles and dips her head again, gesturing toward the sofa.

The way she sweeps her hand sends electric impulses through the boy's body. It's her! She has the cards! The nerves in his neck jump. She's making them sit on the sofa so she can produce the cards and shame him in front of the coach.

She must have spirited into his bedroom while he was sleeping and silently, without even touching the drawer, opened it with her mind! His feet won't move. He looks up at the coach, eyes stinging.

"Ah," Coach says to his mother, "I wonder. Do you think Patrick is well enough to go outside with me and kick the ol' ball around?"

Patrick darts his eyes back at his mother without moving his head. Is she holding the cards behind her back? He tenses, prepares for a blow.

But it doesn't come. She simply smiles sweetly and says, "Yes. I think is okay." Patrick unlocks his head and looks at her. She shrugs like nothing is going on and says, "You must get your shoes and ball."

The boy turns and almost lifts off, down the hallway. Right before he slams his door shut, he hears Coach say, "Wow. I thought that cat was a pillow."

Alone, in the blue room, he zooms over to his desk and jerks the drawer open.

Where? Shuffle. Where?

There.

Yes.

There they are. The cards with a rubber band around them. Right where he left them.

He picks them up, walks over to the open window, cranks open the screen, takes a step back, and pitches the cards out, as far as he can. He watches them clear the big tree and disappear.

Done. He cranks the screen shut and walks over to his bed. Sits. Did

Coach really come all the way here just to spend time with him—a boy who isn't even his son? Patrick pulls in a breath, feeling his specialness. He is the best player on the team. This will make his mother proud.

He stands up from the bed (the Pokémon cards forgotten) and walks over to his closet to get his cleats and ball.

CHAPTER 23

From: FavoriteCoach@gmail.com

To: Manatees   sent Sat, Oct 9 5:20 pm

Subject: YEAH!!! Manatees crush the Dark Knights!

VICTORY!!! THAT'S THE WAY TO PLAY SOCCER, TEAM!!! Welcome back, Patrick Woo!!!! What I was watching out there today was pure poetry—passing, sticking to the strategy, strong defense, dribbling skills (Alejandro, you are a genius!), no calling out the other team, AND everyone running in the right direction through the WHOLE game!!! Who would have thought our little team with only one credible All Star possibility could pull out the stops and crush The Dark Knights (I get it, 5-4 isn't exactly "crushing", but in this case it is because we didn't have a prayer!).

Parents, please share this whole e-mail with your kids tonight! They need to know that each and every one of them made me proud to be a coach. On days like this, I wish that all I ever had to do was coach soccer. This is true job satisfaction, right? Where you put in all of the hard work, all of the inspiring talks and e-mails and quotes, you put in your time and every ounce of your passion and talent, and you get a day like today that's perfect!

Now let me give you all some advice. What used to happen to me was that after a win like today, say in business, or even if I got a girl to go on a date (I'm a happily married guy, but I can still remember the feeling! HAH!). What used to happen is that I would get a win and feel like the ruler of the free world, but the next day I wasn't prepared for the tsunami of bad things that are just part of normal life. So here's my advice, be prepared. Tomorrow is going to be an ordinary day, probably. If you know that now, and you keep it in your mind, you won't be so devastated when you wake up in the morning and nothing has changed.

Good night, mighty manatees! Keep your feet on the ground and life won't be able to knock you over too badly!

I'll see you at practice!

Coach Randy

Manatees never say die

From: PPousaint@mac.com
To: Manatees   sent Sat, Oct 9 5:30 pm

Subject: Re: YEAH!!! Manatees crush the Dark Knights!

Dear Team,

Coach Paul would like to add to Coach Randy's congratulations on a job well done. I can respect his desire to protect you from waking up tomorrow and being disappointed that your whole life didn't change. But this is boys' soccer, after all. Feel free to celebrate your win, and on Wednesday we will discuss what strategies worked and what we still need to work on.

Go Manatees,
Coach Paul

From: PPousaint@mac.com
To: FavoriteCoach@gmail.com   sent Sat, Oct 9 5:35 pm

Subject: Dialing it back

Hey Randy. I appreciate your enthusiasm, but let's keep it all on positives and not on the possible existential black hole that the boys may fall into in the morning. Ten year olds don't wake up wondering why the world hasn't changed, only people over forty do.

I don't know what's going on with you at home, and it's none of my business, but sometimes your e-mails to the team/parents sound uncomfortably zealous.

I'm just trying to be helpful here.

See you at practice!
Paul

———————

From: Visorgrl@mac.com
To: Manatees   sent Sat, Oct 9 5:36 pm

Subject: Great Game, Manatees

Hey team and team parents, you all looked GREAT out there!!!!! ☺ This team was really feeling a lot of love coming off the field and they should because each and every kid was a star!

I just want to say that we don't have to think of ourselves as "crushing" our opponents. Let's just say that this was the Manatees day to shine. ☺

I also want to say that your boys were such gentlemen out there! I give a shout-out to my own kid, Calvin, who didn't kick or refuse to play when the other team got past him. THAT'S WHAT THIS IS ALL ABOUT!!!! LIFE-LESSONS! I noticed that Ben's technique of not talking AT ALL was incredibly effective. I wondered about it during practice, because writing on his white board in between drillswas getting time-consuming, but boy did it pay off today!!!!

See you at practice, everyone! You are all shining stars!

XOXO,
Jacqui

From: MSonnenklar@GSachs.com

To: Manatees   sent Sat, Oct 9 5:38 pm

Subject: Re: Great Game, Manatees

Sorry to miss the game. It was Ben's mother's weekend and she wanted to go. Ben's silent act is directed toward me, with the sole purpose of getting an IPhone. Please do not indulge him at practice or anywhere else.

M

From: Alejandro.Navaro@Pepperdine.edu
To: Manatees   sent Sat, Oct 9 5:41 pm

Subject: Re: Great Game, Manatees

To an excellent team. The boys skills are getting better and better.

Alejandro

––––––––––

From: DPlatt@ca.rr.com
To: Alejandro.Navaro@Pepperdine.edu   sent Sat, Oct 9 5:46 pm

Subject: Today and the future

Alejandro,

I loved our little chat after the game, and especially liked hearing about your decision to come to Los Angeles to study.

I would love to spend more time with you. Would you like to come over to dinner on a weekend that my ex has the kids? We would have plenty of time to get to know each other better.

Diane

––––––––––

From: Alejandro.Navaro@Pepperdine.edu
To: DPlatt@ca.rr.com   sent Sat, Oct 9 5:49 pm

Subject: Re: Today and the future

Diane,

It would be wonderful to come to your home. Do your children stay with you tomorrow?

Alejandro

———————

From: DPlatt@ca.rr.com
To: Alejandro.Navaro@Pepperdine.edu   sent Sat, Oct 9 5:52 pm

Subject: Re: Today and the future

Alejandro,

No, my children will be away tomorrow. You can come by at 1:00pm (445 Benton Way, 90210). We will have the whole afternoon to relax.

Diane

———————

From: Alejandro.Navaro@Pepperdine.edu
To: DPlatt@ca.rr.com   sent Sat, Oct 9 5:53pm

Subject: Re: Today and the future

This will be very good. I have been very lonely here. I wish to talk to a beautiful woman.

Alejandro

————

From: DPlatt@ca.rr.com
To: Alejandro.Navaro@Pepperdine.edu sent Sat, Oct 9 5:54 pm

Subject: Re: Today and the future

Alejandro,

You should know that romantic talk like that is not only unnecessary, it's a turn-off. I just need to get laid and wake up the next day without feeling guilty, sad, or angry.

Diane

————

From: Alejandro.Navaro@Pepperdine.edu
To: DPlatt@ca.rr.com   sent Sat, Oct 9 5:54 pm

Subject: Re: Today and the future

I understand you and can do this with pleasure.

Alejandro

From: FavoriteCoach@gmail.com

To: Manatees   sent Sat, Oct 9 6:03 pm

Subject: Re: YEAH!!! Manatees crush the Dark Knights!

Hey team! I'm sorry if I got a little carried away with advice and every-thing. I'm a very passionate guy, and most people like it! (kidding, you don't have to like it!). But that's me, I can't help myself sometimes.

We all want our kids to succeed (heck, we want ourselves to succeed), but we want to protect them too. That's all I was trying to do.

Go Manatees!

Coach Randy

Manatees never say die

From: RTChampion@gmail.com

To: DPlatt@ca.rr.com   sent Sat, Oct 9 6:12 pm

Subject: From Randy

Hey Diane,

Great game today, huh? I guess you couldn't tell how happy I was from my team e-mail. Just kidding, I know some people thought I was a little over the top. But as I told them, I'm a passionate guy.

It's like I told Patrick the other day. We were kicking the ball around (God, he's a great kid, so polite) and I said, "You have all the skills, but you have to have heart. You've got to want to be the best and you have to love your team." (and your coach). He laughed when I said the part about loving the coach.

Anyway, he said that his parents want him to succeed at everything, not just soccer. Maybe that's why he tenses up every once in a while at the games, it's like he's always aware of his parents watching him.

I think the kid has a hard time fitting in with the others. It isn't only that he doesn't live in Beverly Hills and go to Bev Elem, it's because he doesn't even know HOW to hang out. I'm happy that I can help him with that.

Hey, Missy has a skincare party tomorrow afternoon and I wondered if Aiden and I could come around and hang out with you and the kids?

It was just a thought, maybe you wouldn't like it.

Randy

Manatees never say die

From: DPlatt@ca.rr.com
To: RTChampion@gmail.com   sent Sat, Oct 9 7:42 pm

Subject: Re: From Randy

Hi Randy. Unfortunately, the kids aren't with me tomorrow and I have a prior engagement. That was a nice idea.

I didn't know Patrick doesn't live in Beverly Hills. You should be very careful who you share that with. Some of the dads get pretty aggressive about sniffing these things out the closer we get to playoffs. And I wouldn't want him to get kicked out. He's such a sweet kid.

I think it's great that you are working with Patrick and developing a relationship with him. I hope that you get to spend that same kind of time with Aiden. I worry that because you are keeping secrets from your family, you are isolating yourself. The sooner you are honest with your family, the closer you will feel to them. And they to you.

I've made a ton of mistakes, Randy. And I'm not perfect by a long shot. But I am honest, because when you're honest you at least know what you are dealing with. It's a whole heck of a lot better than painfully wondering what's going on. Of course, you have to know your own mind in order to achieve a level of honesty. That's the tough part. Do you know your own mind?

Best,
Diane

CHAPTER 24

ALEJANDRO AND DIANE ARE DONE, for now. His head rests on her bare stomach. Dark cheek against her pale flesh, his breath rippling the hair of her pussy. The fact that she has ample hair there is a revelation and not an unwelcome one. It reminds him of his mother, who often walked around naked inside their home when he was a child. Diane shifts slightly and he considers raising his head. But she lets out a purr and settles again. He doesn't want to move. Which is also a revelation. Were he to analyze it further, he might recognize this indolence as the closest he's been to contentment since he arrived in California four months ago.

Diane is torn between staying in bed and enjoying the young man's head on her belly for a little bit longer, and getting up to pee. Also, her hip hurts. Also, she suspects that if she moves, he will take it as a sign that he should go. He's a young guy, after all, and only came over to get a little uncomplicated afternoon sex. Which is, of course, what she wanted too.

She adjusts ever so slightly.

"Are you for getting up?" he says.

"No. No. I just need . . . stay right there." She slides her hip out slightly. He lifts his head, and then lays it back down. "Right. Better."

"For me, is good," he says with a little giggle.

"Me too," she says. Then adds (perhaps stupidly, she thinks), "Thanks for coming over."

He giggles again. Which she thinks is cute. Endearing. She hadn't expected this boyishness. Before this afternoon, he had seemed so confident and sexually secure. She knew that he would walk in and take what he wanted. Which was exactly what he did. But she'd forgotten that he was still a kid.

"Do you want to ask me something?" she says, to fill up space. "You don't have to."

"Let me see," he says, nestling his head further into her tummy. She tightens her bladder. "Okay. Yes. I know something to ask. Why is your bedroom not like you at all?"

What does that mean, she wonders. And lifts her head slightly to see it through his eyes. What's he talking about? It's tasteful. The valance, a dusky pink damask. The bureau, an expensive antique. And the painting above it is an original someone-or-other, three blond girls gazing at a book, done in an impressionistic style that is not too derivative or cloying.

Who is she kidding? She didn't choose any of it.

She lets her head drop with acquiescence. "Yeah. Well. I was younger when I worked with the designer and I hadn't a clue who I was or what I wanted. So I guess you're right. I haven't had the energy to change it too much because I probably still don't know what I'd replace it with. And I'm not sure that I care about the bedroom anyway."

"Is very much like all the bedrooms here," he says.

"I'm sure you've seen a lot of them."

"Why not?"

"Yes, of course. Why not?" she says, begrudging him nothing. She raises up on her elbows. "Don't take this the wrong way. But I have to go to the bathroom."

He picks up his head. "Of course. Of course." And stands in one move. "No wrong way. Are you mad that I say this about the bedroom?"

His body is so perfect it almost makes her sad. "Of course not, Alejandro. You're right about my bedroom. You are right about all of our bedrooms."

She swings her legs off the side of the bed and sits, feeling the twinge in her hip again. She suspects that sitting like this makes her stomach look flabby. But what the hell, Alejandro will move on, and she's been satisfied. She stands up and kisses him on the cheek. "If you want to go, it's all right."

Hearing this, Alejandro feels a vague sense of missing something. And he considers grabbing her and pulling her back into bed. But he is unsure. So he stays still and watches her turn. Her ass. The curve of her waist. She walks into the bathroom and shuts the door.

Alone in the room that looks like all the others, he wonders why he wants to stay in this one. He walks over to his bunched-up jockey shorts, grabs them with his toes, flicks them into his hand, and pulls them on. He hears the faucet. She must be cleaning herself. Cleaning him off her. It's a clear sign that she wants him to go. Something in his chest pulls. He looks at the closed door. This is stupid. He shakes the feeling off, leans down, and grabs his jeans.

The door opens and she reemerges, still naked.

"Wow. You got dressed in a hurry," she says as he's pulling up his zipper.

"No. I thought..." he says.

She shrugs. "It's okay, Alejandro."

"What is okay?" He looks at his T-shirt on the floor.

She moves to the dresser and pulls open a drawer. "Anything you want to do is okay. Leave, stay, fuck, eat, watch TV. I have the whole afternoon, with nothing else to do."

She pulls on a pair of striped panties. Practical panties. Not the thongs he's used to. The panties make him want to stay.

"Eat," he says without thinking, and she laughs. "I choose to eat."

She walks over to him, hooks her fingers into his waistband, and pulls him toward her. Their pelvises bump and his cock stiffens. "What do you want to eat?"

He feels her breath on his face. He knows how to play this game. Has played it hundreds of times. But something in him is thrown off. His brain won't produce a clever response. He can only stand there, boner pressed against her, waiting for her to decide.

She stares straight into his eyes and releases his waistband. "All right. Cold pizza." She grabs a silky robe from the back of the door and he follows.

Her kitchen is so clean it glistens. Nothing is out of place, not even a pot left on the stove. It is, he thinks, as if no one lives here. He can't even smell anything. He pulls a chair out from the table and sits, watching her as she peers into the refrigerator. He leans over to look past her ass and he sees almost no food. A few jars in the door. A six-pack of beer on the top shelf and a lime. Three takeout boxes stacked up. A half-gallon of milk. That's about it.

She pulls out a pizza box and slaps it on the table. "I've got water, beer, or half a bottle of wine. Oh, and milk."

"Water is good," he says, opening the box and helping himself to a pepperoni slice.

"I can do that." She grabs a glass that is like all the others off a shelf and presses it against the water dispenser. "Ice?"

"No ice," he says, looking around the room again. The kitchen is cold. He misses his T-shirt in the bedroom and shivers.

Diane sees this.

"Consuela bumps up the air," she says. "I can turn it down. And why don't you get your shirt?" She walks over to the switch while he hops out of the room. When he's gone she turns and leans against the wall to wait. She thinks that she should have let him go. There's nothing to talk about. Maybe he will sense this too and leave. Surely he has something—someone—to get back to. She spots her laptop on the kitchen counter and feels a pang that she's not sitting in the glow of its screen, safely alone, uncompromised.

Shit.

Alejandro pops back in. Shirted and fresher somehow, he slides into the chair and grabs another slice. Now what? She opens the fridge and grabs a beer. "Okay. How about a game of Scrabble?"

"Yes. Scrabble," he says. She was sure he'd make an excuse and fly. Instead he leans back, stretches his legs out, crosses them, and flashes her a wide, white smile.

Holy shit.

CHAPTER 25

From: JHandHRasst@OneStopOffice.com
To: FavoriteCoach@gmail.com   sent Mon, Oct 11 8:36 am

Subject: Set meeting

Dear Mr. Tinker,

Human Resources would like to meet with you regarding several unac-
counted for expenditures on your corporate credit card over the last fiscal
year. Please call to set up an appointment.

Thank you,
Heather

Heather Stanfield
Executive Assistant/Human Resources
OneStopOffice
739 La Jolla Drive
Los Angeles, CA 90042

From: FavoriteCoach@gmail.com
To: JHandHRasst@OneStopOffice.com   sent Mon, Oct 11 9:45 am

Subject: Re: Set meeting

Dear Heather,

Is a meeting necessary? All items were understood to be corporate gifts.
I discussed this in the exit interview.

Randy

Manatees never say die

From: JHandHRasst@OneStopOffice.com
To: FavoriteCoach@gmail.com   sent Mon, Oct 11 9:46 am

Subject: Re: Set meeting

Dear Randy,

This is a matter best brought up with Ms. Hand. When are you available?

Heather

Heather Stanfield
Executive Assistant/Human Resources
OneStopOffice
739 La Jolla Drive
Los Angeles, CA 90042

From: RTChampion@gmail.com

To: DPlatt@ca.rr.com   sent Mon, Oct 11 9:50 am

Subject: (No Subject)

Diane,

I think I really need someone to talk to. No, I KNOW I need someone to talk to. I messed up and I don't know how to go back and fix it. I just always thought that I'd have that job and that they wouldn't look into corporate gifts. I bought them all the time—everyone does. If they want their money back, I don't have it.

What do I do?

Randy

From: DPlatt@ca.rr.com

To: RTChampion@gmail.com   sent Mon, Oct 11 10:53 am

Subject: Re: (No Subject)

Dear Randy,

Your e-mail wasn't very clear. Who is it that wants their money back? Credit card company? A friend? You didn't borrow from someone crazy did you? Some loan shark guy? Are you OK? Are you at the library?

Diane

From: RTChampion@gmail.com
To: DPlatt@ca.rr.com   sent Mon, Oct 11 10:56 am

Subject: Re: (No Subject)

I am at the library and I have 20 more minutes of computer time. It's OneStopOffice—they're asking for an accounting of gifts that I bought that I was supposed to give to clients, but I actually sold. Shit. Shit. Shit.

I don't have the money to pay them back, if they catch it, Diane. I don't have any money at all and Missy doesn't know. I don't know what to do. Why is this happening to me?

I don't know any loan sharks, but I would be interested in meeting one. Do you know anyone who could extend a personal loan of 29,000? Or better would be 35,000, just to give me a little cushion.

Thank you for not judging me, Diane. You're a great sport and a true friend.

Randy

———————

From: DPlatt@ca.rr.com
To: RTChampion@gmail.com   sent Mon, Oct 11 11:00 am

Subject: Re: (No Subject)

Seriously Randy? I have a ton of judgment. And what makes you think that I know loan sharks? I'm so far out of that kind of loop that I don't even know if they're called "loan sharks" anymore. For all I know, they're called "fiscal engineers" or something. Look, I want to help you. But we are not close friends. You are a guy who is down on his luck and I am a single mom who is home all day with nothing to do but push cocktail hour earlier and earlier.

Now, for the judgment part of this exchange. You cannot compound this problem by borrowing MORE money, potentially from people who would have no problem extracting payment in the form of limbs that you hold dear. Stop this craziness and tell Missy. Refinance if you have to. Families pull together, so I hear. Mine didn't, but that was a more hopeless case.

Not to beat a man while he's down, but what did you spend all that money on?

Diane

From: RTChampion@gmail.com
To: DPlatt@ca.rr.com   sent Mon, Oct 11 11:07 am

Subject: Re: (No Subject)

Diane, I'm going to have to get off of this computer in twelve minutes. I don't think the loan shark option is off the table. Maybe if I ask around at one of those quick check cashing places. Also, I could look into selling one of my organs. Off hand, do you know how much I might make?

All I have to do is get another job and then everything will be solved and I can pay back the loan sharks or live with one lung. I'm feeling better already, and I'm thinking clearer. All a man needs is options and you've opened that up for me. You're a good person, Diane. I'm sorry that your life didn't pan out like you wanted it to.

To answer the elephant-in-the-room question: The deck made everything worse. Of course, we were way over our heads even before the deck, and after I lost California Pizza Kitchen, things got really crazy (Missy doesn't know I lost California Pizza Kitchen—she still thinks it's my major account). When Missy first came to me with the plans for the deck, I thought—Whoo Whee, this is going to be almost impossible to pull off!!!! But I got creative and found some guys through a pal at work, all under the table, and things were great until the posts of the deck started sinking into the ground. So then I had to get a licensed contractor and a soil engineer. Who even knew soil needed an engineer? Well, now you know, THIS GUY!!! We had to get this enormous drill and caissons. It looked like we were building a stadium back there, and the whole time I acted like it was all normal so Missy wouldn't know what a first class idiot I was not testing the soil in the first place!!

Missy's younger than me and I know that she loves being with me mostly because I can take care of her. She also thought I was funny, back when we met.

I'm not stupid, Diane. A guy like me doesn't get a girl like Missy unless he can afford her, which doesn't mean she doesn't love me, she does. But lots of what we love about our life together is our house and our neighborhood activities.

I haven't told you before that I had a first marriage before Missy. It was short and in my twenties, but I feel like once Lori began to see my imperfections, BAM, she was out of the gate pretty fast. I learned that you have to maintain being that guy that women thought you were in the first place. Once you show that you're in trouble, you start losing.

OK, I'm shaking this off and getting down to work. I'm going to grab lunch and a paper, and when I get back I'll jump on the computer and research serious options. Thanks, Diane, you are a true friend.

Randy

———————

From: DPlatt@ca.rr.com
To: RTChampion@gmail.com   sent Mon, Oct 11 11:11 am

Subject: Re: (No Subject)

Randy,

I know that you are off at lunch, but I have to answer back. Loan sharks and selling your organs is seriously crazy talk. You need professional help in the form of a therapist or a life coach, or something. You really do, Randy. You can't keep writing to me, thinking that I'm your sounding board. I am incapable of solving all your problems. You keep saying that I'm a great friend. But I'm not. First of all, we've only known each other casually for one and a half soccer seasons. But far more relevant is the fact that I'm a huge fucking fuck-up, Randy. I ruined my own marriage. All by myself. Without any help from T. It was just me. All me. Nobody says that unless it's true. I'll spend my whole life making it up to my kids.

So, sure, I can field a few e-mails and even talk to you on the phone. But I don't have answers. Far from it. I'm the wrecker, not the fixer. Don't get close to me. I mean it.

Diane

———————

From: Kelli.Sonnenklar@Sonnenklar.com
To: KSonn@gmail.com   sent Mon, Oct 11 1:23 pm

dear karen,

i feel like i'm in a movie about a letter that gets lost and is opened twenty years later and the whole movie would have been different if the person who was supposed to get the letter had gotten it in time. i'm ninety-nine percent sure you'll never read this. you made yourself clear about cutting me off when you hung up the phone on me for the third time.

so basically, this is a like the lost letter in the movie. i'm writing it anyway because maybe if you open it twenty years from now, at least you will know i tried.

dear karen, twenty years from now,

i am sorry that i betrayed your trust. you hired me to take care of your son and things should have never started up between mark and i. i don't want to make excuses for myself, but it never looked good between you and mark. not to me, anyways. in fact, they looked kind of terrible to begin with, the first day i worked there. you were always putting each other down and saying mean things behind each other's backs. you would bite mark's head off every time he walked into the room. so when he started confiding in me, i felt sorry for him. that doesn't make you a bad person and I know that mark has his issues like always being right about every-thing and always thinking that all you have to do is just lay down the law and that's that. i know that he didn't respect your job and how stressful it is. even with me, he doesn't care about any of my interior decorating. but that's just him, and i can live with it and you never could.

so, karen twenty years from now, i hope that by now, ben is a thirty year old man with a wife and two kids that he loves to death. i hope you are re-married to someone who helps more around the house (wouldn't that be fun?) and i hope that mark and i are still married and living in palm springs. but what i hope for most is that we are all talking to each other and loving our lives.

i also hope that by now, actually now twenty years later, you have forgiven me for giving ben the iphone. mark forgave me last night after a pretty tense conversation about it. it was the ninth day of ben's silent treatment and banging things in his room, and i didn't think it was good for anyone. we just need some peace back, and i still think that ben needs to see a family therapist, but the first thing is just to get him talking again, which he started doing as soon as he got the phone.

i am including a link about the silent treatment and how it's really emotional abuse: http://hub/How-to-cope-with-Silent-Treatment-Abuse. hopefully, the link will still work by the time you finally open this letter. and when you finally get this please read: dr. phil: http://Oprah.com//Dr.Phil-getting-your-kids-attention and ask patty: http://PattyR/taking-time-for-yourself

thanks for finally opening my letter eventually, karen.

kelli

CHAPTER 26

"ON THREE, WE ALL YELL together," barks Randy above the boys' heads. "Got it?" The boys collectively nod and Diane sees Reece across the field, eyes wide, waiting for the count.

"One!" Randy shouts. "Two!" A pause for effect, then, "Three!"

"All for one and one for all!" they scream with their little-boy voices, and they jump up and down, hugging one another. Individually and in clumps, they throw themselves at Randy, who picks them up and swings them, or smacks them on the back. If Diane didn't know about Randy's troubles, she would never guess.

"That's it!" he yells, holding Dashiell in his arms. His voice is slightly hoarse. "Practice over. See you at the game."

The sun is setting and there is a bite in the air. Diane pulls her light sweater tighter around her waist. She was hoping to make eye contact, at least, with Alejandro, since it has been a couple of days since he came over, with no follow-up. But he isn't at practice.

Next to her, Ben's mom, Karen, starts collapsing her camping chair. Diane watches her wrestle the chair into a canvas sleeve. It's an inelegant operation and Diane smiles to herself. She shouldn't wish a fellow single mom ill, but it's satisfying to see Karen looking inept. Normally she's so put-together that she makes Diane feel like a frump.

Diane tucks a stubborn wisp of hair behind her ear. "Need help with that?" she says to Karen. Her better nature winning.

Karen looks up, red-faced. "Nope. Got it. Thanks." She fusses with the toggle, then appears to give up, tossing the strap of the sleeve over her shoulder with the chair legs still half hanging out. Karen's son (the one who swears and flips off the other team routinely—but who's judging? Well, Diane is, apparently) comes running up to his mother.

"Did you see the scrimmage?" he puffs.

Karen smiles and says, "Of course I did." Even though Diane doubts it. Karen had her head in her phone most of the practice. Not to judge, again.

Diane doesn't have time to dwell on her secret lack of charity, however, since Reece has run up to her and is burrowing into her waist to get warm. She opens up her sweater and envelops him. A moment that makes standing on the sidelines, with not even the distraction of a sidelong glance at Alejandro, worth it.

All over the field, boys are bouncing back to their mothers like balls on a tether, now that the business of being little men on the field is done. Moms call out to each other; water bottles are retrieved and stashed in cloth bags; Beth Paradis shakes out the blanket she brought to sit on. Mako pulls a sweatshirt over Mason's head. The Manatees are the last to leave the park tonight, and the boys' voices ricochet off the wall of the gym and the basketball backboards in the court next to the parking lot.

"Let's get going," Diane says to Reece. He pulls back a bit, poking his head out of her sweater, and with some maneuvering she manages to keep him wrapped up as they head to the car.

Mako and Mason are loading into their Prius and Mrs. Woo is rounding the front of her car, having checked Patrick's seat belt. Diane wonders if Patrick is too old for seat-belt checking. The Woos are constantly fussing with that boy. Next to them, Karen beeps the trunk of her Beamer.

Behind her, Diane hears shouting from the field. The shouts are urgent. Male. Randy. His voice staccato with panic. Yelling what sounds like orders. She and Mako both turn to see Randy racing from the middle of the field toward the recreation center.

Karen runs past Diane, in Randy's direction. She thinks she hears Randy yell, "Calvin!"

Diane starts running, instinctively. She still can't see anything out of place, but is urged on by the primal terror that forever lies below the surface of every mother's skin.

Losing a child.

Mako must feel it too because Diane can hear her running close behind. She looks around for a dad. Where's Paul or Mr. Woo? Or Mark? And Jacqui? Where's she? She's always at practice.

"What's wrong with Calvin?" Diane yells to Karen, who is a few feet ahead.

"He's on the ledge," Karen yells, jabbing the air with her finger.

Diane squints as she catches up with Karen, who has stopped and is looking up. There's Calvin, sitting on the edge of the second story of the rec center's overhang. He has pulled his knees up to his chest. Half of the soles of his shoes jut out over the ledge and they bounce up and down as he rocks, each rock teetering him closer to the brink.

Diane raises her hand, entreating, "Calvin, honey. We need you to stop rocking." Mako is now beside her, bent over gasping.

"Where the hell is Jacqui?" Karen yells.

"At team moms' meeting," Mako says, straightening. Still catching her breath, "She didn't want to leave Calvin here alone. But Randy said..."

Diane glances over her shoulder at the parking lot and sees Reece and the other boys, stone still, staring at Calvin. She looks back up to see a window being raised behind Calvin, and Randy's leg appearing. The rest of him squeezes through and he stands, holding on to the windowsill, looking inhumanly tall and remote against the orange sky.

"Daddy!" Aiden screams.

Diane turns to see Randy's son running across the field, then quickly looks back up to see Randy putting up his hands to stay them all. "I'm fine, everyone!" he yells. He teeters and grabs the windowsill again. "And Calvin's fine too. Right, Calvin?"

Up on the roof, Randy hopes that his voice sounded calm. He's not sure because he can't hear himself over the pounding in his ears. He taps the roof with his shoe. It's tacky and a bit gravelly. But solid enough. Calvin keeps rocking and repeating something Randy can't quite make out.

"Calvin, can you stop rocking for a minute?" he says. But Calvin either can't hear him or won't listen. Randy lets go of the windowsill and takes a step.

The women gasp below and a thrill goes up his spine. He hears Aiden yell up to him, "Daddy?"

"It's okay, son," he says, taking another step, sending a pebble skittering down the incline. His chest clenches, his eyes fixed on Calvin's rocking hunch.

"Randy," he hears Diane say, "for God's sake, stop right there. Someone call Jacqui."

"Daddy!" Aiden's voice pierces the night air.

"Aiden, you're not helping." Again he hears Diane. "Who the fuck has Jacqui's number?" Randy hears the women rummaging in purses and pockets. Phones are retrieved. Keeping his eyes down on the roof's terrain, he tests with the opposite toe, finds footing, and takes another step.

"I don't have it," says Karen.

"Me neither," he hears Mako.

"Jesus. No one has it?" says Diane.

"Well, you don't have it either," snaps Mako.

"For Christ's sake," he yells down to the women, "I have it!" He spreads his arms out to his sides for balance, teetering like a prop plane touching down. "Calvin. Can you hear me? You have to stop rocking. Then we can talk."

"Randy, call Jacqui," Diane implores.

"Can't. Phone's in my jacket on the field." He takes another step, arms waving for balance. The ladies gasp and he feels another tingle of pleasure, all eyes on him. Not that that's why he's doing it. But still.

"Okay. Someone get the fucking phone," says Diane.

"Can we..." says Mako. "Can we pull back on the language? I know we're all tense. But seriously. There are children."

And indeed there are. Randy throws a glance over the edge to see who's watching. All the boys have advanced across the field and now encircle the mothers like the outer ring of Stonehenge. Ben, Mason, Reece. With Aiden in the center of them all, face raised, shining with worry.

"Aiden," he yells down. "You get the phone."

"Got it," Aiden shouts back with more eagerness than Randy's ever heard from him, and the kid starts running.

He hears Diane: "Mako. Can you stop with the constant judgment? We're all doing our best."

"What?" Mako gasps.

"Ladies. Please!" he yells. "Someone tell me if they can see Calvin's face."

"His head's down," Karen yells up.

"Okay," he says. "I'm not sure he's even hearing us. I'm going to have to get closer. Can anyone hear what he's saying?"

"He's saying something?" Karen says.

"Yeah. He's muffled."

"We can't make it out."

"Okay. Never mind." Randy tests and takes another step. Intake of breath from the moms. His arms tip. Aiden races across the field waving the phone. Attaboy. Randy's skin prickles. He feels hyperalive. Hearing is sharper. Eyesight enhanced to the point that he can see a white cat hair on Calvin's collar. He takes another step, wavers, finds balance.

"Aiden," he calls down. "Call Jacqui. She's in 'Contacts.'"

Randy hears the phone boop and he is suffused with pride. He and his boy, saving lives. That's what they do. Working together to get the job done. He judges himself to be about five feet from Calvin, but as he gets closer to the edge, it feels more likely that a wrong move could send them both plunging down. From the second story they'd break some bones at the very least. Calvin sways and mumbles. In this second, Randy's knowledge of physics, athletics, and warfare fuse. His center of gravity needs to be lower.

Of course! Keeping his back straight, he starts bending his knees like he learned in jujitsu. He channels the two classes he took a few years ago, before he broke his toe. Feel the tightness in your thighs. Don't use your back. Or your knees. Imagine a string through your spine, pulling you up as you sink down. Yes, he is a man who only has to learn a thing once to get it entirely. He lowers himself further, like a samurai warrior. Mind and body working in concert.

"Watch it, Randy," Mako yells up.

"You're good, Randy. You're almost there," says Diane.

He's now low enough to plant a hand on the incline and plop his ass down.

"Jacqui?" he hears Aiden say into the phone. "It's Aiden."

Randy yells down, "Tell her not to panic. But Calvin's on a roof, rocking, and saying things."

"Hey, Jacqui. Calvin's on a roof, rocking and saying stuff."

A frenetic, high-pitched string of words bursts through the phone.

"Oh for God's sake," says Diane.

"Aiden," says Mako, "give me the phone."

Randy scoots down on his ass. "Aiden. Tell her not to panic. That's the important part."

"Don't panic," Aiden yells into the phone, which has the opposite effect. The string of words gets louder and less intelligible. Randy scoots down more, the gravel cutting into the palm of his hand. Finally, he is close enough to put his arm around Calvin's rocking shoulder.

"Tell her that I've got him," says Randy. "Guys, I can hear him now. Calvin's saying 'to her, to her.' Does that mean anything? Was he supposed to give anything to her? To anyone that's a female?"

Aiden says into the phone, "Calvin keeps saying 'to her.' Who's he supposed to give something to?"

Randy tightens his grip on Calvin's shoulder and stiffens his arm to stop the rocking. Which works, but Calvin keeps mumbling. "Wait. Wait, I think he's saying 'sugar.'"

"My dad says that he's saying 'sugar,'" Aiden says into the phone.

"Honey," Randy hears Karen say to Aiden, "can you give me the phone?"

"I can do it," Aiden retorts, a stubborn edge to his voice. Then he's back on the phone. A second, and he yells up, "Hey, Dad. Jacqui says he's saying 'sugar.' Sugar calms him down when he's upset."

"That's what this is about?" Mako says. Randy can't tell if this is derisive since Mako always sounds that way.

"Who's got a candy bar?" says Randy. Loud so the moms can hear. But calm, he hopes, while keeping his arm stiff around Calvin's shoulders.

"Who's got a candy bar?" Karen yells into the air.

"I had one, but I ate it," Ben says.

"Dad. Dad," Aiden yells up. "Jacqui says it has to be a sugar packet."

"Seriously?" escapes Randy's lips before he has time to check it. To cover, he leans into Calvin's neck and says, "Don't worry, kid. We're on the case." Calvin lifts his head slightly, but Randy still can't see his face. "Okay, ladies. We need a packet of sugar. Who's got one?"

"Can it be Equal?" says Diane. "I've got a few in my glove compartment."

"You've got to be kidding," says Mako. "You can't give Equal to a child."

"You want me to ask Jacqui?" says Aiden, sounding so grown-up.

"Of course, don't ask her," says Diane, "she's got enough to worry about."

"Anybody have actual sugar?" Karen interjects.

Silence.

"Okay," Karen says, decisively, "let's go with Equal."

"What if he's allergic?" says Mako.

Randy's arm is beginning to ache but he's too afraid to loosen his hold. He feels like the boy is depending on the steadiness of his grip. Almost leaning into it, away from the drop-off.

Diane barks, "Reece. Here are my keys. Go get the Equal."

"Sure," says Reece. Over the edge of the roof, Randy sees him catch the keys and almost click his heels in response to his stated mission. He spins and takes off toward the cars.

"It's in the glove compartment!" Diane yells after him.

"Dad," Aiden calls out, "Jacqui wants to talk to you. I'm going to bring the phone up."

Randy can't believe it. Where was this can-do attitude when Aiden was playing soccer or cleaning his room? He leans in close to Calvin. "We've got your sugar. Everything's going to be all right." Calvin's head rises even more; still buried, but it's a good sign. Randy looks out over the field, which is now dark. He wishes Missy were here to see Aiden and him working like a team. But she never comes to the practices. Oh well, at least the other moms are seeing it.

"I really don't think we should give a kid Equal." He hears Mako's perpetually pissed-off tone. "Especially without asking Jacqui about it."

"Equal is the least of that kid's problems," Diane says.

"What if he's allergic? He's got a lot of allergies. What if he has a seizure?"

"Mako. Let's not skip ahead and imagine the worst. Back off."

Then he hears Karen. "Can you guys zip it? Calvin can hear. And the kids. We're supposed to be modeling. Cooler heads, right?"

"Right," says Diane, with a tone that sounds like she's got a lot more to say. Randy can't wait to hear what she thought in an e-mail tomorrow. He stretches his neck and sees Reece zoom up and slap something in Diane's hand.

"Dad!" Randy turns to see Aiden leaning out the window with the cell up to his ear. He starts to lift his leg through the window.

"Wait," says Randy. Aiden pauses. "Diane," he yells down, "bring up the Equal and give it to Aiden."

"Got it," she says, and disappears through the door. He hears her clumping up the stairs.

Randy turns back to Aiden. "You can relax, son." He likes the way *son* sounds now. He's always called Aiden *son*, but it never felt real before.

"All right. But Dad? Jacqui says that you have to hold Calvin in a tight hug. Tighter than you think. You can start doing it before you give him the Equal. Um... sugar."

"Tell her I'm on it. I'll start the hug now."

"Okay. And I've got the Equal. Sugar. So I'm coming out."

"Maybe Diane should come out instead," Randy says, lifting his ass, tiny pebbles digging into his flesh through his pants, and shifting closer to Calvin. He does not loosen his grip. With his other hand, he reaches across Calvin's chest and clasps him tightly. It's sideways—but it's the best he can do.

"I've got it. I'm coming out," Aiden says. There are fussing sounds coming from Diane, behind the window.

Randy looks over his shoulder. "Take small baby steps, son. And go very slowly."

His boy slips through the window, Diane's hand on his elbow, and then she lets go. Randy watches him carefully with his arms still tight around Calvin, like he can keep Aiden steady with the precision of his gaze. In his arms, Calvin is stiff and unyielding. Randy barely breathes as he watches Aiden take slow little steps toward them. Randy pulls Calvin even closer, hoping to feel some give in his body. He looks down at his son's feet. "Careful. Go slow. Don't take any chances." The gravel of the roof crunches with each step.

"Daddy," says Aiden, stopping and looking up. "I don't think you're supposed to be doing a sideways hug. Jacqui says it has to be super tight. Like you're almost afraid you'll break him. Except he won't break. He'll like it."

"Okay, son. I'll try." Randy twists his waist to look at Calvin, the boy's shoulder poking him in the chest. The maneuver means taking his eyes off Aiden. If anything happens to his son because he took his eyes off his child's feet, he'll die of grief.

But here's the thing, Randy tells himself—his kid says he can do it. Randy holds on to that thought as he turns Calvin's stiff body slightly and pulls him into his chest as tight as he can. Can he break his collarbone? Jacqui said "tighter than you think." He tightens even more, tighter than he's ever held anyone. Calvin softens and turns into the hug a bit, which means Randy can pull him in even closer. The embrace feels so wonderful that Randy wonders why he's never hugged anyone like this before. Like he'll never let go.

He feels Aiden's touch on his head and looks up. "Here's the sugar, Dad."

There is rustling below and he hears a car door slam.

Jacqui screams, "I'm here! Mommy's here!"

"Jacqui's here," Mako says.

"Thanks for the update," he hears from Diane, who must have run back downstairs.

Randy keeps the hug strong. Breathing in the boy. He opens his palm, without releasing any pressure, and Aiden leans over them both to place the packet in his hand. He curls it into his fist, feeling his son now leaning on his head.

Jacqui huffs it to the moms below and yells up another "I'm here! I couldn't find any more sugar packets in my glove compartment. I don't know where they went." Her voice is spiked with fear and self-flagellation.

"It's not your fault," says Karen.

"Jacqui," Randy says down to her. "Everything's under control, I think. It's just...how do I give him the sugar?"

"It's Equal," he hears Mako whisper.

"Equal's fine. Randy," Jacqui yells, "just tell him you have the sugar and you can loosen up. Once he knows he's getting it, he'll be easy! He's really a great kid!"

Randy is afraid to pull back, but he does a little, feeling the warm pocket of air they've created between them. Aiden's hand still rests on his head. "Calvin, I have the sugar."

It's dark now, but Randy can make out Calvin's face as he stares up at him, his mouth opening like a baby bird's. Behind the boy's back, he rips open the packet and eases his hand around so he can tap the Equal in. Calvin's mouth closes and Randy braces himself for a reaction. Who knows what?

But the force is with Randy, as it has been all evening. Calvin smiles and nestles into him as if he is going to go to sleep. Randy pulls him tight again, the mothers cluck, the remaining boys start bopping each other, and it is then that Randy notices. Aiden has wound his arms around Randy's neck and he is crying.

CHAPTER 27

From: Visorgrl@mac.com
To: Manatees   sent Wed, Oct 13 9:17 pm

Subject: Calvin's Hero!

Hello Manatee parents and kids,

I've just put Calvin to bed and I just had to take a moment to thank our awesome Coach Randy for SAVING CALVIN'S LIFE TODAY!!! ☺☺☺ I'm writing to everyone, even those of you who weren't there, because I'm sure you will hear all about it and I want you to know that everything is OK!!!!!! I can tell you that this mom was pretty terrified, but, who knew that I didn't even have to be because Randy was on the scene. It was like he was a trained negotiator, talking Calvin down!!!!!!!

Tonight, when I rolled Calvin into bed (it was so easy because he had already passed out in the car), he opened his eyes for a moment and said, "Can Coach be my Daddy?" And I said, "You already have a Daddy." And then he said, "Yeah, but I really want Coach Randy." I told him that was impossible because Coach Randy and I aren't married, we're just partners like Ben and Jerry.

I'm sending you all a huge group hug and thanks to all of you who love Calvin! It's been a really hard transition from fourth to fifth grade for him. His new teacher doesn't get him yet and he's having a hard time finding his special nitch.

Alright, I'll thank everyone again in person. In the meantime, check your snack schedules and the field—I think it changed from last week!

XOXOXOXOXOXO,
Jacqui

———————

From: Mako@Shakrayoga.org
To: Manatees   sent Wed, Oct 13 9:37 pm

Subject: Re: Calvin's Hero!

Dear Jacqui and everyone,

I'm glad that I was there to help out and cool heads prevailed. Jacqui, I went to this site called www.sweetpoison.com and copied the side effects of aspartame consumption. I know that none of these are going to apply to a one-time ingestion. But just in case you're thinking of it being a permanent substitute, here are the facts:

Eye blindness in one or both eyes decreased vision and/or other eye problems such as: blurring, bright flashes, squiggly lines, tunnel vision, decreased night vision pain in one or both eyes decreased tears trouble with contact lenses bulging eyes • **Ear tinnitus**—ringing or buzzing sound severe intolerance of noise marked hearing impairment • **Neurologic epileptic seizures** headaches, migraines and (some severe) dizziness, unsteadiness, confusion, memory loss, both severe drowsiness and sleepiness paresthesia or numbness of the limbs severe slurring of speech severe hyperactivity and restless legs atypical facial pain **severe tremors** • **Psychological/Psychiatric severe depression** irritability aggression anxiety personality changes insomnia phobias • **Chest palpitations**, tachycardia shortness of breath recent high blood pressure • **Gastrointestinal nausea** diarrhea, sometimes with blood in stools abdominal pain pain when swallowing

Additional Symptoms of Aspartame Toxicity include the most critical symptoms of all death irreversible **brain damage, birth defects, including mental retardation** peptic ulcers aspartame addiction and increased craving for sweets hyperactivity in children severe depression aggressive behavior suicidal tendencies

Goodnight everyone,
Mako

———

From: Visorgrl@mac.com
To: Manatees　　　　　　　　　　　　sent Wed, Oct 13 9:43 pm

Subject: Re: Calvin's Hero!

Thanks for that very useful information Mako! That's it, I'm giving up Diet Coke tomorrow!!!! ☺ Seriously, if you see me with a can on the field, ask me if that ringing in my ears is just excitement or maybe it's the ASPARTAME!!!! Or better yet, just grab the can from me and throw it into a trash-can. I'm serious. ☺

As for Calvin, it was a one-time fix. I would never allow Calvin to have Equal, unless he was on a roof!

XOXO,
Jacqui

———

From: FavoriteCoach@gmail.com

To: Manatees   sent Wed, Oct 13 10:02 pm

Subject: Re: Calvin's Hero!

Hello Team!

I've got to say, I'm a little embarrassed by Jacqui's high praise, especially to those of you who weren't even there! Just in case anyone is confused, Calvin climbed up on a roof and I just happened to be the one to bring him down. Really, anyone could have done it. Could they have made that roof any steeper? One false move and I could have fallen to my death, or been paralyzed from the neck down like Christopher Reeve, or be dead like Christopher Reeve. Or at least lost an eye! But I got lucky!

And I certainly couldn't have done it without my wing-man, Aiden, and back-up singers, Diane, Karen, and Mako!!! Thanks guys, you are the ones who made it look easy. It's like the Beatles say, "I get by with a little help from my friends."

Get a good night sleep everyone. I've been told by a few well-meaning friends to keep my e-mails shorter (Hi Paul!), so I'm going to sign off now!! Who says a man can't change?

Coach Randy

**"You are my superior officer. You are also my friend.
I have been and always shall be, yours."
Spock to Kirk (Wrath of Khan)**

From: MSonnenklar@GSachs.com

To: Manatees   sent Wed, Oct 13 10:07pm

Subject: Re: Calvin's Hero!

I checked and Saturday's game is on the North Field.

M

CHAPTER 28

"Wow," Diane says to her daughter, struggling for a positive tone, "that sounded...I could really hear all the notes being put together into a real tune."

Sabine beams as she rests her wooden recorder in her lap.

"Yeah," Reece says, with absolutely no artifice. "That sounded great, Sabine. Seriously." He and Diane have been snuggled up on the couch, watching Sabine's performance. Diane looks down at him and pulls him close for a second. His natural sense of diplomacy (so like T's) is a quality she already depends upon.

In truth, Sabine's playing was excruciating; not because she's bad at it, but because recorders are torturous under the best of circumstances (what would actually qualify for a best circumstance, Diane can't imagine). Seriously, Diane would do pretty much anything to avoid having to listen to that again with her smile carefully plastered on her face like a clothes hanger. Unfortunately, it's the beginning of a ten-week music program that the school booster club actually raised extra money for. And Sabine is completely captivated. Which, aside from the recorder itself, is a joy to see.

Diane makes a mental note to go back to those booster meetings, even though she hates them, as a simple act of self-defense. That, and possibly get Sabine some flute lessons.

"You want me to play 'This Old Man'?" Sabine asks, already raising her recorder to her lips.

"Bedtime," Diane announces, her voice sounding shrill, even to herself. She takes a breath, summons some of Reece's diplomacy, and says to Sabine in a softer voice, "Why don't you save the 'Knick Knack' for tomorrow? It'll give us something to look forward to."

"Yeah," Sabine says, on a self-satisfied exhale. And Diane congratulates herself for buying some peace and giving parental encouragement at the same time. Masterful.

"Come on, you." Diane leans over and plants a smooch on Reece's still chubby cheek. "Let's get teeth brushed and pick a book."

"Oh, all right." Reece gathers himself, both good-natured and grumpy, winding the blanket that was over both their laps around his shoulders.

Sabine stands up and walks over to the coffee table, where she places the recorder lovingly into its felt pouch. "Let's do *The Lorax*."

"Maybe not," says Reece. "Mom always cries."

"That's why I like it," Sabine says, walking toward the foyer with Reece trailing the blanket behind them.

Diane follows the two of them up the stairs and into the bathroom to watch them brush their teeth and wash their faces. If she doesn't stand there like a sentry, they simply won't do it. But more than this, in the past few hours she has been thanking the universe for these ordinary moments with her kids. She keeps thinking of Calvin on that roof. And Jacqui standing below, breathless and scared. It must be terrifying to have a kid who does things that are so extreme. Diane never thought much about Jacqui last year, when they were on the team together. But this season, she sees Jacqui's cheerfulness as being almost hysterical. Wouldn't it be easier for Jacqui if she could admit that there's something going on with Calvin and get some help? Jacqui's insistence on treating Calvin as if he's simply an eccentric kid has got to require Herculean powers of denial. And that can't possibly be sustainable for Jacqui or Calvin.

Reece and Sabine plop their toothbrushes into the holder on the sink, skid across the hall, and jump into their beds. "Ready!" they yell as Diane scans the bathroom—a clump of toothpaste left in the sink, a damp hand towel on the floor, is that a handprint on the wall above the toilet paper holder? She breathes it all in. The messy ordinariness of it all can really break your heart.

Half an hour later. After bedtime stories—she manages to avoid *The*

Lorax because there's simply no way she's making it through without nonstop snotty sobbing—Diane slips down to the kitchen to pour herself a glass of wine. And after a second and third, she takes her laptop and the almost empty bottle into the living room, where she can write.

To: Visorgrl@mac.com
From: DPlatt@ca.rr.com   sent Wed, Oct 13 11:43 pm

Subject: I'm glad that Calvin is safe

Dear Jacqui,

I know that we don't know each other very well, but I wanted to slet yyou know that I was thinking about you tonight. Maybe it's the fact that we aren't close friends that allows me to feel like I can talk to you honestly about something that is very sensitive. Sometimes friends are the last to be able to speak. They risk so much. The potential cost to me is somewhat lower.

So Jacqui, you know that way that you always talk about Calvin and what he does as, "Hey all kids are like this, right?" Well, and please just take this in, all kids aren't like that. The kicking and rocking and eating rocks and huge tantrums over any little thing isn't what all kids do. Occasionally they do one of those things, but not all of them, and not as often as Calvin. And tonight, when he had to be coaxed down from the ledge by pouring sugar inhis mouth. Soemthing else is going on. I think that it's possible that there's more to Calvin's issues thatn him simply being a sensitive kid.

Have Calvin's teachers suggested that you have him tested to see if there's more that can be done for him? I hope that they have and that my letter doesn't come completely out of left-field.

Anwya, feel free to talk to me if you need to. I truly mean to be supportive. Or if you're mad, delete this whole letter and act like I never said a thing, and I won't bug you.

Warmly,
Diane

In a living room in West Hollywood, Karen sips her lavender tea, even though she'd rather have a scotch. According to her new-agey doctor, lavender is supposed to calm her down. Of course, scotch is more reliable, but she has been consciously avoiding becoming a cliché single mom who stays up half the night boozing and firing off e-mails to her ex. Besides, she used to drink scotch with Mark, and right now, if she were to allow herself to dwell on him, she could end up wrapping a kitchen knife in a dish towel, driving over to Mark and Kelli's, and plunging it into both of their chests.

She sits on the couch, legs folded under her, comfy throw over her lap, listening to some classical station and concentrating on her breathing. Down the hall, Ben's door is closed; slammed shut a couple of hours ago. A poster of Dumbledore lying in front of it, having fallen on impact. Karen hasn't bothered to pick it up. Earlier, she'd had some notion of demanding that Ben put it back up on the door himself. At least she is calm enough now to realize that adding the poster battle to the current war would have been like throwing a Molotov cocktail into an angry mob.

Even though Ben is presumably asleep, she can feel his hatred licking at the doorframe. The iPhone is in the basement of her apartment building, having been tossed down the garbage chute. "I hate you so much I want to kill you!" Ben had screamed, pulling on her arm so hard that she had to drag him out the door into the hall and up to the chute. God, what must the neighbors think? They must have heard it all. She's a monster.

No. No. She's not a monster. Or at least, she didn't used to be. And Ben used to be an easy kid, before the divorce. Cocky, sure. But what did you expect with a dad like Mark?

Mark. It's near impossible for her to remember why she married the man in the first place. There's not a sliver of love or attraction left for him. So what the hell is she fighting Kelli and him for?

She hasn't the faintest idea. All she knows is that she can't let go of her anger. Because what would she have then? A middle-aged body, a tasteful but small apartment in West Hollywood, and no life?

She stretches out her legs. Her bare feet, extending past the blanket, feel a chill. She puts the cup of tea down on the coffee table and reaches down to pull the blanket over her toes. There's a thought that she is refusing to allow herself. To push it aside, she tries to retrieve a list of injustices that Mark has heaped upon her since he took up with Kelli. This list is a constant comfort. But that persistent thought won't let her stay with the list.

Number one on the list, of course, is the lying.

The shadow thought remains, waiting patiently, which is profoundly distracting.

Number two is: *with the fucking nanny—seriously?*

The thought stays, marking time.

Oh hell, numbers three through two hundred will still be there when she wants them.

Then, she allows the thought, because tonight, this fight with Ben, if she's honest, has shaken her like nothing else in this whole dismal saga. She exhales and faces the thought, which is fully formed and ready to be seen.

If you do not let all of this go—right now—you will lose your son.

———

A few miles away, Jacqui lies in bed after sending a thank-you e-mail to the team. Normally, she stays up much later than Steve, organizing and planning for the day ahead. But tonight, a great weariness overtook her after all that drama on the field, and she was sure that she would fall asleep earlier and easier than usual.

She was wrong. As soon as she lay down on her side of the bed, she felt anxious. She tried her usual tricks. She concentrated on a pink heat, warming her from the inside of her tummy and slowly radiating out to her extremities. But she couldn't lie still long enough and turned onto her side. She tried mentally writing her to-do list on a piece of paper, then imagined crumpling it up and throwing it away. But she had a hard time coming up with to-dos, which has never happened before. She always has to-dos. Then she tried imagining that she was at a perfume counter at Nordstrom and Harrison Ford (from the first Indiana Jones movie) spotting her from the men's department, where he was getting a suit fitted. Then, just as Harrison Ford started walking over to her, he vanished and she couldn't get him back.

At this point, she has to admit defeat and do the only thing that ever works: eat a pot brownie and clean the kitchen. She gets up from her bed noiselessly (Steve never stirs) and grabs her slippers from the closet.

Downstairs, she flicks the light on in the living room and shuffles over to her desk, where she opens the drawer and retrieves a key buried in a small cup of paper clips. The key unlocks the file cabinet, and behind the files is a Tupperware container housing the brownies. She takes one out and lays it on the desk before reversing the process, returning the container, locking the cabinet, burying the key, and closing the drawer. It is a routine she has gone through hundreds of times before and it has a satisfying rhythm to it.

Now she sits at her desk, eating the brownie, thinking about Calvin on the roof. How small he looked and how much she wanted to protect him from everyone watching and judging. How she could only stand there and give Coach instructions. The whole time praying that no one thought she was odd or Calvin was being difficult again. She pushes aside the wish that Calvin were someone else. Because that's an awful wish, and she replaces it with the wish that he will get better. Grow out of it. He's so smart. Yesterday he alphabetized the books in his bedroom just for fun. She bends her mind toward the things she loves about him. His spiky hair, his neat handwriting, and his fascination with clocks. And he would never harm anyone. There isn't anything mean about him.

The pot starts to fog her brain and her limbs loosen. Her phone buzzes and lights up on her big calendar blotter. Who could be sending an e-mail so late? She picks up the yellow-framed phone and looks. From Diane. *I'm glad that Calvin is safe.* Jacqui opens the letter. Reads. Her eyesight is a bit fuzzy and her glasses are upstairs. She strains her eye muscles until her tear ducts hurt. *Have Calvin's teachers suggested that you have him tested...* She bites her bottom lip. Yes. There have been teachers and doctors. A lot. The school is even threatening to reject them for sixth grade if they don't agree to an IEP and behavioral plan. Despite the fact that Jacqui is one of their hardest working parents and fund-raisers. But she can't quite—what? She can't quite give in yet. That's what it feels like, *giving in.*

Calvin is a sensitive boy. Yes, maybe he has trouble transitioning. Even ADHD. And other diagnoses she can't allow herself to think about too long. The pot settles into her bones. Finds its groove. She can focus now. Looks back at the glowing phone in her hand. *Or if you're mad, delete this whole letter and act like I never said a thing, and I won't bug you.* Hell, by tomorrow Jacqui will barely remember the letter at all. She swipes her thumb across the phone's glassy face. Delete.

Decisive now. Energy crackles through her. She neatly swipes the crumbs from the brownie off the desk and into the trash can. As she stands, she feels everything click in. She will clean the kitchen for the second time tonight. Then she will feel whole. A clean kitchen is an attainable act and efficiency is her salvation.

CHAPTER 29

From: RTChampion@gmail.com

To: DPlatt@ca.rr.com   sent Thu, Oct 14 9:00 am

Subject: Practice yesterday!

Hey Diane,

How are you this morning? I hopped out of bed like a new man, and today I feel like anything is possible! Last night, on the roof with Calvin, it was like I couldn't make one false move. Why is that, Diane? Why is it that I can mess up my whole life, but come through when it matters the most? I'll tell you why, because there is a reason why all this is happening. I am meant for something bigger than OneStopOffice.

I'm going to spend my time here at the library, writing a list of things that I'm good at—things that I might have forgotten that I was good at. If you can think of anything to add, send it along!! Just kidding. Seriously.

This is going to be fun!!!

Randy

From: JHandHRasst@OneStopOffice.com
To: FavoriteCoach@gmail.com   sent Thu, Oct 14 9:05 am

Subject: Meeting

Dear Mr. Tinker,

Please respond to our request for a meeting regarding questionable expenditures, billed to OneStopOffice. We would like to keep this in house, but are prepared to go through legal channels if necessary.

Thank you,
Heather

Heather Stanfield
Executive Assistant/Human Resources
OneStopOffice
739 La Jolla Drive
Los Angeles, CA 90042

From: FavoriteCoach@gmail.com
To: JHandHRasst@OneStopOffice.com   sent Thu, Oct 14 9:08 am

Subject: Re: Meeting

Dear Heather,

I apologize for not getting back to you sooner. I took my family out for a vacation in the desert. They call it being "off the grid"—there's no Internet or phone service. Have you ever been on the high desert? You should go sometime, Heather. It's a truly spiritual experience.

Of course, I can meet with Ms. Hand. Legal channels are completely unnecessary and I am eager to pay OneStopOffice back if there are any mix-ups. My schedule is pretty full for the next couple of weeks. How about early November? The week of the eighth?

Sincerely,

Randy Tinker

"I've been through the desert on a horse with no name..."
America

From: JHandHRasst@OneStopOffice.com
To: FavoriteCoach@gmail.com   sent Thu, Oct 14 9:09 am

Subject: Re: Meeting

Dear Mr. Tinker,

The week of the eighth is a month away. Ms. Hand was hoping to have some clarity on this in the next couple of days. Please find an opening in your schedule.

Thank you,
Heather

Heather Stanfield
Executive Assistant/Human Resources
OneStopOffice
739 La Jolla Drive
Los Angeles, CA 90042

From: FavoriteCoach@gmail.com

To: JHandHRasst@OneStopOffice.com   sent Thu, Oct 14 9:11 am

Subject: Re: Meeting

Dear Heather,

Of course, I didn't realize that the eighth was so far away. I blame my desert brain. Out there you lose all track of time because you are thinking about your place in the universe, as opposed to the daily grind. You would love it. How about next Monday at the close of day?

Sincerely,

Randy Tinker

"I've been through the desert on a horse with no name..."

America

From: JHandHRasst@OneStopOffice.com

To: FavoriteCoach@gmail.com   sent Thu, Oct 14 9:12 am

Subject: Re: Meeting

Dear Mr. Tinker,

If Monday is your earliest availability, then I will set the appointment for 10 am.

Heather

Heather Stanfield

Executive Assistant/Human Resources

OneStopOffice

739 La Jolla Drive

Los Angeles, CA 90042

From: FavoriteCoach@gmail.com

To: PPousaint@mac.com   sent Thu, Oct 14 10:02 am

Subject: Off the Record

Hi there, Paul. Hope you're OK with an e-mail instead of the old phone, but I've got some time in the middle of the day and I wasn't going to call you at the office with team business.

First off, I hope you're on board with trying Mason on goal for two quarters. I think league regs will allow for it. Hell, if they don't, that means Majors and Zacharian have been breaking regs all season! So I'm going for it.

I've been dropping by the Woo's occasionally and kicking a ball around with the kid, and I can tell you that his issues are mainly mental. As you know, his skills are outstanding, but he tenses up every time a coach yells at him. It's kind of tough to work around, right, so I'm recommending that you, Alejandro, and me work on adding "That-a-boy" or "Got it, Sport?" into our coaching, when specifically dealing with him.

In conclusion, I have a little matter you may be able to help me with. I'm transitioning out of my job here at OneStopOffice and I'm looking for non-traditional ways to enhance cash flow for the interim. Do you know of any such venues? I'm just beginning to put out feelers.

Coach

"I've been through the desert on a horse with no name…"
America

From: PPousaint@mac.com
To: FavoriteCoach@gmail.com   sent Thu, Oct 14 10:15 am

Subject: Re: Off the Record

I'm on board with your e-mail regarding coaching. However, I am unclear about "cash flow venues". Are you looking for a part-time job? By "cash" I assume you mean something that won't affect unemployment? So you mean something like dog-walking? Can you be more specific?

Paul

From: FavoriteCoach@gmail.com
To: PPousaint@mac.com   sent Thu, Oct 14 10:19 am

Subject: Re: Off the Record

Hey Paul. Yes. I am looking for work on a purely cash basis, for a short-term, of course, something that would supplement unemployment for a month or two.

I don't expect to be out of real work for long. Dog-walking seems a little "public" for me. I would like to avoid running into a neighbor in the morning with five dogs on a leash, holding a sack of poop, if you know what I mean. I'm good at sales, but I'm not sure that I would be able to sell that as anything but desperation! Not that I am desperate, but I would like to avoid the APPEARANCE of desperation. I was thinking of something closer to dishwasher or a job in a meat locker, something in the shadows.

Coach

"I've been through the desert on a horse with no name..."
America

————————

From: PPousaint@mac.com
To: FavoriteCoach@gmail.com   sent Thu, Oct 14 10:20 am

Subject: Re: Off the Record

Randy,

I have to admit, your e-mail concerns me. Don't you have savings or a portfolio? Why don't we meet for a drink after work today, so we can discuss the team and your situation?

Paul

CHAPTER 30

PAUL WATCHES RIVULETS OF RAIN cling to the passenger-side window as they drive quietly down the streets of Beverly Hills. Silence sits behind them like an uninvited stranger.

Marianne is an expert driver, and he turns to look at her jawline, glowing softly. He smiles to himself and returns to watch the light glint on the glass. Nothing soft about Marianne silently driving like a cyborg. Her taking the wheel after the party had been a wordless transaction, because he had had several drinks (while she had stuck to her two glasses and stiff black coffee rule) and because all their transactions are wordless these days. Except when the kids are around.

He knows better than to attempt small talk—or even gossip about the partygoers, which she used to love.

In the days following the big confession (was it only six weeks ago?), he'd attempted light banter, reminiscent of the chummy marital accord that they had maintained since the beginning of their marriage. In fact, all the way through his secret affairs, sometimes with the very women at a function they had just left. But since the confession, Marianne had refused to respond to even the smallest of his observations or questions. Refused to pretend that anything was like it was before. Even though, he could have argued, it really was the same. All that had changed was that now she knew.

Earlier this evening, over drinks with Randy Tinker, Paul told him about feeling captive in his own home. Penance for the infidelities he'd racked up following a career humiliation that even now he can't think of without feeling his balls retract. The affairs became unsustainable because Paul had begun to fear for his immortal soul. Damn the nuns. But even more so, because he actually loved Marianne. He takes another sideways glance. Her gaze does not waver from the wet road ahead.

He had warned Randy. Don't blow everything just because of a midlife slump. Look what happened to me. But Randy hadn't made—or *couldn't* make—the connection, because Randy, of course, wouldn't know the first thing about having an affair.

It's not the affairs, he told Randy. A man like Randy spends money he doesn't have for the very same reason a man like Paul nailed pussy he didn't even want. It's the feeling of being outside of yourself that a man goes looking for. Creating a self that is separate from the one who lives at home with his failure. Separate from the self who lives with the woman who *knows* about his failure. It's separation that a man goes looking for, and separation that a man must resist.

Paul didn't say anything to Randy about separation from God. Nothing about being cast out. Discussions like that don't fly at all in such circles, even though he knows a lot about it.

Randy had only stared at him with the dull persistent look of an old dog waiting for dinner. All Randy wanted was some off-the-books job that he could sneak off to. A fix that could only last a month or two before exploding into an existence that was far worse.

Paul finally made some half-hearted promise to check on some tele-marketing work for one of his firm's not-for-profits, and they didn't even get around to discussing the team's drills.

Paul had picked up the check.

Marianne pulls into the garage noiselessly. Extinguishes the head-lights. Her door opens, and closes with a sealing suck after she slips out.

She doesn't wait for him.

He sits in the car and considers rolling back his seat and sleeping right there. Instead of trudging down the long hall to the den, where he changes into pajamas and kneels at the pull-out couch like he did when he was a boy at his bedside.

And prays.

CHAPTER 31

From: Visorgrl@mac.com

To: Manatees   sent Sun, Oct 17 10:22 am

Subject: Picture Day is Coming!!!!!

Well, as if there wasn't enough excitement after our win yesterday!!! ☺ It's PICTURE DAY! So get those haircuts now. ☺ I think that there's only one new family to the league. But in case you have forgotten—at the end of the year, your son will be getting a big team picture in a cute frame that's shaped like a soccer ball, four individual shots to give to grandparents, a yearbook, and a trophy!!!!!! The trophy ceremony is adorable and usually everybody cries.

Our pictures are being taken on Sunday the 24th at 11:30 am on the side of the north field. You may want to talk to your kid about how to smile nicely. There was a kid on another team last year who did that serial-killer grin that some kids do and it kind of ruined their whole team photo for everyone. ☺

I will have some snacks in my bag to head off the "hangries". Sometimes we have to wait awhile and the kids get antsy. I will also have sunscreen and a comb.

XOXO,
Jacqui

From: Mako@Shakrayoga.org

To: Manatees   sent Sun, Oct 17 10:30 am

Subject: Re: Picture Day is Coming!!!!!

Jacqui,

I will be there and can help with arranging the kids. I know from first-hand experience that Mason has to be in the back row. He's so tall that even when he kneels he blots out shorter kids behind him, or he looks like he has a double head.

I know what to do.

Mako

———

From: RTChampion@gmail.com

To: DPlatt@ca.rr.com   sent Mon, Oct 18 9:14 am

Subject: Re: (No Subject)

Hi Diane,

Randy here. Great game on Saturday, huh? Reece is stepping up as a forward. I know he prefers defense, but I see a little forward in his future!!! Hey, that's almost like poetry!

You know what's also like poetry? I got a job!!!!! Paul Pousaint hooked me up. Just like that. The universe is smiling on me. It's just a little side thing (phone marketing) to keep the cash flow going while I hunt for the job of jobs, but how great is that? I'll have to say goodbye to this ol' library for awhile, because I have to physically be in a phone bank room to put in my hours. I bet Irene will miss me. She's the black librarian who teases me about the computer, always cracking jokes about what am I doing on that machine all day. By the way she winks and shakes her hips, I think she thinks I'm looking at Internet porn, which is impossible because it's blocked. Not that I would look anyway. Except once, just to make sure that it is blocked and I can confirm that now.

So how are things with you? You know that if you ever need anything, you can ask me. I don't mean that in a suggestive way. Maybe I would have at one time. But I feel like we sort of know each other now. I've told you things that I couldn't even tell my own wife. And you've told me about your break-up. We can be there for each other.

Well, enough of that, right?!!!!! Way to ruin a friendship! I can keep it light.

Diane, I feel like everything is changing for the good. Aiden looks at me differently since I saved Calvin. Missy is so much nicer lately, and I've got a job selling Baroque music to little old ladies. It's like selling candy to kids who have lots of money. I already made a friend. Maybe she wants to be what they call an office wife. Slam dunk!!! Of course, I still have to meet with OneStopOffice about the big, big money I owe them AND I have to get a REAL job soon!

Love,
Randy

———————

From: Alejandro.Navaro@Pepperdine.edu
To: Missy@skintastic.com   sent Mon, Oct 18 9:29 am

Subject: (No Subject)

My Missy,

I think of you this morning and I worry that you have regret. All the time, I think that you want me and it is good because I want you also. This can never be wrong. But when you cry so much after we make love, I think that this is not so. I think that you love Randy and I must not hurt you any more.

I am sorry, sweet Missy,

Alejandro

———————

From: Missy@skintastic.com
To: Alejandro.Navaro@Pepperdine.edu   sent Mon, Oct 18 10:24 am

Subject: Re: (No Subject)

Dear Alejandro,

Please, please, please, you must not think that my tears were because I love Randy so much. I feel guilty of course, and that is part of it, but mostly I was crying because I have never felt that way before, not with Randy and not with anyone. Please, I don't want to frighten you away.

I hope you can believe that I've never done anything like this. I have tried very hard to be a good wife and mother and that includes not cheating and generally being upbeat. I guess if I'm honest, I thought that being a good wife and mother would instantly make me happy and make anything else I dream about fade away.

Before I met Randy, I hung out with a group of girls from work. I was a make-up artist for TV and film. When I look back on it, I realize that it really was pretty glamorous. We hung around with stars and pretty much everyone loves their make-up person, because we're the ones who make them look less old or tired or fat. Anyway, I went out to bars a lot and had a few boyfriends, but none of them made me feel the way you do. They all were thinking of something else when they were with me, like, they thought about their own careers, sports, how to make more and more money, and, yeah, they thought about sex all the time. They didn't take the time to talk to me the way you do, like there's nowhere else you want to be. They weren't good with kids the way you are, and after one or two dates, they wanted to be dating someone else. Sometimes I see one of them out on the street with their kids and wives who are younger then me and I wonder how I missed it all. How come one of them didn't want to marry me?

Maybe I wasn't very good at sex. I know that I felt self-conscious about my body, and I never wanted them to see me naked, because my stomach poofs out a little and my knees touch.

So all of the sudden, I was thirty, and everyone on the planet was already married. That's when I decided that there was something definitely wrong with me, and that was when Randy showed up. We met the usual way, at a bar, but from the beginning, he was different. He was dressed in a suit and he was older than most of the guys I usually dated. He was standing with a bunch of men from work who were all laughing at his jokes, and I could tell he was one of the ringleaders.

After a few minutes, Randy came up to us group of girls and said, "You see those men over there? They bet me that I can't get one of you to talk to me for a whole fifteen minutes." We all laughed and I don't know why

I said, "I'll talk to you." I still remember Randy looking kind of stunned, which I thought was cute.

When I think about it now, I think we both had this excited feeling like it was meant to be. I mean, who meets like that? Randy had been married before and that woman had stomped all over his heart. He wasn't expecting anything at that bar, and I hadn't ever gotten married and figured no one would ever ask me, so I wasn't expecting anything either, and here we were.

Then you came into my life, and now I can't think of anything else but when we will be together again. It's like finally finding this thing you never knew you needed so much, and you can't get enough. Your afraid you might never get enough. It scares me how much feeling this is bringing up. I can literally shake from it, and that's why I was crying. Its like I can see what is possible now and now I know what I was missing, and if you leave, what am I going to do with all those feelings? I can't stuff them down and pretend they aren't there.

I can't go back to before, please don't leave me.

Your Missy

CHAPTER 32

THEY ARE IN THE LIVING room. An empty box on the coffee table waits to be filled. Flaps untucked, it is a receptive maw. Diane places a large orange glass object into its center.

"What is that?" says Alejandro, with a now familiar punctuating giggle. He is stretched out on the couch, shirtless, in jeans, watching her with a slice of pizza lying on his stomach.

"It is," says Diane, straightening her back, pretending to be a proper lady version of herself, "a work of art."

"Yes. I know this. But what *is* it? A wave from the ocean?"

"Not everything has to be a something, Alejandro. The artist is very famous."

"Why?"

"Why is he famous?"

"No. Why this thing?" He picks up the slice and lowers the floppy end into his mouth. She watches him take a large greasy bite and has to close her eyes for a second. His sensual idleness almost pains her.

"Ah yes," she says, opening her eyes and reverting to the glass thing. Which is not painful to look at, and in fact evokes no emotion at all. "Excellent question. I have this thing because our designer, at the time, thought that corner of the room was too dark. Hence, a glass reflecting *thing* to brighten it up."

"Hence?" asks Alejandro, the way he has repeated several of her words before.

"That is why," she explains. "That is why I paid for it and the designer brought it here." She regards it. "I should have fired her."

He chuckles. "There are many glass things such as this you can choose. Why this one?"

She maintains her playfully arch tone. "Clearly, you don't understand anything about designing the upscale American home. The items we choose advertise our taste, our wealth, and most important—how powerful we are. The fact that I could get this glass thing when the designer assured me others could not expressed all three. Which I thought was important at the time."

"Now, not so much."

"Now, not so much."

He lifts up the slice again. To avoid staring, she looks around the room for another object to get rid of. This domestic purging started last week when she decided that Alejandro was right. The house did not express her at all. It didn't even express T, who probably would have gone with a more standard Crate & Barrel artfully distressed look. And while she wasn't entirely sure what *would* express her, she thought that the effort of finding out might tell her a little bit more about herself.

She reaches out and picks up, "Look at this. A candle thingy."

He lays the slice back on his stomach, his mouth full. "What?"

"You put out the flame with it. A—what's it called?

"A thingy, you said." He smiles.

"A snuffer. That's it."

"A sniffer?"

She waves the long black metal object in front of her. "Not sniffer, dummy. You can't use this to sniff." She stretches it out and covers his nose with the small hood at the end of it. "See. You can't smell anything, can you?"

Again he chuckles and bats it away. The fact that she amuses him touches her. Not simply because it draws him back to her, what, five times already? But because it is a part of herself she thought she had lost. Or that T had taken with him. A playfulness that makes her feel tender toward herself. "Snuffer. I said 'snuffer.' See, you snuff out candles with it." She glances around the room for a candle, to demonstrate.

"You do not have candles," he says preemptively.

"Right. You see. I have no candles." She spreads her arms out, metal snuffer barely missing a lamp. "That is why it must go," and she pops it into the box, next to the glass thing.

Alejandro lifts the pizza to take another bite. With his mouth still full, he asks, "Why you have this snuff thing and no candles?"

He watches her turn to take in the whole room. He doesn't care how long it will take for her to answer because, whatever she says, it will be interesting. Or funny. It never occurred to him that a woman could be so funny. She is less like a woman and more like a friend. He stares up at the bright white ceiling. A vast lid. His mother would wonder, *Why all this space? What do they do with all those big rooms?*

He feels a weight press down on the cushions of the couch. Like a cat jumping on. Shifts his gaze and sees that it's Diane. Sitting beside him, hip to his hip. Her hair hangs in front of her face and she tucks one side of it behind her ear. He stares at her, trying to remember what she looked like to him before he knew her. Her skin is downy in the light. And there are little wrinkles around her eyes and mouth that you don't see at first. But that make her different from the rest.

She reaches out and places a cool hand on his forehead. "There are no candles in this room, because I don't live in it."

"What is the room where you live?"

She looks up past his head, out the window. "The TV room, mostly. It's smaller and can hold me closer; box me in. The children's room when they are here. Never when they are not. They feel too empty."

She shivers, her face looking pale and sad. Annoyed that thoughts of her children are pulling her away from him, he reaches up and puts his hand on her breast, but feels only the cushiony mold of her bra through her T-shirt. Why did she get so dressed up after they made love?

She looks at his hand on her breast, then at him. But her gaze is unseeing. "I'm sorry," she says wistfully. "I ruined the mood, didn't I? We were having so much fun."

Why can't she be here with him? He has seen her do this before. Her mind floating. Almost always when she talks about her children.

No. He yanks her to his chest, clamping his mouth on hers roughly to stop her from talking about her kids or anything else that has nothing to do with them in this room. Here. Now. His erection strains against his jeans. She raises herself up, sliding one leg to the floor, and fumbling with too much speed, unzips his jeans. He pulls at her pants and she stands, one-footed, as he yanks them down. She pushes him back on the couch, falls down on his chest, reaches between her legs to find him, forcing him into her not-wet-yet, tight, jagged almost, cunt. Raising herself up, breasts still bound by her bra and T-shirt, she grinds and strains, shoving him deeper into her. He grabs her thighs, hoping for bruises, marking her, owning her.

He can't get deep enough. Writhing under her, lifting his ass, ramming, ramming. Again and again. When will it be done? He cannot stop. Fuck her. Fuck her till she's nothing. Her eyes are closed. He needs her to see him. Him. Not a dream. Damn her. Look at me, bitch. Love me. Fuck you, I can't. Can't be what you want. Don't leave. *Madre.* I want. I want. Christ.

Arching. He cries out. Finally, the end. Everything stops. She opens her eyes. Sees him. Yes. That is what he wanted. Fuck. All he wanted. He falls back. Breathing heavy. Can't see. Can't see until there it is. The blank ceiling.

Now this. The postfuck drift. After all that intensity, the freedom that comes from being nothing to anyone. For only a few moments. He's nothing to her. Nothing to his mother and sisters walking to the bank on Fridays to get his money. Nothing to those white bitches at Pepperdine. Nothing to Missy or the other mothers on the team. Nothing to his dead father. To Colombia or his priest. His friends. Boys he grew up with. Played soccer with. Far away. He is nothing to all of them.

He drifts, feeling her rocking on him. Wet and soft. Back and forth. He is at sea. Slipping in and finally out. She rubs against him, back and forth. The fuzz of her. Faster, until he feels her clench. And again. Again. Waits for her. Waits. Now.

Her head lowers slowly onto his rib cage. Her body now loose. No air between them. Sweat. Her hair silky, tickling his neck. He feels his heart beating under her damp cheek.

Diane's face against his chest, she opens her eyes and sees the room sideways. Her world askew. Everything upended like a shipwreck. That seems about right to her. Nothing is going to be as it was. She has spent the past few days in a ritual of acceptance. Throwing things out. Saying it to herself out loud. T is never coming back. She knows it now. Has stamped it on her bones. T is never going to walk back into this house and pick up where they left off, as if the past two years were a blip in their lives together.

She feels this boy's hand stroking her hair. Yes, she deserves to be comforted. Because the acceptance of this truth is still a shock. Even after all this time. And it is a shock to her that it is a shock. Because she must have known it all along.

She feels a slight hitch in Alejandro's chest. And then another. She lifts her head and sees that he is crying. "What's wrong, Alejandro?"

A tear drips off the end of his nose. He wipes it and his cheek, and looks at her, watery-eyed. Boyish. Do men cry? They must, although T barely ever did.

"I am a bad person," he squeaks.

"Oh, honey," she says, collecting herself as much as she can, pants-less. She shifts and adjusts until she's sitting up next to him. "Are you talking about this? Us? Because I understand what this is. I don't expect anything."

"No. No." He shakes his head. "I am bad for everyone. I do bad things."

"We all do bad things."

"Very bad things."

She takes his hand and turns his palm upward, pressing her thumbs into it, wanting to calm him. "Maybe we need to define *very* bad. Have you started any wars or betrayed your country? Sold secrets to the enemy?"

Alejandro pulls his hand away and inches himself up against the back of the couch. "Don't make this a joke."

Her regret is instant. She reaches again for his hand. "I'm sorry. I was being awkward. I can listen." Although it flashes through her brain that maybe she doesn't want to hear what's coming next. What if he killed someone? Maybe not on purpose, but still. Accidentally drowned someone? If it's really bad, she doesn't want to know.

Alejandro's eyes darken, rimmed with tears. He pulls himself up even farther and reaches down to the floor to pick up a pillow, which he places neatly over his penis. She also moves—to the other end of the couch, tucking her feet under her bare haunches.

"I should no be here," he says in a soft voice.

She tries to match his tone. "Okay. Do you mean 'here' at my house?"

He shakes his head.

"'Here,' Los Angeles? Or do you mean it in a bigger sense? Like 'here,' in the world?"

"Here in the States," he says, scrunching his eyes closed. As if to blot out the misdeed.

"Are you here illegally or something?" she prods, curiosity trumping her instinct to keep things simple.

"My sister, she need me," he says, eyes still tightly shut. "And I am here in air-conditioning, fucking a lady." He opens his eyes as if to say, *There, I said it.*

She checks her impulse to smile at the bare-bones hilarity of his statement, as well as the unintended (she is sure) slight. "Do you feel bad about your sister or fucking the lady? Because the lady is just fine."

He opens his eyes and looks directly into hers, unblinking. "I should not have fun, while my little sister works and has no school."

"I'm sure she understands," Diane says, knowing that she knows nothing of the sort. It's simply the kind of soothing thing she says to her own kids. She shifts slightly with the uncomfortable thought that she's treating him like a child.

"Adriana. The little one. She cry when I leave."

"I'm sorry about that. But you came here to make a better life so that you can help your family. That's what you said, right?"

"Yes. But I should work harder. Take classes faster so I can get the job."

"In forensic dentistry?"

"For the police."

"Yes. You have said." She pauses, again thinking that his degree doesn't seem to fit the nude soccer god on her couch. There is so much she doesn't know about him. And come on, isn't that part of the attraction? She thinks about pulling her shirt on again but doesn't want to seem dismissive. "Do you want to tell me about your sister?" she asks.

"Adriana."

"Yes. Adriana."

"She is six. My other sister is older, like me. Adriana, she has"—he lifts a hand to his mouth and pulls out his upper lip—"a cleft palate. Do you know what this is?"

"Yes, of course."

"Hers is very bad. She has one operation, but there must be others."

Diane's nakedness gets the better of her. She can't discuss cleft palates without clothing. Holding his gaze, she reaches down to pick up her tangled pants. She quells the need to fidget, placing the pants on her lap. "I'm sorry," she says, unable to think of anything else and afraid to elicit further information. She really shouldn't get this caught up in the boy. There's no future in it. Already it's too . . . too what?

Alejandro tosses the pillow off his lap and grabs his jeans. "I should go now," he says, standing and thwacking the jeans to loosen them. Teetering, he works a foot through the part of the leg that is inside out, bare ass bouncing. The jeans finally on, he snaps them and looks back at her. "I am sorry. Is not you."

She reaches up and grabs his hand. "Alejandro. Don't worry about me. Look. There's a lot of pressure on you. You shouldn't feel guilty about feeling good and having a little sex now and then. It doesn't make you bad and it doesn't hurt your sister."

"It *is* bad," he cries out, his voice ragged. Pulls his hand away from her. He plops down on the couch, covers his face, and cries. Full on. She scoots next to him and slides her arm around his back, just like she would with one of her kids. And lets him cry. She puts her lips on his shoulder and murmurs, "You're good. You're okay." Nuzzling him. "You're good."

And he shakes his head, crying and crying in great waves. Diane rocks with him back and forth. "You're good. You're good."

Until, finally. Finally, he rests. Slumped on the arm of the couch.

After a time, Diane reaches over and snatches her bunched-up pants from the other end of the couch, pulls out her panties, and shimmies into them before getting dressed once again. She grabs the flaps of the box on the table and folds them in for something to do, wondering if he is going to sleep. She walks over to the window and looks out. It is still sunny. Sabine and Reece's bikes lie on their sides in the driveway even though the kids are at their father's. She likes the bikes lying there, ready to be picked up upon the kids' return. Their life at her house only paused, not ended.

She turns and walks over to Alejandro's end of the couch, crouches next to him, touches his hair. He stirs. She says, "Do you think, maybe, we should stop doing this?"

He picks up his head and looks at her, seeming not to understand. "Why?"

"I thought"—she strokes his hair—"maybe I should get back to figuring out my real life. And... maybe I'm not good for you. Maybe you need to find someone younger. Someone you can have a real relationship with."

"No," he says quickly. Definitively. "Here I am not a bad person. It is with another one that I am a bad person."

She quietly takes her hand from his head and puts it over his hand. "There is a woman who makes you feel bad?" She lowers herself to her knees, keeping her hand over his.

"I think it is just a game," he says, looking for something in her eyes. "A game where I catch the woman and we both have what we want. Like I do with all the married women. We fuck and it is simple. They go back to their husband. Yes? Is easy."

"I guess," she says, thinking that nothing is ever quite that easy. But from his perspective it probably has been.

"But now I am a bad man because this woman will be hurt." He closes his eyes against the image of—what? Her? Himself as a bad man? Which seems to be all wrapped up with him being a bad son and brother, somehow.

"So she—this woman—she didn't understand?" she says, adopting a maternal tone that she's not sure she likes.

"No. I am afraid she will ruin her life. Leave her husband. I am so stupid."

"Well, maybe her marriage wasn't very good to begin with." Her knees twinge and she takes her hand away, shifting her legs to the side.

"I make a big mistake, Diane. Everybody will be angry with me. Can you help me?" His eyes are round, imploring. What the hell is he asking from her?

"I'm not sure. What could I possibly do?"

"Talk to her for me."

He looks so hapless that she can barely connect this version of him with the man who fucks her so masterfully, she can come just thinking of him. "Alejandro, I'm not sure that two women who are sharing a man are going to communicate that well."

"But I cannot talk to her. She cries and then she begs me. I am very bad." He keeps his eyes on hers.

Damn it. Seriously? Is she going to cave on this? She hates this weakness in her. A propensity for getting drawn into other people's troubles. Every single time, she simply walks right in like the last girl alive in a slasher movie, inching her way down the basement stairs. Don't go into the basement!

She looks away from him, down at her lap, and sighs. "Okay. Okay. Maybe I can do something. Is it someone I know?"

Alejandro flops against the back of the couch, eyes to the ceiling, like a teenager asked to do the dishes. "I cannot tell you." Jesus Christ. What the hell is going on? It occurs to her that maybe the kid is homesick. For all she knows, his sister's cleft looks like a mild overbite. And Alejandro's other woman was simply PMSing and completely understands the game. What are the odds of a Beverly Hills wife not understanding the rules of fucking the paid assistant coach?

Diane grabs on to the end of the couch and pulls herself up. Standing in front of him now. "Alejandro. You are the one who asked me to help. I am not going to play a game of extracting her name from you. Tell me or don't tell me. But don't drag me through a long exchange just to make yourself feel better about betraying her."

She watches him stare at the ceiling and wonders: Is it someone from their team? The young one—what's her name—Kelli? Or Paul's wife, maybe. She's a cute little number. Diane's seen her a couple of times, sitting apart from the other moms at the games.

Alejandro lifts his head to look at her. "It is Missy. The coach's wife." He closes his eyes and drops his head back again.

"What were you thinking?" Diane gasps before she can stop herself.

He squeezes his eyes tight. "I think that it is a game. When it started, it sounds like she knows that we will fuck eventually. And that is what happens."

"No. No. No," Diane says, walking over to the mantel. "You can't do this to Randy. He trusts you. I can promise you that he has absolutely no idea that this is going on. He won't recover."

He doesn't move. "You make me feel worse."

"One look at Missy and you can tell she's not a player."

"She ask me to help teach Aiden."

"And you thought that was her opening move?" She plops down on the couch next to him and stares straight ahead. Diane's assessment of Missy comes only from what Randy tells her and what she's noticed from a distance. Missy seems to be slightly wary of Diane (a vibe she's not unaccustomed to). From both Randy and her own observation, Diane senses that Missy's ubiquitous half-smile is evidence of a somewhat medicated and foggy inner life. Not that Diane's judging how a woman gets through her days.

"Okay." Diane exhales. "So Missy cries, because?"

"She tell me that I am the first time she has been with another man. At first, I did not believe. Because it was a game. It was fun. She act so innocent. It was a chase."

"And now she knows that you do this with several women?"

Alejandro covers his face with his hands. "I have to tell her. I am afraid she will leave Randy and it will be my fault."

"All right." Diane leans forward, elbows on her knees. "Have you ended it?"

Alejandro keeps his hands over his face. Like he's hiding from some all-seeing eye. "I keep trying to tell her," he squeaks. "Can you help?"

That young, helpless voice. God damn it. Once you see the complexity in a guy, it's hard to get back to the simplicity of a good fuck.

"Look, Alejandro," she says, carefully using her *Mom can fix this* voice. "I'm pretty sure that it would be a bad idea for me to talk to Missy. From what you say, she doesn't strike me as realistic. If she's going to be forced into looking at her life and her marriage honestly, I don't think it should be from her boyfriend's mistress."

"I am not her boyfriend," he says, not unkindly. Simply frustrated.

"I'm not your mistress either. But that is the way that Missy would see it," she says. "I may be able to help you, though. Just a little. The main thing for you is to cut it off with her. Be kind, but firm. You can be honest. Tell her that you thought she knew that it was a game."

"It hurts when they cry," he says, crumpling again.

She watches him, attempting to marshal some grown-up objectivity. But it's no use. Her throat hurts with unshed tears. Who for? Him? Missy? Herself? All of them? And then she thinks. Holy fuck. That's it. There's a link. His sister. Missy. Both needing what he cannot give. And this guilt. Tearing at him. Such a good Catholic boy.

"Alejandro," she says as she slips off the couch and onto the floor. She crawls in front of him and slowly parts his knees. She raises herself up and rests her head against his chest, where she listens to the beating of his heart. "You are a good boy. You really are."

CHAPTER 33

Things I am Good At
by Randy Tinker

I am a people person
SELLING   - most of the time
            - especially when I believe
            in the product
- also the OneStopOffice bowling team
  - and the Abbey softball team

KARIOKE (We are the Champions, For All the girls I've
Loved Before, The Devil Went Down to Georgia)

grilling
Telling Jokes (making people (most people) laugh)
My extensive knowledge of movies
math
thinking outside the box
decent dancer
My album collection (I still have a turntable)
Not Addictive
A pretty good Dad

                              ...to be CONTINUED

"Goal!" Randy yells. Patrick has gotten another one past him. How many does that make, five? In the space of fifteen minutes?

"That's it. Keep the ball close to you," Randy says. "If it gets too far away, you're asking for a forward to grab it. Don't let it go until the goal kick." Randy has been watching soccer training videos and has picked up a thing or two from Alejandro. Now, he tells himself, he is not merely inspirational and a manager, but an honest-to-God skills coach too.

Patrick pumps a fist into the air and does the celebratory shuffle that Randy and Aiden perfected together recently. Randy slaps Patrick on the back, hands him a water bottle, and gestures to their usual spot on the stoop of Patrick's apartment building.

"See?" Randy says. "When you focus on the ball and the other players, only on that, you're unstoppable. Don't think about the crowd." He sweeps his hand out, indicating an imaginary crowd. "Only listen to me. No one else." Patrick nods his head.

Sitting on the steps, side by side, Randy is reminded of just how small this boy is. The smallest on the team. He puts his arm around Patrick's shoulder and gives him a short squeeze.

Patrick doesn't do his shy pulling-away routine this time. In fact, Randy feels Patrick slip his hand halfway across Randy's back.

"I'm sorry about missing the goal last Saturday," Patrick says for the fourth time.

"Don't have to be sorry at all," says Randy. He feels large with magnanimity. "Every great athlete has bad moments. Even whole games when they feel off. Hey, I told you about Michael Jordan, right? Lost more games than he won. And he's one of *the* greatest athletes of all time."

"Yeah, but Jordan was such a star that everyone knew he would win the next time."

"He wasn't always great. It took a lot of hard work." Randy looks down at Patrick, who is staring straight ahead.

"I'm still afraid about Sunday's game," Patrick says in a small voice, burrowing into Randy's side a bit.

"Well, you know what Will Smith says in *After Earth*," Randy says. Patrick shakes his head, still staring ahead. "I haven't told you that one?" Another head shake. "Okay. This is good. He says, 'Fear is not real. The only place that fear can exist is in our thoughts of the future.'"

"What does that mean?" Patrick asks.

"Um," says Randy, thinking it over thoroughly for the first time. "It means that right now, right here, you're safe. You only get scared when you think ahead. So don't think about the game right now. Think about it when you're in it."

"Yeah," says Patrick, smiling and looking up at him. "I get it. You have to train your mind. I can do that. I can train my mind to get myself out of situations."

"I guess. Sure, that's kind of what I mean." Randy pauses. He, Randy, should listen to his own advice. After all, what he needs to do is mentally train himself not to think about the mortgage, for example, until it's really a problem. Who knows what can change in a month?

"I have special powers," the boy says.

Randy looks down to find Patrick looking directly at him, his eyes shining.

"Sure you do," Randy says, patting his shoulder.

"I really do."

"No one's arguing. Once you filter out everyone's voice but mine, you're gonna kill at that game."

"I mean, I can find things that are lost."

"Okay," says Randy, now zeroing in on the kid's actual words. "What do you mean, exactly?"

"I can find things with only my mind." Patrick's voice is frenetic, squeaky. Randy feels a stone of apprehension in the base of his throat. The boy is too excited. "I can leave my body and fly anywhere I want."

"Like a superhero," Randy says.

"No," says Patrick, confused.

"No, no. Seriously, I get it. Like Superman."

"No, not like you're thinking!" Patrick says quickly, definitively. Randy thinks he sees something turn off in the kid's eyes. Like a switch.

Patrick's shoulders droop and he turns his head and stares back across the yard. "Right," he says flatly. "Like Superman."

What happened? Patrick's body pulls away. Randy takes his arm off the kid's shoulder and rests his elbows on his knees. The confusion Randy feels is familiar to him. He often finds himself here, standing on the precipice of real connection only to be yanked to safety by his own inability to jump in. God damn it. Why can't he ever get closer?

Patrick stands up, his back to Randy. Everything in his stance saying that they are done here. Randy has failed somehow. He knows this. Mentally kicks himself for a fault he cannot name. Just like Aiden. Just like Missy. Always pulling away from him. Damn it. Not again.

"Patrick," he says, fumbling. Say something, he tells himself. Anything. There must be a right thing to say. And if there isn't a right thing, maybe just a comforting thing. And then he finds it. "I believe you. I believe that you can fly."

CHAPTER 34

From: DPlatt@ca.rr.com
To: RTChampion@gmail.com   sent Wed, Oct 20 9:29 am

Subject: Re: (No Subject)

Hey Randy,

I'm sorry I let your last letter slip through the cracks. That's great about your job and your potential office wife! Although, I'm guessing you will need more than that eventually. But, hey, it's a start. It's great that you think things might be getting better between you and Missy. I hope they are. But I worry that Missy may be in a lot of pain right now. I only say that because I see my own situation in yours. A successful husband, great house, enough hired help to free up my time, beautiful kids—in your case, Aiden—who is also beautiful. Because, at the risk of sounding like wacky Jacqui, they are all beautiful. But what does Missy have that's hers? What does she DO? What does she WANT? In my own case, I didn't have a clue back then. And maybe Missy doesn't either.

I thought that marrying a man who could support me easily would give me time to devote to my kids and pursue a passion. But I just got bored. Did I get a degree? Get a job? Nope. I used to be into photography. But I didn't even go back to that. Did I try to do anything else that was meaningful? Volunteer at a soup kitchen? No, and why? Because I didn't know who I was or what I liked. I married pretty young and I depended on other people to tell me who I was.

And in some fucked up way, that's why I tortured T with dalliances that couldn't even be counted as affairs, because they never got that far. "Tell me that I'm beautiful," I would be thinking, before putting my tongue in a man's mouth. "Tell me I'm witty," I would be hoping, while I slid my leg against a stranger's at a dinner party. You've seen me like this, and I'm sorry about that.

T caught me numerous times and kept forgiving me. He actually loved me, the poor slob. And I hated him for it. Because he was in love with a person who was kind of like a non-person, and he didn't even know it. It has taken me two years to understand that I had to become impossible to be around, and drive him away, so that I could start to become someone fully formed.

Talk to Missy. Tell her what you need. Tell her about your big dreams and your disappointments. Encourage her to tell you hers. And if she doesn't have a dream, help her find one. Was she really committed to the skin care thing? Maybe you can help her.

Good luck, Randy. And, hey, great game on Saturday! I think you're right about Reece playing offense.

Diane

To: Visorgrl@mac.com
From: DPlatt@ca.rr.com   sent Wed, Oct 20 9:45 am

Subject: Re: I'm glad that Calvin is safe

Hi Jacqui,

Since you haven't responded to my e-mail about Calvin, I'm assuming that

I overstepped some boundaries. Clearly, that's my special talent. Please accept my apologies. I'm sure that you know what's best for Calvin.

Diane

From: FavoriteCoach@gmail.com

To: Manatees   sent Wed, Oct 20 10:11 am

Subject: Keep breathing

Hello everyone. Coach Randy here with your weekly pep talk! That final non-competitive game was a squeaker, but we prevailed because of our great spirit. Here is a quote that you probably want to read to the kids. It's from "Cast Away"—the movie where Tom Hanks is all by himself on an island. Which is the way all of us feel at some point. So just in case your kids are scared about the playoffs or being competitive, think about this: "I know what I have to do now. I've got to keep breathing because tomorrow the sun will rise. Who knows what the tide may bring?"

Anyway, it's normal to be scared. Heck, I was scared on that roof the other night. I may have looked like I had it under control, but seriously, I threw up when I got home. Don't tell Aiden!!!! And I probably wouldn't have thrown up if I had remembered to "keep breathing" like Tom Hanks.

So that's my pep talk. Paul's been suggesting that I keep it short. So, here it is:

"Keep breathing."
Coach Randy

Keep Breating

From: Visorgrl@mac.com
To: Manatees   sent Wed, Oct 20 11:14 am

Subject: Re: Keep breathing

I'm breathing!!! ☺ Also, just a reminder that someone forgot snacks last weekend. I'm not going to say "who" because that's blaming. A big thanks to Mark, for saving the day by ordering pizzas so the kids didn't totally melt down.

Please, please people check the schedule, it's really not hard! In our Team Mom Meeting, we talked about penalties for forgetting snacks, and maybe a smaller penalty for not providing a healthy option. Nothing is firm yet. I'll let you know. ☹

XOXO,
Jacqui

From: DPlatt@ca.rr.com
To: Manatees   sent Wed, Oct 20 11:20 am

Subject: Re: Keep breathing

Hi Jacqui and all,

My apologies AGAIN for forgetting the snack. Jacqui, thanks for your non-blaming way of blaming me. I tried to reimburse Mark for the pizza, but he gallantly refused. I will be taking his snack day instead. Where does everyone stand on Pirate Booty as a healthy option? Don't answer. I'll bring kale balls.

Oh, and Randy, you misspelled "Breathing" in your sign-off. Just thought I'd let you know since it's kind of the literary equivalent of having your fly open. And only those who truly care will tell you!

I'm breathing too.
Diane

From: ParadiseB@gmail.com
To: Manatees   sent Wed, Oct 20 11:36 am

Subject: Re: Keep breathing

We're all breathing over here. But I have to say, Dashiell is beside himself with excitement about the playoffs. It's a little scary that his hopes are so high. He'll be devastated if we don't go on to the tournament. Is there some way that we can prepare them for losing without dampening their enthusiasm? I'm just putting it out there. By the way, I'll be running late to the game. Can someone take pictures of Dashiell whenever he gets near the ball? His nanny will be there, but whenever she takes photos of the games, Dashiell looks the size of a bug.

Beth

From: FavoriteCoach@gmail.com

To: Manatees   sent Wed, Oct 20 11:42 am

Subject: Re: Keep breathing

Hello Manatees!

Coach Randy, here. Beth, I can appreciate your concern about a possible loss, but I won't be preparing the kids for it on game day. I will be giving a stirring, inspiring speech about taking the field and being warriors (don't worry, I'll lay off of "focused rage"!). Remember, we have four playoff games. So even if we lose this one coming up we still have three more games to earn enough goals and points to get into the tournament.

After my big speech, I will be playing Queen's "We are the Champions" for the boys on my IPod. That song is like steroids for ten-year-olds. The first time that I played it for Aiden he charged outside and ripped a branch off of a tree so that he could beat the ground with it.

In the event of an unlikely loss, I will probably hit the kids with some words from "Braveheart".

Keep breathing and thanks Diane, for pointing out my spelling mistake. I fixed it.

Coach Randy

Keep Breathing

From: Visorgrl@mac.com

To: Manatees   sent Wed, Oct 20 12:13 pm

Subject: Re: Keep breathing

Dear Coach and team parents,

I think that Coach's decision is a good one for most of the kids, but some of us have kids who are more sensitive. It's not anything that we parents did, it's just the luck of the draw, and I wouldn't trade my beautiful boy for anyone!!!! ☺ I know from experience that preparing Calvin ahead of time can often prevent some of the behaviors you have seen in the past. In fact, his doctor has told us to go through possible scenarios with him before an event, so that he doesn't become hyper-focused on one result. "Hyper-focus" is a condition that Calvin has. Many high achievers in history have had it, like Abraham Lincoln and Houdini!!! ☺

I'm sorry to over-share. But since Calvin's incident on the roof, I thought I should give you some information so that you can understand better!!! Trust me, Steve and I are on it and Calvin is going to grow up to be an impressive man!!!!

XOXOXOXO,
Jacqui

———————

FROM: KARENSONN
TO: KELLI SONNENKLAR

I am ready to meet regarding Ben.

FROM: KELLI SONNENKLAR
TO: KARENSONN

that's great, karen! don't mention to
mark. i'm sure that we ladies can make
a difference working on this together.

FROM: KARENSONN
TO: KELLI SONNENKLAR

Meeting does not = forgiveness. It just
= what's best for Ben. Tomorrow. Starbucks. Wilshire + SM. During practice.

FROM: KELLI SONNENKLAR
TO: KARENSONN

OK

CHAPTER 35

KAREN IS THE FIRST TO arrive, having dropped Ben off at practice early. She wants to get her coffee before Kelli gets here, so that she doesn't have to stand in line making small talk with a woman she routinely imagines stabbing. There is a smattering of young people on laptops and a couple of businessmen probably getting their caffeine fix before going back to their offices for another few hours. Thankfully, she doesn't know anyone. Not that she envisions losing control, but you never know. She smiles to herself. The only knives here are plastic.

She is wearing her work gear. Slick pegged pants, heels, and a silk blouse. The other female attorneys at her firm wear skirts, but Karen's legs aren't that good. Instead, she rocks her cleavage. She could have run home to change into something more casual, but has calculated that this outfit gives her an advantage.

She picks up her French roast skinny latte and sweetens it with Splenda. Ever since Mako's e-mail about aspartame, she's been thinking about cutting it out. Peptic ulcers? Blood in her stool? No thanks. She stirs her coffee, making figure-eights with a stirrer in the foam. The trouble is, she needs the sweetener and she can't get fat. Mark would enjoy it too much.

She finds a table at the back, facing the door so that she can see Kelli before Kelli sees her. Crossing her legs and hearing the satisfying swish of lined pants, she wonders if she should busy herself with her phone. Leans back. No. She'll wait with—what was it? "Hyper-focus." Jesus, she should stop reading all those stupid team e-mails; they're occupying way too much brain space.

The door swings open. A young woman. Karen's stomach clenches. But it's not Kelli. Relax. Breathe. Keep breathing. Shit. She sips a little of the foam. She needs to remind herself of her objective here, which is to keep Ben close to her. That's all.

The door swings again. And it's her. Karen stiffens, uncrosses her legs as if to get up. Kelli scopes the other side of the shop, which gives Karen enough time to catch herself. Recross her legs. Lean back. Wait.

Kelli turns, sees her, and waves. Karen waves back, reflexively. Kelli points to the counter. Karen nods. Nothing in the exchange to indicate enmity. Quite the opposite. And Karen remembers coming home one evening to find the indoor kiddie tent in the living room. Kelli and Ben giggling from inside it. Elbows poking at the yellow nylon, making it look cartoony. Kelli emerging from the tent, hands up to smooth her hair, jeans loose on her waist, a ready smile. And Ben standing up beside Kelli. God, he was four. So young. Both of them looking at her as she tossed her keys on the side table. This is the image she returns to over and over again. That particular afternoon with the tent. Because it is the feeling she remembers. Gratitude. My baby is all right with this girl. He's taken care of. He is safe. I have made the right decision.

Karen takes another sip of her latte. When she looks up, that memory of Kelli diffuses and rearranges itself into the confident woman walking toward her, Starbucks cup in hand. Karen sees betrayal in the swing of those hips. She puts her coffee down so Kelli won't spot the vengeful tremor in her grip. Fixes the smile she uses in the boardroom. Thin-lipped, purposeful.

Kelli pulls out a chair, hangs her bag on the back, and plops into it. "I'm so glad that we're doing this," she says, smiling. Looking loose, relieved.

"Well," says Karen, "we have to move forward. Right?"

"Right."

"So where do you want to start?"

Kelli looks startled. Karen is purposely skipping the usual niceties. The toe-dipping before jumping into the pool. It's a shock to the system and Karen knows it.

"Um." Kelli wiggles in her chair. "Well, as you know, I'm worried about Ben."

"What do you think is wrong with him?" Karen lays a hand on the table.

"Well, for starters, you could say he's angry. And it's pretty scary."

Karen places her other hand on the table and crisscrosses her fingers. Prayerful, thoughtful. "So, this is something I don't understand. Ben does get angry, yes. When he doesn't get what he wants. We all do, correct?" Kelli nods. "So what is so scary about that?"

"It's…" Kelli bites her lip, looks past Karen. "It's, it's, um, just how big his tantrums are. How long they last, I guess. It's kind of like he's angry all the time."

"He throws tantrums because they are effective. They get him what he wants. In the most recent case, an iPhone."

"He wouldn't talk to me for days. He'd walk right by me as if I was invisible."

"Yes. And now he knows that that is all that's needed. It's not rocket science. You need to be on the same page as Mark and me." Karen involuntarily shakes her head at the thought of Mark and her on *any* page together. "You are undermining everything we are trying to do."

"Mark has forgiven me for the phone."

"Good for him."

Karen watches this land. Kelli's eyes get watery. There's the bite of the lip again. Kelli takes the plastic lid off her cup, blows into it. Karen can see that the girl is trying to collect herself. And what's that she feels for her? Pity? Softness in Karen's core? A dangerous moment for any attorney. This is when she needs to be most ruthless.

"Look," says Karen, leaning forward, fingers still interlaced, "all it will take is for you to leave decisions concerning Ben up to Mark and me. Once Ben knows that there are firm boundaries, he will accept realities like homework and sportsmanship."

Kelli's lips press together and a tear slips down her face. But there is determination in the set of her face. "I'm not like you, Karen. I'm not like you and Mark and Ben. You're all alike. You're *all* scary. How much you hate each other." Another tear. Red-faced now, with the effort it takes to put thought into words. She wipes her face. Karen can barely allow herself to hear what Kelli is saying. Something about how much they all hate each other. But that's not true. She loves Ben. Loves her son.

But Kelli isn't done. "All you do is take stuff away. And punish." She gulps. "Maybe I was wrong. Yeah, probably. I shouldn't have given him the phone. But I thought that if Ben got the one thing he wanted it would stop him from being so mean. Stop him from being…like you…and Mark." She wipes her face again and stands up. Her chair scrapes and she bumps her knees against it as she turns to get her bag. And turns back again to Karen. "I can't do this anymore. I'm not good at being mad and mean and spiteful like all of you. Like it's a sport. Like you enjoy it. You. And Mark. I'm sorry I hurt you. I'm sorry for everything. But stop punishing Ben for it."

Kelli doesn't know enough to stand and watch her winning, irrefutable argument find its mark, leaving her opponent without rejoinder or an offensive move. Instead, she spins around like an amateur and practically runs out the door.

Karen watches until she's out of view. She lifts her cup of coffee, but her hand is shaking too much. She puts it down again and shuts her eyes, waiting for her body to calm the fuck down.

———

Practice has ended and there is an orange strip on the horizon, beyond which the Pacific tides crash against the western shore of the continent. But here, on the soccer field, the evening brings nothing more dramatic than a slight chill. The boys welcome it. They have been running for over an hour. Their hair is damp and sticks to their necks. The moms have claimed most of the players and now only four of them are left, kicking a ball by the bleachers. Aiden, Reece, Patrick, and Ben running over to join. They are waiting for the adults to finish talking. Mr. Woo is smiling and talking to Coach Paul. Reece's mom leans against a chain-link fence, talking to Alejandro. And Ben's mom is late. Which is often the case.

"I'm not talking to her anyway," says Ben, about his mother. He slices the ball to Patrick, who flicks it up and bounces it off his shoelaces.

"Because of your phone?" says Aiden, who is a big boy, and slow-moving. He raises his knee to block Patrick's pass, but is too late and has to run after it.

"She's a bitch," says Ben, catching Aiden's throw-in with this chest. The ball bounces into the middle. The boys scuffle and Reece kicks it loose, running down the field. Ben, Aiden, and Patrick watch him go.

"Do you call your mom that to her face?" asks Aiden.

"Sure," says Ben. "What's she going to do that's worse than throwing my phone down the garbage chute?"

"You could have gone down to the basement and gotten it," says Patrick, who bets that he's the only other teammate who lives in an apartment.

"What's a garbage chute?" says Aiden, proving Patrick's theory.

"It's a hole that you dump garbage into," says Patrick. "And it ends up in a big dumpster in the basement. In a room with metal doors and rats." He sits on the lowest bleacher and watches Coach Paul put his hand on his father's shoulder.

"Score!" yells Reece from way down the field. He has kicked the ball neatly into the corner of the net. Reece's mother looks up from her talk with Alejandro to whoop for him and pump the air with her fist. Kind of lame, since there's no goalie.

"Yeah, like I'm going to go down to the basement by myself," says Ben, puffing out air like he always does. "Rats." He shivers.

Aiden crosses in front of Patrick and plunks down next to him. "I bet my dad could go down into a basement with rats."

Patrick knows that there are other ways of going down into the basement. Ways in which you leave your body behind. He wants to tell the boys about how he can sail through the world invisible. Not only that, but he has eyesight that zooms in on small details. Movements that give a person away. When his mother's right eye twitches, she is about to smack him. Right now, all the way down the field, Reece is dancing around the ball in front of the goal and Patrick can see the red abrasion on his cheekbone, gotten from a tumble this afternoon. And, over by the chain-link fence, he even sees the back of Alejandro's hand brush against Reece's mom's wrist. Now he sees Ben's mom's car pulling into the parking lot. Ben sees her too and darts behind the bleachers.

"What are you doing?" Aiden says to Ben through the space between the steps.

Patrick watches Ben's mother get out of the car and stride toward them. There are dark smudges around her eyes that look like messed-up makeup. And a thin gold chain glints on her neck. He wants to touch it.

"Don't tell her I'm here," hisses Ben from behind the bleachers.

"I can't lie to your mom," Aiden whispers back.

"Besides," says Patrick, "she already knows you're here."

Karen comes to a stop right in front of the boys and places both of her hands squarely on her hips. "Ben. I know that you're back there. Come out. We're going home." Her voice sounds hard and weary.

Patrick hears Ben rustle behind him, but he does not emerge. The necklace on Karen's neck rises and falls with her breath, which Patrick notices is fast and shallow. This means that she is angry. He tenses, primed for violence. But also feels a thrill that is connected to Ben's defiance. Can boys do this? Disobey their mothers? And how will Ben survive the beating that will surely come tonight?

Karen's lips press together in a thin, mean line. Then she parts them just widely enough to say, "Ben. I am too tired for this bullshit. If you don't come out from there, I am going to call your father and have him deal with you."

Patrick is transfixed. Terrified and fascinated. His heart thumps so loud that he is sure the others must hear it. Without turning his head, he glances to see how Aiden is reacting. The big boy is loose-limbed, supporting himself between two elbows resting on the step behind him. Aiden doesn't look scared at all. In fact, he looks distracted. His head lolling to one side. How can he not feel the electric threat sparking off of Ben's mother?

"Ben," Karen snarls. Her electricity jolts Patrick and he prepares to run. Feet itchy, he slowly slides one in front of the other. Come out, Ben, he thinks. You're only making it worse. Come out now and get it over with, he prays.

But instead of marching behind the bleachers and yanking Ben by his ear or hair, Karen does something so shocking to Patrick that he can barely find his breath.

She cries. Plops down beside Patrick. Nudging him down the bench with her hip. She slumps and covers her eyes with one hand like she's ashamed. Her shoulders bob up and down with each quiet sob. Patrick has never seen anything like it. His breath kicks back in and he turns to Aiden, who hasn't changed positions. Ben's mom takes a big breath and her shoulders start to shake. What should he do?

He lifts one of his hands off his lap and tentatively puts it on Karen's tweedy thigh. She grabs it and squeezes. It's remarkable. In an infinitesimal moment within this extraordinary moment, he feels that he's never been closer to anyone in his life. And he wishes it could stay like this. Wishes that Karen would take him home instead of Ben. To her little apartment, where it is safe.

He pulls air into the spaces between his ribs as Karen tightens her grip. His hand is damp. But she doesn't seem to mind.

Now Ben appears in front of them. Red-ringed eyes. Green stains on the knees of his sweatpants. Contrition rounding his shoulders. "I'm here, Mom," he says.

Patrick's eyes sting and he pulls his hand back. He hates Ben. What does Ben ever do to help the team except mouth off and lose sportsmanship points? Karen stands up and he feels the coolness in his leg, where her thigh was. He watches her pull Ben into her arms.

Past the two of them, Patrick sees his father walking toward him, and he stands. His stomach is a big black stone, weighing him down as he starts to walk. Making his legs heavy and his gait plodding. Every lumbering step the boy takes narrows the space between them.

CHAPTER 36

From: RTChampion@gmail.com

To: DPlatt@ca.rr.com   sent Thurs, Oct 21 9:36 am

Subject: Re: (No Subject)

Hey Diane,

Randy here. I really appreciate your thoughts on Missy and even you giving me insights into mistakes that you made in your marriage. In some ways I feel closer to you than anyone else right now, which is strange because we almost never talk in person. Thank you for letting me write to you and work things out. You can tell me your darkest secrets if you want. It could be fun and I promise I won't tell anyone.

The window of time where I could have told Missy about the job and the money has slammed shut. I went in to talk to HR and my immediate supervisor was there. Sam (for the purposes of this letter, let's call him "Judas") was the jerkoff who leaked an e-mail that I sent privately to him about work particulars—thus leading directly to my firing. Asswipe. Sorry, but I feel that I can talk to you this way.

Anyway, HR is questioning some of my expenditures on the corporate card. I seriously don't know why they care anymore. Granted, there were a few Lakers Tickets and a private winery tour, but those are nothing unusual. They are asking me to write down a list of clients I gave the perks to. I'm supposed to be going through my notes right now, but I'm not because I know exactly who I gave those tickets to, and it's not going to make me look good.

You know, I'm going to stop dwelling on the negatives. Did I tell you that I made $432.00 in commission just last week? I can sell the crap out of classical music. I'm trying to get on the "Mad About Mozart" campaign coming up after this gig, but I'm not sure they're hiring anyone new. But, Mozart, come on—that guy practically sells himself, he's like the Shaq of classical music.

I don't mind telling you that I feel terrified and also totally alive! It's like anything is possible. I could survive this whole thing without a scratch or lose everything and blow my brains out! Don't worry. I'm nowhere close to blowing my brains out. That's just a figure of speech. And I don't even know how to use our gun. I just keep it to scare burglars—which is funny, since the most scary thing to burglars now would be that they spent all that effort robbing people who don't have anything. Hah!

Hey, by the way, I think that the black librarian has a crush on me!

Love,
Randy

————————

From: DPlatt@ca.rr.com
To: RTChampion@gmail.com   sent Thurs, Oct 21 10:08 am

Subject: Re: (No Subject)

Randy,

Seriously? Don't mention guns, it really scares me. It sounds like you were making a joke. And I get it. But nothing that you are dealing with is that drastic. And even though your plan sounds stressful (the part about keeping your secret), it does sound somewhat viable. Although, at some point you're going to have to find a job that pays more than $600ish a week.

I hear you on being terrified and feeling alive at the same time. I am finally, finally letting go of the belief that T will come back to me. And in some ways that's liberating and I feel lots of options floating around out there. But in other ways it's terrifying to be a forty-five year old single mother with no job. Frankly, I'm not worried about money, because I get enough from T. But I feel the need to do something with my life, besides being a mother. And I haven't a clue what that is right now.

You're back at the library? I thought you were working full-time.

Diane

———————

From: RTChampion@gmail.com
To: DPlatt@ca.rr.com   sent Thurs, Oct 21 10:28 am

Subject: Re: (No Subject)

Diane,

I AM working full time, but the hours are all over the place. It's great! Sometimes I don't start work until 2pm. My office wife (I have to tell you more about her sometime because it's pretty weird) gets there before me and starts a new pot of coffee. Can you imagine? There's so much you can do before 2pm. Yesterday, I saw the Avenger movie and the only people in there were me and a mom with a baby sleeping on her shoulder.

Yesterday, my shift started at 7am (to call folks before they go to work), and I was out by 3pm. I went over to Patrick's place and kicked around a ball. The freedom is incredible!

I could live like this forever, except that I know that I can't. Sometimes I wonder if things should be simpler like this all the time.

I remember when Aiden was about two and I had just started at OneStop-Office, but I didn't have anywhere near the responsibility and stress that led to that fateful e-mail to Judas. Missy and I took Aiden camping. Can you imagine that? We would never do that now, but we thought it would be fun to be in nature with our little guy, so we rented this tent and headed up the coast, to a little campground on the beach. We set up camp and had some boxed wine while Aiden toddled around collecting rocks. Missy was wearing a speckled green turtleneck sweater and she had pulled down the sleeves so they covered her hands, and she leaned against me when we were sitting on top of the picnic table. I remember thinking that this was the closest I had ever been to having a perfect day. But then something happened that made it even more perfect. A Mexican fisherman was out in the ocean and he came toward us with something in his hands, and he kept shouting, "For the boy. For the boy." Missy and I hopped off of the picnic table. I guess we somehow trusted the fisherman, and Missy grabbed Aiden's hand. We had to walk over a thin stretch of rocky beach to make it to the shore, and by then, we could see that the man was carrying a small speckled shark that he had caught. It was like the size of a loaf of bread. Aiden jumped up and down, and Missy and I clapped, and the fisherman held the shark out for Aiden to touch, and Aiden wasn't scared at all. The shark flopped around a bit, but Aiden reached out and touched its back. Then the fisherman laughed and threw the shark back into the sea. It was like the shark was only there for us and then it returned to nature. That was my last perfect day. I guess everyone has that ideal day like that, when everyone is completely there with each other and there's no other place to be.

I don't know why I'm telling you that story. Maybe because in the last couple of weeks, I've started to think that it's possible to get back that feeling! Maybe, I should take one of my afternoons off and drive up the coast to find that same spot on the beach, and just sit there imagining nothing going wrong and everything turning out that perfect.

The librarian let me have twenty extra minutes on the computer. She definitely does have the hots for me! Don't worry, I won't do anything about it.

Love,
Randy

CHAPTER 37

RANDY HAS AN HOUR TO go before signing out and heading home. He's sorry to miss soccer practice, but Paul and Al can handle it. Other than that, he enjoys the work at this place. Low pressure. He closes 35 percent of the time. And his bosses told him that no marketer in the five-year history of Going Baroque has had those numbers. It's only been a week and a half, and he's already getting noticed. He stretches his legs and cracks his knuckles.

"Ew, don't do that," says Laney next to him. Even though this is an admonishment, she makes this sound flirty, with her eye roll. Randy shakes out his hands and shrugs his shoulders. He still can't figure out Laney's gender situation. But he's decided to go along with "she" because Laney looks like a fairly attractive woman, with long blond hair and a love of tube tops. Still, she sounds like a man. Really. With a deep, unmistakably male voice. A pretty unusual office wife, that's for sure. He's thought about telling Diane more about Laney, but he's worried it might change Diane's opinion of him.

Randy checks the last call off his roster. N/A for *No answer*. He should power through the next ten calls. He has given himself a quota for each workday. The two managers don't seem to care about the number of calls each marketer makes; after all, it's primarily a commission-based business. But Randy has always been a man who needs a goal.

"Lord," Laney says to him, "I'm wrung out. Wanna hit the break room for a shot of caffeine?"

Randy glances at Laney's long fingers twirling the ends of her hair and mentally pinches himself for feeling a bit turned on. "Sure," he says. Glancing at his roster. If he doesn't get to all the calls today, he can tack them onto tomorrow's quota.

Laney rises from her chair—all six foot three of her—and sashays through the swinging door to the right of a row of marketers. Randy gets up to follow. You don't run into people like Laney in Beverly Hills. Which is another part of this job that's pretty entertaining. He's already met an Iraq War vet with PTSD, a girl with blue hair who says she plays "found instruments" like water bottles and tires, an old black guy who talks endlessly about his chemo treatments, and the two managers, who sweat a lot and look like they're in middle school. Each person Randy's talked to has a story that they're surprisingly eager to tell. In great and often intimate detail. It's like being on a reality TV show.

When he walks into the kitchen, Laney is already at the coffee machine, pouring. She puts down the pot and carries her cup over to a table, slipping into a seat with what Randy considers exaggerated femininity. He wonders if Laney still has a penis. She pats the chair next to her and he obliges. Only once he's seated does it occur to him that she might be hitting on him. Nah. Couldn't be. But why not? People like Laney have fewer options and might think he's pretty hot. Randy feels his chest expand.

"It's been a good shift for me," he says. "I sold two new subscriptions and one was to a woman under fifty." He smiles, hoping he sounded charming rather than cocky.

"You are all work, mister. Just so you know, no one gets rich in telemarketing."

"You never know," he says, stretching out his legs and crossing them at the ankle. He likes this pose because it shows off his height. "I heard that some of the LA Philharmonic people make six figures. Besides, I'm counting on winning that bottle of champagne when we knock off in December."

"You probably will. But let me warn you, it's almost always shitty champagne." Laney flips her hair over one shoulder.

"Sounds like you've done telemarketing for some time."

"It pays the bills, and has the added benefit of being on the phone instead of in person." Of course, Randy thinks. Maybe the employees here are like him, wanting a job where they won't be seen. On the other hand, that doesn't seem to be true for Laney, or why would she dress that way? Why dress like a woman at all? You have to want the attention. "That tells you a bit about me," she says coyly, "but what about you? You aren't a career telemarketer." She leans forward and sniffs. "I can smell it."

Randy thinks of her penis and pulls himself up in his chair. "Well, not telemarketing per se, but sales. I've been in sales all my life."

"Oh. That's why you're so good!"

"Yeah. Well, until I got myself fired," he says, surprising himself with this candor. But it's also a relief. Who would Laney tell? Diane is the only other person who knows his secret. And even though he trusts her, sometimes he has a hard time looking at her on the soccer field. He can only be honest with her through e-mail. He'd never say some of the stuff that he's written to her out loud.

"I'm sorry about that," says Laney. And her eyes look soft, like she really is sorry.

"Ah. I screwed myself over. Got too cocky. You know salespeople. The thing is, my wife doesn't know about the job. Right now, she thinks that I'm there. Not here."

"I see," says Laney.

"Right now, she thinks I'm working late at the office."

"Wow. That must be hard. Keeping up appearances."

Randy pauses to think about that. Because of a thought that has flitted through his mind a couple of times. It *should* be harder to pull off the charade. He's terrified, of course, about the possibility of everything blowing up at once. The company suing him. Losing the house. Losing Missy. Aiden. But the part where he has to come home and pretend to have been working at OneStopOffice, making up office stories for Missy in the kitchen while he uncorks a bottle of wine—that doesn't feel much different from the way it's always been. At least not so far. And something about this realization nags at him. Although he can't say why.

"I guess it's hard, pretending," he says noncommittally.

"I bet," says Laney, maintaining a steady, though kind, stare. He waits, thinking that she's going to give him advice, like women always do. Even when they don't know a thing about the situation. But Laney simply smiles.

Huh, maybe that's because she's a man.

CHAPTER 38

From: FavoriteCoach@gmail.com

To: Manatees   sent Fri, Oct 22 9:02 am

Subject: How true are Vince Lombardi's words

Hey Team! Coach here with one simple thought about the game on Sunday (note that it's Sunday, not Saturday!):

"The only place success comes before work is in the dictionary." That's by Vince Lombardi. For those of you who don't know, Vince Lombardi was a great athlete and later, he was an even greater coach for The Pack. He's famous for his motivational speeches to his players. So I can't think of anything more perfect than quoting the great man himself to your kids for the next couple of days.

I'm working on keeping it short (thanks for the tip again Coach Paul!). So that's what I'm doing. Get lots of rest and remember to quote Lombardi!

Coach Randy

Keep Breathing

———————

From: MSonnenklar@GSachs.com
To: Manatees   sent Fri, Oct 22 9:04 am

Subject: Re: How true are Vince Lombardi's words

The dictionary is also the only place where divorce comes before marriage!

M

————————

From: FavoriteCoach@gmail.com
To: Manatees   sent Fri, Oct 22 9:05 am

Subject: Re: How true are Vince Lombardi's words

I hear you, Mark! Or gain before pain!

Coach

Keep Breathing

————————

From: MSonnenklar@GSachs.com
To: Manatees   sent Fri, Oct 22 9:05 am

Subject: Re: How true are Vince Lombardi's words

Or trophy before victory.

M

—————

From: Visorgrl@mac.com
To: Manatees   sent Fri, Oct 22 9:06 am

Subject: Re: How true are Vince Lombardi's words

Or happiness before love! ☺ I can play this too!!!!

XOXOXO,
Jacqui

—————

From: FavoriteCoach@gmail.com
To: Manatees   sent Fri, Oct 22 9:07 am

Subject: Re: How true are Vince Lombardi's words

Or leaping before looking. I guess it kind of loses something if it's the same letter, right? I couldn't think of anything else.

Coach

Keep Breathing

—————

From: DPlatt@ca.rr.com

To: Manatees   sent Fri, Oct 22 11:49 pm

Subject: Re: How true are Vince Lombardi's words

Or orgasm before sex!

Diane

——————

From: DPlatt@ca.rr.com

To: Manatees   sent Fri, Oct 22 11:52 pm

Subject: Re: How true are Vince Lombardi's words

I crossed a line there, didn't I? Sorry, it's late.

Diane

CHAPTER 39

ALEJANDRO STANDS BEHIND THE KITCHEN island, hands folded across his chest, like the big, fat liar he is.

Missy's heart beats so fast that she has to hang on to the counter so she doesn't pass out. She hears Aiden clunking around upstairs, making all his after-practice sounds. The ball smacking the floor as he tosses it in his closet. The hamper slamming shut in the bathroom. This domestic low-level din is the only thing stopping her from screaming right now.

"Tell me why again. And tell the truth this time," she rasps. Furious at herself for the tears streaming down her face.

He looks at the floor. "I tell you already. You say you want to be with me forever. You say I cannot leave you. And…but, I cannot do this."

But didn't he say *forever*? He had said *forever*. Lots of times.

"You said…" Missy snarls. She can't remember exactly what he said. But it was a lot of promisey stuff.

Alejandro lifts his head and looks at her and she feels like her legs are going to give out. His eyes don't look mean. But they do look faraway. "I tell you this," he says, "and is true. I am sorry. I thought we were playing a game. Sometimes women act like this is a first time they have an affair."

"Women?"

"Yes. All the time."

"*All the time?* You do this *all the time*?"

"I'm sorry," he says, and steps forward.

She pulls back, even though there's nowhere to go. The edge of the sink presses against her lower back, holding her there. Through her clenched jaw, she makes herself say, "You told me that you never felt like this before."

"I lied," he says.

The air goes out of her. She tightens her grip on the counter.

"So what if…" She can't believe she's saying this. "What if we just kept…" She stops to take a breath. "What if we just kept going?"

She hears a door close upstairs, but keeps her eyes on Alejandro.

He unfolds his arms, which she doesn't think is a good sign. It makes him look more sure. "Missy. It would hurt you. I know this. You are mad now. But it will be better."

"How can it possibly be better? I can't go back to the way things were before. You can't just open a door and show me what it's like to feel something. To finally feel like I'm a breathing person who matters and then shut the door and say, 'Oh, that feeling like everything is so alive and everything feels so impossibly good. That feeling you were feeling, well, you don't get to feel that anymore. Bye-bye. I got what I needed. But you… You get your…'" She's gasping. She has moved away from the sink and the counter. She's standing on her own, although in seconds she could be crumpled on the floor. "'You, Missy. Guess what you get? You get your old life back—when you barely felt a thing.'" She takes a step closer to the kitchen island. His barricade. "I'll do anything. I don't care about the others."

"Missy," he says with faraway eyes. "There is only one other woman now. And she is important to me. I care for her. I cannot play a pretend game anymore."

Her shoulders stiffen. One woman? One *special* woman.

She stares at him hard. Wishing him intense and swift pain. She coils. Gathering strength. To swipe. Scratch. Punch. Stab. "Who is she?" She hears her voice, high and screechy.

A door bangs upstairs and Missy flinches. Aiden. She pulls back. Stops herself from instinctively dropping to the floor to hide. Instead, she stuffs every impulse down inside her. Smashes it all down. All that rage. She steadies. Focuses only on Alejandro's eyes. Her voice guttural now: "Who is she?"

Clumping down the stairs.

"Who is she?"

He shifts.

"Who is she?"

Then he does this thing. He throws up his hands like it's no big deal. Like all this was nothing and he says, "Diane. Is Diane."

———————

Randy drives home, high as a motherfucker. He hasn't smoked pot since before he married Missy. And back then, he only did it occasionally to be sociable. Whatever giggly state he managed to achieve had never been worth the feeling of being watched—which was a bad enough feeling when he was completely sober.

But smoking with Laney tonight was different. It was true liberation. No one on the planet knew where he was. And if they did, they certainly couldn't have guessed that he, Randy Tinker, had been getting high with a transvestite in downtown LA.

Seriously. He, Randy Tinker, is higher than fuck and has almost made it home without making a single mistake. God is smiling on him. Getting fired has been the best possible thing in the whole damn universe. Why didn't he get fired earlier?

He pulls into the garage flawlessly. Look at that! Gets his keys out. No problem. And slips them into the lock on the first try!

The inside of his house hums. The lamp in the foyer has been left on and down the hall he can see the kitchen illuminated by the pendant lights that hang low over the butcher block island. He turns off the lamp and slips down the hall, thrilled by how sure-footed he feels.

In the kitchen (it took, like, no time at all for him to get down the hall), he turns up the dimmer. The light is a shock. His eyes slam shut. He shrinks and turns down the light again. All he needs is the tallest, clearest, coldest glass of water that any civilized man has ever consumed. He would pay hundreds of dollars for it. But he doesn't have to! It's here! He grabs a tall bumpy tumbler from the cabinet and programs the fridge for crushed ice. Presses the glass against the back pad and, presto, lots of crunchy ice. Whoops. Almost too much. He pulls the glass back. Reprograms for simple water. Life-giving. Clear. Like a mountain stream. It flows into his glass, which he pulls back at just the right time. He holds it up. It's perfect. Lifts it to his mouth and gulps and gulps and gulps.

He thinks that there isn't anything that can't be made better by water. Hey, he'll bring a glass up to Missy. He puts down his empty glass and gets one filled, just as perfectly, for her.

The upstairs hallway is completely dark. Usually there's a slip of dull light under the bedroom door, indicating that Missy is on her iPad or watching television. Could she already be asleep? He slides his hand along the wall so that he won't veer off course and spill the water. The door to the bedroom is open. His toe catches and he has to lean against the doorframe for a second. But it's no big deal.

In the slight lunar glow, he sees a round lump in the middle of the bed. Is she on top of the sheets? His neck tenses. Is she awake? He takes a big breath to clear out any leftover mental fog and carefully places the glass on her nightstand. He feels like he's watching himself in a movie. He sits on the edge of the bed and slides a hand over to her. She is warm and breathing and, as he first suspected, uncovered. She's pulled herself into a tight ball. Her round back is damp and tense.

"Is that you?" she says, her voice thick with mucus.

"Ah. Yes. I brought you some water." He slides into the center of the bed and curls himself around her. Maybe he should have taken his clothes off first. But there was something receptive in her voice and he didn't want to lose the moment. She smells salty. He nuzzles her tousled hair. Her shoulder gives in to him. Missy always washes her face and combs her hair before bed. There is no evidence of this usual routine. He doesn't know what to make of it. But whatever it is has softened her back into his torso.

"Is something wrong?" he asks, because he knows he must. But he doesn't really want to know the answer. It might require action from him. And while he feels, in this moment, he would do anything for her, he doesn't feel confident that the fix would be within his power to achieve.

Missy lets out a pouty sob. "I had a bad day." It's adorable, really. And he hopes that "a bad day" is all it is. Frustration with the housekeeper, a tangle with Aiden over homework, the back door sticking, or a girl-friend of hers criticizing something. Randy rubs her shoulder, knead-ing it with his thumb, until she shakes him off. Usually when she does this, she quickly scoots to the far side of the bed, all the way to the edge, leaving a vast area of unoccupied mattress between them.

This time, however, she rolls over and puts her arms around his neck. Pressing her face into him. He is afraid to breathe. His lower back clenches, but if he makes an adjustment, it might trigger her scooting thing.

"Is Aiden all right?" he asks, not wanting that answer either. But showing concern might keep her in his arms longer.

Missy coughs out a short laugh that cuts through the mucus. "Oh yeah. He spent the night in his room, killing people on *Warcraft.*"

"Well, I'm here now," he whispers.

"I feel so bad," she says into his chest, and whimpers. She crooks her leg over his so he can inch closer. Takes her hand from around his neck and places it over his heart. But her hand is not flat, it's like a paw, and he realizes that she's holding a crumpled-up Kleenex. Which she now uses to dab her nose.

Randy knows that he should be ashamed of being grateful for the troubles that have fused her against his side. That have brought her arms around him, her leg over his, so that his prick pushes against her soft belly. He is afraid of taking advantage. Of blowing the mood, as they say. Each move he makes is furtive. Exploratory. Can I put my hand here? On your breast, held in by spandex and one of those annoy-ing shelf bras? Yes? But how to get in? He removes his hand, careful, and slides it back over her shoulder, stealthily smoothing it into the back of her yoga pants, under the panties. There's skin. She wiggles to get closer to him. She does not deflect. She sniffs. Poor thing. Poor Missy.

He gives her ass a few squeezes and pulls her even closer. Her cheek is wet against his chest. He rubs his crotch against her, while considering how to unleash his cock without telegraphing his intent.

"I'm so sorry you're feeling bad," he whispers roughly into her ear. She lets out a mewl. Kittenish. Hot damn. He risks it. Flops onto his back, unbuckling his belt, while keeping his voice soft. "Let me make you feel better."

Miraculously, he feels her hand slide over his shirt, finding his earlobe. A move she hasn't made in years. She rubs it between her thumb and forefinger while he wriggles out of his pants, rolling back toward her, jouncing on the bed, thinking of how to get her out of her spandex casing. He moves in for a kiss. But she places a hand over his mouth. Without taking it away, she gets onto her knees, jiggling the mattress. Wobbling, she pulls the straps of her tank top down with one hand so that her breasts bounce out. He lifts his head to suck them, but she pushes him down with her palm, still against his mouth. His teeth cut into the insides of his lips. His cock seeks her out. Will not be denied. He raises his hips. Whoosh. Now her pants are off. He doesn't know how. She straddles him. He tries to sit up. She pushes him down. Slides him into her. Already wet. Hot. Gets a rhythm going. Faster and faster. Ferocious. He wants her to slow down so he can think. Remember this. Savor. But she pumps faster and faster and faster. He is raw. Can't. Take. It. He cries out. Where is she? Erupts. She arches and strains. They convulse with each other. Holding on to each other's arms. He tries to pull her against him. But she pulls away. Her body suddenly hard and angular. She lifts herself off. And disappears.

Alone, he reaches over and grabs her balled-up pants, brings them to his mouth.

She is already in the bathroom. Running the faucet.

———————

"You told her it was me?" Diane says. Her voice is tremulous and semi-controlled, instead of a full-throated yell. It's got to be past midnight. The kids are sleeping upstairs. She hopes to God they're sleeping.

Alejandro stands in front of the window, still wearing his jacket, arms dangling. Lit only by one lamp next to the couch.

"Is better to be honest," he says. "You say to tell her the truth—that I think it was all a game."

"But not the whole truth, for Christ's sake!" Diane plops onto the couch and puts her head in her hands. "The part about me is totally irrelevant. And don't ask me what 'irrelevant' means."

"I know what it means," he says, stepping toward her.

She lifts her head and looks at him. What the hell has she gotten herself into? Alejandro was supposed to be a drama-free arrangement. Uncomplicated sex. And here she is smack-dab in the middle of some *Real Housewives* episode. Within minutes, Missy could be on her doorstep ready to yank her hair and scratch her eyes out, waking the kids with wild accusations. Reece and Sabine running down the stairs screaming, "What are you doing to my mommy?!" Jesus.

Alejandro kneels on the floor beside her. His eyes are soft. "You are not irrelevant," he says. "You are the reason I do this. I am not married. You are not married. We are real. We do not have to be a secret."

"Ah, Jesus," escapes her. She puts her hand on his cheek. "It's not that simple. It's not simple at all."

"Why? It could be simple." He takes her hand from his cheek and sits back on the floor looking up at her. "I understand when women are playing games behind the husband's back. And it is fun and sometimes I think the husbands—they know anyways. But that is not what I want with you. We are free to be what we want."

"Alejandro. I don't think...that's not what I signed on for." Which is a dumb phrase, but it's the best that comes to her mind. She winces. Did she know that this was coming? That he had—God, she can barely think it—that he had fallen in love with her? Had she wanted him to? To prove something to T? To herself? Could she be that fucking selfish?

"I think we are both surprised," he says.

"Maybe." Which is true. She's certainly surprised at how much she's come to care. "But even if that's true, it doesn't mean that we could work."

"You are so limited."

Her laugh here is humorless. She looks back at him. "Yes. You have no idea how much. First and foremost because I am a mother."

"I don't want for you to stop being a mother. I only want for you to be who you are and for me to be who I am."

She sighs. It's so damned late. "We're not going to solve this tonight. Alejandro," she says. "I am begging you not to tell anyone else about us right now. Really. I need you to promise." Maybe Diane will get lucky and Missy won't say anything to anyone. Not to the other moms on the team. Not to Randy. Shit, Randy. God knows how he'll react.

Her head hurts. She leans forward to look straight into his eyes. "Promise me."

He holds her gaze. "I promise."

"Now you need to go home."

He squeezes his eyes closed, and tears start running down his cheeks.

Her gut clenches. "Oh, honey," she says. "I'm sorry. I'm so sorry. I made a mess of things." She reaches out and strokes the side of his face. "I should have left you alone."

"I don't want to go home," he says, crying.

She's so goddamned weary. Mostly of herself. Of how she wrecks everything with her whims. With impulsiveness that's supposed to be fun, but is really silly and plain stupid and heartless. She looks down at the top of Alejandro's head. His shaking shoulders.

"Alejandro," she says. "Listen to me."

He raises his tearstained, incredibly young face to meet her gaze. She hopes that the smile she returns is reassuring.

Okay. She's going to have to fix this. Be the adult for once. He's not simply a hot Latin lover, he's a human being with complicated needs just like everyone. For one thing, he's still a kid. His sexual confidence isn't an indicator of some unique maturity, which she's talked herself into believing he possesses. He's clearly longing for his family. Longing for his—she can say it to herself, at least—longing for his mother. Jesus, it's all too classic and she walked right into it.

"It's late," she tells him. Copping out, but helpless against her baser instincts. Primary right now, surprisingly, is sleep over sex. Which is the only pure need she can identify. "Why don't you sleep on the couch until early morning? Can you set your alarm for five thirty? Before the kids get up?"

She expects some resistance to sleeping on the couch rather than in her bed, but instead he nods. She leans forward and chastely kisses the top of his head.

"It will all be okay," she says. She stands and leans over to turn off the lamp. Moves past Alejandro and starts toward the stairs without looking over her shoulder. She feels the tightness of foreboding at the back of her neck. It's a familiar sensation and therefore doesn't mean much of anything. A sensation she usually drinks away.

She dims the lights in the hallway and ascends noiselessly.

———

Patrick can't sleep. He sits on the edge of his bed. It is the first competitive game tomorrow. Everything counts now. Every goal. Every foul. Every missed opportunity to score. He must be perfect. Patrick is a boy who already lives with pressure like a Clydesdale's harness. But this night is worse than any other. The weight and pull of it is unbearable. He looks at the clock by his bed. Three oh four. If he does not sleep, he will not have strength. He *must* sleep. He squeezes his eyes shut and falls back on his bed. Sleep. Sleep. Balls his fists. Sleep.

It used to be that all he risked was his mother's fury and his father's helpless silence. These he has endured before. These he can manage. But what if he loses the coach's confidence? The boys' respect?

It's easier to sleep when no one cares. When no one sees you.

Sleep. Sleep. He imagines Coach lifting him up after the game. The way he does when he's proud of you.

Sleep.

Nothing.

He sits back up. Stares out the window to where he must go to get relief. He imagines himself there. Tightens his stomach and forces himself to take quick short breaths. Until he can lift away from his body. Separate from that fleshy frame that always lets everyone down. He floats above the human boy below. Drifts over to the windowpane. Emotionless now. Weightless. He slips through the glass, out into the black. Not many souls awake. He can tell because there are almost no lights on. He swoops and soars. Past homes, tall buildings, swimming pools, tennis courts, parking structures. Out. Out. To the beach. The crashing waves pulled by the moon. And beyond.

Out there, between the earth and heaven, the moon is fat and round. He dips close to the water, hoping to catch a glimpse of the speckled fin, the flat glistening head of a small leopard shark. The one that Coach Randy told him he saw on his last perfect day.

CHAPTER 40

From: FavoriteCoach@gmail.com

To: Manatees   sent Sun, Oct 24 11:47 pm

Subject: Manatees raise the roof!!!

Helloooooo Team!!!!!

Coach Randy here. I could not be prouder of everyone than I am right now! Our first competitive game this morning and we crushed it!!! We crushed it like the warriors we are and will continue to be. Winning feels sweet after all our hard work. Breathe it in, men!

Jacqui, I saw you taking some video. If you got footage of either of the two goals, can you post it on youtube? Just make sure to cut out any player or parent flipping the bird. We don't want evidence of misconduct out there!

I don't know about all of you, but I'm so pumped that I can't even sleep! That's why I'm writing to you all so late. Maybe you guys are still up too! I kept imagining us getting the first place trophy, which is much bigger than the normal ones they give out. Dan Majors has two of them in his downstairs bathroom, and I'm telling you there isn't a soul that goes to his house who doesn't take notice. Unless they don't go to the bathroom while they're there. But even then, he's put a mirror behind them so that it looks like four trophies and you can still see their reflection through the window onto his back porch.

Now, next week is going to be critical in keeping our boys focused and hungry for another victory. I recommend a lot of rest and inspirational movies. Just don't show them "Dead Poets Society". First of all, it's about poetry and not soccer. But mainly, the suicide at the end is a real let down for kids, and hard to explain. You want to keep everything optimistic. Try "Breaking Away" or even "Frozen"—which isn't about sports, but IS about overcoming enormous odds. In this case, eternal winter. Hey, maybe I'll play "Let it go!" at practice, to pump the boys up. We can all sing along. At their age, they can even hit those high notes, while I have to take it down a couple of octaves! I bet Jacqui can hit those high notes too, right Jacqui?!!!

As for keeping our young men fit and ready for anything, I recommend cold showers in the morning, for toughness, a raw egg blended into their orange juice like in "Rocky", daily laps (building up their stamina is going to be key), and dribbling practice every time you can squeeze it in.

Parents and boys I am depending on you like I've never depended on anything or anyone before! I'm seriously pumped!!! But I still have to get some sleep so I'm going to have to let it all go!!!!!!!!!!!

LET IT GO—RIGHT????

Coach Randy

Keep Breathing

———————

From: Visorgrl@mac.com
To: Manatees   sent Sun, Oct 24 11:55 pm

Subject: Re: Manatees raise the roof!!!

Hi Randy and everyone else who may be up tonight (or reading this tomorrow morning like sane people!). Congratulations to everyone!!! ☺

Coach, sometimes I think that you are reading my mind. More than anything, I need to be told to "let it go" right now, because if I don't I could have a heart attack! Now that I've had a taste of winning, I can feel what it's like to want more!!! But we can't want winning so bad that we lose sight of what's really important. Which is our beautiful boys who have exceeded all our expectations ALREADY!!!!!!

We have to remind ourselves that just because we won this one doesn't mean we will win again Although I kind of feel in my bones that we probably will!!!! Seriously, though, when you let expectations of winning go, you can accept whatever comes your way!!!! I mean, even if our boys are as perfect as they were today, sometimes it's just not the team's moment for whatever reason. Call it G*d or the universe or luck. It's moments like this, when we feel like life is unfair that we have to remind ourselves that these are really small things compared to Ebola or ISIS.

So when things DO go our way like today, we need to enjoy it and really take it in. Tonight, when I tucked in Calvin, I told him that he was a wonderful player, a smart boy, very sweet when he's had enough to eat, and I will love him win or lose, even though I think that losing might not happen now!!!☺☺☺

XOXOXOX,
Jacqui

———————

From: DPlatt@ca.rr.com
To: FavoriteCoach@gmail.com, Visorgrl@mac.com
                                        sent Sun, Oct 24 11:59 pm

Subject: Off topic

Hey Randy and Jacqui,

I had to double check that I was sending just to you two. Hey, I know that I'm problaly the guiltiest fo drunk-emailing to the whole team. But I thought I'd make just a friendly suggestion to save your e-mails as drafts and then read them over the next morning, before sending them out. It might save you soundling a little over the top. No offense. Seriously. With only the best intentions, Diane

CHAPTER 41

MISSY LIES IN THEIR BIG bed, spread eagle like a sacrifice. Which is pretty much what she feels like right now. Randy is downstairs, probably sending out his congratulatory e-mail to the team. This morning, she awoke thinking of ways that she could get out of going to the game. She couldn't imagine sitting there with the other moms, cheering on their sons and giggling about Alejandro's rock-hard thighs. She has been between those thighs.

She could have gotten out of it by saying that she had food poisoning, which no one usually questions. Especially if you spend a lot of time in the bathroom, running the faucet. But Aiden was so excited about his first competitive game, she couldn't bear to disappoint him. And Randy had been so sweet and grateful for the sex last night that she couldn't stand to see his eyes get that droopy and defeated look that makes her want to punch him. And, who cares about her feelings anyway? Seriously, who *does* care? Randy hasn't noticed that she's walking around like a woman whose heart was just ripped out of her chest. In fact, Missy thinks, he's looking like things are the best they've been in a while.

She rolls onto her side and draws her knees up. The thing is, she had tried to resist Alejandro. Tried to keep it just a friendship. But he had seemed to need her so badly. He acted like she was causing him physical pain when she denied him. And when he looked at her, it was like he was climbing right into her soul. No man has ever looked at her like that. If Randy could climb into her soul, he would know she was miserable.

She squeezes her eyes tight. Foolish. So dumb. This is what Alejandro does all the time. He seduces women. And she fell for it. Fell for it all. Her mind keeps wanting to replay moments from their four times alone together. Only the last one without clothes. Seeing him naked. God. But she won't let herself think of those moments. Because each time, she would have to think about what an idiot she had been. And, worse, she would have to think about whether she encouraged it.

She rolls onto her back, in the middle of the bed again, and covers her eyes. Maybe that will stop the images that keep popping up.

So, yes, she had gone to the game. Wearing sunglasses and looking exactly like the rejected lover who had been up all night crying. She had no choice. She was a mess. Let Alejandro see her, she thought. See what he had done to her. And, in fact, she thought that she had seen some softness in his eyes when he noticed her setting up her chair next to Karen. He had waved.

She had tried to stop herself, but couldn't help scoping the sidelines for Diane. She had never given Diane much thought. Honestly, Diane scared her a little bit, saying sarcastic things that could be put-downs; you were never quite sure. Through her sunglasses, Missy saw her talking to Coach Paul and Mark. Diane didn't hang out with the women much. There was something frazzled about her. She always looked like a piece of her clothing was being held together by a safety pin. This morning was no exception. Diane was wearing loose-fitting jeans, with a boxy oxford shirt that made it difficult for Missy to make out her figure. And she had really needed to know if Diane's figure was better than hers.

She takes her hands away from her eyes and pulls her knees up to her chest. Her gut hurts. Gnaws. Maybe if she makes herself walk around, the pain will subside.

She jettisons from the bed and grabs her sweater from the armchair.

Randy is in the kitchen, as she suspected, laptop open on the countertop. But instead of being huddled over it, he is at the window with a half glass of wine in his hand, staring out at the deck. As soon as he hears her, he turns and gives a foggy smile, then turns back to the window. Funny thing, Missy thinks, because the lights aren't on outside. Randy must be simply staring at his own reflection. She remembers his manic energy after the game. His insistence that Aiden slow down and describe every pass leading up to his goal. Maybe he's been admiring himself.

She feels a slight undertow of revulsion that's becoming familiar to her. But with a short breath she manages to shift her focus and look for the positives. A trick she learned from her *Happiness Workout* handbook. She scans his clothed body like she has infrared vision. Nothing. And then, there it is. The positive thought. He has nice hands. He's always had nice hands.

"I thought you were already asleep," he says without turning around. She stares at the back of his pants, shapelessly loose over his ass.

"I was tossing around too much. I thought, maybe a glass of wine."

His body animates quickly and he bounds to the overhead rack to grab her a glass. "Yes. Yes," he says, picking up an open bottle and pouring. "We should celebrate. Great idea." She pulls a stool up to the island and he places the glass in front of her with an exaggerated flourish. "Tell me what your first thought was when the final whistle blew."

Missy's stomach sags. She doesn't want to talk about the game. It reminds her too much of Alejandro picking up each boy and throwing him into the air.

"I was relieved," she says.

"Right. I understand that. Relief, and then the joy of winning."

She watches him reclaim his own glass. He leans against the counter with one of his satisfied looks. He can't ever let a success simply be. And there's no difference if the success is big or small. It could be something small at work like Sam giving him a compliment. Or something social like getting a maître d' to give him a table that was reserved for someone else (which he does pretty often). And on the soccer field? Winning the game, a compliment from a parent, the opposing coach conceding—he has to relive all of it. Over and over. And then, he almost always has to follow it up by spending a lot of money doing something showy.

"You know, we should take Aiden to Paris this summer," he says.

There would have been a time when she would have jumped at Paris. Randy is pretty fun on vacations, because he wants to do everything and go to the fanciest restaurants. But now the thought of all that fills her with dread. It would demand a level of pretending that she's not sure she could pull off. And she's been a pretty good pretender in the past.

"Were you writing to the team?" she deflects.

"Yeah. The coach's recap. They all look forward to it. What do you think happened to Patrick out there in the second half? It was like he just shut off."

Missy shrugs. She doesn't get involved with the players or the families much, and she probably knows the Woos least of all. "Everyone can have a bad day," she says.

And even that he doesn't pick up on. *I'm having a bad day!*, she wants to shout at him. But he's staring out into thin air, obsessing about the Woo kid. In seconds, her mind pings back to Diane.

Randy gazes at his wife, feeling a surge of warmth from his toes up. And it's not just the wine. This is so much fun, he thinks. This is what it's supposed to feel like, hanging out with your wife after your team wins their first competitive game. Shooting the breeze. Talking about the other parents. It feels like he and Missy are getting past something. Even though he doesn't know what.

"Don't you think it's funny that Diane's ex doesn't ever come to the games?" Missy says.

Diane's ex? He has to stop and think about that for a moment. He must have met T at some point. He's Reece's dad, after all; even the Sonnenklars, who hate each other more than Israel and Palestine, switch games so they can see Ben play. "Huh," Randy says, "I guess it is pretty strange. Did he ever come to a meet-and-greet?"

Missy shakes her head.

"Maybe he hates soccer," Randy muses.

"More like he hates Diane," says Missy in a voice that sounds, to him, harder than usual.

"I guess." He puts his glass down. "But Diane is pretty broken up about the divorce. I think she'd do pretty much anything to make it up to him."

"How do you know?" says Missy. Randy bristles a bit. Her tone is sounding suddenly combative.

"Diane talks to me every once in a while." He shouldn't have to feel defensive, he tells himself. He never did anything. *This very kitchen. Diane's hand on his dick.* Yeah. He thought about it. What man married for twelve years wouldn't pause? But did he follow up? No. Well, sort of. But only because he had been so flattered. He doesn't know if he would have done anything if she had followed through. Which she never did, so he's in the clear there.

"She talks to you?" Missy says in that same hard tone.

"I'm an approachable guy. Lots of people talk to me," he says.

Missy practically snorts. "Like who else?"

His mind flashes on Laney, legs up on her desk, a flash of thigh. Their stoned talks. He feels a kind of giddy pride that someone as exotic as Laney likes to spend time with him. Is genuinely interested in him. And he wants to share it with Missy. *Yes, there is someone who talks to me. Who is interested in what I have to say.*

"Um. Sam Reidel at work. I'm still in touch with Mike Terry. His dog just died," he says. "And. Okay. Jacqui talks to me."

"Jacqui doesn't talk to anyone," says Missy, taking another sip. He thinks she should slow down. Maybe it's just the wine that's making her voice sound sharp and her face look pointy.

"Jacqui talks all the time," he says.

"Sure. But she doesn't *say* anything."

"I don't think that's true."

"Okay. Calvin's autistic?"

Why is she asking it like it's a question? "What does Calvin's autism have to do with anything?"

"She never says anything about it."

"Maybe that's private for her. There are lots of things that *you* don't talk about," he says. "You're a big mystery." It's out before he can take it back. He thinks he sees a flash in her eye. Then it disappears. Why the hell did he say that? Sure, he wants answers, but then she'd get her chance to hurl her own questions at him.

"Anyway," he says quickly, "we don't know that Calvin is autistic. Steve's an odd guy. Maybe he's just like Steve."

"All I'm saying is that you can't count Jacqui as someone who"—she air quotes—"'talks to you.'"

Randy senses an inherent silliness and even a bit of potential danger in this exchange. But he can't stop himself. "Okay. How's this? Paul Pousaint talks to me. He told me that he had a string of affairs and his wife hates him and he lives in that house with his hating wife because he's Catholic and he can't leave his kids."

He looks to see if this lands. Missy flinches and stares at him wide-eyed. "Wow," she says. "Really?" He can't tell if she's shocked or impressed. Or both. "He told you that? Why would anyone tell *anyone* that?"

There. Randy is vindicated. He watches Missy mull over this new information.

"How many affairs?" she asks slowly. The sting in her voice gone.

"Lots and lots, apparently. And I think I may be overstating it when I say 'affairs,' sounds more like one-night stands."

"Why?" she asks. The dimmed track lighting makes one side of her face glow, like she's wearing a *Phantom of the Opera* mask.

"He got passed over for a promotion at work."

"That's all?"

"It sounds like that started a whole chain reaction."

Randy thinks that this might be the best conversation he and Missy have had in a year. Last night they had pretty great sex by anyone's standards, and now they're having a deep talk. Who else can he tell her about? Paul was a juicy one.

"So yes," Randy says. "People talk to me."

"And Diane is one of them."

"Sure. Diane talks to me."

"So then, you must know that she's been sleeping with Alejandro?"

"What?" he says, before he can stop himself. What? Diane? *Diane?* Impossible. A month ago she was here, right here in this kitchen. Right here. Her breath in his ear. Her hand on him. All her e-mails. Begging him to be honest with Missy. Her anguish about her divorce. At practices, giving a random hug or two. She even patted his behind once. Or maybe he imagined that. Sure, you could say they didn't talk much face-to-face, but that didn't mean they weren't close. How could she have kept this from him? How could he not have guessed?

Missy is talking. He hears "such an asshole." But he can't bring his mind back to the conversation. He is reviewing every exchange he can possibly remember with Diane. "I'm the wrecker, not the fixer," she wrote once. Had she been warning him? Warning him about what? Diane hasn't exactly betrayed him. But yes, she has. She owes him. He told her everything. And he assumed, just *assumed* that she was telling him everything too. "Goes against some code of ethics," he hears Missy say.

And she rattles on and on and on as they turn off the lights and stash their wineglasses on the draining board.

Up the stairs, he follows his wife. Her narrow behind swaying above his head as his mind replays every image he has of Diane—like a funeral video of a deceased loved one.

In the bedroom. Lights dimmed, clothes off, and pajamas on. "Of course, Alejandro probably isn't the only one," she says—and more—taking breaks from her teeth brushing and rinsing.

Later that night, Missy and Randy will lie on their backs. Close but not touching. Unable to sleep. Thinking of others. Missy of Alejandro. Randy of Diane. And all the signs that they missed.

CHAPTER 42

From: FavoriteCoach@gmail.com
To: Visorgrl@mac.com, DPlatt@ca.rr.com   sent Mon, Oct 25 7:55 pm

Subject: Re: Off topic

Hi Diane (and Jacqui). Randy here. I guess I should thank you for warning Jacqui and I about getting too enthusiastic in our e-mails last night. No one else called us out for it, so I guess it's kind of the way that you read it, and don't forget that Jacqui and I are kind of like the Mom and Dad of the whole team, and we get a little "verklempt" at seeing our boys triumph! And Jacqui (Hi Jacqui!) I know, worries about how they will react if they lose (notice I used the word "if"). We take different roles and even do a good cop/bad cop routine, like we've had to do with Ben when he calls the other team douchebags and assholes. I come down hard and then Jacqui cleans up by being understanding. By the end of us double teaming him like that, he's sorry and won't do it again. It works!!!!

Teams work best when we think of them as a family, including the parents. Which is something to think about. Should one member of our family be sleeping with another member of our family? Only you can answer that.

There's probably more to discuss. But I will leave it at that for right now.

Go Manatees.
Coach

Keep Breathing

———

From: Visorgrl@mac.com
To: FavoriteCoach@gmail.com, DPlatt@ca.rr.com

                                                     sent Mon, Oct 25 8:01 pm

Subject: Re: Off topic

Hi Randy (and Diane),

I'm a little confused about "sleeping with"? Are you talking about league regulations regarding sexual relations between parents? Is this a real situation or something you are anticipating? Let me know so that I'm informed at our next Team Mom meeting! Plus, I'm just curious!!!! ☺

XO,
Jacqui

———

From: FavoriteCoach@gmail.com
To: Visorgrl@mac.com, DPlatt@ca.rr.com   sent Mon, Oct 25 8:07 pm

Subject: Re: Off topic

Hi Jacqui (and Diane),

Don't worry about bringing anything up at the meeting, Jacqui! Seriously, don't! I'm just talking about families and what we're striving for here in the league. Good clean family fun and a family type atmosphere where adults behave accordingly, right? I mean, I can't smoke a joint after practice, right? That wouldn't be responsible behavior as the dad of my team "family". And I can't make-out with someone's mom right in front of them. We don't do that in families!!! Unless you're Italian from Italy (not the states). But Italy and France have their own rules and we don't live there!!!

Randy

Keep Breathing

From: Visorgrl@mac.com
To: FavoriteCoach@gmail.com, DPlatt@ca.rr.com

sent Mon, Oct 25 8:09 pm

Subject: Re: Off topic

Hi Randy (and Diane),

Oh yes, I love all those Italian and French movies. and I agree that it's a whole different culture. ☺

XO,
Jacqui

CHAPTER 43

DIANE READS RANDY'S LOONY LETTER to her about not sleeping with someone from the team "family"—cc'd to Jacqui. What a mess. Missy must have told him about Diane's relationship with Alejandro. Which she had initially feared, but maybe it's for the best. Cards on the table.

Diane sits back in her desk chair and exhales. Spins around to review what was the den, and is shortly to be her office. T's entertainment center has been pulled out by a couple of guys she found outside Office Depot. The exposed wall is battered and three paint swatches are taped up next to the light switch. Jamaica Bay. Gutsy Grape. Forward Fuchsia. She still can't make up her mind. She wants to be gutsy, but will probably settle for the safe sky blue of Jamaica Bay.

It occurs to her that the state of her house accurately reflects her state of mind in general. There are plenty of beliefs she should be purging along with old things. Beliefs about how a life is lived. She decides that she'll give that more thought later and spins back to her desk.

She takes another sip from her glass, and rereads Randy's letter before she answers.

From: DPlatt@ca.rr.com
To: FavoriteCoach@gmail.com   sent Mon, Oct 25 8:53 pm

Subject: Re: Off topic

Dear Randy,

First of all, notice that I have taken Jacqui off of this thread because your emails seem specifically addressed to me, regarding a relationship I am having with Alejandro.

I am sorry I didn't say anything about A. No, forget it, I'm not sorry. I feel like I'm supposed to say that. But really, Randy, it's none of your business. I'm an adult and even though A is younger, so is he. You know what, it's not even a "relationship". We're simply having a few laughs. And, as someone who has said that I deserve to be happy (I think you said something like that once), you should be glad that I'm not my miserable, cranky self.

My situation with A will play itself out eventually, as these things do. So it's hardly worth talking about. But I do think that maybe this gives me a chance to talk to you on a more honest level. I mean, either you are going to continue being my friend (and be somewhat supportive) or you are going to act like we never confided in each other. I can live with either.

So here's the deal, Randy. Regardless of how fucked up my life might seem right now. Screwing a 23 year old and tearing apart my whole house, at least I am MOVING FORWARD! I'm not criticizing you, I'm really not. But Randy, you have to stop burrowing yourself into the ground and praying that life will fix itself around you.

According to you, you have no money, no real job, and a wife who is clueless. And your son now thinks that you can solve everything like a damn superhero. What is going to happen when it all blows up? Take action.

Talk to Missy. Have a plan. Sell your house or refinance, if that is what it takes. Admit where you are and lean on each other.

And when life hands you a moment of deep understanding, take it! I had several of those moments just recently, in re-doing the house. Moments when I fully understood that T isn't ever, ever coming back to me. Ever. Ever. Ever. And that this house thing was an almost ritualistic act of moving on. It's painful to face reality, but it's also a relief. Stop writing lists about what you are good at, and write a list about what is true for you right now.

That's it, Randy. That's all I've got.

Diane

_____

She sends, raises her glass, and spins in her chair to face the room again. The swatches by the light switch. Three stacks of papers to be thrown out, towering up from the Persian rug. A collection of ceramic eggs in a box by the door.

Her dismantled past. There is so little that's worth saving. Which might have felt sad to her, weeks ago. But now she feels this great sense of making space for things that *do* matter. And, right now, there are only two.

Reece and Sabine.

_____

Steve is still reading when Jacqui gets up to the bedroom. Downstairs, she signed off of the computer—had a brownie—and now, she might feel like having sex. The pot helps a great deal in the sex department, ever since Steve started growing hair out of his ears and nose and gaining weight from all the cooking he does.

"I think that some of the parents on the team might be having affairs," she says for an opener, walking past him and into the closet to take off her shoes and skort.

"Who?" Steve says loudly.

That got his attention. She pulls her T-shirt over her head and lets it drop. "I don't know. Randy just mentioned it in an e-mail."

"How on earth would Randy know?"

Steve's voice has that superior sound that he always gets when he talks about Randy or anyone else she volunteers with.

"He's super involved with the team," she says, deciding to take off her panties as a subtle invitation. She pulls on a short nightgown.

"Right," he mumbles.

She walks into the closet, hearing some jostling on the bed. He's probably turning out his light. She reaches into her drawer, finds the massage oil, and pours it carefully into her palm, trying not to spill any on the carpet. "Who do you think might be having an affair?" she asks behind the closet door, keeping her tone casual but staying on the topic of sex.

She places her oily palm between her legs and rubs, slipping her fingers into her vagina. Sparking desire so that Steve will have to do very little to finish things.

"How should I know who's having an affair?" he yells. "I barely know any of them. What about that single mom? The one who's always late?"

"Diane?" She slides her finger out and glides it over to her clitoris. Swirls it around. Tightens her butt as she grabs on to the dresser. Imagines hot breath down there.

"Yeah. I think so. She's got the look."

Jacqui widens her stance and pushes her hips forward. "What look?" she says, seeing Diane's face. Diane, touching her breasts. Someone else's hot breath between her legs—a stranger who just happened to walk into the closet.

And a man behind her. Paul Pousaint, maybe, pressing his penis against her ass. No, not Paul. Alejandro, pressing his cock into her ass.

His strong arms strapped across her chest, while Diane continues to run her tongue around her nipples.

"That look that says she would have sex with almost anyone who asked," he yells.

"Well." She gasps, removing her hand before she comes and wiping the oily excess off on her thigh. "I'm not sure how many people would ask." She smooths down her nightgown and walks into the dark bedroom, wet and throbbing.

She slips between the covers. The mass that is Steve adjusts. Her hand travels over and under soft cotton to find him.

"Listen," he says in a different tone, "I went ahead and scheduled a sit-down with Applebaum and the school psychologist next week. We should start working on this before he goes to middle school."

She stops her hand. Everything retracts. Even the wetness between her legs seems to dry up instantly.

"Okay," she says tightly. "I don't think Applebaum..."

"Let's just hear what they have to say," says the mass.

"I said 'okay.' Okay?"

Now it is his hand that travels, over her thigh. But Jacqui rolls away from him and draws her knees up to her chest.

CHAPTER 44

From: MSonnenklar@GSachs.com

To: Manatees   sent Tues, Oct 26 8:45 am

Subject: Re: Manatees raise the roof!!!

The kids deserved their victory on Sunday and hats off to the coaches. I suggest hiring Alejandro for an extra hour after practice for all the playoff weeks.

M

———

From: PPousaint@mac.com

To: MSonnenklar@GSachs.com   sent Tues, Oct 26 11:03 am

Subject: Re: Manatees raise the roof!!!

I'm in

———

From: Visorgrl@mac.com

To: MSonnenklar@GSachs.com   sent Tues, Oct 26 11:04 am

Subject: Re: Manatees raise the roof!!!

What a great idea!!!! ☺ We're in!!!

From: Alejandro.Navaro@Pepperdine.edu
To: MSonnenklar@GSachs.com   sent Tues, Oct 26 12:11 pm

Subject: Re: Manatees raise the roof!!!

I will do this, with pleasure.

From: MSonnenklar@GSachs.com
To: Manatees   sent Tues, Oct 26 12:17 pm

Subject: Re: Manatees raise the roof!!!

Great. I'll set it up.

From: ParadiseB@gmail.com
To: MSonnenklar@GSachs.com   sent Tues, Oct 26 12:20 pm

Subject: Re: Manatees raise the roof!!!

Dashiell will love it!

From: JWoo@DesignX.com

To: MSonnenklar@GSachs.com   sent Tues, Oct 26 12:24 pm

Subject: Re: Manatees raise the roof!!!

This is good for Patrick and his skill.

———————

From: DPlatt@ca.rr.com

To: MSonnenklar@GSachs.com   sent Tues, Oct 26 12:36 pm

Subject: Re: Manatees raise the roof!!!

Count Reece in!

———————

From: Mako@Shakrayoga.org

To: MSonnenklar@GSachs.com   sent Tues, Oct 26 12:39 pm

Subject: Re: Manatees raise the roof!!!

Yes. We're behind Mason and the team 100%. This is a good way to model "going that extra mile"

OneStopOffice
CORPORATION

Mr. Randy Tinker
42 S. Maple Street
Beverly Hills, CA 90212

Dear Mr Tinker,

Listed below are several charges to your corporate credit card account that need to be verified.

Please give the name of the account, lead executive, and a brief statement of purpose for each charge that is flagged.

While OneStopOffice does not require advance clearance for purchases, we reserve the right to verify when charges appear excessive or unrelated to company business. We will review your response and contact you if the accounting department determines any charges you have made to be invalid. We will require you to immediately compensate the company for any and all such charges and interest accrued on the account due to these charges.

We look forward to your response to this inquiry within five business days. Thank you for your swift response.

DATE	REF	VENDOR	AMOUNT
08-17	WT1487349	UNITED AIRIN FLT SVC – UA347	$16.40
08-17	WT1480021	HILTON DEN CO GST 34987-AR	27.90
08-17	WT1489132	JAY'S TKTS VEN 47658T9079 DEN CO	789.00
08-17	WT1486194	TKT MSTER EVENT DEN342 DEN CO	875.00
08-17	WT1482241	BBQ WILLIE'S DENVER CO	267.46
08-17	WT1489081	BRIGHT EVENT VENDORS CRS FD DEN CO	47.00
08-17	WT1484627	HILTON DEN CO GST 34987 AR	47.69
08-18	WT1487797	JAY'S TKTS VEN 476793R9090 DEN CO	650.75
08-19	WT1481239	HUDSON EXPRESS STORE 5674 – LAXT3	34.13
08-22	WT1482768	TKT MSTER EVENT LA8172 LA CA	290.90
08-24	WT1485177	COFFEE SHACK CULV CITY 90232 EE499	29.49
08-25	WT1487388	HILTON FLAGSTAFF AZ GST 34987-AR	27.97
08-25	WT1487090	TKT MSTER EVENT FL145 FLG AZ	275.00
08-26	WT1482005	AZ FUN TKTS FLAGSTAFF AZ VEN 998034	175.00
08-26	WT1481744	HILTON FLAGSTAFF AZ GST 34987-AR	23.50
08-27	WT1481334	HUDSON EXPRESS STORE 5674 – LAXT3	28.15
08-29	WT1487007	CHEAPTX4U.COM 783992878289 FARGO ND	210.00
08-29	WT1481444	CHEAPTX4U.COM 783992878376 FARGO ND	380.00
08-29	WT1488281	TKT MSTER EVENT LA8281 LA CA	245.65
08-30	WT1483338	TKT MSTER EVENT LA8297 LA CA	190.65
08-30	WT1481433	TKT MSTER EVENT LA8306 LA CA	247.65
08-30	WT1487163	COFFEE SHACK CULV CITY 90232 EE499	28.44
08-31	WT1486616	COFFEE SHACK CULV CITY 90232 EE499	10.80

Regards,

Ray Blackburn

Ray Blackburn
Accounting Department
OneStopOffice Corporation
739 La Jolla Drive
Suite 222
Los Angeles, CA 90042

WELLS FARGO
ADVISORS

CONFIRMATION OF TRANSFER OF FUNDS

Mr. Randy Tinker
42 S. Maple Street
Beverly Hills, CA 90212

Dear Mr. Tinker,

This letter is to serve as confirmation of the requested transfer of funds from:

WF4087 297-TIN-3008 CD   Fund Type: Long Term

AMOUNT: $27,480.31 (Account Liquidated)

Transferred to:

WF 02937146   Account Type: Private Checking

This account (WF4087 297-TIN-3008 CD) is now considered closed.

Wells Fargo thanks you for allowing us to be your bank for all your financial needs and concerns. If you are in need of any further assistance with this transfer, please do not hesitate to call us at 800-990-7100 or visit us on the web at www.wellsfargo.com/accounts.

Thank You,

Charlotte Simmons

Charlotte Simmons
VP Investments
Wells Fargo Bank
333 S. Grand Avenue
Los Angeles, CA 90731

CHAPTER 45

JUNG-AH WOO WATCHES THE COACH pace in the grassy area behind their apartment building. He wonders why the coach hasn't simply left already, but the motivations of this man are always mysterious. Jung-ah quickly glances toward the kitchen to make sure his wife doesn't catch him looking outside. If Mi-ran realizes that the coach hasn't left yet, she will go down and invite him back upstairs. She feels that it is an honor that Coach Randy takes such an interest in Patrick and she would be angry that Jung-ah was letting the man pace out there all alone, in the dark.

Jung-ah does not share his wife's opinion. Of course, he is happy that Patrick is the star of the team. He is also happy that Coach Randy spotted the boy's talent in the Hancock Park league and introduced himself after a game, offering the plan of using Jung-ah's work address as a home address, so Patrick could play in Beverly Hills. All this, as Mi-ran says, is the way to get ahead. But Jung-ah feels that Randy's interest in his son is too conspicuous. Draws attention to the boy and to the family. And, while the Woos are doing nothing that many other families aren't doing, lying about their residence (lying about anything, really) makes Jung-ah feel vulnerable.

Not that he would say anything like this to Mi-ran. Weakness is not a thing she understands—or *allows* herself to understand. He has seen her eyes get soft, even tearful. But as soon as she feels him looking she adjusts her face, like a mask.

Jung-ah hears her start the dishwasher and quickly moves away from the window. He finds himself standing in a strange place between the coffee table and the black chair when she comes in. She stops and looks at him. There is no reason for him to be in this spot and he isn't thinking fast enough to make something up.

She asks him if Patrick has started on his homework yet. And Jung-ah leaps on the thought. Yes, he tells her, he will check on Patrick now. And he starts down the hall before she can ask him why he is standing next to the coffee table with nothing to do.

Outside Patrick's door, he pauses to knock softly. Jung-ah has noticed that when he enters his son's room unannounced, the boy seems unusually agitated, like he's been doing something wrong. But what can a ten-year-old boy possibly be doing that is so wrong in his own bedroom? Patrick is just jumpy. He's always been jumpy. The type to look over his shoulder all the time.

Jung-ah opens the door and Patrick is at his desk already with his books open. He is still wearing his cleats from having practiced with the coach. Mi-ran would tell him to take them off, but Jung-ah is not going to mention it. What's important is that the boy is already at work.

Jung-ah tells him to put on the desk light. There is not enough light from the overhead. Jung-ah walks over to switch it on, and sees what Patrick can see from his desk. The coach is still out there. He has stopped pacing and is simply standing, looking across the street. Not moving. His pose suggesting that he's making a decision or trying to remember something. Patrick must have noticed that the coach is still there.

Jung-ah turns on the light and chooses not to say anything about the coach. He pats the boy on the shoulder and reminds him to put the cleats in the closet when he gets ready for bed.

Yes, his son says. He won't forget.

Jung-ah stands for a moment, gazing at his boy. He puts his hand back on Patrick's shoulder and says, "Your mother and I enjoy watching you play soccer."

Patrick turns, looks up at him, and gives him a slight smile. Jung-ah smiles back before he turns and walks out the door, closing it gently behind him. He walks down the hall and into the living room to watch TV with Mi-ran. She is watching her religious show on the Korean channel. He tells her that Patrick was already working on his math. He doesn't tell her about the cleats. And he sits in his chair.

On the screen is an evangelical minister whom Mi-ran particularly likes. She sends him money for his lunch program in the orphanages. Even though her daughter would be thirteen by now and adopted by someone who had the actual resources to take care of her, he knows that Mi-ran still thinks that she might be sending her own girl some food. He knows that she lost part of her heart when her parents took her daughter away. Mi-ran can be hard, but Jung-ah knows that it is because of what she learned then. Softness only brings you pain.

Jung-ah takes off his glasses and pinches his nose. The images on the screen are fuzzy now. But he doesn't need glasses to know that Mi-ran is scanning faces of the orphans, looking for someone who could be hers.

Outside, Randy considers where to go next. He's already texted Missy that he's working late. This not only relieves him of the burden of acting sunny after having finally drained their savings account entirely, but also gives her the impression that work at OneStopOffice is busy and, therefore, good.

He bounces on his toes, thinking about his practice session with Patrick. What would it be like, he wonders, to be that undeniably good at something? People would love you automatically because of it. If Patrick becomes a big soccer star, he'll get girls, money, guy friends who want to be around him all the time. Why are some people blessed and others not? Why wasn't Calvin given that kind of talent? Or Aiden? Aiden's got the raw material. Strong legs, stamina. But not the God-given talent. Randy takes out his phone and scrolls through his contacts.

FROM: RTINKER
TO: PPOUSAINT

Are you available to meet and go over
plays?

In his den, Paul picks up his phone and reads the text. Marianne is upstairs in their bedroom, watching a Disney movie on TV with both kids snuggled on either side of her. Envisioning the scene turns him inside out with loss.

FROM: PPOUSAINT
TO: RTINKER

Sure, where? Or over the phone?

He hears one of the children walking down the hallway to the bathroom. "Don't start it again until I'm back." Claude's voice. A click of a switch and light spills down the staircase.

FROM: RTINKER
TO: PPOUSAINT

Can I come over there?

FROM: PPOUSAINT
TO: RTINKER

Really? After everything I told you about
what's going on here?

FROM: RTINKER
TO: PPOUSAINT

Right. OK. A dark bar?

FROM: PPOUSAINT
TO: RTINKER

Why dark?

FROM: RTINKER
TO: PPOUSAINT

Right. A light one then.

FROM: PPOUSAINT
TO: RTINKER

Where?

FROM: RTINKER
TO: PPOUSAINT

PINZ

FROM PPOUSAINT
TO: RTINKER

The bowling alley?

FROM: RTINKER
TO: PPOUSAINT

Beer and pizza there.

———————

The bathroom light goes off and he hears Claude running down the hall. Paul pictures him jumping back into bed, Marianne putting her slim arm around his son's shoulders and picking up the remote to start the movie again. He stands up from his desk and grabs his keys.

———————

As Paul suspected, the roster and plays are not what Randy really wants to talk about. Although what is actually on the man's mind is hard to say. They do manage to make a couple of substitutions and change the formation from a 4-2-2 to a 4-3-1.

Randy ordered another pitcher when Paul went to the john and now Paul feels stuck, enduring a vague sense of responsibility for the guy along with the ambivalence he now realizes comes with having nothing to go home to. The beer isn't cold enough and Paul looks around for a soothing curve of breast or ass to rest his eyes on.

None. Except on the bartender, whose sharp movements project fatigue and all-business. Paul turns back to Randy, who is saying, "...but Aiden's always been that guy. He waits until the last minute and then is surprised when there's a ton of work left to do." What's Randy going on about? "I mean, the kid doesn't know that life isn't going to just hand you the keys, am I right?"

"Right." Paul wishes he could check his phone for the time without seeming rude.

"Sorry." Randy reaches over and touches Paul's arm. "I'm not much of a drinker, so I'm feeling a little. You know." He raises a finger and loops it around his ear.

"It's okay," Paul says. "Although you should probably Uber."

Randy pours himself another glass. Balls thunk and roll down alleys. Pins are knocked down. Paul hears, "Hell yeah!"

Randy sips and looks out at the bowlers. "God, it must be easy to be them."

And even though Paul's instinct is to avoid being drawn in, he's here and he can practically smell the man's suffering. "Oh, I don't know," he says. "Everyone has their own burden."

"They don't look very burdened."

"Looks are deceitful," Paul says.

"Huh. I guess that's true." Randy seems to consider the thought like it's brand-new to him. Then he quickly throws back another swig of beer and says, "Did you know Diane was sleeping with Al?"

Paul flinches at the unexpected left turn in Randy's thinking. "No. But it doesn't surprise me."

"It doesn't?"

"For all I know, Alejandro is bagging half of the moms on the team. I would, in his shoes."

"There should be rules about that." Randy takes another sip and sets down his glass. His upper lip glistens.

Paul feels for his phone in his jacket pocket. "How's the job going?" he asks in a *let's wrap this up* tone.

"Oh. Great. Great. Thanks for that one. I owe you. I'd love to get on the Mozart drive once Baroque is over."

Paul doesn't say anything. Makes no promises to intercede.

"You going?" Randy says, a bit foggy. But not too far gone, Paul figures.

"I was thinking about it. You want a ride home?"

"No."

"Honestly? You shouldn't drive."

"I'll Uber," Randy says, pouring more beer from the pitcher.

"You're sure you will?"

Randy points his fingers at him like a gun and fake-shoots the air. "Oh, I'm a man of my word. I really am."

"Sure," Paul says softly. Feeling kind. "I believe that."

"You're the only one," Randy says on a laugh.

These are the jokes men tell each other and don't mean. Paul knows the groove, so he counters as he slides out of the booth, "That's why you're paying me the big bucks." He glances down at Randy to say goodbye.

Randy looks up, his face is soft, and says, "I made a mess of things, didn't I?"

Paul pats him on the shoulder. "See you later, sport."

Before Paul can get his hand away, Randy reaches up and holds it. Paul feels compelled to stand there for a moment waiting for Randy to continue. Which he does. "I wish I could start over, you know?"

Paul slides his hand from Randy's grasp. And in a moment that will keep him up tonight in the den, replaying it until he gives in to sleeplessness and turns on the light and the TV to blot it out, he says, "Don't we all."

CHAPTER 46

From: KSonn@gmail.com
To: MSonnenklar@GSachs.com   sent Tue, Oct 26 5:38 pm

Subject: Co-parenting/The same page

Hello Mark,

I'm writing to you to open a cooperative dialogue between us regarding Ben and what he needs. I may never be able to forgive you for such a classic, mid-life betrayal of the wife who wasted the best years of her life on you—but I do recognize the need for us both to come together for our son. It is very hard for me to admit that our open fighting has infected Ben and is probably the primary reason that he has anger issues. Of course, it should have been obvious, but I let Ben see my pain because I wanted him to know who the guilty party was in all of this.

I am going to stop sharing my resentment of you and Kelli with him, and I respectfully ask you to stop sharing your feelings about me with him. I think that's the best place to start.

Secondly, I think that you and I should make joint decisions about discipline and expectations. When Kelli gets in there, things get confusing. I'm not saying this out of anger (although there's plenty), but out of practicality.

Thirdly, we have to start thinking about Middle School placement. Ben probably needs a tutor for the big test. I suggest that you and I split payment for that.

Please let me know that you received this and please add your thoughts about moving forward in a way that benefits our child.

Karen

_____

From: Visorgrl@mac.com

To: Manatees   sent Tue, Oct 26 5:44 pm

Subject: Extra practice with Alejandro YAY!

It looks like almost everyone is IN for Alejandro's special soccer clinic (I'm calling it that!) after our usual practice this week. So make sure that you pack a snack and extra water for your kid. I'm not going to assign an extra snack shift for the three soccer clinics that we have scheduled because, I can't keep reminding people about that on top of all the other reminding I do!!

Mark is collecting the money for Alejandro, so if you haven't gotten to him yet, don't forget!!! I can't keep that list and keep up all my duties as Team Mom, it's too much! I'm serious! I hope everyone understands. Thanks Mark!!!!!

XOXOXO,
Jacqui

_____

From: MSonnenklar@GSachs.com
To: KSonn@gmail.com   sent Tue, Oct 26 5:50 pm

Subject: Re: Co-parenting/The same page

K,

I am confirming that I got your e-mail and also that we are on the same
page. I will share your plan with Kelli. I'm sure she will comply, since it is in
line with what she has been proposing for a while.

Let me know if you can switch this coming Tuesday with Thursday. Kelli
and I have a dinner. If you can't, we will get a sitter.

M

CHAPTER 47

THE PARENTS HAVE DECIDED THAT the boys will take a half-hour break between practice and Alejandro's clinic. Lately it's been getting dark before the practice ends. They can only see the darkness on the periphery, however. Here on the field, the night has been flushed out by floodlights, paid for by the municipality of Beverly Hills.

Reece feels his mother watching him as he tips the ball back and forth to Patrick, Ben, and Aiden. She's standing next to Alejandro, who keeps whispering in her ear. Reece is pretty proud of the fact that Alejandro comes over to practice English and play Scrabble with his mom sometimes. He bets the other kids would like their moms to hang out with the coolest semiprofessional coach in the league. But when Reece told Ben and Aiden about it, Ben made an inappropriate sexual gesture with his hands and Reece decided it was better not to mention it to kids who obviously don't understand.

Reece misses Aiden's sorry pass and has to go running after the ball. As he dribbles it back, he turns his attention to his crew. Patrick was just telling them about how he can find Aiden's *Minecraft* book. It mysteriously vanished from Aiden's backpack when he brought it to practice three weeks ago. Everyone looked for it, even under the bleachers. But nada.

"I'm telling you. I can find it with my mind," Patrick is saying again, when Reece gets back to them. Patrick side-passes to Aiden without looking. Aiden misses, of course. And Reece has to stand there waiting for him to run after the ball. He glances over at Ben throwing his hands up at having to wait for Aiden and parking himself on the bottom bench of the bleachers.

"You can't find a book with your mind," Reece says to Patrick while he watches Aiden huff it.

"I can too," says Patrick, feet apart with his hands on his hips.

Ben, on the bleachers, snorts and tosses his head.

Reece's shoulders stiffen at Ben's obvious scorn for Patrick, who is a better soccer player by far, *and* a much better person.

"Okay," Reece says to Patrick, giving the guy a chance. "Prove it. Go ahead and find the book right now, and we'll watch."

Patrick raises his hand to Aiden dribbling the ball back. "Hey, pass!" And Aiden kicks the ball. Patrick stops it clean with his foot and reaches down to pick it up. "Follow me." Reece catches Aiden's eyes halfway across the field, nodding in Patrick's direction, and Aiden nods back. Then he glances back at the bleachers to find that Ben is apparently interested enough to get up off the bench and follow.

Behind the bleachers it's a lot cooler. Shaded from the floodlights, it feels like a damp basement. Patrick turns to look at Reece and Ben. Aiden appears between the two of them, breathing heavily.

"Patrick's going to find your book," Reece announces to Aiden. And immediately he regrets saying it like it's a done deal. Because if Patrick doesn't succeed, Ben will never let him forget it.

"How's he going to do that?" says Aiden, getting hold of his breath.

"It's a trick," Reece says, figuring he might as well double down. "You'll see."

"Okay," says Patrick, getting their attention and holding up his hands like a magician settling the crowd. "You have to be quiet and be still the whole time. Until I come back into my body."

Reece looks over at Aiden and they both shrug. "Okay." "Whatever."

Ben says, "Yeah, right," but stays planted.

They watch Patrick sit on the ground cross-legged.

Reece makes himself stand still even though he feels nervous for Patrick. He watches as Patrick begins to breathe very quickly. He sees the boy's tummy going in and out really fast. Reece feels a tingle of excitement in his own belly. Wow. Patrick's doing *something*, all right.

Reece steals a quick look at Ben, who is staring transfixed. Then he slides his glance over to Aiden, who is watching openmouthed. And back to Patrick, whose body is breathing faster and faster, faster and faster. Like he's going to pop his mind right out of the top of his head. Reece starts to worry that Patrick's going to just pass out and that will get the parents all crazy. His mom, for one, is going to ask a million questions. She never, never lets things go.

But then.

It stops. Patrick's heavy breathing stops.

Or seems to stop.

Patrick's face goes blank, like he's not even there.

Reece can barely breathe himself. His heart pounds while he watches, waiting for some ghostly-looking thing to rise like smoke from Patrick. But nothing does. The only thing that's freaky is the totality of Patrick's stillness. Like he's a sitting-up dead person.

Reece darts his eyes sideways. Sees Aiden's hand twitch. Past him, Ben is stone still. Beyond the bleachers, out there somewhere, Reece hears Alejandro rounding the boys up for the clinic.

His body wants to obey and run back to the field, but he doesn't know how to leave Patrick. What should he do? The adults will wonder what's going on. They'll come looking. Should he go up to Patrick and say something? Like what? *Hey, buddy, hope your mind comes back soon, but we have to run?*

In that moment of deciding, however, Reece sees a change come over Patrick. His face starts to move. His back arches slightly. He takes his hands off his knees in a floaty way, like they aren't attached, and opens his eyes.

Thank God. Reece's shoulders relax and he's starting to turn back to the field when Patrick smiles and says, "I found it!"

"You did not," says Aiden. He looks almost scared or something.

Patrick jumps up from the ground, acting jittery, and starts leaping and skipping over to a recycling bin. They all run after him.

Something inside Reece lifts up as he's running. It's like crazy hope. Hope that this is all real. What if you can really slip outside of your own body? Then you wouldn't have to be stuck in only one place, doing only one thing. Just think. He could be doing his homework while he's entering a computer game with his mind. He could be eating dinner downstairs while his mind listens to iTunes upstairs. He could even be at his father's house and his mother's all at once. The possibilities go on and on.

Patrick gets to the recycling bin and positions himself beside it. He faces the boys, who line up in front of him, ready to affirm his powers once he follows through.

Patrick raises up a hand with a flourish, then way too slowly reeeeeeeeeaches behind the bin and—

Behold! Pulls out the olive-green *Minecraft* book and holds it up.

They all gasp. Reece shoves away the thought that it could be any- one's *Minecraft* book. He wants that much to believe.

Then, like a dramatic librarian about to read, Patrick lowers the book to present it to Aiden. Before he hands it over, however, Patrick flips open the cover, beckoning the boys with his free hand.

They inch close. Closer. Finally, Reece is close enough to see.

There it is. In the upper-right corner of the first page. Aiden's printing:

AIDEN TINKER

MASTER GAMER

ULTIMATE RULER OF THE UNIVERSE

CHAPTER 48

WHISPERING PINES
A New School for a New Age

Mr. & Mrs. Randy Tinker
42 S. Maple Street
Beverly Hills, CA 90212

Dear Mr. and Mrs. Tinker,

Hello from Whispering Pines.

Regretfully, we have not been able to process the monthly payments on the credit card you have on record for the past 3 months. We have tried repeatedly to resolve the matter over the phone, but as yet we have been unable to reach you in person, and our messages have not been returned.

As a consequence we would like to meet with you both to see what can be done to resolve the matter. If satisfactory arrangements cannot be made soon, we will be forced to terminate Aiden's enrollment at Whispering Pines – an outcome I am sure none of us want.

Please contact the main office ASAP to schedule the meeting to clear up any difficulties and to keep Aiden's academic progress uninterrupted.

Thank you for your swift response,

Cassandra Fortgang

Cassandra Fortgang
Chair, Finance Committee
Whispering Pines School
9201 Del Vado Ave.
Beverly Hills, CA 90210

Integrity Trust Fortitude Light

CHAPTER 49

From: Visorgrl@mac.com

To: Manatees   sent Sat, Oct 30 8:08 pm

Subject: Remember, there are two games left!!!!

Hello team and parents,

The team was awesome today and so brave!!! I was proud of our boys for playing in the rain, and I was also proud of our boys shaking the hands of the other team so nicely, right after losing! ☺ Shaking hands when you're soaking wet is the kind of sportsmanship we're all about!

So let's all give our fine boys extra love tonight for keeping cool under pressure, and remind them that they can still get into the tournament. We only have to win two of the four games and we already won one, so do the math!!!!

Remember Alejandro's clinic this week!!! Alejandro—don't think that all your hard work was wasted just because we lost. Coach, don't stop all of your inspirational speeches just because of one game! I loved the call and response of "WE ARE WHAT?" "UNDEFEATED". Because even if we are defeated on the field, we really aren't in our hearts! ☺

XOXOXOXO,
Jacqui

———————

From: MSonnenklar@GSachs.com
To: Manatees   sent Sat, Oct 30 8:51 pm

Subject: Re: Remember, there are two games left!!!!

What are the regs about playing in the rain? I didn't say anything because I didn't want to lose game points for defying the refs—or whatever the technical term for speaking your mind is. But is there a way to retroactively void the game since the kids shouldn't have been playing anyway?

Drizzle I understand, but that rain was full on.

M

_____

From: DPlatt@ca.rr.com
To: Manatees   sent Sat, Oct 30 9:00 pm

Subject: Re: Remember, there are two games left!!!!

Mark,

Spoken like a true republican! If you don't like the outcome, find a random reason to manipulate the results. The kids lost. Let it go.

Diane

_____

From: MSonnenklar@GSachs.com

To: Manatees   sent Sat, Oct 30 9:17 pm

Subject: Re: Remember, there are two games left!!!!

Diane,

Are you nuts? What do my politics have to do with it? I talked to Randy about the rain before the game even started. My reasoning wasn't then, and isn't now, random. And I don't appreciate wild political aspersions that have no place in a conversation about Junior Soccer League.

M

_____

From: DPlatt@ca.rr.com

To: Manatees   sent Sat, Oct 30 9:18 pm

Subject: Re: Remember, there are two games left!!!!

Hey Mark,

Right you are. Let's leave politics entirely out of it. I shouldn't have had to hear your insanely uninformed riff on the evils of Obamacare before the game today. I was keeping quiet because kids were around and I know how to be polite. In the future, at practices and games, please keep your political opinions to yourself.

Diane

_____

From: MSonnenklar@GSachs.com
To: Manatees   sent Sat, Oct 30 9:19 pm

Subject: Re: Remember, there are two games left!!!!

Diane,

In case you didn't notice, I wasn't talking to you. I was having a personal conversation on the sidelines. I have no interest in talking to you about anything. Much less, politics.

M

From: DPlatt@ca.rr.com
To: Manatees   sent Sat, Oct 30 9:19 pm

Subject: Re: Remember, there are two games left!!!!

M,

Unfortunately, I can still hear your assholery across the entire length of the soccer field.

D

From: MSonnenklar@GSachs.com

To: Manatees   sent Sat, Oct 30 9:20 pm

Subject: Re: Remember, there are two games left!!!!

That is physically impossible. I was speaking in a normal voice to Steve Hirshorn. You could have moved and not heard anything I was saying.

M

———————

From: DPlatt@ca.rr.com

To: Manatees   sent Sat, Oct 30 9:58 pm

Subject: Apologies

Dear team parents,

My deep apologies for taking Mark to task over this group e-mail. I was angry and should have talked to him directly, instead of involving all of you.

Best,
Diane

———————

From: MSonnenklar@GSachs.com

To: Manatees   sent Sat, Oct 30 9:59 pm

Subject: Re: Apologies

Thank you for your apology Diane. I would like to simply state to everyone, that this was not a thread that was started by me. All I was doing was asking about the rain policy, before I was attacked without provocation about my own personal opinions.

M

_____

From: Visorgrl@mac.com
To: Manatees   sent Sat, Oct 30 10:47 pm

Subject: Re: Apologies

Hello everyone,

Let's all take a page from Coach's book and just BREATHE!!!!!!! ☺ I'm getting the feeling that we are blowing off steam because the loss was hard on all of us today. I know that I had to come home and decompress with a long bath and a lot of sugar that I don't need!!!!! I think we need to trust our boys. Calvin is handling all of this pressure better than I am! He's really matured during this season. We're starting a new thing that you might want to try with your boys too. I have him write down any bad feelings he has on a piece of paper, and then we burn the paper, and throw it away before it can set anything on fire. It really works!!! Just remember to have a glass of water close by for safety. I throw the lit paper into a metal saucepan in the sink, but you can also use the toilet. Anyway, Calvin didn't even have to burn his feelings about the game today. He processed them all by himself!!!

I say BREATHE or burn your feelings!!!!!!! I'm sure that Coach Randy will add his inspiring words very shortly.

XOXOXO,
Jacqui

From: PPousaint@mac.com
To: DPlatt@ca.rr.com   sent Sat, Oct 30 10:56 pm

Subject: M Sonnenklar

Diane,

I hope that you don't mind my reaching out to you as the assistant coach and also as a casual friend. Maybe "friend" is overstating it a bit. How about, "fellow parent"?

Now that I've struggled to create context, I can barely remember my point (if I were Jacqui I would put a smiley face here).

Ah yes, my point is that Mark Sonnenklar is a first class dick. But even worse, he's an agitator who simply enjoys getting under people's skin. So attacking him is giving him exactly what he wants.

As a fellow parent, I recommend that you don't engage him further. Also, there are more republican parents in the league than you would probably guess. Even though BH is a seemingly liberal bastion, you'd be surprised at how many people secretly vote their pocket books.

I sympathize with you politically and regarding M's "assholery" (apt term, by the way).

All the best,
Paul

From: DPlatt@ca.rr.com
To: PPousaint@mac.com   sent Sat, Oct 30 11:11 pm

Subject: Re: M Sonnenklar

Hi Paul,

Thanks for your gentle admonishment (received) and your sympathy.
You are a diplomat and a man of reason. Maybe I should try Jacqui's
technique of writing down evil thoughts about Mark and burning them in
my toilet!!! ☺

Warmly,
Diane

_____

From: MSonnenklar@GSachs.com
To: Manatees   sent Sat, Oct 30 11:23 pm

Subject: Re: Remember, there are two games left!!!!

Seriously, I still would like to be clear on the league's rain policy.

M

_____

From: RTChampion@gmail.com
To: DPlatt@ca.rr.com   sent Sat, Oct 30 11:54 pm

Subject: (No Subject)

Hi Diane. Randy here. I was wondering if you were still up. I think that I might need a friend to talk to. Everytime I think of the situation I've gotten myself into, I start to feel so sick I think I'm going to pass out. I need to do something about this anxiety, and maybe just talking it out with you would help.

I would call, but I don't want to wake you up if you are already asleep. If you get this and you can talk, feel free to call me, if you want. And, of course, feel free not to call me if you can't, I understand. I'm really sorry about what I said about you and Al. Don't worry about me if you get this. I'm fine, it's no big deal and I can talk to you later, unless you are up right now, which would be great.

Never mind what I just said, maybe I'm not that fine. I thought I was when I wrote that, and now I'm thinking that I'm going to override myself and say that it would be great if you could call ASAP. I'm having a fluttery thing in my chest, which I don't think is my heart but just anxiety that's kind of out of control.

Thanks,
Randy

CHAPTER 50

DIANE CAN'T SLEEP. SHE'S TOO amped up from taking on Mark on the e-mail thread. At the game, he and Jacqui's milquetoast husband were yakety-yakking about Obama, spewing their misinformed right-wing, patriarchal rhetoric like ejaculate all over the sidelines. Her bystander pissed-offedness had been even more fueled by the fact that she had been honoring the constraints of the setting, while they were ignoring them completely—meaning, the males, Mark and Steve, were saying whatever the hell bullshit they wanted in loud, bombastic voices, while the women had to passively listen, because the only other option would be to start a big-ass political argument on the sidelines and risk losing sportsmanship points or getting kicked off the field.

Fuckers.

So yeah. It feels good to let Mark have it. And she doesn't give a shit if it was "appropriate" or not. At least she let him know that she wasn't a simpering female who was just going to stand there and let him jizz his ignorance all over without repercussions.

Right now, she stands in her almost empty living room, distancing herself from her upstairs office and the phone and the computer. Even though she feels entirely justified, Paul's levelheaded e-mail has cooled her off a bit. And staying out of her laptop's orbit means less possibility of her continuing to spar with fuckwad Mark.

She breathes in, touches her temples, consciously willing herself to disengage. It's no easy task. Because, if she's honest with herself, she has to admit that she gets a charge out of these confrontations—a jolt of energy that is almost sexual. Hell, it *is* sexual. It's connection at its downest and dirtiest.

She closes her eyes for a moment, inhales, and drops her shoulders. Feels the charge in her, still, radiating from her pussy. Exhales. Looks around for something—or other—to rest her mind on.

The room looks larger without the bookshelves, which held only art books with fat spines displaying artists' names, Matisse, Kandinsky, Vermeer. She can't remember ever lifting one of them off the shelves and perusing it.

She sits on the edge of her couch and stares at a blank wall. The ghostly outline of the bookcase barely visible. Old life. Old wife. She smiles to herself.

She hears a couple of taps on the front door. Seriously? At this hour? She knows it's him. Although he always texts to make sure the kids are asleep or away. Her phone is upstairs, however. At least he knows enough not to ring the bell. Good boy.

She quickly goes for the door, soles of her feet meeting slick, cool wood. Despite her best efforts, she's been unable to cut things off entirely with him. Okay—maybe not her *best* efforts.

She peers through the peephole, steps back, and unlatches the top dead bolt. The moonlight shimmers dewy around his head and shoulders. He is shadow but also substance, stepping into the foyer without saying a word. She closes and bolts the door behind him.

"What if I hadn't been sitting down here?" she asks. "What would you have done?"

He turns and shrugs in the dark. "I did not think of that."

Of course he didn't. "Do me a favor, don't ever throw rocks at my window. It doesn't work like it does in the movies."

"I texted."

"I'm sure. I'm trying to get away from my phone. It's upstairs."

He walks into the living room and over to the only lamp left. It's on the floor. Pointing to it. "Can I?"

Diane reflexively glances upstairs. "Yeah. I guess. Sure. They're not going to wake up now."

Alejandro bends to turn it on. And there he is. Illuminated like a gift.

She pulses with desire. Even though she has promised herself she will resist him. Promised herself she will make things right. Set him free, for God's sake. She is not what he wants, but the poor kid doesn't know it. She is tired of feeling duplicitous. For leading him on with motherly comforts. Food. A cool hand on his brow. Occasionally tucking a blanket around him while he dozes on the couch. True, she did not do these things to ensnare. But that has been the result.

It occurs to her that he is not speaking. He is only standing there, looking at her. And for a second she feels a thrill—*he's going to break it off and save me from having to cut the cord!* Absolution.

But it can't be that simple. And instead of ending things, he crosses his arms over his waist and pulls his shirt over his head, dropping it to the floor. Diane's breath is cut short. He is lit from the side, from below, and looks like a statue that she could have found in one of those heavy art books she donated to St. Vincent's yesterday. Adjectives elude her. He is simply, objectively, beautiful.

She stands still, the sweat on the soles of her feet warming the hardwood. Without taking his eyes from hers, he kicks off his shoes. The pulse in her neck jumps. He slides his thumbs into the waistband of his shorts and pulls them down, kicking them easily to the side.

She has to sit. Walks over to the couch and sinks down. Alejandro's cock stiffens. He places his hand on it. She lies back and slips her hand into her pants. She is damp, sliding a finger against her clit. Slippery. Ready. With her other hand she pulls up her T-shirt, showing him her breasts. His hand tightens around the base of his cock.

Slowly, he walks over to her on the couch. Stands above her as she rubs herself. Then sinks to his knees and tugs at her pants. She wiggles free and he parts her legs, placing his hot breathy mouth on her bush. Tongue swirling, he finds the right spot and she gives over, raising her hands above her head and resting them on the back of the couch. He pushes her knees wider apart, lifting her legs over his shoulders and burying his face deeper between her thighs.

There is no reason, she thinks now, why this ever has to stop.

CHAPTER 51

From: FavoriteCoach@gmail.com

To: Manatees   sent Wed, Nov 3 9:39 am

Subject: Some inspiring words from your Coach!!!

Hey team. I forgot to give you some inspirational words to think about for the next three days!!!! Remember to get a good sleep this week, and on Saturday morning eat a good breakfast (but not too much!), and fill up those water bottles. Saturday, we face the Tigers and we've beaten them before, so I'm not worried at all, and remember, even if things start off badly in the game, like they did last week, remember Mark Wahlberg's words in 'Lone Survivor', "No matter how much it hurts, how dark it gets, or how far you fall, you are never out of the fight."

The key phrase is, "You are never out of the fight."

Go Manatees. Keep fighting and I will fight with you!!!!!!

Your coach,
Randy

———————

BRETT PAESEL

From: Visorgrl@mac.com
To: Manatees   sent Wed, Nov 3 9:46 am

Subject: Re: Some inspiring words from your Coach!!!

I heard that Mark Wahlberg is super short in real life, which tells you that even rappers who were famous models and then movie stars, have their problems to overcome!!!!! Nobody looks at Mark Wahlberg and thinks about his shortness. They think about his talent and his arms! ☺

Go Manatees!

XOXO,
Jacqui

From: DPlatt@ca.rr.com
To: Manatees   sent Wed, Nov 3 10:13 am

Subject: Re: Some inspiring words from your Coach!!!

When some of us think about Mark Wahlberg, we think about his arrest and conviction for assault and robbery.

D

From: KSonn@gmail.com
To: MSonnenklar@GSachs.com, Kelli.Sonnenklar@Sonnenklar.com

                            sent Wed, Nov 3 10:30 am

Subject: The game on Saturday

Dear Mark and Kelli,

In the spirit of our new co-parenting agreement, I thought that I would recommend that we attend Ben's next game together, instead of alternating
games. I can get there early and grab a spot close to the sidelines. I think
that it would do Ben good to see us being united in support of him.

Sincerely,
Karen

———————

From: Kelli.Sonnenklar@Sonnenklar.com
To: KSonn@gmail.com, MSonnenklar@GSachs.com

                            sent Wed, Nov 3 10:39 am

Subject: Re: The game on Saturday

dear karen,
we would be super thrilled to be at the same game as you! i'll bring some
pita chips and hummus. also, we have a great umbrella that you can share
with us. well, of course, mark can never sit still during a game, so it will be
just you and me under the umbrella.
this is going to help ben so much! AND mark and i have a surprise for you!

love,
kelli

_____

From: KSonn@gmail.com
To: Kelli.Sonnenklar@Sonnenklar.com, MSonnenklar@GSachs.com
                                sent Wed, Nov 3 10:41 am

Subject: Re: The game on Saturday

Kelli, you might not remember since it's been a long time, but I don't handle surprises well.

Respectfully,
Karen

_____

From: MSonnenklar@GSachs.com
To: KSonn@gmail.com, Kelli.Sonnenklar@Sonnenklar.com
                                sent Wed, Nov 3 10:45 am

Subject: Re: The game on Saturday

Kelli, thanks for trying to make this fun. But Karen is right. She hates surprises. So I think it's best to tell her straight out that you are pregnant.

M

IT TAKES DIANE A FEW seconds to adjust to the dark bar in the middle of the afternoon. She stops right inside the door to get her bearings. The windows are entirely blacked out. A couple of young people (with tons of chains hanging off their jackets) sit on bar stools. No Randy. The girl serving drinks inclines her head and says to Diane, "He's back there."

"Well, thank you," Diane says, in a way that makes her feel like one of those prim but well-meaning nuns who walk the streets trying to rescue prostitutes from "the life."

He's in the last booth, already hunched over a beer. Were she to photograph him, he would be a study in defeatism. The pose is heartbreaking. She had called him after she finally opened his distressed e-mail last night. The one she hadn't read earlier because she had assumed it was another weigh-in on her sex life or another rambling justification for inaction. Over the phone, he had asked to meet her downtown, where she never goes. And she's here against her better judgment (getting more involved in a situation she probably can't do anything about) because it feels cruel to turn down such a naked plea for help.

He looks up and gives her a half-smile. "It's you."

"Of course," she says, still standing.

"I wasn't sure you'd come."

She looks back at the bar. "Let me get a drink."

"It's okay," he says, looking past her and signaling to the girl. "What do you want? They know me here."

Diane slides none-too-smoothly onto the sticky bench opposite him. "Pinot grigio. Or just white wine. Do they have a white wine?"

"Not sure," he says, and starts negotiating with the girl over Diane's shoulder. Apparently they don't have wine at the bar. But they do have three airplane-size bottles of pink zinfandel in the back.

While they wait for two of the minis to be unearthed, Diane glances over her shoulder half a dozen times and lets herself babble about the streets she took downtown. He tells her that his marketing job is located just around the corner. She finds herself wishing that the small talk could go on and on, even though she simultaneously wants him to cut to the chase. Truth is she's only really *known* Randy through his e-mails. In person, they've never transcended superficial niceties, other than the drunken kitchen incident (and one could claim that even that was a superficial encounter). So she's not sure how to turn the conversation toward Randy's e-mail, or even if she wants the conversation to turn. Maybe the crisis has passed and he simply needs to chat about nothing.

The minis arrive. They are room temperature, but she pours two of them into a big red–wineglass that the girl brought while the conversation skims.

"Midafternoon hours are the best for closing a sale," he is saying.

"Of baroque subscriptions? Why? Because you're getting bored housewives?"

"Exactly. Selling the dream that their husband is actually the kind of guy who would want to spend an evening sitting in a cold church, listening to a small ensemble playing classical music, all dressed up with maybe another couple."

"Hmmm. I guess that makes sense." She takes a sip of the godawful wine. "Selling a dream."

"Right," he says, getting more animated now that he's on familiar conversational footing. "It's always about tapping into what you think they want and making your product fit that fantasy."

"Sure," she says. "Sure. Sure." She slides her finger over the lipstick stain on her glass. What little light there is glints off the pink wine, making it glow a bit. She tilts the glass and watches it slide up the side. A dream. That's certainly what she was buying when she married T, wasn't it? An idea of what a happy life is supposed to look like.

"...so I can't stall anymore."

She places the glass back on the table. "I'm sorry. 'Can't stall'?"

"Yeah. The cat's about to jump out of the bag."

"What cat?"

"Did you hear what I just said?" he says, a little louder.

"Selling the dream, right?"

"Right. I was talking about *our* dream. Missy's and mine. To send Aiden to Whispering Pines."

"Oh, right. Of course," she says, taking a sip. She and T had considered Whispering Pines, but for two kids it would have been insanely expensive. Even though they had the money, there were better investments.

"But, of course, I haven't been paying tuition now for three months."

"Of course."

"And now..." He hangs his head again. Diane leans closer to hear him. "Now they want to meet with both Missy and me next week."

"Ah," she says. "Well, there are payment plans, I'm sure." Was she really here to talk about Aiden's tuition? Randy's e-mail had sounded so desperate. She takes a big swig of wine.

He looks up at her. Even in the dark, his eyes shine. "You don't understand."

"I guess it's slightly embarrassing. And I'm sorry about that. But you won't be the only people who have ever been in that situation, I'm sure."

"That's not it. The point is that Missy will know."

"Oh, right." She slides her finger down the stem of her glass. "Can't you go into the meeting alone?"

"They are demanding that we both come in, together."

"Hmmm." She speaks her thought out loud: "They've probably been through this *exact* situation before. With both parents there, it's harder to make excuses."

Silence. Randy rips off part of the napkin under his drink.

Here it is. The price of secrets. The reveal. The moment when the secret takes on a life of its own and cannot be denied.

"Well," Diane says to Randy, who has been studying his half-full glass of flat beer. "Is there any part of you that is just a tiny bit relieved?"

The look in his eyes is so pained that it's clear he hasn't even entertained the thought.

"So what you are saying," she continues—although he hasn't said a thing—"is that it's more comfortable for you to keep pretending."

He nods.

"Right." She shifts around and unsticks her yoga pants from a spot on the bench. "Got it. So I'm not sure what I'm here for."

"What do you think I should do?" Randy says, staring into her eyes for an uncomfortably long time.

She tries to muster some of the sympathy she had walking into the bar. But it's fast fizzling. He asks for advice but then only continues down the destructive path he's willfully chosen. And while she knows something about destructive paths, or maybe *because* she knows a lot about them, she finds herself incapable of humoring him with anything less than the truth.

"I've got nothing new to say, Randy. You know that. I've got nothing other than telling Missy everything *before* the school meeting. I'm sorry to sound so cold about it, but I don't know what else to tell you."

"Maybe I could write it all down in a letter?"

"Maybe."

"I could write it down and take a long walk while she reads it."

"Or. You could say it."

He scrunches his eyes tight. "I don't know how to do that."

Dear Lord, she wants to reach across the table and smack him. She takes another sip. "You just fucking say it, Randy. How do you say anything unpleasant? You blurt it out. You take a good couple of swigs of whiskey, or whatever, and you go for it."

He opens his eyes but avoids looking at her, training his gaze somewhere else, near the bar.

This could take forever, she thinks. "Okay, look," she says, not even bothering to soften her tone. "Let's rehearse what you're going to say. Then I have to pick the kids up from their after-school thing."

He looks back at her. "I should rehearse. Yes."

"Pretend I'm Missy. And say it no matter how imperfect it sounds. Just get it out there."

Randy pulls himself up. Obviously this is an idea that appeals to him. "Got it. This is good. You're Missy, and I'm me. Can you look like you're scrolling through your phone or something, so I have to work to get your attention?"

"Seriously?"

"Never mind. I guess we can start from where I've already gotten Missy to pay attention."

"Right," says Diane. "So talk to me. To Missy. Me as Missy."

Randy wiggles around and pushes his glass to the center of the table. "Okay. Let's also assume that Missy has had some food, so she's not cranky. Maybe we're having a glass of wine and I say, very casually"— Randy cocks his head and takes on the role—"'So Missy. I've got some good news and some bad news.'"

Diane can't stop herself. "Really? That's great, Randy. What's the good news?"

Randy drops the act and says to Diane, "You know I don't have any good news. I'm just saying that to warm her up."

"Okay," Diane says, leaning in. "But what if she actually thinks there's good news? I wouldn't say that unless you can deliver. Start again." She pulls back and assumes a Missy-like vagueness.

Randy takes a sip of his beer and squares his shoulders. "Right. Hello, Missy. How's the wine? Good. Well, that's great because I've got some bad news, I'm afraid."

"Bad news? What is it?" Diane says, raising her pitch a little and drawing out the vowels.

"Yes. Sorry about that. You see. We're out of money because I lost my job. And I'm pretty sure we're going to have to sell the house."

Diane drops the Missy voice and holds up her hand. "Okay, Randy. I think you can split the difference between making false promises and pummeling her with the worst news ever right out of the gate."

"I could start with the fact that I haven't cheated on her or stolen anything."

"Charmer."

His face flushes. "This is stupid."

"Well, it is *now*," Diane says. "How do you two usually talk about hard stuff?" The blank look on his face tells her everything. "Got it. You never talk about hard stuff."

He smiles with half his mouth. "That's why I need you."

She takes a deep breath. Lets it out and takes another. "All right. Let's try this again. Then I really have to go. If I'm late for pickup, they call T and I really don't want to get into that."

"Good. Good. Let's do it. Thanks, Diane. You're a real friend."

"So, here's how you start." Is she really giving marital advice? Fuck it. "First you take responsibility. You admit that you've done something that you don't feel proud of." Yes, that's how it goes. She remembers.

"And then," Randy says, "I have to say that I wasn't cheating. Or she'll think that immediately."

Lord, she can imagine where Missy's mind will go at the mere mention of cheating. "I guess, start however you want. But then quickly get to the part where you tell her how you feel and what you're going to do to make it better."

Randy claps his hands together. "That's good. Good, yes. Got it." He clears his throat and Diane makes her face go soft.

"Missy. Hello. I've done a terrible thing that's not cheating on you."

"Really, Randy? What could be so terrible?"

"First," he says, reaching across the table and grabbing her hands, "I want to tell you how much I love you." He gazes into Diane's eyes.

A door swings open somewhere behind them, and light falls across the table for a couple of seconds. Then it's dark again. Diane checks her impulse to turn and see who has walked into the bar. Instead, she doubles down, squeezes Randy's sweaty hands and stares back at him. "I love you too," she says sweetly. But adds, as Missy probably never would, "Is there something you need to tell me?"

Randy pulls his hands away and brings them to his face, covering his eyes. "I can't believe what a complete mess I've made of things," he says. "I spent too much money trying to make you happy. Well, and me too. I wanted to be happy. And Aiden. But then I got fired and didn't tell you. And now we owe a lot of money and it's all my fault. And we're going to have to—" His hands slide down his face, pulling at his skin and making him look preternaturally old. His eyes are wet and earnest as hell. "Please don't leave me. I'll make it better, I promise. I don't think I can live without you."

The door opens again; a stream of light and the dark follows. Randy continues to look at Diane. Abject. Laid bare. She can barely hold his gaze. In fact, she drops her eyes down to her pink drink and clears her throat. "That's it, Randy. That's all you can do."

CHAPTER 53

Is THERE A SINGLE FUCKING man on the whole goddamned earth who is faithful to his wife? Karen doubts it. Because if any such man did exist, certainly it would be Randy Tinker, wouldn't it? The guy is so eager to please. So childlike. But there he was in some hipster dive bar downtown, holding on to a woman's hands and crying. Karen has to hand it to him—or his mistress—no one would ever have seen them there, except that she needed some club soda ASAP for a red wine stain she discovered after a client lunch down the street.

Karen stews. Her blouse is still damp. She can't concentrate on the brief in front of her. It's a rare gray day in the city, adding to her funk and the feeling that she should be in bed, under a mound of covers, feeling sorry for herself. Kelli is pregnant. Mark gets to redo his family life. He gets another shot at being a great dad, loving husband. Hey, he fucked up the first time, but now he gets another turn. This time he can be sweeter, more present, come home earlier from work. While Karen is still stuck with her old mistakes.

She takes her eyes off the angry sky outside the window and focuses on the brief.

The thing is that we wives—we cast-offs—we fucking take it. We wait until the man has used us up and gone on to someone younger, prettier, bouncier, firmer, more adoring, more stupid, more agreeable, more dependent. Dewier. Softer. Who still gets wet down there. Not fucking dried up from listening to all his bullshit. We wives wait until it happens. And when it does, we are shocked. Flattened. Docile. It's not just that he—that they—are such first class dickwads, assholes, heartless bastards. It's that I—that we—are so clueless. Stupid. And helpless. Simpering. Needy.

Karen looks out the window again. Rain pours through a black gash in the gray clouds, down onto the Hollywood hills. Her anger is fuel and she should be channeling it into her work. A civil case. One couple suing another couple for being injured on the first party's boat. A case that is hardly going to elicit the jury's sympathy. The injury was two broken toes on a rich woman's foot. And, because the outward circumstances are not compelling, Karen will have to create a sympathetic narrative from whole cloth. The broken-toed plaintiff, Karen's client, will be rendered as a trusting wife who had overcome her boating trepidations at the insistence of her negligent hosts. The hosts have ulterior motives for wanting broken-toed wife on the cruise. They mean her ill somehow. And the only person who cares, besides broken-toe's hapless husband (and he is hapless; Karen has met him) is Karen herself. Defender of sucker wives.

She sits back down at her desk, stares at the paperwork, but can't focus.

There must be something she can do. Something to stop another feckless bastard from getting everything he ever wanted.

From: KSonn@gmail.com

To: Missy@skintastic.com   sent Wed, Nov 3 3:51 pm

Subject: Urgent from Karen Sonnenklar

Hello Missy,

It's Karen, Ben's mother from the team. Forgive me if the subject line was over the top. I wanted to make sure that you read my e-mail and didn't think it was simply a request for a playdate with Aiden.

I am sorry to be writing this e-mail, but I feel that it's important that we women not be kept in the dark about certain things. I have personal experience that compels me to tell you what I am about to tell you, and I feel that what follows is better told by a distant acquaintance rather than a friend. This way, you can get mad at the messenger (me) and still keep your friends close. Because you will need them.

Please forgive me for being so blunt, but I can think of no other way.

This afternoon, I saw Randy in a bar downtown. It is a place that is somewhat out of the way, so I'm sure that he and the woman were being careful not to be discovered. They didn't see me, as they were deep in conversation. The woman's back was toward me, but I did see that she had long straight, slightly stringy hair. He was holding her hands across the table, and he appeared to be crying. And it looked to me like he was pleading with her. I watched for only a couple of minutes.

Anyway, Missy, I thought you should know. Perhaps the whole thing is innocent. My guess is that this revelation (so sorry, again) will either speak to some gut intuition or not. In my experience, we suspect before we know.

Please call or write me if you have any questions. While I am an attorney, I don't handle divorces. I can, however, put you in touch with several excellent lawyers. I recommend a woman.

Forgive me for interfering. I do so only because I wish I had gotten a letter like this so that I could have been more prepared.

Good luck.

Karen Sonnenklar

CHAPTER 54

From: RTChampion@gmail.com

To: DPlatt@ca.rr.com   sent Wed, Nov 3 4:13 pm

Subject: You're such a good friend

Thank you, thank you, thank you, Diane for being there for me through this whole mess. I feel totally pumped to tell Missy everything and to take anything she throws at me (let's hope it isn't anything super heavy like the beer stein I got in 2013 for top regional sales!). Seriously, I just have to stay loose and keep telling her how sorry I am (and make sure I'm light on my feet!). I also think that picking the right moment is going to be key. If we win the game this Saturday, for instance, that would be perfect! We'll be celebrating and I can tell her on the deck after Aiden's asleep.

When life is at its worst, you just have to keep your mind on a picture of how perfect life can be. Because we've all had a taste of it. We've all had a day or a moment when everything fits into everything else and you're not thinking of being anywhere but where you are right then. You just have to keep reminding yourself that it can be that way again. It's not like you're never going to have a great day again. Right?

Thanks again, Diane. You have many wonderful qualities that you don't even know you have. Let's get together again, soon.

Love,
Your friend,
Randy

Diane closes his e-mail. Maybe things will turn out fine after all. Is that possible?

She gets up from her desk, stretches, and walks over to the rickety side table she just bought at a little hole-in-the-wall junk shop she found on Fairfax. It's beat up, but she likes the texture. The flaking wood finish. Grooves of wear on the legs. Maybe a dog gnawed on them fifty years ago? Stuff has already piled up on top. She runs a finger along the edge of a photograph that she recently found in her files. One of the last that she took before the whole photography obsession faded away.

It's a picture of Reece at age one or so, holding on to the edge of a table for balance. His diaper sagging. The image is sentimental. She knows that, but she's going to frame it anyway. She looks at the wall where it will hang with several more pieces of hers that aren't completely terrible.

She sets the photo back on top of the pile and sits in her desk chair, spinning around so she faces the room. She likes it now—the room. It's honest and reflects her. Ragged and in need of a paint job. Pardon her dust while she figures shit out.

There's something sweet about the room too. It's a shambles, not pretending to be anything more than a mess. Which, in fact, makes her feel tender. It's a feeling she knows she's felt before, but has never much thought about. Never actually located it or identified it as a state of being.

Tenderness.

The last time with Alejandro was a moment of weakness, but not without tenderness. Hell, the afternoon with Randy was maddening, but not without tenderness. Lately, every night she gets to spend with her children—microresentments pinging between the three of them, and often suffocating. But not without tenderness.

Tenderness.

She reaches over to her laptop and shuts it, leans back, and closes her eyes.

CHAPTER 55

From: FavoriteCoach@gmail.com

To: JWoo@DesignX.com   sent Fri, Nov. 5 4:56 pm

Subject: Patrick and the game this Saturday

Dear Mr. and Mrs. Woo,

It's the coach here, Coach Randy. I wanted to thank you for allowing me to come over and coach Patrick privately this week. He's one heck of a player and we're depending on him to carry the team to victory this weekend. No pressure! Seriously, I mean that! Even though we all know that he's a big part of the team, he doesn't need to feel that. Teams lose all the time and Patrick should not feel the burden of our hopes and dreams on his shoulders.

Having said that, I have some thoughts on what might help him focus during the game. One, of course, is a good night's sleep. I wouldn't mention the game at all tonight, because he said he has a hard time sleeping if he worries about it the night before.

Obviously, he'll need a big, hot breakfast in the morning. While he is eating his eggs and pancakes, I think that you can keep the conversation light and don't let him feel any pressure at all. Talk about something that is fun like golden retriever puppies or how funny penguins are when they walk. In short, you can talk about anything that puts him in a good mood and doesn't make him overthink the game ahead of him.

Then, right before you're leaving for the game, you might casually say something like, "You know it's a good thing you're not a penguin (or a puppy, or some reference to the conversation you just had), because if you were, you wouldn't be such an awesome soccer player." This is when you start pumping him up. You can tell him what a great kid he is and how he would still be a great kid even if he wasn't a soccer player. Remember, keep all of this really casual.

When you get to the field and he's suiting up, you can go all inspirational. You may want to reference a folk tale or a movie or a poem, at this point, something that dovetails into how great players never give up. You can't go wrong with anything by J.R.R. Tolkien.

OK, I've gone on long enough here! The point is to keep him relaxed and focused. He's a great kid, regardless of his skills. I wish we had more like him.

On to Victory!
Coach Randy

CHAPTER 56

JUNG-AH WATCHES HIS SON EAT dinner while he mentally sorts through possible topics to discuss. Mi-ran has been silent, heeding the instructions that were sent by the coach. They are not to talk about the game tomorrow. Jung-ah wonders what his wife is thinking now, since she almost always gives out orders at dinner on how to prepare for the next day.

Mi-ran lays down her spoon and makes a sound as if to say, *That is that.*

Patrick keeps his eyes on his plate, moving his pasta around. Jung-ah clears his throat and asks about the math test that Patrick took earlier today. He asks in Korean, to include Mi-ran. Even though he knows his son prefers English.

Patrick doesn't look up, but he pauses long enough to say that he is sure he got an A.

"You can never be sure," says Mi-ran.

"That is true," says Jung-ah, "but the boy has studied and gets an A every time, so we can trust that he is probably telling the truth." Jung-ah winks at Patrick, who is looking at him from under his heavy eyelids. He thinks he sees a flicker of gratitude from his son, and Jung-ah smiles.

Mi-ran stands and picks up her own dish. Jung-ah and Patrick stop moving and their breath is shallow until she disappears into the kitchen.

"Your mother wants the best for you," Jung-ah says in English.

"I know," says the boy.

"She wants you to be successful so that you won't suffer. It's her way of protecting you."

"Yes," says the boy, "I know that's true."

"And you are her only child," he says. "You are her only chance to get it right."

He thinks of the other child, Mi-ran's daughter. Of grainy TV images of children in an orphanage with a phone number flashing below, telling Mi-ran where to send her money.

"Do you want to see my watch?" Jung-ah asks his son.

The watch is new, and some of the working parts are exposed beneath the glass, which Patrick enjoys. Jung-ah extends his forearm over to his son, who immediately touches the crystal.

There is still so much of the little boy in Patrick's gesture that Jung-ah feels a lift in his chest. "Here," he says, taking the watch off and handing it to him.

Dishes clatter in the kitchen even though Jung-ah and Patrick are not finished eating. This usually means that there is something that Mi-ran is not saying.

Patrick turns the watch over and inspects the back. The curious etchings like hieroglyphs. The boy runs his thumb over the markings.

The door of the dishwasher closes. The dial ratchets, and the hum starts. In the dining room, Jung-ah looks toward the kitchen, anticipating Mi-ran's reemergence.

"All I want to say," she says in Korean, standing in the doorframe with her arms crossed, "is you cannot take things for granted. The world will not hand you anything that you don't work for."

"We know, Mi-ran," he says. "Sit down with us. I was just showing Patrick my watch again."

He turns and the boy is looking at him with a big grin across his face—and no watch.

"Where is the watch?" Jung-ah asks.

"I took it," says Patrick. With a twinkle of mischief.

Jung-ah laughs, sharing the joke with his wife. "See what a talented kid he is? He made the watch disappear."

"Okay," she says. "Where is it?"

Patrick reaches behind his father's head and pulls his hand back with the watch, presto, dangling in his grasp. He beams with accomplishment.

To Jung-ah's delight, Mi-ran claps. Yes. That is Jung-ah's girl.

"That is a good trick," she says. "Let's see what you can do tomorrow at the game." She is smiling still. Jung-ah feels his son's body getting smaller.

Patrick hands the watch back to his father, who sees the boy's face change. The look is not necessarily unpleasant. But it unsettles Jung-ah, as it does every time he sees Patrick do this. It is almost as if he's disappeared.

CHAPTER 57

Visorgrl@mac.com

To: Manatees   sent Sat, Nov 6 2:39 pm

Subject: Don't lose heart!!!

Hi Team,

I am sure that Coach Randy is going to weigh in pretty soon with some great words of wisdom from the movies, so I'm not going to steal his thunder!

While we are waiting for word from our fearless leader, I wanted to keep up morale by saying that even though the boys lost today, they can still make it into the tournament if they win the game next week. It's super important that you all understand that. We lost the game, not the playoffs! It's a forest and trees deal!

ALL IS NOT LOST!!! ☺☺

Although, you know me, even if it all stopped right here and we never went any further (or farther?), I would still think that this was the best season ever! Calvin's confidence has grown and he was even talking about playing forward next year!

Anyway, I'm sorry it was rough out there. As Coach says, the Tigers are fierce. And even though the Manatees can be pretty fierce themselves, the Tigers were just fiercer this time.

Don't give up!

XOXOXO,
Jacqui

––––––––––

From: Mako@Shakrayoga.org
To: Manatees   sent Sat, Nov 6 2:50 pm

Subject: Re: Don't lose heart!!!

Thank you Jacqui, for such a quick follow-up. Mason feels very strongly that the first foul called, was a clear mistake and cost us a goal. I know that there is nothing we can do about it now, but I do know that ref and we should remember to put it in his record for next year. The lack of consistency with refs is very frustrating.

And, Jacqui, it is "farther" in that case. "Farther" implies physical distance, whereas "further" implies figurative distance. For example, "I wish that umpire had come further in his training before being allowed to call a game."

I am also not convinced that "fiercer" is a distinction one can make. You are either fierce or you are not.

Mako

––––––––––

From: MSonnenklar@GSachs.com

To: Manatees   sent Sat, Nov 6 2:53 pm

Subject: Re: Don't lose heart!!!

Mako, "fiercer" is fine. I looked it up. It's better than "more fierce", which sounds British.

I do, however, agree about the first foul and the ref. He's an acquisitions agent over at CAA, I believe. His name is Dave and I'm fairly sure that his last name starts with a "B".

M

————————

From: ParadiseB@gmail.com

To: Manatees   sent Sat, Nov 6 3:06 pm

Subject: Re: Don't lose heart!!!

I have to admit that Dashiell is pretty torn up about the game. Unlike Calvin, he says he doesn't want to play ever again. I know that children have to get used to losing. I really do, but it hurts even more if it's because of one random referee.

Regards,

Beth

————————

From: Visorgrl@mac.com

To: Manatees   sent Sat, Nov 6 3:13 pm

Subject: Re: Don't lose heart!!!

Dear Beth and others,

Don't get me wrong, Calvin was pretty upset too! So if your little ones are crying, please know that you aren't alone! Calvin had said that thing about being a forward, last week. Today, he told me that he needed some time to get mad about the game and then he would come out of his room. That's called "dealing with your own anger" which is also a really positive thing!! While I'm waiting for him to come out, I'm making ginger cookies! It's very therapeutic, because making them is calming, and also ginger is good for depression and sea sickness.

XOXO,
Jacqui

———————

From: PPousaint@mac.com

To: Manatees sent Sat, Nov 6 4:05 pm

Subject: Re: Don't lose heart!!!

Hello Parents and Team,

I'm sure that Randy is being held up by work obligations, or maybe he is simply taking time to mull over the game and what he wants to say. In the meantime, let me clarify. Because we are dependent upon parents to referee, the system is inherently problematic. We must accept that there is a lack of uniformity in the league, in much the way that we accept the rule that "everybody plays". Why do we accept these realities? We accept them because the league favors playing and learning over winning. I want to remind you all of that, as we go into the last game of the playoffs next week.

All the best and see you at practice.

Paul

———————

From: Mako@Shakrayoga.org
To: Manatees   sent Sat, Nov 6 4:11 pm

Subject: Re: Don't lose heart!!!

I'm going to let it go, because it's a small thing. However, I still believe that "fierce" is an absolute. Despite what "Yahoo ask" says.

Mako

CHAPTER 58

RANDY HAS BEEN WALKING UP Wilshire Boulevard for a couple of hours, occasionally wandering into a store for no particular reason except to listen to snatches of conversation or, once, pretending to admire ties while watching a young couple try on hats. Their ease with each other fascinated him.

Randy has an extraordinary sense of being outside of normal goings-on, which is both exhilarating and terrifying.

The loss to the Tigers this morning seems to have caused a fissure in his brain. He could almost hear a pop of release when the final whistle blew.

They could still win the playoffs, so his reaction couldn't have been only about the loss. It was more than that. He hadn't realized until that moment that he had been hoping that the win would redeem him somewhat. It would have been something at least. Ballast for the conversation with Missy. Now he feels the lightness of having nothing to lose.

It is a cool day, but sunny as he turns up Canon Drive. He looks out of place with his sweats all damp and musty, and his thin hair sticking to his pate. But a defeated man doesn't care about these things. A defeated man is unseen. Even his cell phone stays silent. Obviously his wife and son don't feel his absence.

He considers getting a vodka martini at Nic's but suspects that if they don't have an actual dress code, there is an informal one that doesn't include athletic attire and the smell of postgame funk. His state of mind is not unpleasant, but he is sure that he will crash as soon as he walks into his front hallway. So he should have something. A drink, a joint, anything to sustain him through dinner and (after Aiden is asleep) his confession.

He hears Diane saying, *Just tell her how you feel.*

I feel awful. I lied to you.

He stops outside a store that says Puruti and peers through the window. There don't seem to be any customers and the inside appears calm. On either side of the center aisle, he can see colorful handbags and briefcases displayed on sleek blond shelves. He wipes his hands on his sweatpants and opens the door.

The smell is clean. Leather. Moneyed. The light subdued. His pulse slows. People take their time here. He glances at an older Indian man in a suit and a turban, behind a glass counter. The man smiles but goes back to a chain he is handling. Plainly uninterested. You either have the money or you don't, his demeanor says.

Randy picks up a glossy purple handbag. It looks like crocodile or alligator skin. He turns it over, watching the light bounce off it. He's never bought a handbag before, but Missy likes them. She's always asking if he likes her new one. How much can this one be? Maybe a couple thousand? He imagines himself arriving home with a gift. A purple reptile purse. Unique and thoughtful.

I feel awful about what I have done. But I care about you so much. Here is a bag that I bought you.

He turns to the man and holds up the bag. "How much is this one?"

The old man looks up and, without hesitation, says in a heavy accent, "Thirty-three thousand."

Randy almost drops it. He would have been surprised to hear fifteen thousand. But it wouldn't have completely floored him. Thirty-three? That's half the price of his deck. Seriously? For anything to cost thirty-three thousand, you should be able to live in it.

He places the handbag oh-so-carefully back on the shelf and steps back. Maybe he simply picked the most expensive signature item in the store. The purple color is highly unusual. Maybe if he chooses something more subdued and smaller, the price will go down significantly. He lets his fingers drift over a couple of items that are still probably too pricey, only to indicate his viability to the man behind the counter. Meanwhile he scopes, out of the corner of his eye, for a more suitable object. And there at the end of the long middle shelf, in the corner, are some clutches in earth tones. Slowly he makes his way toward them.

He picks up a brown one and opens it. The insides are a surprise, a satiny pink that makes him think of sex. He feels a flush coming on and puts the bag back down. The green one next to it is black inside, which is far more serious. But lacks the fun of the first. And he returns to the brown one, feeling foolish about having been turned on.

He turns to the man with the sexy clutch and asks, "How much?"

"All of those are forty-eight hundred."

God damn it. Randy has about that much left on his card, the bank having refused to raise his limit. But it would max him out. And besides, he thinks, bristling with irritation, is he being taken? Does the man behind the counter think that he is a fool? In his splotchy sweats. Obviously out of place. Is the clutch worth forty-eight hundred? Would he go lower for a man wearing Armani?

Randy drops the purse and moves on to a glass case, where he finds a few desk items. A business card holder (too small), an alligator stapler (too odd), and a blue speckled pencil holder. He picks up the pencil holder. Missy's desk in the bedroom is light blue.

I feel terrible about what I have done. I lied to you. To Aiden.

He lifts up the pencil holder and admires it.

"That is ostrich leather," says the old man.

"Huh," says Randy, "it's definitely unusual-looking."

"Yes. It is a different texture," the man says, sounding formal, as if he is talking to a kid who doesn't understand.

"And how much is this?"

"Eighteen hundred."

"Really?"

Randy mentally kicks himself for sounding so delighted. But seriously, how cool is that? An ostrich pencil holder? No man in the world buys his wife an ostrich pencil holder. It shows his whimsical side. The side Missy liked so much that she married him.

"I'll take it," Randy says, modulating his voice to a more businesslike tone. "And can I get a box for it?"

The man smiles. "Of course. Of course," taking the pencil holder from him and disappearing through a door. Leaving Randy bouncing on the balls of his feet.

————

Missy tries to concentrate on *Project Runway* instead of her thoughts. But even after half a Xanax, the show isn't doing its usual job of settling her mind to a dull purr. And, on top of her mind going around and around and around, she regrets the Xanax. She'd rather have a glass of wine. Maybe she should take the other half.

The drapes have been drawn since it got dark at six. The family room is cozy, and Missy pulls the throw blanket up higher on her chest. Aiden is upstairs on some device, having thrown a fit when Randy failed to appear after the game. She tried to comfort him by pointing out some of the good plays he made, in spite of his missed goal. But he wasn't very consolable. He really needs reassurance from Randy. Ever since Randy "saved Calvin," Aiden and his dad have been close to the point of Missy now being the outsider instead of Randy. Which would pain her more if she weren't already in such pain.

Tim Gunn praises an off-the-shoulder minidress that looks hard for the average woman to carry off. Of course, that's part of the point of the show.

Missy's tongue feels fat. She swallows.

She hasn't called Randy because she doesn't want to see him. She can't stop thinking about him with the woman in the bar. Is she someone from the office? How long has it been going on? And what else doesn't she know about Randy? What has been going on the whole time she has been obsessing over Alejandro—thinking only of him? Dying to check her e-mail. Dying for Randy to leave her alone so that she could relive a recent memory of her secret lover.

Back to the TV, she stares at Heidi Klum, thinking that Heidi's actually pretty big for a model. Now she wears a red gown with a bow and a slit that goes all the way up to her waist, letting you know that there is absolutely no way that she is wearing panties.

Honestly, what could it possibly do to her to have one glass of wine on top of half a Xanax? The worst that could happen would be that she would fall asleep. And the best that could happen is that her chest might loosen up and she might feel more optimistic.

She tosses off the blanket and stands up. And instantly, she feels better. Her skin feels cool without the warmth of the chair and the blanket. Her bare feet smack the floor flat-footedly as she walks down the hallway to the kitchen.

What is she really upset about? Sex with Randy hasn't been satisfying for years. She can still do it with him. But she usually has to psych herself up somehow. So what does she care that he's seeing someone else?

She grabs an open bottle of merlot and finds a glass. Pours.

Would she care so much if things between her and Alejandro had worked out?

She shoves the cork back into the bottle.

Aha, she thinks. What really bothers her is that it's like Randy has been saving up everything that's maybe interesting about him for someone else.

She takes a big sip. It goes down easy and makes her think of sitting in front of a fire. She takes another swallow, grabs the bottle, and heads back to the family room. Feeling a little sway in her hips.

Back in the chair. Forget the blanket. She's warm.

Five designers stand in a row, having to defend their work. The only straight man on the show stands at the end. He's got an accent like Alejandro's. In fact, he looks like he's from the same part of the world. The same casual stance. Like he was born knowing things about women and sex that most American men never learn.

Why, why, why did Alejandro break up with her so fast? Had she given in to him too early? Was she bad in bed? She was probably bad in bed. She couldn't do things that women like Diane probably do all the time. They embarrassed her. Besides, she was too worried about getting the basics right.

She picks up her glass and takes another sip. It feels like the alcohol is sharpening her thoughts. Either counteracting or working together with the Xanax. This is good. She takes another sip.

You know what really sucks? she thinks. Randy still has someone else and she's stuck with Randy. Not even regular old Randy. But a cheating Randy who lies to her.

Everyone lies to her. Alejandro lied.

Men lie to get you into bed, almost always.

Everyone lies. Fuck lies.

She hears the front door open and Randy's keys clink on the plate on the sideboard. Her whole body tenses. She feels like hiding. Feels like he's an intruder. About to find her in here with her wine and her *Project Runway*. She quickly grabs the remote and clicks off the program. Right before they decide who's out, damn it.

Her hearing is sharp as she listens to his feet clumping past her and to the kitchen. He hasn't seen her through the open door. Or doesn't want to see her yet. She feels an erratic fluttering in her neck. Listens to him making noise in the kitchen. Opening the refrigerator? That's what it sounds like. She should call out to him, otherwise she's going to seem guilty when he finds her here.

She holds her breath.

Clump, clump, toward her.

Clump.

"Randy?" she says.

Clump. Stop.

"Oh, hi," he says.

"Where have you been?" she says.

"Out," he says.

"Oh. Did you get some dinner?" she says.

"No," he says. "I was just walking."

"There's some pasta in the fridge," she says.

"Okay," he says. "Where's Aiden?"

"Upstairs," she says. "He got mad when you didn't come home."

"Shit," he says. "I lost track of time."

"It's been five hours."

"Really? Sorry."

"Maybe say that to him."

"Right. I'll go up in a minute." He comes into the room a bit. She looks at him and sees that he is carrying a glossy red shopping bag. "I got you something," he says. He is smiling but it doesn't look real. He looks pained.

"Oh," she says, sliding her legs off the ottoman and tucking them under her hips.

Randy sits on the vacated ottoman and reaches into the bag. He pulls out a shiny black box that has a name that starts with a *P* printed in fancy white script on the side.

The box looks like it came from a luxury shop. Oh God. What's he going to say?

He holds out the present and she stares at it.

"What's it for?" she asks.

"I felt like buying you something," he says.

"Is that because you're going to tell me something?" she says.

Randy's eyes widen like he's a man found out. He stands and places the bag on the ottoman. "You can open it while I go see about Aiden," he says. And he's gone.

She reaches for the box. It looks too big to be a tennis bracelet, which is the traditional cheater's present to his wife. She feels the weight of it. Too light to be a vase or a piece of art glass.

Get it over with, she thinks. Open it and be done. Open it and hope that he doesn't feel like he has to tell her the truth. She doesn't want to hear his truth right now. Because if she does, she might just tell him hers. Why should he get to think that he's the only one who got to escape their regular lives for a few weeks? Her brow feels sweaty. Probably the wine. Fuck it. She lifts the top off the box and sets it down on her lap so that she can remove the tissue paper.

And there it is. A light blue cylinder with weird dots on it. She lifts it out, turns it around, and sees that it's covered in leather. Ostrich. Some of her friends have bags made of ostrich.

She turns it around in the other direction. It looks like a vase. She already has tons of vases. But no. Wait. Water would bleed through, wouldn't it? Huh.

Hang on. She's got it. That's it. It's a pencil holder.

What's she supposed to do with a pencil holder?

She places it on the ottoman and takes another sip of wine while she thinks of nice things she can say about it so they can avoid any conversation that could lead to a bad outcome and go back to everything being fine.

———————

Randy sits on the edge of his bed in his bedroom. So far things are okay. Not great, but okay. She knows he's going to tell her something, and probably knows that whatever it is isn't good. Otherwise he would have brought her champagne and flowers instead of an expensive pencil holder. She's as prepped as she's ever going to be.

He can't quite make himself face Aiden. So he's sitting here waiting for the present to take effect. She must have opened it by now. Still he waits. Oh God, what if she hates it? That hasn't occurred to him until now.

Surely he can return it. He hadn't even asked.

Or maybe she hasn't opened it yet, and she's waiting for him to come back down to watch her open it. He prays that isn't the case. He doesn't think that he can bear the slightest hint of disappointment right now. Which is a weird thing to think, since he's about to give her the mother of all disappointments, financial ruin, in a few minutes.

Come on, Randy. Get it over with. He stands and shakes out the tightness in his shoulders.

Downstairs, he finds her staring at the pencil holder on the ottoman, a glass of wine in her hand. He sneaks up behind her. "What do you think?" He means for his voice to sound lighter than it does.

"I like it," she says thickly. Dully, like a book dropping. "It's a nice color."

His gut is a fist. He walks around the chair and faces her. "I feel terrible," he says. "I've disappointed you. I feel awful."

She looks up at him; her eyes are wet from having already cried. And at first he's grateful. Tears are softer than words. Tears can be loving and forgiving.

But it takes only a second to see that her gaze is anything but that. It is hard. Mean. And her lips are pressed together in a way that he's never seen before. She looks like someone who could leave him. *Will* leave him. A woman who wholly despises him. His thoughts careen.

"I feel terrible," he says again, dropping onto the ottoman in front of her. Feeling the ostrich pencil holder drop onto the carpet. He starts to sob. Shoulders shaking. Hands up to hide his face. Words sputtering out. "I feel—" He can't find the words that can begin to explain all they have lost.

Even though someone might say to him, even now, *What is it you have lost? Your wife sits in front of you and your boy is upstairs. You are warm. You have food to eat.* His sobs heave with everything unshared. His burden. And Missy watches.

"You are not the only one," she says to him. Her voice sounds metallic. Weaponized.

"What? The only one?" he whimpers. "What?"

"I have lied to you too."

"Lied to me?"

"Alejandro and me."

He looks at her. "Who?" As if he barely recognizes the name. Can't, in fact, place it.

"We—" she says, looking past him, dreamily at the blank TV screen. "Anyway, it's over."

"What? You and Alejandro?" He wipes his eyes, looks around the room. His foot nudges the pencil holder and it rolls to the wall. He shifts onto one hip and pushes himself off the ottoman.

"What were you going to tell me?" she says in the same hard voice.

He looks at her. Searches her face. Sways slightly. And says, "It doesn't matter."

"Yes it does," she says.

He turns and clumps into the hallway. Clump, clump.

In the family room, perched on the edge of an overstuffed chair, Missy braces for the slam of the front door. Which is how it goes in almost every movie she watches on TV. The slam that says this is not over—not by a long shot.

Missy holds her breath. Waiting. Listening to the scraping sound of keys being retrieved from the dish. Her hand grips the armrest as she waits. Hearing the whooshing of the door being opened, and then—closed with a quiet and deliberate *click*.

It is the little click that tells her nothing is ever going to be the same.

CHAPTER 59

From: RTChampion@gmail.com
To: DPlatt@ca.rr.com   sent Sat, Nov 6 7:49 pm

Subject: Last letter from the Library

Hey Diane. This is coming from Randy here at the library. Libraries are weird at night, I just noticed. One thing that's different is no line for the computers. It's too bad my flirty librarian isn't here. She always cheers me up, and I guess I need cheering up.

I tried taking your advice, and telling Missy all about the money. I want you to know that I really tried, but it turns out the money isn't our biggest problem. I guess it never was, and I just didn't know it.

I'm writing this to you because I want you to keep thinking the best of me. I know I'm not the smartest, handsomest, most athletic, funniest (OK, maybe the funniest), nicest guy you've ever known, but I try not to hurt people. You could always say that about me.

Goodbye for now and see you on the flip-side!

Your friend,
Randy

CHAPTER 60

MISSY WAKES UP ON TOP of the covers, still dressed from last night. Light splashes onto the bottom of the bed, warming one of her bare feet. She lifts her head to look around the room. Something is off, but she can't quite think what. For one, the room is too quiet. What day is it? She lets her head drop back down and closes her eyes to concentrate. Where is she? In her bedroom. Who else is here? She opens her eyes and looks to her side. No one. How old is she? For a second, she believes she is her younger self. Single and alone. But this makes no sense, since this is the house that was bought by Randy. Who is, she remembers, her husband.

And now she remembers everything.

She rolls over onto her stomach and raises up on her elbows. Maybe Randy's back by now. Sleeping on the couch or making coffee in the kitchen. She drops her head between her shoulders, letting it hang.

How will they go on from here? Are they going to stay married? What will happen to Aiden? How can they make it through all the talking and truth-telling that will have to happen now, when they've never done anything like that before?

She lifts her head and sniffs. Now she sees what is off about the room. It is completely undisturbed. How can she and Randy have split their marriage in two yesterday—slashed right down the center of everything they ever built or owned or believed—without knocking one thing over or shaking anything loose? The stillness in the air feels unnatural.

She rises from the bed, her joints achy, and walks over to her vanity to look in the mirror. Her reflection is not of her younger self, but of Missy as she is now. Vaguely pretty, tired. The skin around her eyes loose and slightly discolored.

It is Sunday, she remembers. And decides to pee before facing Randy and Aiden. As she steps into the bathroom, she considers going downstairs and pretending that nothing happened last night. It's entirely possible that they could move on from this as they always have, by simply acting like everything is all right. She reaches for the toilet paper. But nothing this big has ever happened before. She flushes and pulls up her pants.

Missy finds her relative calmness slightly disturbing but doesn't know what to do about it. Shouldn't a woman on the verge of losing her whole life feel worse? She walks over to the bedroom door, which she must have closed last night, and opens it.

The air in the hallway is cooler and now she realizes that she didn't look at the alarm clock and doesn't really know what time it is. Still, given the sunlight, it's got to be at least eight. She stops outside Aiden's door, turns the handle, and leans in to take a look at him sleeping. On Sundays he can sleep until nine or ten, having stayed up late playing on his phone.

Her gaze falls on the rumpled bedsheets, but he is not there. She freezes. Pulse jumps. But she shakes it off. Telling herself he must already have gone to the kitchen. Quickly she scuttles downstairs, her breath tight even though she is sure he must be there. Where else would he be?

And he is. Of course. Sitting at the island, leaning over the iPad. She takes a breath and glances at the oven clock. It is 11:42.

How could she have possibly slept that late?

"Where's Daddy?" she asks her son.

Aiden shrugs. "I haven't seen him yet. I thought he was sleeping."

She looks around the kitchen for signs of Randy. The coffeemaker is unplugged. His habit—and Randy is a man of habits—is to immediately turn on the coffeemaker in the morning. Missy feels another stab of not-rightness.

Conscious of Aiden, she affects a casual air as she walks down the hall to the front door. Glances down at the table where Randy tosses his keys. They're not there. But, strangely, his phone is. Why would he take the keys and not his phone?

She turns and walks back toward the kitchen, her neck aching. All she has to do is wait. He'll come back and then she'll know what's going to happen next. Waiting isn't that hard. In fact, it's a thing she's especially good at.

CHAPTER 61

JACQUI STANDS IN FRONT OF the mirror in her master bath, having downed two Percocets. Last night she had resolved to throw the whole bottle away. She had taken three pills after Calvin threw a royal fit when they got home from the game. The pills had numbed her out, but they also made her nauseous and unable to sleep. Finally, she dozed a little in the early morning. And now, in the light of day, she realizes that she doesn't need to toss them entirely. All she has to do is regulate how many she takes at a time.

She looks at her reflection. Her hair recently cut short and pixie-like, close to her skull. Her eyes large. She doesn't like their expression right now. Too lost. Too unguarded. She takes another sip of water, swishes it around her mouth, and spits it out.

If only they had won the game. Calvin had been doing so well.

No, he hadn't.

He hasn't been doing well at all.

Enough of this. She places the cup on the side of the sink. Looks at the cabinet to her right. The one with the junky drawer full of nubs of lipsticks, skin cream samples, nearly empty bottles of pills, and even a one-hitter way in the back. It's a drawer she has promised herself to clean at least once a week for a decade. Easily the most crapped-up square foot of the house. The only one, really. And why has the drawer escaped her organizational zeal? Who knows. Maybe it's because it's only her who sees it. Steve wouldn't dream of snooping. Which she's pretty sure she hates him for. Signaling his general lack of interest in anything having to do with her inner self.

She pulls out the drawer and runs her hand across the forgotten objects. Finds a Chanel lipstick. Surely it's still good. Uncaps, and rolls it up. There's only a sliver of color left. A matte peach. Ah yes. She bought it for a school fund-raiser. To go with a backless jumpsuit that was a different shade of peach. She knows not to be too matchy-matchy. Calvin was in first grade. Jacqui was one of the new ubercompetent moms on the scene.

She couldn't have imagined, then, what happened this past Friday. Sitting across from Calvin's teacher, Ms. Lowry, going on about how kids on the spectrum can be socialized and achieve just as much as their peers.

Jacqui had smiled through the whole meeting. Even patted Steve's hand every once in a while to let the teacher know that they were a united family. A family that would do what needed to be done, without any hysterics. Because, of course, they loved their child.

Every parent loves their child.

Jacqui looks at herself again and starts to apply the peach lipstick, the rim of the tube slightly scraping her upper lip.

There. She looks good in peach. She *is* a peach. She's moved into rose tones lately. Maybe she should go back to peach.

Of course, she had heard everything Ms. Lowry was telling them before. But Calvin had been so young then. It was hard, the other experts had said—or Jacqui *remembers* them saying—to diagnose.

Jacqui presses her lips together. Looks at herself again. Fusses with her short bangs. The night of that fund-raiser, wearing the peach lipstick, was the first time that she really noticed Sarah. Before that, they had been on the haunted house committee together, but Jacqui had found Sarah to be quiet and slow to volunteer. So she had written her off as another mom who says she's there to help, but really isn't. In short, she was like all the others.

But at the fund-raiser, Sarah seemed to light up. She was animated as she flitted from one group to another, even pressing some of the husbands to bid higher on silent auction items. Maybe, Jacqui remembers thinking, Sarah could be groomed to be a committee chair.

Which is exactly what happened. Sarah and Jacqui had been a

powerhouse team all the way through fourth grade. At last year's Spring Fling, they had raised $650,000 in one night. The two of them had snuck out onto the balcony to toast their success. Sarah laughing with her eyes, hanging on to Jacqui's arm. Doubling over. Jacqui couldn't remember any other moment in her life so storybook perfect. The curve of Sarah's back. Champagne fizzing on her tongue. The feeling of being so known by another person that nothing, not even death, could scare you.

Until it became unbearable. The happiness. Jacqui felt such a pain in her chest that she had run back into the dining room. Grabbed the first chair she could find and passed out. Woke up slumped over. Steve shouting to everyone to give her room to breathe and could someone get her inhaler?

Jacqui stares at her face. Reaches over and rips off some toilet paper. Wipes her peach lips, till they look raw and blurry. Like a drunk sorority girl's.

She caps the lipstick and throws it back in the drawer.

Sarah stopped volunteering after that. She said that she had to put her efforts into a math tutoring program at her oldest kid's middle school. But Jacqui knew that wasn't why. Jacqui knows that when you have a moment like that—pure connection, like you're almost inside the other person—you can't go back to the way things were before and pretend it didn't happen. You either have to follow that happiness or black it out. Cut it out of yourself.

She looks down at the open drawer, junked with the past, and shuts it. She'll go through it all some other day.

CHAPTER 62

WHAT TIME IS IT? MISSY opens her eyes and peers around the room. Blue light from the street shines onto the end of her bed and the carpet. Okay, yes. That's right. It's Monday morning. Early. Too early. Last night was Sunday and Rosa has Sundays off, so she wouldn't have pulled the blinds down completely. It's Monday. School. Aiden is at an overnight. Did she coordinate his morning drop-off at school? She must have.

She pulls herself up, swings her legs to the floor, and walks across the glowing carpet—it looks like water—and stares out the window. No car. No Randy.

She crawls back onto the bed. Her stomach is tight and she feels on the edge of throwing up. She's felt like this for hours and nothing has happened. Even though her unsettled tummy is telling her she's upset, she still can't figure out how she feels.

She's worried. Yes. That's true. Very worried. But what, exactly, is she worried about? It's been a day and a half, and now it's occurred to her that Randy might have honest-to-God left her and moved in with his girlfriend, whoever she is. Is that what is making her nauseous? Or is she more upset about the possibility that he'll walk in the door any minute and that they'll have to talk? That she'll have to explain all about Alejandro and then he'll have to come clean about the woman and there it will all be—out in the open?

She stuffs a pillow behind her so she can sit against the headboard and reaches for her phone. Taps it and sees in the glow that it's 4:42. Too early—or late—to call anyone.

Except.

She stares at his number. Why not? He should know, shouldn't he? It's not like he's an innocent bystander.

Her back stiffens and she pulls herself up higher against the pillow and the headboard. She feels a rush of something she can't quite name.

She doesn't have to be alone in this, and she sure as hell doesn't have to take all the blame.

She presses his number. Three rings, and he answers.

"Missy?"

"Alejandro," she says. "I thought that you should know." She speaks deliberately. "Randy has been missing for two days."

CHAPTER 63

DIANE PULLS ON A T-SHIRT. Alejandro has turned on the lamp. He's been talking into the phone for a minute or so. Sharp, short answers, mostly. "Missy" and "No" and "I don't know." And a couple of "I'm sorry"s.

She looks at his tense, bare back. "Why did you tell him this?" he is saying. She can't hear Missy's words, but the tone of her voice through the phone is clear. Accusing. Unyielding. "When did he leave?"

Diane pulls on her panties and stands up. Fully awake now. Her temples hurt already and she doesn't even know the whole story yet.

She walks around the bed and stands in front of Alejandro. "Missy—" he says into the phone as he looks up at Diane. He holds his hand up, as if to stop Diane from talking. But she wasn't going to say anything. She points downstairs—then points in the direction of Reece and Sabine's room and puts a finger up to her lips—*Don't wake the kids*. She grabs yoga pants from the chair, pulls them on, slips out the door, and slinks down her own stairs like a one-night stand.

She turns on the light in the kitchen, pours herself a glass of water from the fridge, and sits at the table, feeling surprisingly clear-headed for five in the morning. But then, she thinks, she'd be waking the kids in an hour and a half for school anyway. And the only good thing about getting the call from Missy is that Alejandro will be out of her room by the time she gets the kids up for school. It's the only time she has let him sleep upstairs when the kids are home. The way he stretched out on her bed after sex last night made her think that he was enjoying the domestic scene as a new normal, rather than what she considered it—a gift while she looks for the least explosive, least painful way to end things. As usual, her willpower has been the problem. She keeps giving in to Alejandro because it's simply the easiest thing to do. And because, if she's honest, she's avoiding pain. Her own and his.

She takes a long drink of water. From what she could make out on this end, Randy didn't come home last night. Why would Missy think Alejandro would know anything about it? She gets up and starts filling a coffee filter. Maybe Missy was using the crisis as a way to pull Alejandro back in. *Come over and comfort me.*

She clicks the filter into place, pours in the water, and flips on the machine. Poor, dopey Randy. What has he done now? She had thought of answering his "see you on the flipside" e-mail right away, but decided to wait. At some point, she figured, Randy needed to work this out with Missy alone. The e-mail had sounded sad, but also like he was beginning to accept some realities, which would ultimately be a good thing.

She feels Alejandro slip into the kitchen behind her, even though she didn't hear him come down the stairs. Good man. Good stealth. The kids' door is closed upstairs and they never wake before she jostles them. But still.

"So what's going on?" she says quietly, without turning.

She feels him move closer. "Randy is gone for two nights now," he says.

She turns. "*Two?*"

"Yes." She turns to see him leaning against the counter. His mouth is tight. Eyes dark. And it looks like he might have been crying.

"Two nights? And she can't find him?"

"He left his phone at home."

"Shit," she says. Her gut tightens. The coffeemaker hisses. She turns to take another cup out of the cupboard, and thinks. Randy must have left on Saturday night then. That was the night he sent that e-mail.

She holds her hand over the coffeemaker to feel the heat and juju it into going faster. She sees Alejandro staring at the cups. "She—Missy—" he says, "—told Randy about us. And he left the house. Like that. Without saying anything."

Diane's head starts to whirl. "Missy told Randy about the two of you?" Fuck. That's all Randy needs. One more loss to add to his mountain of losses. "Why the hell would she do that now? After it's over?" Her throat catches.

Alejandro gives an unconvincing shrug, like he's playing at being casual. "She says that he is having a girlfriend too."

"What? Randy?" she hears herself say. Too loud. But seriously? Randy would have told her. The librarian? No. He wouldn't have been able to help being more explicit about it. She leans closer to Alejandro and lowers her voice. "Did Missy say who it was?"

Alejandro throws up his hands. "Why does this matter?" He pounds the counter, turns toward the cupboards, bangs his forehead onto one of the doors and leaves it there. "It does not matter who it is," he says into the door. He rolls his head away from her. "It is only that he is gone and I am the bad one again. I am the bad one."

A small detached part of herself sees Alejandro's dramatics as being beside the point. But clearly, this is where she is now. "God damn it," she says to him, leaning in close to his face. "You are not bad. You're twenty-three."

Alejandro lifts his head from the cupboard, avoiding her gaze, and lets tears roll down his cheeks. God, he thinks. If something happened to Randy, it is his punishment. Crying feels good. Upstairs, his neck had been tight and painful from holding it all in. Now everything loosens and his shoulders start to shake.

He doesn't want Diane to see him like this, though. She already thinks he's a child. He covers his eyes with one hand and helps himself with the other, over to a chair. Lets himself sink down on it. Sag. And cry some more. His body shaking like he's six years old.

Through his phlegmy sobs he hears her firm, practical voice say, "I'm only asking because maybe Randy is staying with this girlfriend. If he has one. Isn't that the main thing? To find out where he is right now?"

On the landing upstairs, Reece is unheard and unseen. He has wandered out of bed and is listening to the voices in the kitchen below. They have a whispered, hard, adult-only sound that makes him want to hear even more. He eases himself down onto the top step and tries to make out the actual words.

Below, Diane's arms are around Alejandro's shoulders now, as his sobbing haltingly subsides. She's on her knees in between his legs as he sits at her kitchen table. And even though he's been carried away on a river of grief that is all his griefs, he begins to nuzzle her neck. Desire can grow out of any strong emotion. He has always known this.

She pulls back. "No," she says simply.

He looks into her eyes. "Is all I want. To be with you." How can she not see his passion? How much he is willing to leave everything—even his manhood—at her feet? What woman can deny this?

"You are confusing many things, Alejandro." She sits back on her haunches.

"No," he says through his teeth. "It is *you* who confuse many things. *You* who want to fuck and say it is nothing. *You* who treat me like a boy—like some exotic thing that is not real—who comes when you call and leaves when *you* decide."

He stops to see if she hears him. He pleads with his wet eyes while she presses a cool hand against his forehead.

"Yes. Maybe I do treat you that way," she says. "But the part about you being a *thing*. Something exotic. That's not true. I see you, Alejandro. I really do. I just—I'm sorry I let it go on too long."

Diane gets up on her feet, even though she feels shaky. She pulls out the chair opposite Alejandro. She looks at his bowed head. His tousled black hair. She closes her eyes, resisting the temptation to plunge into guilt and longing, which leads to self-loathing, which leads to what-the-fuck, which leads to fucking. An endless, inescapable cycle, unless—unless she simply doesn't give in.

Unless she lets him hate her. Right now.

"Alejandro," she says. "You need to leave now. I have to find Randy."

"I do not want to talk about Randy," he says, baring his teeth.

"I'm not going to talk about him." She stops. Takes a breath. "I can't make sense of most of the shit I've done yet. But in this moment, I can do the right thing—even if every other thing I did was wrong. I can let Randy know that someone gives a flying fuck about him. And I can tell you that it's time to go, and get on with your life."

Alejandro jumps out of his chair and yells, "So this is it? You are finished with me?" He stands above her. Roots himself to the floor in front of her like some iconic Greek (Colombian) god. But she refuses to look up at him. Keeps her eyes fixed on the oven dials. Hears something scraping in the hall.

"You do not even talk to me!" Alejandro screams. "All you are worried about is Randy. He does not even care for you. He is a selfish man who cannot take care of his woman!"

She keeps her eyes on the oven. Past his hip, which almost blocks her view.

Don't give in.

"You are selfish too, Diane. You are like all of them! Okay. Go find Randy. Send him back to his wife who does not love him. Find another boy next year who will fuck you and not ask questions! You are right. Is better for me. Fucking Americans! Fucking, stupid. Stupid Americans and their stupid fucking lives!"

His voice is cracking. *Don't give in.* Don't look up. She squeezes her eyes shut. For a second there is no sound. Then she hears him stomp into the living room and grab something. "Fucking stupid!" he yells again, then slams the front door.

In the kitchen, Diane brings a hand to her mouth. *Don't give in.*

Upstairs, back in his bed, Reece has pulled the covers over his head. He scrambled away as quietly as he could when Coach Al started yelling. Yelling makes his tummy hurt. And his head. And makes him want to cry. But worse than the yelling is the slamming door.

CHAPTER 64

FROM: RPLATT
TO: BEN, WUMAN

Hey, any of you know where Coach
R is? My mom is looking. Aiden
the Ultimate needs our help.

Reece.

FROM: BEN
TO: RPLATT, WUMAN

Maybe he was bummed after the game
and drank to much

FROM: RPLATT
TO: BEN, WUMAN

I'm serious.

Reece

FROM: BEN
TO: RPLATT, WUMAN

So am I or maybe he has a girlfriend.
thats where they go usually

FROM: RPLATT
TO: BEN, WUMAN

Coach R is too old.

Reece

FROM: BEN
TO: RPLATT, WUMAN

Hes my dads age and my dad had a
girlfriend and now shes my stepmom

FROM: RPLATT
TO: BEN, WUMAN

This isn't helping. Where's Patrick?
Patrick?
Text back when you're there.

Reece

FROM: BEN
TO: RPLATT, WUMAN

I dont get why your worried

FROM: RPLATT
TO: BEN, WUMAN

Coach Al was over here and my mom
and him were both upset. Its big.

Reece

FROM: BEN
TO: RPLATT, WUMAN

Al was over there, dude?

FROM: RPLATT
TO: BEN, WUMAN

Him and my mom are friends.
Reece

FROM: BEN
TO: RPLATT, WUMAN

Uh huh

FROM: RPLATT
TO: BEN, WUMAN

Stop it Ben. I shouldn't have brought
you into this. Except you're friends with
Aiden, and I THOUGHT you would want
to help him.
Reece

FROM: BEN
TO: RPLATT, WUMAN

I do
forget what I said

did anyone do the obvious and call the
guy

FROM: RPLATT
TO: BEN, WUMAN

They must have.

Reece

FROM: WUMAN
TO: RPLATT, BEN

HE PROBABLY DIDN'T TAKE HIS PHONE

FROM: RPLATT
TO: WUMAN, BEN

Why wouldn't he take his phone?

Reece

FROM: BEN
TO: RPLATT, WUMAN

Hey Wuman hows your lead foot? Sorry
about the game

FROM: WUMAN
TO: BEN, RPLATT

HE WOULDN'T TAKE HIS PHONE IF HE
DDN'T WANT ANYONE TO FIND HIM.
BUT I CAN FIND COACH RANDY.

YOU CAN'T TELL ANYONE.

FROM: BEN
TO: WUMAN, RPLATT

You're going to find him by yourself?

FROM: RPLATT
TO: BEN, WUMAN

Sure, if anyone can, Patrick can!

Reece

FROM: WUMAN
TO: BEN, RPLATT

I WILL TEXT YOU AFTER SCHOOL.

I NEED SOME TIME

CHAPTER 65

From: DPlatt@ca.rr.com

To: RTChampion@gmail.com   sent Mon, Nov 8 2:44 pm

Subject: Re: Last letter from the Library

Hi Randy,

I'm sorry that I'm only now reading this and getting back to you. I'm writing in the hope that you will read this either at the library or wherever else you are.

Look, I know that you have been gone from the house for a couple of days and I wanted to let you know that people are very concerned about you. Especially Missy. Please let her know that you are all right. Whatever is wrong is fixable.

People care about you, Randy. Please call Missy or me so we can talk.

Your friend,
Diane

If anyone were to ask, Diane wouldn't be able to tell them what she did all day. She moved a few boxes from one room to another. She walked up and down the stairs a dozen times, carrying objects: laundry; a book Sabine left in the kitchen. She did some worrying about Randy; kept listening for the phone. She thought about Alejandro a couple of times, but quickly trained her mind elsewhere.

Mostly, however, she thought about all the people who had moved in and out of her life and why some stayed and most left and how they had all changed her. And wasn't that a remarkable thing?

Before Diane knew it, it was three o'clock and the kids were about to walk in the door and still no word of Randy. Damn it, she really should do something more proactive than simply worry.

Upstairs in her bedroom, she calls Paul Pousaint. "Paul, it's Diane Platt. How are you?"

"Okay. I guess. What's up?"

Huh. Apparently, Paul isn't one for chitchat. She sits on the edge of her bed. "I have a rather delicate thing to ask."

"Delicate?"

"Hell, Paul. I don't know how to say it. It's private. You can't tell anyone I'm asking."

"Okay."

"It's just. I know that Randy has been working at a job you set him up with."

"Yes. He told you?"

"It doesn't matter. Look, Randy has been missing for a couple of days and I know that there was a woman he was friendly with at the job. He called her his office wife. And I thought—maybe she would know where he went."

"Do you think he's okay?"

"I'm trying to find that out. I can go back and check Randy's e-mails and see if he mentions her," she says. "But that could take time. You want to just ask the manager or whoever?"

"He e-mailed you that much?"

She scoots back onto the bed and tucks one leg under the other. "Paul, there isn't a big story here. Randy was depressed."

"Aren't we all?"

Something in Diane catches. *What? Are we? Are we all?*

Paul says, "Sorry. That was a bad joke. I know he was depressed. I just didn't think it was this bad."

"Can you make that call?

"Understood. I'll call right now." She is about to sign off when he breaks in with an afterthought. "By the way. How did you find out about all this?"

Stumped. Does she mention Alejandro?

"Missy," she says fast. "She was calling around to see if anyone had seen him."

"Huh," she hears him say, and in the pause that follows, she can almost hear his brain trying to put it all together. Instead of digging herself deeper into an implausible lie, she waits. Breathing. And is rewarded when he seems to actively choose credulity.

"All riiiiiight," he says. "I guess I'll make that call."

"Thanks, Paul," she says, possibly too quickly, and hangs up.

She walks over to her laptop on the dresser. Her mail is open. She types *RTinker* into the search bar. Goddamn, look at how many e-mails they exchanged. Although far fewer recently, she notices. A jab of guilt. What had she been thinking the whole time Randy had been writing her about his deepest insecurities and worries? Had he really been having an affair? It still doesn't sound right. Had she been compassionate? She remembers that she felt sorry for him, tried to be helpful. But she had remained distanced too. What if he's gone and killed himself—will that distance have been worth it?

She lifts her hand from the computer. Shit. It's the first time she's let her mind go to the worst possible thing. Is that what she's been thinking the whole time? No. Yes. How could she have ignored it?

She bites the inside of her cheek and shakes her head. *Not now. Not now. Blame yourself later.* She's good at that. She starts scrolling again. Looking at the dates. Guessing at when he started the job. Hoping that the woman at the job had been kind to him. *Is* being kind to him. Kinder than Diane.

A couple of taps at her door. She startles. "Yes?" Glances behind her. The door noiselessly inches open and Reece peeks his head in. His hair so every-which-way, it makes her heart hurt. "Yes, my love. What is it?"

The boy softly steps into the room and stops in front of her. His eyes are watery but intense. He is there to say something that is important to him. She knows the look.

She reaches out and strokes his shoulder. "Is there something you need?" Usually this would be all it would take to get him to lean into her, wrap his arms around her neck, and have a good cry. Before telling her about a mean thing someone said to him, or a test that he bombed.

But he stands there, stiff and resolved.

"Honey?" she says again.

He clears his throat. "I heard what you and Coach Al were talking about." His eyes close for a second as if waiting for a rebuke.

She continues stroking his shoulder. But her mind scrambles. What the hell did he hear? She cups his cheek. Damn it. *Damn it.* "I'm sorry, honey. That was adult stuff. Adults have arguments sometimes too. Coach Al is a friend."

"No," he says, swatting her hand away. "I heard about Coach Randy."

"Oh." She replays some of what was said, but can't remember an order to it. Maybe he only heard the part about Randy. She takes a breath. "You're worried about Randy?"

Reece looks down. "Yes."

Keeping her voice soft, she says, "Well, I am too. But I bet he'll be all right. A lot of adults need time to get their thoughts together."

"Right." He shuffles. "It's just. I know where he is."

"What?" She jumps. "You know where he is?"

He shuffles more. "Not exactly. But Patrick knows."

He thrusts his phone at her.

———

FROM: WUMAN
TO: BEN, RPLATT

I KNOW WHERE COACH IS. I SAW HIM.

———

Her shoulders drop.

Thank God. He's okay. Randy's okay. All that worrying for nothing. She hands the phone back to Reece. "That's great. Did Patrick say where he saw him?"

Reece shakes his head. "It's not like that."

Sometimes her son can be maddeningly opaque. "Never mind. It's still great. Give me your phone."

"Why?"

"I'm going to call Patrick. Can you pull up his number?"

"I guess," Reece says, swiping his phone and handing it back to her. "You should know that it's gonna sound a little weird."

CHAPTER 66

PATRICK JUMPS WHEN HIS PHONE buzzes. Reece is actually calling him? Of course he is. Patrick's revelation is a big deal and will nail his status as a kid with very special powers.

But it's a woman's voice. "Patrick?" He startles and hangs up. Places the phone on his desk and backs up. It buzzes again. He watches it. It stops. Then buzzes again.

He's going to have to answer. It's an adult. He picks up the phone slowly. "Yes?"

"Patrick. It's Reece's mom."

He almost drops the phone. What did Reece do? Tell her? Stupid Reece. Adults don't understand. "Uh. Hi, Reece's mom."

"You can call me Diane."

"Okay, Reece's mom. Miss Diane."

"So Reece says that you saw Coach."

Patrick looks down at his feet on the carpet. "Yes."

"That's great, Patrick. Where did you see him?"

He thinks extra hard about the words he should use.

"Patrick?"

"Yes."

"Can you tell me where you saw him?"

"On a beach."

"Wow. That's great. Really? You saw him on a beach? Was this yesterday?"

"No."

"Today? Today you went to the beach?"

"Right."

"Patrick, are you sure you went to the beach? It's a school day."

He slides one foot along the carpet, in front of the other. "I didn't exactly go there." He hears her sigh. Most of him wants to tell her everything. But you have to be very, very, very careful who you tell.

"Patrick. Sorry, honey. I really need to know if you actually saw Coach or didn't. It's important."

"I know."

"So?"

He slides his foot back to meet the other one. "Yes. I saw him. He's there."

"On the beach."

"It's the beach he told me about," he says. "The one where he saw the leopard shark."

"Yes. Yes. I remember that story. He told me that one too. And that's where you saw him?"

"Right."

"You're sure?" she says.

"I'm sure."

"What beach was it?"

"I don't know the name of it."

"Can I talk to your mom?"

Patrick's heart starts pounding. "Why?" His voice catches.

"Because she might know the name of the beach that she took you to."

"She can't speak English."

"Can you ask her, then?"

Patrick walks over to the window to get as far away from his bedroom door as possible. He lowers his head and whispers, "She won't know the name of it. I know she won't. That's all I can tell you. Coach is at the beach with the leopard shark. That's all I know."

There is a big silence that his brain can't find words to fill. So he waits and holds his breath. Finally, she says, "Okay, Patrick. Okay. Thank you. You've been very helpful. Really."

He exhales. "Okay. Bye."

He hangs up quickly and looks out the window. His breath now quick and shallow. His pulse flutters in his wrists and his face is hot. In the past, an undercurrent of emotion like this would be unwelcome. A sure sign of present danger. This feels different, although he can't think how.

He pulls out his desk chair, sits down, and waits to hear that everything with the coach is all right.

CHAPTER 67

DIANE HAS A FEELING OF being outside of her body and, at the same time, being completely conscious of everything around her. As she drives over to Randy's, her mission seems perfectly clear. Get the name of the beach from Missy and drive out there to talk some sense into Randy. If he's there.

Her mind keeps returning to the picture of T's face as she dropped Reece and Sabine off after school, minutes ago. She had wanted to tell him, *See, I'm a better person now. I am not supremely selfish, like you said. In fact, I'm going to rescue a person I barely know, simply because it's the right thing to do.* Which is silly, she knows. Not only because it's massively immature. But because getting the credit for being selfless nullifies the generous impulse and proves that it's still all about her.

She erases T's face and concentrates on the road. She thought about calling or texting Missy. In fact, these options were her first and, let's face it, safest choice. But lately it feels like all these texts and e-mails pinging around the team, and especially Randy, have gotten in the way of more honest conversation. Plus, the chances of Missy picking up the phone or engaging in a reasonable text conversation with Diane, the stealer of Alejandro's affection, are about nil.

Diane feels something close to virtuous as she waits at a light.

The light changes.

Patrick's story was all over the place, but something about it makes sense in her bones. Where else would Randy go? To a bar? A hotel? Okay, maybe. But no. Randy, with all his yearnings for a time when everything wasn't so complicated, a time when he was loved (even if it was all an illusion), would go back to his last perfect day. He had told both Patrick and her about it. She can feel him thinking—if he could only get back there, he would be able to start over from that point and not fuck it up this time. She even remembers him saying something about going back to the beach in one of his hundreds of e-mails.

Her phone buzzes. She picks it up, reads the contact sideways, and answers, "Paul. I'm driving."

"Sorry. I'll be brief. I found the woman at Going Baroque and she doesn't know anything about where Randy went. Although she didn't seem surprised. She also thinks that he's been very depressed."

"Thanks." Diane pulls onto a side street. "I think I may have figured it out anyway."

"You found him?"

"Not yet. But I have reason to believe that he's gone out to a favorite beach spot."

"Really? Huh. Why would he do that?"

"I'm driving, Paul. But trust me."

"Which beach?"

"I don't know yet. I'm about to find out."

"Wait, Diane. One last thing. The woman Randy was working with. I don't know if it's relevant to anything. But she's a man."

"A man?"

"You know. A man who dresses and acts like a woman. Trans-whatever."

She pulls into Randy's driveway. "Okay. I can't think about that now." She hangs up. What the hell is that about? Randy never mentioned that she was a he, which is the kind of thing he *would* mention. Is she about to find a whole trove of things about Randy that spin this mission in a shocking direction? Has she been too eager to dismiss the idea of Randy having an affair? She's been quick to decide what kind of guy he is—but maybe she's been entirely wrong.

Before her resolve fades, she gets out of the car and strides up to the front door. Stomps on the welcome mat to bring her thoughts back to her first task. Rings the bell.

Clutches.

What if Aiden answers? Or the housekeeper. What does she do then?

The door opens and there is, in fact, the housekeeper. Young and pretty, in a sweatshirt and tight faded jeans. "I would like to speak to Mrs. Tinker." The girl flashes a perfunctory smile, nods, and steps aside. Diane nods back and whisks by her. "My name is Diane."

She's in, and the girl leads her into the living room. Where she is left to wait. She hears steps being climbed. Hears the girl knock on a door and speak in a low, professional tone. Hears the door close again and footsteps coming back down to her.

She glances around the living room that she saw last at the barbecue when Alejandro did his stripper dance. That scene, remembered—the adults singing karaoke, kids running around the yard and some hanging around the edges, even her grabbing Alejandro's ass—takes on an innocence in light of what has happened in the past couple of months.

The housekeeper reemerges. "Miss," she says, gesturing for Diane to follow her. They climb the stairs like burglars. Quiet, careful, determined.

In the upstairs hallway, the girl knocks lightly on a door, opens it noiselessly, and nods back at her. Diane slips through, into the room.

It is the master bedroom, light blue, shades half-drawn. Sunlight spilling through the bottom third of the windows. And in the middle of the rumpled bed is a balled-up Missy, her back to Diane. Her hair is dirty and tangled, splayed across the duvet.

"What are you doing here?" Missy says, not turning to see her. Her voice is gravelly. And even without seeing her face, Diane can picture it. Ruddy, damp. Dark eye sockets. Her prettiness rubbed out.

Diane clears her throat, although she doesn't need to. "Alejandro told me about Randy and I want to help. I have an idea of where he could be."

Missy's shoulder moves as she makes a derisive sound. Diane stands firm and waits. Making herself breathe.

The air in the room doesn't move. Diane tries to imagine Randy in here. His rangy tallness against the feminine scallops and flounces. She watches as Missy rolls over, taking time and arranging herself so she's sitting on the edge of the bed. Keeping her head down as she does this, Missy avoids eye contact. Fair enough. "Why would you have any ideas about Randy?" she says with a rasp that sounds far more worldly than Diane has ever heard her. "Did you sleep with him too?"

Diane shakes her head. Jesus, she doesn't need any of this. But she squares herself, pressing on. "No, Missy," she says, banishing the image of the crotch grab in the kitchen. "I never slept with Randy."

"Yeah, right."

Everything in Diane wants to throw her hands up and be done with it. Why is Missy making it so goddamned hard to help her? Diane takes a purposeful breath. "Look, I'm very worried about him." Missy's arm reaches out to snatch a crumpled tissue from the folds of the covers. "Are *you* worried about him?"

Missy stares up at Diane. "Of course I'm worried about him," she says through tight lips. "He's my husband."

Diane takes a breath. "Have you called the police yet?"

Missy finally looks directly at her. "You think I should call the police?"

Diane's lower back hurts. She reaches behind and rubs her tailbone with a fist. "Uh. Yes. If we are all this worried, I think we should call. Yes."

"We?"

She digs into her lower back muscles with a knuckle. "Yes. You. Me. Alejandro." She doesn't say "Paul." Keep it simple.

"So Alejandro is worried that Randy might"—she blows into the Kleenex—"hurt him?"

"Hurt Alejandro? No. I don't think he's worried about that." And now it hits her like her recurring dream of finding a whole room in her house that she never knew existed. Randy hasn't told Missy anything.

Anything! Not about the money, getting fired, the marketing job, coaching Patrick, the library, the woman (or man) from work. His whole secret life. Missy knows absolutely nothing. She thinks that all this is a reaction to her affair.

Diane pulls over a wicker chair and sits, wondering how to proceed. "I think that I need to tell you some things," she says, leaning forward and feeling the wicker lip of the chair dig into the back of her thigh. What is the bare minimum she can divulge while still getting across the seriousness of the situation? "Is it okay?"

"Is what okay?" sniffs Missy.

"Okay if I tell you some things about Randy that might help you?"

"Don't tell me anything you think will make me feel worse."

Diane sees Missy from the side. The C curve of her back and her stringy hair hanging down. Absolutely everything she can tell Missy will make her feel worse.

"Nothing improper has happened between Randy and me," Diane says, dropping her register on the word *improper* like a mother superior. "But I need you to know that he has confided in me. Mostly through e-mail."

Missy turns her head and looks directly at Diane. "Why you?"

Diane struggles to maintain her gaze. To look away would seem guilty. "I don't know why he started writing to me. Maybe because I wrote back? I was lonely. My house was empty half the time when my kids were with my ex. I don't know." She shifts her weight on the edge of the chair. "But what I do know is that Randy is very unhappy." She quickly holds up a hand. "Not about you. In fact, you were the one thing that he felt good about. You and Aiden. Well, mostly good. Except he didn't think that you loved him." She's bothered by slipping into the past tense, as if Randy is dead. She shifts again. Takes a breath. "He loves you. Maybe that's why he couldn't. Can't. Tell you about how unhappy he is."

Missy listens. Seems to take it in. "I don't know what to do," she says in a whimper. The sound is one of total abdication. And also, Diane notices that she hasn't asked what Randy was unhappy about. She sees the bottles of pills by the bed.

Of course. Unhappiness is a habit that Missy and Randy have shared, without saying a word. Diane thinks of T. Of herself. And the cottony safety of not having felt much at all, for so long.

"Well. I've thought of what to do," Diane says, taking up the reins Missy has shoved in her direction. "First, I think that you should call the police and just tell them that Randy is missing. Maybe they can't do anything yet. But at least we—You. At least *you* will have done the right thing." What is the right thing? Diane can't stop to consider. "And second, I need to know which beach you were on. When Aiden was a toddler and you saw the little leopard shark?"

Missy shoots up from the bed. Stands thin and brittle. "Why do you need to know that?"

Diane pulls back at the unexpected kinetic jolt, but presses on. "This is going to sound strange."

"Damn right it's strange. Why do you have to know about the beach? What does it have to do with anything? What did Randy tell you?" She kicks a piece of clothing aside and stomps into the closet or the bathroom, Diane can't tell which. But she can still hear her. "He told you about the beach? He talked about me? I don't have to tell you anything. Not one fucking thing."

She emerges with a sweater hastily pulled on, her hair staticky, floating away from her head like filament. She is all energy. "What else do you know about me? What did Alejandro tell you? Did you laugh about how I fucked?"

Diane stands, finding herself a bit unsteady. The curled-up, damp ball she found mourning in the middle of the bed has uncoiled and she hasn't had time to reassess. On she presses. "You have to believe that Alejandro told me nothing about you."

"Nothing? I can't believe that."

"Okay. Not nothing. He told me that he felt bad. That he thought the two of you…" She pauses, light-headed. "He thought at first that the two of you were playing a game. A seduction game." She's talking too fast and tries to slow down. "You know. Where you act innocent. And he gets aggressive." She looks at Missy, who is now stone still, except for the hairs, which haven't settled. What was she saying? Words. "And later. He realized, later, that you weren't playing a game. But he was. And he felt bad. And had to end. It. Because." She pauses to take in air. "Because he didn't want to hurt you anymore."

She feels herself sway a little. Then bam. A pillow hits her in the face. Another. And another. Missy is pulling them off the bed and hurling them at her. Stunned, Diane holds up a hand and ducks. Seizes a round thing from the desk and flings it at Missy. She hears it thwap against Missy's forehead. Fuck! But before Diane can ask if she's okay, Missy's crawling across the bed to grab a pillow from the other side, pitching it in Diane's direction.

Diane ducks again.

The pillow knocks over a vase thing. Diane sees her moment and pounces onto the bed. Crawling over to Missy, she body-slams into her. Smashing her into the mattress with her weight.

For a moment nothing happens while Diane lies on top of Missy, feeling how small she is.

Then in one move, Missy arches. Lifts herself up on all fours with Diane swaying on top of her, trying to get balance. Missy bucks. Diane slides off. Missy crawls to the other side. Diane reaches out to grab her leg and pull, slamming her onto the mattress again.

Missy reaches back and gropes, trying to find some part of Diane to yank or hit, and screams, "You are a biiiiiitch!" Tears in her voice, it catches and she starts to sob. She heaves and lets out a wail. Then abandons herself to weeping.

Diane lets go of her leg and Missy pulls it into herself, moaning and crying. Slowly, shakily, Diane lifts herself up and crawls off the bed. She teeters over to the window shades and pulls on the cord, lifting them, and the light rushes in.

She is breathing hard. Hot. Damp everywhere. She lifts a hand to her cheek. Raw. Turns to look at Missy in her knot of grief. "You're right," she says, moving around the bed toward the door. "I am a bitch."

Diane slams the door and stomps down the stairs. Pounding her feet with as much force as she has left. God damn it. God fucking damn. She hits the hallway and starts for the front door. Is about to fucking leave this crazy, fucked-up house. Reaches the living room on the left, where she sees the housekeeper vacuuming.

And stops.

Is this it? Is she done? Giving up when it gets hard or boring or seems pointless?

She chews her lip while the housekeeper mows the carpet, back and forth. Back and forth. What did she hear? Diane wonders. What does she think of us? Of me? Standing there, dripping with sweat. Her hair— God knows what her hair is doing. Her cheeks burning.

Diane clears her throat and shakes her hair out of her face.

The housekeeper stops the vacuum. Turns it off and looks at her.

"Mrs. Tinker is upset," Diane hears herself say in a gravelly voice. "Would you tell her that I'll be waiting for her in the kitchen?"

––––––––––

Diane has been standing at the kitchen sink for ten minutes. She heard the housekeeper go up to the room and back down, twice. Aiden's not back from school yet. Maybe he's at a friend's. At one point the house-keeper ducked into the kitchen to say that Mrs. Tinker would be coming down. Diane has no idea if that's a direct message from Missy or simply the housekeeper's assessment.

She taps her hand on the counter by the sink as she looks out the window. Come on. Come on. It's almost three o'clock. If she doesn't get started soon, it'll be dark. Maybe she should call Patrick again. See if he remembers more about the beach.

Tick, tick, tick, tick—Diane hears in her mind.

Footsteps in the hall. Purposeful clicking. She turns and Mis-sy's there. On the other side of the island. She's combed her hair and changed her shirt. Looking at Missy all cleaned up, Diane feels even more of a mess. Feral. Smelling of sweat and something sour.

"I called the police," Missy says.

Diane's neck tightens. Calling the police makes it real. "What did they say?"

"They asked about the circumstances and I told them that Randy—I told them we had a fight." Missy shrugs and looks away.

Diane keeps her face as neutral as possible. Hoping that Missy doesn't guess that Alejandro has already told her what happened.

Missy drops her head. "Anyway. I e-mailed them a picture. They put all his details in the system." She reaches out and absently picks up a fake green apple from the decorative arrangement in front of her. "In case he turns up."

"Turns up?" The picture of a body washing up onshore flashes through Diane's mind. She shakes it off.

Missy picks out another fake apple. Holding one in each hand, she looks at the permanently perfect fruits as if she doesn't know where they came from. "Maybe he's disoriented, they said. He could have amnesia."

Diane watches Missy stare at the two fruits in her hands, her breathing shallow. Is Missy thinking about lobbing them at her? "Do *you* think he has amnesia?" Diane asks quickly.

Missy puts the apples back in the bowl and Diane's shoulders loosen a bit.

"No. I don't think it's amnesia. I think he's angry and thinking about what to do next."

"Probably."

"I think that that's what the police think too. Once I told the sergeant about our fight, I could hear it in his voice. He thought it was my fault." Missy stares at the bowl of fake fruit with great concentration. Diane stares at it too, thinking about how to move this along without shutting Missy down.

"Point Mugu is where we saw the shark," Missy says.

"Oh. Thanks. That's good. That's helpful." Diane tries not to sound too businesslike, but she's itching to move. She steps forward.

Missy takes a counterstep and eyeballs Diane with a flat, unsparing look. "Why do you need to know about the beach?"

Shit. "Well, this is where it starts to sound a bit strange." Diane attempts a collusive *we're just girlfriends here* tone. She doesn't want to set Missy off with any suggestion that she might know more than the wife. "But Randy is very attached to that memory and I think it's a possible place that he would go to be by himself and think. I know it sounds crazy. Unless you can think of other places he usually goes." She shoots her what she hopes is an inviting smile.

"He only went to work and home," Missy says. "Or Starbucks, but they'd never let him sit this long. He never went to bars. Or at least I didn't think so until—" She stops to think. "Wait. Maybe." She closes her eyes and says quietly, "I didn't think. But maybe. There's a woman he might—might have been—" Her eyes open. "He might have gone to her."

Diane wants to ask her how she knows about the woman. How could she know that much and not know all the rest? But all this speculation isn't getting them one bit closer to Randy.

"I'm pretty sure that the woman is just a friend," Diane says in a re-assuring tone. "Randy told me about her and he didn't sound like he was hiding anything. And usually with Randy you can tell." She checks Missy's face to see if this is too much of an intimacy to share. Their common understanding of Randy's MO. If he were having an affair he would have gone overboard with explanations. Or wouldn't have men-tioned her at all, for fear of exposing his secret.

Diane inches forward slightly. "Look. If it's okay with you, I'm going to drive up the coast to see if Randy's there."

"You're going to go up there?" Missy steps to the side, imperceptibly blocking Diane's easy path to the hallway.

"Someone should go. Is it that campground off the PCH, right after Malibu? It's not far."

"I'm the one," Missy interrupts Diane's calibrations. Her voice is shaky and suddenly louder. "I'm the one who should go and talk to him."

They stare at each other, the air quivering between them. It would be the easiest thing in the world to walk away and let Missy take it from here. But something's still nagging at Diane. What if it's the worst possible thing? She keeps her voice even. "I don't really know if he's there, Missy. It's just a hunch. Are you sure you shouldn't stay here and wait?"

"No. It's our beach. He tried to talk about that day sometime last week."

"He did?"

"Why are you doing this?"

They are squared off, to the side of the island. Diane would have to shove Missy aside in order to get past her.

"Look," Diane says, unsure of what's going to come out of her mouth next. "You're right. It should be you. But there's Aiden, right?"

"Rosa can watch him."

"Okay. But should you drive alone? You're upset."

"I can manage."

And right now, Missy does look like she can manage. But what about later?

And what if?

Diane stops her thoughts. "I'd feel better," she says, "if we both went together. I won't get in the way, I promise."

Missy cocks her head. "I can't think of a single reason why I should say yes to you."

Diane closes her eyes, draws a breath and lets it out slowly. "I don't know. Maybe because we both want the same thing. For Randy to be—" What? "For us to know that he's okay." She opens her eyes and looks directly at Missy. "Look. He might not be okay, is what I'm saying. And if he isn't . . . then you might need someone like me."

Missy stares back, then quickly spins and starts to walk out of the kitchen. For a second, Diane thinks she's going to walk right out the front door without saying a thing. What does she do then? Run after her? This all seems so silly. Yet the feelings are real. They're in Diane's neck and bowels and shaky voice. She's about to go after Missy when

Missy turns on the threshold of the kitchen and says, "Okay. But I drive, and if he's there, you keep quiet. I do the talking."

Before Diane can say anything, Missy pivots again, striding out of the kitchen in a way that makes no promises of polite conversation or even forgiveness.

CHAPTER 68

FROM: DPLATT
TO: PPOUSAINT

Since you're the only other person who
knows about Randy, I'm letting you know
that Missy and I are driving up to Point
Mugu, in the hopes of finding him there.
Also, police have been informed about
his disappearance, but not about our
Point Mugu hunch, in case it's nothing
and we look a little crazy. Should only
take a few hours or so, there and back.

"I'm sorry, it's just. I couldn't help overhearing you on the phone this
afternoon."

Paul startles, and looks up to see Marianne in the doorway of the
den. Her long hair is wet from a shower and her tank top skims lightly
over her breasts in a way that fills him with longing for the past.

"What's going on?" she asks, as if it's the most normal thing in the
world for her to be talking to him like this, instead of it being the first
time she has asked him a direct question (about anything other than
the kids) in months.

His eyelid twitches and he's suddenly aware of the pile of linens on
the couch, where he sleeps. He moves into the center of the room in an
attempt to pull focus away from the countless artifacts of their fractured

marriage. The array of toiletries on the edge of his desk. A couple of shirts hanging off the bookcase. Empty yogurt containers in the trash can.

"Randy Tinker has been missing for a couple of days," he says.

"Really? Who were you talking to?" She leans against the doorframe, raises one foot and places it over the other in a move she's made for more than fifteen years.

"This person he works with. I got Randy a job a few weeks ago."

"You got him a job?"

He feels awkward—unmoored—standing in the middle of the room. But he's afraid that moving might give her the opportunity to leave. And he needs her there. Needs to look at her a little longer. With her eyes not hating him. "Randy got—no one knows about this by the way—Randy got fired a couple of months ago and he needed some income, even if it was small. And a place to go, I guess."

Marianne crosses her arms. What does that mean? Is it a judgment? "Missy doesn't know?"

"Not from what Randy told me," he says, shifting his weight slightly onto one hip. "He was hoping that he'd land another job before he had to tell her."

Is he imagining the softening of her face?

"Ah," she says, pulling away from the doorframe and planting both feet. "That kind of sneaking around rarely works."

His forehead hurts, but he keeps his eyes on her. "You're right," he says carefully. "Especially when you feel terrible about yourself."

They look at each other, holding their gaze for longer than is comfortable. Finally, she breaks it. Looks down and uncrosses her arms.

"Well," she says, "I hope you find him."

"Right," he says, as she turns and starts walking away. "Thanks," he calls after her as she disappears into the kitchen.

He looks up at the ceiling, kicking himself for thinking that she'd somehow give him credit for helping a guy like Randy out.

That's not how this is going to work, he reminds himself. The road to forgiveness is going to be fucking long and torturous. The more so, the greater the reward. Keep that in your mind, buddy. Keep only that in your mind.

CHAPTER 69

DIANE AND MISSY HAVE BEEN driving in silence (except for the sound of traffic, and now the ocean) for forty minutes or so. The sky has been overcast since they left the city, and Diane wonders if it might rain. If they make good time, they'll reach the campsite right before sunset. If Randy's there, she hopes they find him before it gets completely dark and they're scuttling around on the beach like a couple of clueless teen detectives.

Diane gives Missy a quick glance. Her expression has not changed since they got in the car. It's as steely as Missy can manage. Diane remembers again the lack of definition Missy's face always seems to have. She'd be hard to describe to a police sketch artist.

The volume of everything they are not saying occupies the most space in the car. After all, Diane's and Missy's stories have intersected for months, but they've never had one direct exchange about it before today. Hell, they never even had an *indirect* exchange. How can that possibly be?

Diane looks out her window, wishing she were smarter. More able to articulate her feelings, or at least better at drawing Missy out. This—right here—is an opportunity for the two of them to change the narrative. Do two middle-aged conquests of the same gorgeous twenty-three-year-old soccer coach have to play their parts to the very end? Is their only option a reality-TV-like catfight? Or could one of them say something that, like a train switch, could send them in a completely different direction?

Missy is aware of every small adjustment, every sigh or itch that Diane makes. And she most certainly noticed the side glance Diane sent in her direction. Missy's guess is that Diane has been waiting for her to say the first word. But why should Missy make anything easy for her? There isn't one time that Diane has ever tried to engage her in a conversation about anything. Not even about something small, like nail polish or middle schools. And the whole time she's had no problem talking up a storm with Randy.

She hears Diane clear her throat and say, "I think you should know that I am not seeing Alejandro anymore."

Missy shudders. Why's Diane bringing this up now? So she can be the better person in all this?

"It doesn't matter to me," Missy says.

"Well, good. I just thought—in case it does—that it might make things easier for you to know that it's over between us."

"You're free to do what you want. I'm free. He's free."

"Okay, fine," Diane says. She guesses they're sticking to their roles. She stops herself from saying, *Seriously? If I am so free to do what I want, why were you throwing shit at me in your bedroom?*

A few drops fall on the windshield. Of course, Diane thinks, because nothing about this could be easy, right? She looks at the darkening sky ahead and has to admit that there's something satisfyingly atmospheric about it. But then she remembers that this is a real story, not a book or TV. There's a real man out there somewhere. If not in Point Mugu, then somewhere. A person who asked her for help many times. She stops herself from going back and parsing through the range of her responses from adequate to dismissive.

Fuck it. She might as well try to have an honest conversation. What does she have to lose? "Are you scared?" she asks Missy.

The windshield wipers swish.

"Scared of what?"

"I don't know," Diane says. Although she does know. But if the thought hasn't occurred to Missy, she's certainly not introducing it. "Finding him, I guess. Not finding him."

"Yes," Missy says.

Swish.

Swish. The drops stop, but Missy doesn't seem to notice.

"I have this feeling that whatever happens," Missy goes on, "nothing will be the same as it was. And that's scary." She turns the wipers off.

"I understand," Diane finds herself saying. And she does, because there is nothing more terrifying than uncertainty.

"Damn it," Missy says.

"I know. Right?"

"No. I thought I could hold it. But I really have to pee."

"We're almost there."

"I know. But if we find him, I don't want to be talking to him while I'm thinking about having to pee."

"We could pull off to the side, instead of taking an exit. I'm worried it's going to get dark soon."

"Right," Missy says, slowing down and pulling onto the gravelly shoulder. She looks into the rearview mirror, sees her moment, and opens the driver's side. Diane watches her cross in front of the car. The dim light from the headlights catches her; then she's off, into the tall grass.

Fuck it. Diane has to go too. She pushes the car door open and is hit by the cold. In a split second, she thinks of closing the door and suffering. But the pull in her bladder won't be denied. She hops out, yanks her pants down, and squats.

Over the stream she hears yelling and turns to see Missy bounding toward her. She can't make out the words. And can't stop herself from peeing to stand up. What the hell?

Missy reaches the gravel. Stands in front of her, panting. "I didn't look for the gun!"

"What?" God damn it, she probably just peed on her shoes. "What gun?"

"Our gun!" Missy yells. "What if he took it? I didn't even think about it. He keeps it in the garage. Why didn't I check?" The wind has wound Missy's hair around the lower part of her face. She starts walking in a tiny circle on the gravel muttering, "Oh God. Oh God. Oh God."

Diane is almost down to a trickle. She shakes her ass. Stands before she's sure she's done and pulls her pants up.

Missy stops circling; cars whiz by. "I crushed him. I should never have told him."

"Come on," Diane says. Fuck, it's freezing. She throws herself into the car seat and yells, "Get in the car, now!" But Missy doesn't move and Diane feels like she can't close the door.

"What if he hurts himself?" Missy says, her arms crossed, rubbing her hands up and down for warmth.

"We don't know anything right now." Diane reaches for the hand rest. Jesus, can she just close the door?

"I can't believe I was so stupid," Missy says, not moving.

Diane's teeth are starting to chatter, but she forces herself to stay with Missy.

"You weren't stupid. You were just trying to be happy," she says.

"How do you know that?"

"Because that's all anyone ever wants."

The wind whips while the women stare at each other.

"Now, let's go," Diane barks and slams the door closed.

She watches Missy standing stock-still for a second, then jogging in front of the car. The door opens. Missy's in. Slam. They belt up. And just like that, they are on the road again. Ominous sky, but not raining. Not yet. Still some light.

Diane blows into her fists. Eyeballs the GPS and the road signs. "He's going to be all right," she says to Missy, pointing to their exit. "Really. He's got to be. All of this worrying and running around has to count for something." She attempts an encouraging smile in Missy's direction. But Missy's eyes are on the road.

CHAPTER 70

RANDY'S JEEP IS ONE OF only two in the lot, since it's not camping season. And even though Diane has been hoping to find him here all along, she still can't quite believe that they've done it. Her pulse pounds as they pull into a parking spot. For a second, she can't find the door handle. By the time she does, Missy is already out, her head bobbing up and down as she peers into Randy's front and back windows, hand to her forehead. "He's not in there!" she yells and runs across the lot, heading for the beach.

Diane consciously slows herself down. Her movements. Her thoughts. Don't get ahead of yourself, she says to her body. Put one foot in front of the other. Don't think about what you might find. What has happened up until this moment has already happened. You can't change it. She pulls her sweater tightly around her, walking steadily across the lot, looking at the ground. Not looking ahead. Deliberately not looking ahead. *Don't think about the cold. Keep your head down.*

A gunshot.

Diane hears Missy. "No! No! No!" How is it that her voice isn't more carried away by the wind as she runs toward the ocean?

They are both running. Missy clacking across the rocky beach. Diane behind her. Where the hell are they going? Out to sea? Where did the sound come from?

"Randy!" Missy screams. "Randy!" into the wind. Waves crash. She makes a sharp right along the shore.

Diane stops. Pants for breath. Looks in the direction that Missy is running.

There. On a pile of boulders. A football field away. Is that a figure? Fuck. Could it be him? Sitting? Please let it be him.

"Randy!" Missy runs toward the big rocks.

Diane follows. Slow. Trudging. Breathing hard. She sees Missy start scrambling up the big rocks. Her lungs hurt and she stops again. Looks up to see Missy reach the figure, her hair flapping. Sees the figure move. It is him. Thank God and God damn him. Even with his hood up, Diane can tell it's him by the way he's sitting and the way Missy is standing in front of him, furiously flinging her arms around him.

Diane starts walking again. Step by step. So he's fine. He's alive. Was it a gunshot? Did he miss? Fuck, what now? She tromps up to the boulders, grabs the top of one, and hoists herself up. Her hands numb with cold. Teeth rattling.

"Are you kidding me?" She hears Missy shout over the pounding waves. Diane bends and plants her hand on another boulder to guide herself over to them. Straddles two boulders. Wobbles until she finds balance, pulls her back leg up, and finally jumps onto a patch of packed sand in the middle of some stones. Missy's back is to her. Randy leans out to look around his wife.

"Hi, Diane," he says.

Missy turns to look at her, and Diane can see him fully now. His face is puffy, hangdog, and wet from the ocean spray. They are all wet.

Missy points back at him and yells to Diane, "Mr. Brilliant here was in the middle of faking his own suicide!"

"What the hell?" Diane says.

Then she sees it. The gun. Lying next to Randy's thigh. Holy shit. He's got the fucking gun. A fucking loaded gun. Jesus Christ.

"He just shot the gun into the ocean!" Missy yells and turns back to him. "Do you know how scared we've all been?"

Randy folds his arms across his chest, tucking his hands under his armpits. "How's Aiden?" he says. "Is Aiden okay?"

"Aiden's fine," yells Missy. "No thanks to you. Now you're suddenly worried about him?"

"Look," Diane says, holding up her numb-as-hell hands, "can we just...?" What? Just what? "Look. I'm super uncomfortable with that gun sitting there."

"I told you we shouldn't have a gun," Missy spits through the tangle of hair across her face.

Randy picks it up: Diane flinches. "It's empty," he says. "I only loaded one bullet."

"Okay. Okay," Diane says, looking away. "Can you put it in your sweatshirt or something? I'm not capable of normal thought when it's there."

"Sure," he says.

Diane looks back as Randy is pocketing it. She takes a deep breath through her chattering jaw. "And now. Can we please, please, please get into the cars or meet in a bathroom or something? We can do everything we need to do—yell, apologize, make up, confess—I really don't give a shit—but can we do all that inside somewhere?"

"Fine by me," Missy shouts, and marches past Diane. They watch her stumble across the beach. It's now almost entirely dark, but the shore is lit by the moon and the glinting ocean—which Diane would appreciate on any other evening.

"I really fucked up, didn't I?" Randy says, standing up.

Diane pushes herself off a boulder. "We already knew that, Randy. The point was not to make it worse."

She leads as they carve a winding path down. On the beach again, stones grind under her feet as she walks with crossed arms, head down. Randy catches up to her.

"Have you been here the whole time?" Diane finally asks.

"I've been driving around. Pulling off the road to sleep and think. I got here last night."

She lifts her head and sees the light from Missy's car shine as she gets in. Randy stops walking. Rocks crunch. Diane stops. They stand together, staring at the car as the light goes out.

"I was going to do it," he says.

Her breath catches. "God, Randy."

"And then I couldn't."

She shivers even more than she's been shivering. "Well, good," she says, at a complete loss. Because, even though Randy is standing here now, he might not have been. He might have gone somewhere other than this beach. Might have summoned up the courage after a fifth of Jim Beam to end it all. He had thought about it. He had brought the gun.

"I'm a coward," he says, standing still despite the cold. Staring at Missy's dark car.

Diane stomps a little to get the blood going. "I don't know what that means, Randy. Most of us are scared shitless all the time."

"And then I thought of faking the suicide instead. They'd find the gun and it would look like I got washed out to sea. And then I would start over somewhere else. North Dakota, maybe."

"North Dakota. Jesus, Randy. Nothing's in North Dakota."

"Exactly. It's the perfect place to start over."

She stares at him, every part of her body shaking. Seriously? What goes on in his brain?

She turns and walks again; he trips after her. "Did it ever once occur to you that things weren't that terrible?" she yells over her shoulder.

"She cheated on me."

"Which sucks. And hurts. But, Randy—" She stops again and turns back to him. "How big are your problems, really? How big are any of our problems?"

Randy throws his hands up. "They're pretty damn big, Diane. They're big to me!"

"We live in Beverly fucking Hills!"

"Did you come all the way out here to make me feel worse?" he says, spitting. "'Cause you're doing a fantastic job of it." And she sees that he has been crying. Tears have left tracks down his cheeks, and the loose skin around his eyes is even puffier.

They are on the edge of the parking lot. They are on the dark curve of the earth under the limitless sky. She's come all the way here, made all kinds of promises to be a better person—and she's blowing it. She's yelling at a man who almost killed himself.

The cold is making her face feel like it might fall off, but she tries to hold his gaze in some kind of freaky, wordless solidarity.

"Got it," Randy says, "I'm on my own!"

He trudges past her, and she yells after him, "That's not what I meant!"

He raises an arm and keeps walking toward the Audi.

"I'm sorry," she yells. "I really am sorry, Randy."

He keeps going but waves his upheld hand in a way that could be interpreted as forgiveness. "Hey, Randy!" she yells louder.

He stops. Turns. "What now?"

"Can you throw me your keys? I'll wait in your car."

He pats himself down, finds them, and tosses. The keys hit her chest and fall to the ground.

CHAPTER 71

MISSY WON'T LOOK AT RANDY. She stares straight ahead while he fusses in the passenger seat, making more legroom and throwing some receipts from the floor into the back. After he's done this, however, there's nothing more to do and he has to settle. He leans the seat back a bit and waits.

He hardly felt the cold outside, but Missy's been running the heat on low and the dank warmth inside is almost too much for him. He slides his hand over and lowers the window a half inch.

"Don't do that," she says.

He raises it back up. Pulls at the collar of his hoodie. Would she let him take it off?

Wait a minute. Why is he acting like the guilty party here?

He pulls his seat up straighter. "Okay. Let's start with how long you and Al were together."

"No," she says. Her voice sounds older than usual. "Let's start with what this was all about."

"What 'this'?"

"You know what 'this.' Scaring me and disappearing like that. Faking your own death? What the hell would I tell Aiden?"

He winces at the thought of Aiden. Of course, he had thought about him. Had even thought that the boy would be better off. He can feel the weight of the gun in his sweatshirt pocket, resting against his belly. God, how stupid.

"And it wasn't just me cheating, anyway," she goes on. "What about you? I wasn't the only one."

His face flushes. And his gut hardens.

Has she known the whole time? Watched him walk out the door every morning in his suit and tie? Knowing it was a lie? Damn, it's hot.

He lowers the window halfway.

"I told you not to," she growls.

He turns to face her. She's blotchy and her hair's all tangled into a snarl on one side. "I have to. I don't want to throw up!"

She crosses her arms, turns away from him, and stares out her window. He breathes in the fresh air. He can make out Diane's profile sitting in his car.

"Okay. Okay," he says, taking in more air. His sweatshirt sticks to him. Itches. He shivers. "I'm sorry I lied to you. I thought... I thought I was protecting you. I know how you get when things go wrong at work. I knew you'd completely lose it if I told you."

She looks straight at him. "Something's wrong at work?"

He stops breathing. What did she think he's been lying about? His mind bounces around. What is she thinking? What does she know? Does he still have to tell her everything, or can he just tell her some of it?

"What's wrong at work?" she says.

"Okay. Okay. I'll tell you." He wiggles around like he's trying to get comfortable, but he's buying time.

"For starters," he says, "Sam betrayed me."

"Just tell me what the hell happened."

"It's a long story."

"Just tell me!"

He closes his eyes. "I got—I was let go."

"When?"

He can't look at her. "Over a month ago, I guess." Squeezes his eyes tight.

He waits. For her to scream or hit him with her fists.

Eyes tight, he contracts. Primed for impact.

Instead, nothing.

Then the door swings out. A rush of air. Slam. He opens his eyes and she is gone.

From the relative peace of Randy's Jeep, Diane watches Missy stumble toward the ocean. Her first impulse is to get out and follow. But she checks it when their car light goes on again and Randy emerges. His tall frame outlined for a second before he shuts his door. He follows at a much slower pace. But still follows. And Diane feels a swell of something like pride, watching him walk determinedly after his wife.

She takes another bite of some god-awful meat jerky thing that she found in a brown bag on the passenger seat. She had the choice between it and a half bag of M&M's.

She watches the undulating thumb-sized figures of Randy and Missy pacing back and forth, dwarfed by the rolling tide. Her hands have almost completely thawed and she feels strangely righter with the world than she has in days, other than her gnawing stomach. She takes another salty bite.

Feeling righter is a relative thing, since nothing has felt right for years. But as she watches someone else work through the frayed remains of a marriage, she feels the pragmatic calm that comes with being on the other side of a crisis. Yes, it still stinks, but Jesus, it's great to be done.

She should mark this moment somehow, she thinks. She should celebrate the absence of pain and the budding of satisfaction that comes with having helped a guy out. Even though Randy probably doesn't see it as "helping out." Yet.

She raises her ass off the seat and twists herself on a knee to look into the back. With any luck, Randy bought himself some beer. Her hand gropes around a bunch of takeout bags as she dangles over the seat back. Come on. He must have gotten something. Who runs away from home to end it all, one way or another, without some liquid courage?

But no. She slumps back down into her seat. Sees Missy and Randy still on the beach. How long is this going to take? She hadn't factored in the waiting, and she wonders if she should check in with T to see how the kids are doing. Or text Paul about Randy. She definitely should let Alejandro know that Randy is safe. But it hurts her chest to think of contacting him. *Don't go back. Don't go back.* If she talks to him, her resolve might fizzle.

Jesus, when is she going to stop being such a fucking wimp? She reaches into her pocket to get out her phone and text. Holds it in her hand for a minute, then thinks—Fuck it. Be an adult.

She dials. Barely breathes as she listens to it ringing, and as it switches to voicemail she feels instant reprieve. Only for a second, before she makes herself speak.

"Hi, Alejandro. Sorry to leave this message on your voicemail, but I thought it was better somehow to call instead of texting." Out the window, Randy is following after Missy, who is walking away from him, along the shoreline. "I just want to let you know that I found Randy. Well, Missy and I did—" She pauses, not sure what else there is to say. Although now that she has made the connection, she is reluctant to hang up. She watches Randy catch up to Missy.

"To review your message, press one. To end your call, press two..."

She hangs up, and redials before she can back out. Holds her breath again while it rings. Voicemail again. "I just wanted to say that you weren't just a fling to me. It started out that way. I admit that. But then you started talking about your family and your feelings and then—just like that, I started caring." She pauses. What more can she say? "Maybe I'm not as good at flings as I thought I'd be. Or—and this is probably more accurate—you're not fling material."

"To review your message, press one. To end your call, press two..."

Oh hell. Nothing more pathetic than three voicemails in a row. She dials again, feeling like a teenager. "Okay, I have to keep this short. Have a good life, Alejandro. I'm saying that in case we don't talk in person before the end of the season. I understand if you don't want to." She pauses, hoping she doesn't get cut off again, and quickly adds, "You're a kind person, Alejandro. Don't stop being kind."

Done. She hangs up and quickly tosses her phone into the driver's seat. What the fuck did she say that for? Maybe she should have texted after all. Shit. She should have planned things out and texted. Less chance of saying something dumb.

She looks up to see Missy marching toward her car, with Randy jogging after her. Diane sinks lower in the seat, as if to stay out of view.

CHAPTER 72

ALEJANDRO LISTENS TO DIANE'S MESSAGE while he sits on the edge of his bed in his dorm room. Two suitcases lie open in front of him. They are almost full.

"Don't stop being kind," she says before she hangs up.

This makes him want to curl up in a ball on the bed. Diane says this to him because she knows it is his weakness. He has told her that he thinks his worst sin is that he has been selfish all his life. Loved the most by his mother and sisters even before his father and Sergio died. Sergio, who had been the firstborn. The one to take care of all the rest. And now it is Alejandro who should do the taking care of. Instead he is thousands of miles away, fucking women and playing soccer.

He gets up and walks over to his desk to look at his textbooks again. He has to store them or sell them. And right now he can't decide because he doesn't know if he will come back.

When he told his mother on Skype that he was coming home early, instead of staying and saving money over Thanksgiving and the winter break like they had planned, he thought he could see a worried look in her eyes. Even though she was excited. Even though she clapped her hands and cried a little. Had she figured out that he was skipping a ton of classes to get home as soon as he could? To ensure that he wouldn't try to get in touch with Diane again?

Is it possible that she can tell across all that distance that his heart is broken? Not only because Diane does not want him, but because he is not the person his mother would expect him to be. He is not pure in his heart.

He would like to call Diane. Just to hear her voice again and maybe to make her think about taking him back. But he knows that all he would do is cry.

He picks up an anatomy book and flips through it. Staring at cross sections of various parts of the body. Here are the muscles of the neck and throat. If this is all we are, tissue and bone—animals who eat and sleep and shit and fuck—why do we suffer from so much feeling?

He closes the book.

Is there a way to avoid the feelings? Would he want to? He had come to Pepperdine thinking that he had left everything that mattered back home. Those first couple of months at school, and starting to coach, had felt like flying. Nothing had been tying him down. Except an occasional thought of his family. This floating feeling was what he thought he wanted. And then, Diane. It's like he walked toward complications. *Looked for them.* Maybe he is a man who longs to get tangled up in the mess that always comes with caring for another person.

He puts the book back on top of the pile and stares at the light bouncing off of the black windowpane.

Randy must despise him. They coached side by side the whole time that Alejandro was seducing his wife. Even worse—the whole time he was doing it, Alejandro never gave Randy a thought.

He sits back down on the bed. Looks at the plastic bag on one of the piles of clothes in the brown suitcase. In it are two baseball caps for his sisters, and a thin scarf for his mother. Each one says *Pepperdine.*

He bows his head and thanks God that Randy is all right. And he prays that Randy hates him completely. He couldn't bear forgiveness.

CHAPTER 73

THE AIR INSIDE MISSY'S AUDI is stuffy, since she's been running the heat. She and Randy have been sitting in near silence for minutes. It's not total silence, because every few seconds Randy sighs or *hmphs*, like he's still arguing in his head. Missy glances over to Randy's car, where Diane has been waiting and is probably asleep by now. She'd feel annoyed with Diane for snoozing through a big life moment like this, if she had the energy—but she is wrung out.

Missy is wrung out in a way that feels good and terrible at the same time. Good, because this soggy emptiness that she feels after having sobbed and screamed her guts out is preferable to the fog she's been slow-walking through for days. Okay, years. Terrible, because now she has no idea what comes next and one of the huge comforts of life with Randy has been predictability.

"You're telling the truth about not having an affair?" she says, making herself establish a point where they can both feel okay. The muscles in her throat are thick and sore. Her face red, she's sure.

"Yes. No affair. I don't know where you got that idea from," he says.

"Maybe I got the idea from you sneaking around," she says reflexively. More to punish him than to solve anything.

"Maybe you got the idea because that was what you were doing, so you thought everyone else was too," he says.

She's about to come back at him about the money and his lying, but stops herself. If only for now. Because it could go on like this for a long time; Missy senses this without putting it into words, even inside her head. Their marriage could go through a long, long period of mutual punishing while they struggle to recover all that was lost. Which isn't just the money and the house and his job. Which isn't even the trust that's been destroyed by a brief affair. Because she senses—again, without being able to fully form the thought—that if they jimmied their life back together and it looked like it had before, he would get over it. And she would, again, get consolation from a life that seemed enviable. On the outside. Their beautiful son, their home, the job, their routines, good cars. And while some might say that there's more to life than simply *seeming*, who can really disparage the lulling comfort of normalcy and a life that promises (even if it doesn't always deliver) the sweet absence of worry?

Yes, after they'd punished each other enough and leveraged every advantage they had, they could get back to that place of seeming. As long as they kept it together on the inside too. As long as neither one of them pushed it. As long as neither one of them got too drunk or too angry or too bored or so terrified of the future that they opened up everything all over again.

They could go on like that. Many have.

"Well," Randy says, adjusting in his seat, "it's a good thing the season's almost over and you won't have to—we both won't have to—see Alejandro again."

His turn to establish a mutually agreed-on starting point: the Affair. Neither one of us has to face the proof of it again, he's saying. Alejandro will disappear.

"Yes," she croaks. "That will make things easier."

So this is where the reconciliation is supposed to begin. After the initial recriminations (there will be more, they both know it) and some tentative truth-telling. Missy starts to reach over and touch his wrist and say something like *It will be all right*. It is time for the reassuring gesture. But she stops herself.

Missy can't because she can't. It's not that she's pining for Alejandro. Not right now, anyway. But she is longing for the feeling she had when she was with him. The aliveness that rose from following her own desires. That terrifying freedom that made her feel giddy with possibility. Could she get to that feeling on her own? Is there a place beyond seeming? A place worth risking all her comforts for?

But as quickly as this thought emerges, the present moment takes over. Like it always does. Sealing up the windows, fogging the windshield, and locking the doors. The present moment, which says to her, *What kind of woman leaves a man when he's at his lowest point?* What would that say about her? She loved him once, didn't she? *Didn't she?* He had taken care of her, given her a son, and made her feel safe. She looks over at him, covering his eyes with his hands again and breathing softly like he might go to sleep.

Didn't she love him once?

And from the part of her she has never paid attention to, she hears the answer: *No. No. You never did.*

CHAPTER 74

DIANE HAS STOPPED SNEAKING GLANCES over at Missy and Randy. Instead, she stares ahead resolutely, the empty bag of Randy's M&M's crumpled in her hand, trying to ignore her insistent and acidic stomach. She focuses on the dark sky and the sound of the ocean slamming onto the beach.

She hopes like hell that Randy is coming completely clean. Not likely. True, she hasn't known him that long. However, all she's known of him so far reveals a man who practically cannonballs out of any situation that requires facing an uncomfortable truth.

She can sympathize. Truth hurts like a motherfucker. How long had she avoided admitting that she had willfully, systematically destroyed T's love for her? And even after she faced it, how much longer did it take her to admit that she hadn't done it because she felt undeserving, but because she hated him for knowing himself? For being so goddamned sure of what he wanted. Unlike her.

She is looking down for a place to stash the M&M's bag when the driver door opens and Randy hurls himself into the seat.

"Well, that's it," he announces. "I probably ruined my whole life right there."

It takes a second for her to adjust to the total shift of energy in the car. The blast of cold air. The musty smell of his sweatshirt and the boom of his voice. But also, the pronouncement. So final. Fatalistic.

She takes a moment to drop the scrunched bag at her feet and looks at him sideways. "Randy, you really don't know what's going to happen yet."

"I've never once seen her this pissed off," he says, buckling his seat belt and starting the car. "And now she's just sitting there, saying nothing like a ticking bomb."

"Hold on. We're leaving?" she says, placing her hand on his arm. "What about Missy?"

He lets the engine run but sits back and looks at her. "She says she can't look at me right now."

"But we can't just leave her here."

"She wants to be alone. She was clearer about that than I've ever seen her, ever."

"I'm going to check on her," Diane says. She hops out and jogs over to Missy. Knocks on the window. Missy lowers it halfway.

The skin under Missy's eyes, under her nose, looks raw.

"You okay?" Diane asks.

Missy starts to laugh and snort.

"Do you need me to ride with you?" Diane says.

"No," Missy answers through her snuffling.

"Uh. Okay." Diane shifts her weight from foot to foot, feeling the cold now and blowing into her fists. "I have to say, I'm a little worried about you driving while you're upset."

"I drive upset all the time." Missy half smiles and raises the window slightly.

"Okay." Diane glances back toward Randy's car. She sees the dark outline of his body, waiting.

"Diane?" Missy says, and Diane looks back. "After I drive out of here, will you tell him that I'm going to my sister's?"

"Okay. Um. Does your sister live close?" She shivers.

"New Mexico," Missy says, her gaze steady. Weird smile gone.

"*New Mexico?*"

"Just tell him, please. After I leave."

"All right. I guess," Diane says, rubbing her upper arms through her sweater. "When are you coming home? He's going to want to know."

"Just tell him, my sister's," Missy says, rolling up the window yet another inch. "I'll figure out the rest when I get there."

"Just. Okay. Just promise you're not going to disappear. You have to give him something."

"I'll call Aiden. Tonight," Missy says as she rolls up the window. She starts the car and eases out of the lot.

Shit. "Missy!" Diane yells, running after the car. It screeches to a halt as Diane catches up and Missy rolls down the window. "My purse," Diane says, breathing hard.

Missy's head bobs down as she fishes for the purse. She emerges again as she hands it out the window. Diane reaches for it, but Missy hangs on to it for a brief moment, saying, "This isn't about the money, you know. I'm not like that. And I won't leave Aiden alone for too long. I'm not like that either."

"I never thought…" Diane stomps her feet.

Missy lets go of the purse, raises the window, and takes off. Diane cups her hands in front of her mouth again and breathes into them. Glances back to Randy in the car, the engine still running; he appears to be in the exact same position as he was when she last checked. Like he's bracing for a blow.

Diane walks toward Randy's car, through the beam of headlights to the passenger side, and gets in. "Let's go," she says. And Randy looks over his shoulder to start pulling out. He doesn't ask what she and Missy were talking about. And Diane's not ready to say anything more.

Randy pulls onto the road and shortly merges onto the highway. The moonlight must be bouncing off the waves to their right, but she doesn't turn her head to take it in. The two of them breathe only as much as is necessary, keeping their eyes on the glowing median.

Diane's mind catches on Missy saying, "I'm not like that." The phrase rolls and repeats in rhythm with the median. *I'm not like that. I'm not like that. I'm not like that.*

But we're all *like that*, Diane thinks. We're all *like that* sometimes. We're capable of being and feeling contradictory things. This very moment, in fact, Diane feels the glow of righteous compassion for both of them, while still resenting the fuck out of being hungry and tired and deeply unappreciated. She leans her head back against the headrest and closes her eyes and thinks about all the choices that led to her being in this car, sitting next to this hapless man as he drives down the coast in the dark night, and wondering whether or not to deliver his wife's message. Which will surely cause him great pain.

Her throat tightens and her closed eyelids start to sting. This is crazy. Why does she hurt for him? Is it that his problems are so compelling? So dire that no breathing human could remain unmoved? Hardly. His problems are, in fact, ordinary and puny. Minuscule and of his own making. She shouldn't be aching for him. What about Gaza? Syria? Starving children everywhere? For fuck's sake, this man was born lucky.

She rolls her head toward the window so he won't see if a tear rolls down her cheek. Keeping her eyes closed, she still denies herself the glinting ocean. Can she isolate the moment when she started to care about him? It must have been somewhere in the mass of e-mails. Something he wrote. She remembers phrases. She remembers that he kept calling her a friend. Kept telling her more and more. Kept asking her for help. Kept telling her his secrets. Fuck. That's it!

Her eyes pop open. Her breath has fogged the window.

He became human, became whole, by revealing himself to her. And once you know someone—know their fears and loves and yearnings— it gets much, much harder to walk away. She doesn't know any starving children in Syria. She knows him. *He* is her starving child.

The car jogs sharply to the left and Diane whips her head around. Randy is already righting it.

"You should slow down," she says.

"Sorry. I thought you were asleep."

"No. Just thinking." Which is true. Come on. Tell him about Missy and get it over with. "What are you going to do when you get home?" she asks.

"I don't know. Start looking for a job. Sell the house."

"Start again?"

"What else can I do?"

"I guess I was asking about what you are going to do differently, instead of what you're going to do the same."

"Selling the house isn't the same."

She shifts, relieving a soreness in her hip. "It's an outside fix. Don't you think you need to—"

She looks at his profile. It betrays nothing, which is unusual for him. She has thought him to be infinitely readable. "Don't you think you need to," she starts again, "think about your life completely differently?"

"Well, not yet. I mean, I've *been* hoping that if I can ride it out, everything will come back to me."

"Yeah. I don't know."

"You don't know what?"

"I don't know if going back to the way things were is what we're supposed to do."

"All I know is that before all this happened, things were pretty perfect."

Really, Randy? Really? She turns away to look back out her window. How can he possibly think that? How can he think that a life that led to him almost shooting himself on a desolate beach is anywhere close to perfect? Is even in the ballpark of perfect?

"I'm going to have to work extra hard to get it all back," she hears him say. "It might take a couple of years. Three years, tops. I could probably keep up the telemarketing as a side gig."

Get it all back. She remembers these words. They beat rhythmically through her brain every day after T left. Not that she tried much to actually make it happen, other than write him e-mails that she never sent. That said, what she didn't know then, and what she knows now, is that trying to get everything back only means returning to where your troubles were seeded in the first place. The very reason why you lost whatever you think you lost is buried in your seemingly perfect past.

She turns her gaze back to the road ahead. "Randy," she says quickly, "Missy wanted me to tell you that she's going to take a break. She's not driving home."

He turns his head to her, and the car jogs again. Her heart stops for a second. Then, immediately, his eyes are back on the road. She waits for a bit. Median dashes, slicing evenly to their left. She presses on. "Missy said she's going to drive out to her sister's in New Mexico. I'm sure she'll want to talk after she's cooled off." In an instant, she regrets the impulse to offer hope. It's cowardly.

"What am I supposed to do about Aiden?" he asks.

"Right now all you have to do is get him to school this week, and work things out while you're alone. Missy said she'll call him tonight."

"You think she'll be gone the whole week?"

"I don't know, Randy. She didn't say."

"Laura hates me," he says.

"Laura?"

"The sister. Her sister hates me."

"You don't know that." She keeps it simple.

"Yeah. I do," he says, slowing the car down and pulling onto the shoulder.

"You're stopping here?" she says. Her lower back tightens with a vague worry that some new revelation or a complete meltdown will require more energy than she feels she has left. He reaches down and turns off the engine. Fuck.

"I just—" he says. A car races by. The Jeep shudders. Diane looks at his profile, which is only slightly darker than the sky behind him. "If she's going to Laura's, she's never coming back."

"Yes," she says carefully. "It sounds like that's possible."

He turns and looks at her. There is a breathless moment before his face completely changes. Becomes grotesque. Forehead scrunched. Mouth stretched from ear to ear, he lets out a sound that is somewhere between a screech and a moan. His shoulders shake as he lowers his head and starts to sob.

She can't think of a thing to do. The noise he's making. The sheer helplessness. She feels strangely embarrassed for him. Maybe she should simply look out the window and wait for it to pass.

He covers his face for a second, sputtering into his hands. Then he uncovers his face, throws back his head, and howls.

What does she do now, she thinks, in the very same moment that she knows exactly what she must do.

She scootches closer and puts her arm around him. He doesn't pull away. The image of him holding Calvin on the roof flashes through her mind and she turns with some adjusting of her elbow and her left hip, clasping her other arm across his chest and pulling him in as tight as she can.

He shakes and cries, but she doesn't loosen her grip. In fact, she pulls even tighter. "No," he whimpers. "I want"—he gasps—"her."

"No. No. No," she says softly into his hair. "It will be all right. I promise. I promise."

She starts to rock him slightly, ignoring the edge of the seat digging into her leg. Stupid. She can't promise a goddamned thing.

And yet she rocks. Pulling him as close as she can. Desperate to ease his pain. "I'm so sorry. So sorry. So sorry." She whispers and rocks. Tears running down her cheeks, she wipes her nose on his shoulder. "So sorry," she says over and over. And she is.

CHAPTER 75

BEFORE SHE OPENS RANDY'S E-MAIL, Diane goes over to the fridge to get herself a glass of water. It's been a week since the beach, and in that time, she's seen him at practice (no time for a big talk there) and had a couple of short exchanges over the phone. One in which he was actually quite straightforward, which is rarely the case. "What do I do now?" he had asked her, and she had given him some practical suggestions (after-school programs for Aiden, for one). According to Randy, Missy has been in touch with Aiden and the kid's been soaking up the extra time with Dad. They've started some huge Lego project that sounds like it's taking up a lot of space in the living room.

Randy still sounds lost, though, and she told him to give it time. She wonders if her small comforts were too generic. Should she have gone deeper? Hard to know. She tells herself that she's following his lead. Letting him decide what he's ready to discuss or not.

She peeks into the living room to check on Sabine, who is still buried under blankets on the couch, reading. If Sabine's sniffle gets any worse, she may have to keep her home from school tomorrow. Diane is sure that she's not supposed to derive such pleasure from the thought of ministering to her daughter by watching movies in bed together all day long. But she does.

She dips back into the kitchen, walks over to her open laptop, and sits down to read.

From: FavoriteCoach@gmail.com
To: Manatees sent Sat, Nov 13 4:49 pm

Subject: It's not whether you win or lose!!!!

Hello Manatees and Manatee families! It's me, your coach, Randy!! I had to write as soon as I got home from the game to tell you what an honor it has been to be your coach and your friend, and that's even after the crushing loss we experienced today. Some of you were crying too hard to hear, but let me make it clear that we will not be playing another game because once you lose three playoff games, you are eliminated. We will not be able to go on to the tournament. A couple of you asked if there was anyone we could beg, pay, or even offer up a parent's time share in Big Bear for another shot, but that's not the way The Beverly Hills Junior Soccer League works. So I think that Jacqui's ritual of burning our feelings on the sidelines was initially a good one, I just should have thought about the fire and the refs were right to stomp it out!

Thank you for the Starbucks cards, the Yoda action figure, the basket of hard and soft cheeses, and certificate for a facial—I've never had one before, but I'm told they're very relaxing and that my skin will feel like a baby's butt afterwards and who doesn't want that! I also read every single thing you wrote in my thank-you card and I want to say, "Back at you" to all of you! It's really those heartfelt notes that keep coaches like me going!

I owe you all thanks, but there are a couple of people I have to single out. The first, of course, is the best team mom in the league, Jacqui Hirshorn!!!!!! I can't believe that I got you two seasons in a row. If there's a place in heaven next to "insert your name for God here"—Jacqui's going to be right up there! She might need a ladder, but she'll get there! Just kidding, Jacqui! She gets tired of the short jokes, but I figure I wouldn't be me if I didn't make one last one!

The second person I have to thank is Paul Pousaint! What a great assistant coach he was!! This is a man who does everything you ask him, and then he's there for you in personal ways too!! I can't thank him enough.

The third person I have to thank is Alejandro, who is already gone for his winter break.

I'd also like to make a personal thank you to my son Aiden, who improved this season and who helped me out with a lot of things at home. Aiden, my man, you are my rock! Now get to bed!!!! Hah!

Last, but not least, I'd like to thank Diane Platt—who knows everything that she did.

And even more last than that, I would like to leave you all with this quote from 'The Titanic' which has been going through my mind for a week:

"Rose. Promise me you'll survive. That you won't give up no matter what happens. Never let go of that promise."

Don't give up, Manatees!!! Even though you're not playing as a team anymore. You can still keep this promise in your hearts!

Your favorite coach,
Randy

———————

From: MSonnenklar@GSachs.com
To: Manatees　　　　　　　　　　　　sent Sat, Nov 13 7:06 pm

Subject: Re: It's not whether you win or lose!!!!

Am I the only one who wants to know what Diane did?

M

Diane quickly closes the laptop on her kitchen counter so as not to get sucked into the exchange. She knows its pattern clearly by now. The rah-rah from Jacqui, the smackdown from Mako, the douchey insults from Mark, and one or two other predictable chimes.

She aches a little for Randy, emotionally crouching behind his usual coach banter. Although doesn't everyone do that? Present themselves to the world with their best bona fides? *This is who I am*, we say. *Look at how I walk and talk and pick up the check. Did you notice my shoes, my charitable donation, my loving attention toward my children?* All while balling up in bed at night, hoping someone will see past it all and fucking love us?

What a painful construct—building barriers to any real connection while desperately hoping that someone (the right someone) will bash them down.

She takes a sip of water. Outside, she can hear the occasional thump of Reece kicking a ball against the wall of the garage. She reaches out and picks up a handful of bottle caps that lay next to a stack of magazines she is planning to toss. Alejandro had flattened the caps and played some solitary game with them one day when the kids were at T's. She had watched him flip one, then gather one, two, three of the others before he caught it—like Jacks. She had wondered if it was a game he had played when he was younger, or one that he was simply making up on the spot. Why hadn't she asked him?

She slides the caps into a box on the chair next to her. Stands and puts the pile of magazines in there as well. Done. Lifts the box and walks into the foyer, out the front door, past Reece dribbling the ball over the lawn, and sets it down on the curb.

She turns and watches her son toss the ball and start nudging it over the grass. She watches him. Really watches him. The side of his foot against the ball. Reddish knees. His short, quick breaths. Teeth biting his lower lip. Concentration tensing his brow. She watches him line up a shot. He kicks and the ball hits the wall with a smack. He jumps up, fists in the air, and starts his victory run. Arms outstretched as he hears the fans in his stadium cheering.

———————

It is a perfect day in Los Angeles. Crisp colors so cinematic, it's hard to believe that an artist hasn't played around with the contrast and saturation. The palm trees on Diane's street are impossibly tall. The curbs are shiny white. Clouds puffy. Ah yes. It is the kind of scene that Patrick flies over often. The power to release himself from any physical claims gives him a vantage that few enjoy. In fact, seeing it all from such a distance gives him that sliver of wisdom many don't get until they are much, much older (if at all). Which is simply this: Most of us end up being fine in the end.

There he is right now, soaring overhead, watching Reece race around his front lawn. Diane standing next to some boxes on the curb. He banks and picks up speed. Soon he's swooping through the halls of Calvin's school as Jacqui picks him up from his tutoring session. Then fluttering in Paul and Marianne's bedroom as Paul moves his bedding and toiletries back upstairs from the study. Gliding by Karen and Kelli and Mark's first stiff attempt at sitting together in Ben's school gym. Floating over the park where Coach and Aiden have started practicing regularly (afterward grabbing a smoothie at the strip mall across the street). And even climbing higher so he can see all the way over to Colombia. There's Alejandro sitting at a long table with his family, who all tell stories noisily and at once.

Things change a lot, but not very much. Which is a contradiction, but Patrick understands contradictions very well. We are not one thing or the other. He is, after all, a good son and a thief. There are stories hidden in everyone's soul, and even as we choose one thing over another, one lover over the rest, a place to live, a job, to have children or not—we are stunned by our helplessness in the face of circumstances that simply choose us. Circumstances yielding both calamity and grace.

Patrick tumbles through the universe. We all do. Weightless and yet tied to one another. Aware of our separateness and still maddeningly dependent upon small and large kindnesses. Yearning to ascend far above our daily existence. But scoping, always and forever, for a safe place to land.

ACKNOWLEDGMENTS

Thanks to my editor, Amy Pierpont, for her thoughtful and rigorous notes. The novel deepened because of them. Thanks also to Alexis Hurley, my agent, who read several iterations and got the manuscript into readable shape. In the end, we cut a few storylines and 35,000 words! And always, my profound thanks to Adam Peck, my manager. His unflagging faith in me has truly changed my life.

Many friends and fellow writers read various drafts, or bits of drafts, and gave me invaluable feedback. They are Claudette Sutherland, Kerry Haynie, Bob Odenkirk, Stephanie Young, Cathy Mathews, Milly Charles, Erika Schickel, Aliza Murietta, Sarah Stanley, Hilary McGregor, Jill Ackles, Andrea Goyan, Leslie Jordan, Shelly Kramer, Charlton Pettus, Roy Samuelson, Frank Sharp, Kathy Miller Kelly, Jennifer Ashe, Jennifer Winslow, Holly Palmer, and Jenna Jolowitz.

Thanks to Hedgebrook Writers' Retreat. I started the novel in earnest in a little cabin on Whidbey Island. The community of women around Hedgebrook's dinner table is the kind of magical juju that I hope every artist gets to experience at least once in a lifetime.

My sons, Spencer and Murphy, helped me with the soccer references and actual game recaps. But more than that, they took my work seriously and celebrated all the big and small victories ("First Draft, yay! Let's go to dinner!") along the way. They are my heart and soul.

And all my love and thanks to my husband, Patrick Towne, who, like Diane, knows everything that he did.

AUTHOR'S NOTE

A few years ago, due to some maternal zeal to get my son on his best friend's team, my family landed in the Beverly Hills AYSO soccer league. We weren't supposed to be there. We were supposed to be in the neighboring league that used a literal dust bowl as a field, no doubt causing many cases of lifelong asthma.

I'm not going to lie. I loved sitting on the green grass in the shade of a leafy tree, watching my sons kick a ball around in Beverly Hills. Life seemed easier there. Greener. More relaxed. But the endless e-mail chains I got from the coaches and parents started to reveal a different story. Ostensibly about soccer and scheduling, these cyber missives revealed so much more: personal details, conflicting views on parenting and politics, unfocussed (dare I say often "unmerited") pride in their progeny, dismay at losing—and something else I had a hard time identifying—a vague but pervasive sense of subterranean shame without any clear source. These e-mails were heartbreaking and hilarious at the same time. Initially, I planned on parodying them in a short story, but throughout the season I found myself empathizing with the parents more and more. They were, in fact, me. All of us longing for connection, intimacy, and approbation.

So the short story became the novel *Everything Is Just Fine*, a social satire in which the characters consistently look for love in the wrong places. Some look for it in material wealth and other trappings of success. Some look for it in meaningless sex and career advancement. And one mistakes a relationship that is played out almost entirely in e-mails to be one of the closest friendships he's ever had.

I find such longing deeply human, even when it's misguided. And what I learned when I got to know my characters better is that the connection we all yearn for can only be found when we are completely honest with each other and, oh so much more terrifyingly, with ourselves.

ABOUT THE AUTHOR

Brett Paesel is the author of the *Los Angeles Times* bestseller *Mommies Who Drink: Sex, Drugs, and Other Distant Memories of an Ordinary Mom* (Warner Books, 2006). Her work has been published in numerous collections and national publications including the *New York Times*, *Los Angeles Times*, and Salon.com. In Hollywood, she was a consulting producer on Amazon's television series *Transparent* and *I Love Dick*. She has developed and written shows for HBO, ABC, Fox, Comedy Central, WB, Lifetime, and Nick at Nite. As an actor, she was a cast member of *Transparent* and HBO's *Mr. Show with Bob and David*. She lives in Los Angeles with her husband and two sons and was, in fact, a parent with kids in the Beverly Hills AYSO soccer league.